Rabbits and Moons

A Novel

L. Wendell Vaughan

Grosbeak Books
New Bedford, MA
USA

This is a work of fiction. Names, characters, places, and incidents are products of the author's imagination or are used fictitiously and are not to be construed as real. Any resemblance to actual events, locales, organizations, or persons, living or dead, is entirely coincidental.

 Printed in the United States of America. For information, address Grosbeak Books, Small Press Publishing PO Box 1507, New Bedford, MA 02741

www.grosbeakbooks.com

Library of Congress Control Number: 2020909825
Library of Congress Cataloging-in-Publication Data
Vaughan, L. Wendell
Rabbits and Moons: a novel/L.Wendell Vaughan 1st ed.

Grosbeak Books may be purchased for educational, business, or sales promotional use. For information please email: info@grosbeakbooks.com

Book cover design
Photograph by Hisbeth-Rodriguez
altered by Grosbeak Books

ISBN 978-0-9702979-1-4 paperback
ISBN 978-0-9702979-3-8 digital ebook

To my grandmother,
Louise Beachamp Vaughan,
who hated the phrase— I *can't*

"If I advance, follow me.
If I stop, urge me on. If I retreat, kill me."
— *Henri de la Rochejaquelein*

Chapter 1

The Bus Ride

The three children had gooey noses and small, bright faces. They stood swaying with the jarring bumps of the bus, staring at me, heads just above the seat edging, wide-eyed and toothy, never skipping a beat, never seeming to blink as they jiggled back and forth, curious and amused.

"What's so funny?" I asked them in Spanish which made them disappear, then bounce back up giggling, never uttering a word, just laughing and exuding shyness. I watched them pee into plastic bags that the mother threw out the window and munch on torn pieces of corn tortillas. The mother, young with a button nose, her dark skin freckled, several times had turned toward me and smiled while asking if I wanted some food. I would smile back and point to the orange and jicama I had brought. One time she touched the white, untanned skin of my lower arm and said, "*Suerte*." My response was to sweep my eyes over her family and say, "Why, you have luck." Not that I really thought that; I didn't want children.

Five of them, the father silent and pensive by the aisle, were pinned in tightly into one seat. I imagined them living in a generic thatched hut made with corn stalks, smelling of corn while they ate corn, and everyone else in the village living in similar houses with smoke peeling from their thatched roofs in unrefined swirls scented with corn. Then there were the beans and rice, day after day after day after day. The constant cleaning to keep the dirt floor pristine—understandable but redundant, sweeping dirt onto dirt. It never ceased to surprise me how neat and pressed their clothing appeared—even their oily hair, coiffed and colorful with bows and ribbons yet smelling like corn, but a soured corn as though it had been picked and peeled and thrown into a bag for way too long. Lives constantly threatened by cold, heat, humidity, vermin, another child being born, a goat dying, a drunken husband, the unexpected arrival of the military. I was fine being just with me, I thought, fumbling around in my bag for chewing gum.

The bus I was on was a yellow Blue Bird school bus built for elementary-aged kids. I sat with my knees bent sideways, the unforgiving chassis causing every ditch, pothole, and ravine to send me flying into the air, making it impossible to read. The windows were shut to keep out the dust, and the air was clogged with sweat, corn, and too many mouths breathing. My only solace was the undulating ruminations of whatever came into my head. My thoughts random and obsessive at times when thinking of my family back home, words I wished I had said to an unfit ex-boss, a past lover's touch.

For an entire year, I'd been keeping myself chaste. No sex, no crushes, just me. I liked my freedom. Freedom from entanglement and commitment was enlightening. My only responsibility was to myself. My happiness, my desires, my wants and needs—when I could figure them out. It was all trial and error, but then how else was I going to know what I wanted and didn't want? Who I was and desired to be? And what fun I'd been having traveling around Mexico and Central America, being carefree, making friends yet never a commitment. But lately, something odd had begun to stir, to wake up inside of me. A visceral gnawing or should I say, craving for, well—I kept telling myself, 'if nuns could remain celibate for life, why couldn't I remain for years?' It was so freeing not to be enslaved to another's touch.

But I was no nun. A church was something I only went to when drunk on Christmas eve or in foreign countries to observe the insane architecture. More noted, the lack of sex was beginning to have some peculiar side effects.

For instance, there was a lanky Swiss fellow across the aisle. He had an entire seat to himself because he was too long to sit properly. He was trying to read the newspaper *Las Noticias*, a regional paper filled with car crashes, murders, bribery, and, now and then, the odd story regarding witchcraft. Every time the bus hit a ditch, swerving and yanking itself over it, the paper would smack him in the face. It made me laugh, a haughty laugh that caught his attention.

When the bus stopped at a village so the driver and his assistant could sell the wares they kept on top of the roof, the Swiss came over and sat with me. The legroom was unaccommodating, so he maneuvered his body halfway out into the aisle. I could tell he was one of those travelers that didn't use deodorant. A strong odor of peed-on kitty litter emanated from his hairy, drippy pits. When he put his arm up over the back of the seat for comfort, I couldn't help but cough and wave my hand in front of my nose. He wore faux Central American clothing, which no one wore except hippy types, gringos wanting to seem cool, but weren't because they were trying too hard. He had a weak jaw and the full lips of someone a few years younger than me. I placed him in his early twenties, with clean, white teeth and crystal-clear blue eyes.

He didn't like Americans, "Americans think they're better than everyone else."

"So what?" I said, thinking, how unimaginative since every European I'd met said the same thing. Then to make matters more distressing for me, I imagined what it would be like to have sex with him. As he stretched sideways, leaning in, his back against my shoulder, his wispy, blond hair fluffing next to my right cheek, sweat beading on his forehead, I imagined kissing him. But when he yawned without covering his mouth, revealing food encrusted between his back molars, it was obvious to me that sex with him would be spastic, smelly, and quick. However, it would give me great pleasure to tell him, afterward, that Americans were much better at satisfying their partners than the Swiss.

Goofy and petulant, I asked him to move back to his seat. "Too hot," I said. His response was to sniff the air and pucker a bruised, rejected ego at me before moving away. He did give me the paper he had been reading. He said he was done. This made me snicker. I knew he hadn't read it, and he had the ink marks on his nose to prove me right.

It wasn't long after my episode with the Swiss that the bus began to crawl up into the mountains. The ubiquitous military with their maroon berets and AK-47s, stopped the bus every fifteen minutes. It was nothing terrible, just mind-boggling because the same men were told to get out each time as though they had become different people. It was also very time consuming which put me on edge. To arrive in El Puente in the middle of the night was not a pleasant thought. I'd been told the town was more like an outpost. Few people lived there which meant there wouldn't be any hotels. The town closed for the night, I wouldn't be able to get a taxi to the orphanage either and would find myself left out in the dark until morning.

I was to be a *niñera.* I had volunteered, back in the city, to work with the three- and four-year-old children in an orphanage located on a river in the middle of a rainforest. This position had come about because I had grown tired of attending Spanish

Language schools. When a classmate of mine suggested I work at an orphanage, it piqued my interest. She told me her sister had become fluent in Spanish by working in one. The idea of becoming fluent in Spanish by doing something useful seemed wonderful. I jumped at the suggestion and began searching for orphanages in the region. Yes, I know that I said I didn't want children, but working with them and having them are completely different. If I didn't like it, I could leave. And since leaving situations when they became boring or distasteful had been part of my journey, along with learning to speak Spanish, the volunteer position seemed perfect. My timetable, unknown. I had few expectations but was hoping for the best. Yet, at the moment, sitting on the bus watching the police wave at the driver to stop, all I could think was—not again.

The military police, from what I could see, were a bunch of kids playing cops. Some even looked like they were ten or twelve. They kept their index fingers on the triggers of their assault rifles. Their night goggles flapped in front of them and cigarettes hung out of their mouths. They talked to each other about women's boobs and made bad jokes about the clothing of the men they were harassing. Some men wore *vaquero* attire, loose jeans on thin bodies, torn slacks, cowboy boots, and hats; thick leather belts with big metal buckles, some with rhinestones, heralding bucking horses, the lone star. Others wore traditional clothing, striped chinos tied on with ropes knotted at their waists, and loose-fitting cotton shirts. A few more had on T-shirts with farcical sayings in English like, 'I don't need a hairstylist, my pillow sets my hair,' and, 'If people are talking behind your back, fart.' These T-shirts with their ludicrous sayings were compliments of the USA. Boxes of them could be found in the markets and on the streets. They were sold on the cheap and given out for free by charities. The non-English speaking recipients got to walk around inexpensively dressed, but comical.

The men all had one thing in common: they looked indigenous, poor, and scared. At these inconvenient stops, the men, except for the lanky Swiss because they weren't looking for foreign white people but only their own kind, had to get out of the bus. Yet, the Swiss always got out too. He was the only one that seemed to enjoy the harassment. He even giggled whenever the *niños militares* bumped the nose of their blunt guns into his back or arms. Often looking around and grinning, I think he wanted someone to take his picture.

Sometimes the whole shakedown took so long that the men relieved themselves like patient burros onto the grasses below. The first one would lower his hand and take his penis out, then another, causing a swoosh of splattering urine followed by a mild shake as they zipped back up. The boys with their guns snickered as they commented on dick sizes. The Swiss, who now appeared to be chinless, would pee, too, but when he peed, he let out a big sigh causing everyone to look at him. No one commented on his penis size even though I saw many of the men looking at it. I imagined it small, like the pink lobes of his ears, or long and thin like the fingers he kept combing through his hair.

At each checkpoint, I watched it all from the sanctity of a thicket off to the side of the bus where I also peed. The jostling bus wreaked havoc on my bladder. Once back on the bus, within minutes I'd have to go again, even though my water intake was limited to oranges and jicama. But I felt lucky; no one ever bothered me while I squatted off to the side or even looked at me. Being a *gringa*, I was a nonentity. Not part of the dance, just a mere apparition passing in and out of their lives. In a different place or situation, being invisible wasn't as easy, but on buses, I was never harassed or even particularly noticed.

Once we were out of the mountains, twilight crept into the sky; we drove without a hitch along a smoothly paved road with a dry, cracking desert on both sides. Somehow on this wonderful pavement, a tire went flat right at the only village I'd seen in hours. It did occur to me the villagers may have booby-trapped the road for business. But then why think negatively, I had to go to the bathroom, and I was positive the village had one somewhere.

Since there wasn't a spare tire, the driver and his assistant went off to find one. This was another delay compiled on a delay. It rattled me more than all the other delays because it seemed like it would take the longest. If the Swiss had still been on the bus, I would have complained to him about my situation, but he had gotten off a while back by a sign that said, 'Bus Stop.' I had no idea where he was going and didn't care. Left without a fellow foreigner to grouse about my rankled nerves, I merely shrugged; it was one of the dilemmas of traveling alone.

Just my luck, a foreigner was standing by an embankment near the back of the bus. He was tall and ruddy-white. His body sinewy, he wore a beige, felt fedora that dipped over his left eye. He was nibbling on a piece of hay like a hungry rabbit which gave him the appearance of either being very bored or nervous. His square chin and flattened cheekbones somehow made him handsome the way an oddly shaped rock appeared captivating. I placed his age to be somewhere around fifty and figured he would be much better in bed than the Swiss due to experience, but I wasn't in the mood for imagining sex with strangers anymore as there was a more pressing issue.

Charging up the embankment to the village, I looked around for a restaurant or sign saying *banos*. A dusty place with unpainted cement buildings, rebar sprouting like rogue hairs from unfinished second stories, dirt pathways, and, in the middle of the square, a small, stucco church with Christmas decorations and lights around the door. It wasn't Christmas. The people in the region were just very fond of multi-colored bulbs; blinking, hanging off of fences, placed strategically around biblical paintings, or bloody sculptures of Jesus.

I found a tienda with an outhouse in the back, which the owner let me use for what was equivalent to a penny. It was neat and clean with a deep hole. The minute I bent over to pee, a swarm of black flies came in, making the ordeal uncomfortable.

When I returned to the bus, the foreigner was still milling around chewing on hay. Eyeing him more closely, I saw that his clothing looked rich. I assumed he was the type of fellow that shopped at fancy stores for people who wanted to appear casual but wealthy. He wore pressed blue jeans, a collared, long-sleeve shirt, and had a leather jacket slung over his right arm. I thought it odd he was waiting for the bus as it was a bus for the poor. If so, he wasn't being very patient. He kept kicking the dirt and circling as though he didn't know if he should stay or go.

I walked over to him to say hello. He must have sensed I was coming toward him because he immediately glanced my way. His coral blue eyes, barbed and flecked, jabbed at my inner soul like darts. He then put the flat of his hand in the air indicating he didn't want me to come any closer. I stopped in mid-step. Standing frozen in place, I stood staring at him and thinking he could be a madman. Then possibly, because I didn't shy away, his jumpiness boiled over, and he took off up into the village. I was happy to see him leave and hoped he wasn't coming back because—who needs crazy? Hungry, I went over to a vendor stirring a big steel barrel of steamy water. I bought a waterlogged tamale and a tepid Coca-Cola from him. Sitting on a hefty boulder by the bus to eat, I pulled the newspaper the Swiss had given me out of my daypack and began to read.

After going over the comics section, I read a terrible story about a kidnapping gone wrong, then an opinion piece about the United States invading Kuwait and the upcoming election between George Bush and Bill Clinton. The article favored Bill Clinton; I hadn't thought much about the elections back home but thought Bill seemed a bit cooler than George. Flipping to the front page, the headline was about a corrupt government official. The head of the Ministry of Interior had been caught falsifying land deeds, but the government wasn't filing charges because the Minister of Interior was the president's cousin. Below the story, was another head-liner with a picture of a man wearing a fedora. He looked a lot like the man who had just run off into the village.

Holding the paper toward what was now, an orange, fading sun, I realized the picture had to be him, the penetrating eyes were a dead giveaway. I looked around to see if the man had come back, but he hadn't. I read the article. It wasn't good. He had recently been acquitted of murder even though all the evidence stated that he had committed the crime. His acquittal was due to him bribing the judge in charge. This admittance of bribery and murder met with impunity, had me shaking my head. The article also stated that the murdered victim was a fifteen-year-old boy; the grandson of a Doña Yenara Pinola Alvares. She lived in El Puente the town I was heading for. Creepy, was my first thought. Then due to the town being on a river, I mumbled, "Drama on The *Rio*." It was a great movie title but then changed it to *Asesinato en el Rio* because it seemed much more grabbing. Reading further, it appeared Doña Alvares' brother, Don Edmund Poco Pinola, had been framed by the man wearing the fedora for the boy's murder. The story then went into the gruesome details of how the boy had been shot, dumped into the river with cement blocks attached to his feet. But cement floats in Central America, and he floated into a patch of mangroves. His bloated, decomposing body was eventually discovered by a young orphan who resided at the orphanage I was going to. 'Poor thing, what a horrible sight to see.' And 'what am I getting myself into?' I grumbled putting the paper aside and finishing my meal.

With nothing left to read or eat, I got up to see if the driver and his assistant had returned. To my great joy they had, and the tire repair was all set. Staring off over the desert, which was flat for miles until it ran into a long mountain range, I could see that the disappearing sun had left traces of pink and gray in the sky. The scene was beautiful, breathtaking. Secretive, remote, and mysterious as the earth submissively rolled into darkness. We had a good six hours to go, which meant I was going to arrive in El Puente somewhere between midnight and the wee hours of the morning.

Chapter 2

The Arrival

The town was pitch black when I stepped off the bus. There were no lights on anywhere, and the sky was without glitter, which punched another hole into my fragile psyche. I could taste dampness in the air, and the disheartening idea of rain swept over me. I then scolded myself for getting off the bus. I should have stayed on until the last stop. I could have slept on the bus until morning and then jumped on another at daylight and come back. But I hadn't, so here I was, a solitary, vulnerable human set adrift in a lightless town without an umbrella or a bench to sit on. I kicked a pebble out of frustration and listened to its echo as it bounced down the potholed road, but then quickly regretted it because what if I disturbed something bad? What if I awoke or caught the attention of some ill-minded people? I then chuckled at the foolishness of my thoughts. What good were they? Pointless.

Then the clouds must have moved, exposing a sky the darkest of blue and full of sparkling stars. Turning 360 degrees,

I searched the heavens for the moon, but there wasn't one. A moonless night, I frowned. The thought of the night without a moon seemed troubling, like when a light switch in a room doesn't work. The Milky Way dotted with green and orange and clustered strips of white turned the rooftops of the only three buildings in the town the color of ash. It also highlighted the dirt road that broke off at the jungle's edge. The jungle looked like a child's cutout, black and jagged, and uninviting.

With the brilliant galaxy blinking above, I no longer felt as though I were the only person alive on the planet or even in the universe, and my nerves began to calm down. Taking in my surroundings, I noticed a cement bridge to my left. It crossed over a rushing river, cascading white, gurgling swirls that made sucking noises as though slurping up the mud from the bottom. Below the bridge, there was a dock with several canoes with outboard motors, and a dog with white spots was sniffing at an overflowing trash bin. I listened in earnest over the churning river to hear a human voice or some laughter, but there was nothing promising, just the dog crunching on something hard and brittle.

Walking over to the three cement buildings, I peeked behind them. The first floor of the middle building had a light on. I felt a sense of relief and smiled at the possibility of good fortune. Walking carefully over the dips in the dirt pathway, I went up to the door and knocked. Nothing. Not one sound came from within. I knocked several times again, and each time my knock grew louder. Finally, something shuffled from within, followed by footsteps that came right up to the door. "*¿Quién es?*" asked a woman's voice, cautious yet stern, from behind the door.

"*Me llamo Eleanor,*" I said, my throat raspy from lack of speaking. "*Necesito alquilar una habitación por la noche.*"

Silence.

Clearing the phlegm, I said, "*Yo pagaré mucho.*"

The woman fiddled with the lock, then opened the door,

but only enough to expose small, squinting eyes. A dank odor of rotten corn and animal came from within, causing me to step back, but the woman thrust her hand out and grabbed my arm and clenched it with her gnarly fingers. I would have ripped my arm away, but then again, where was I to go? I let her pull me inside and as she did; she peeked around to the outdoors; I gathered, worried there may be others.

She stood approximately a foot shorter than my five feet and seven inches, and her face, shadowed by the backdrop of a dull, yellow light, was that of a withered old lady. But when she moved closer and smiled, she displayed high, rosy cheeks and calculating eyes that sized me up. A woman of many faces, I thought, and thrifty as she had let me in. Her black and white hair in its loose bun made me realize I had woken her up. When our eyes met, hers narrowed. "*Cinco dólar,*" she said.

"*No problemo.*" But before paying, I asked about a boat to the orphanage up the river and if there was anyone, in the household or in the area, willing to take me there tonight. She shook her head no while holding out her hand, but I paused once again. Looking around the room, I saw the floor was swept clean. The walls tarnished with what appeared to be overwashed grime, possibly the hazard of too many layers of cooking oil. There were only two blue plastic chairs and a lopsided wooden table. I had been hoping for a couch but would be fine sleeping in the chair with my head on the table. I was just content to be inside a building with a door.

Satisfied, I once again went to hand her the money, but it was then that a tattered, diminutive man burst through the door, pushing me aside and throwing my body against the doorjamb. The woman grabbed me and held me against her body. Her small but meaty frame felt like mealy down, and I quickly re-pocketed the money and pulled myself away. The man reeked of garbage, and his breath, which had brushed my cheek, was bitter and tangy and soiled no doubt by the rotgut he had been drinking.

His presence threw the woman into hysteria. She ran over to him, taking hold of his oversized coat with both hands, and shook him from side to side. She was strong, I thought, watching her berate the drunkard, placing her face and harsh words inches from his. She spoke rapidly in a language that sounded like upside-down French, filled with shushing words and ticks that swallowed each other. The man barked back in the same tongue, only he was sloppy and slow. Finally, his desperation to get away failing, he slunk down onto one of the plastic chairs, placing his hands over his ears, his eyes downcast, his thin face with its loose skin miserable.

"Christ," I mumbled. All I wanted to do was sit at that table and go to sleep, but I couldn't stay here. I wanted nothing to do with their domestic squabbles. I quickly turned and left. The cool, damp air was a relief as I hurried down the path, not sure where to go. But before I could make it around the corner of the building, I heard a shout from behind. I turned and saw the woman's squat silhouette in the doorway and a skinny boy of only twelve or possibly fifteen years coming toward me. The boy walked lazily, twisting his legs, and rubbing his eyes. "I take you," he said in heavily accented English. "*Orfanato.*" He then told me a price. I knew it was high, but I would have paid ten times what he was asking to get out of this town. Waiving him over, I smiled. What luck, I thought, the family was in the water taxi business.

The boy came up to me and gave me a toothy grin before taking my backpack off my shoulders and slinging it over his skinny body. He wasn't much bigger than the bag, and for a moment I thought to take it back but dismissed the urge as not to offend him. Beckoning me to follow with his hand, we went down to the dock and the rows of canoes. Turning back, I saw the woman, yards away, waddling like an obstinate rat and humming an off-key tune that I found unnerving. She was following us. I wished she would just go away.

Settled in, I sat down on the middle bench and breathed in the river and the mud-scented air. My back had a pinch around the lower lumbar, no doubt from the jarring bus. I twisted back and forth, trying to get rid of the pain while I watched the woman wobble over. She had on ethnic clothing, but different from what I was used to seeing in the country. Instead of a *huipil* and a heavy black, wool skirt, she had on a cloth skirt and blouse, and a vest with decorations in the middle. I turned to the boy and asked if they were *Mam* or *Q'eqchi*? He said, "No, *Mapuche*."

"*Mapuche*," I repeated and shrugged. I'd never heard of the *Mapuche* people before and wondered if they too, like many of the other groups in the area, were transplants from the north, but asking more questions seemed too tiring, so I let my curiosity slide away.

The woman, having reached us, was looking down at me. She huffed, smacked her lips, and said in stilted English, "Tell Cleef to see me. Yena."

"Yena?" I questioned.

"*Me llamo Yena.*"

The name sounded familiar. I had seen or heard it recently, but where? But before I could ask any questions or acknowledge her request, the boy slammed the boat into gear, and we shot backward, then forward into the rushing river. Glancing back at the woman called Yena, her body a cryptic blur, I watched her grow smaller and smaller as we pushed with haste up the river, a river painted white with hints of orange and yellow lit by the silver streaks of the stars. On each side, I could sense more than see the jungle and the foreboding sense of awe it emitted. It was moments like these, the ugliness of the town contrasted with the beauty of nature, discomfort overshadowed by rapture, and fear replaced by glory, that filled me with exultation for life.

At the dock, I paid the fare and threw in an extra *dólar* for the boy. I thanked him, and he sped off behind a thicket of mangroves, leaving nothing but the high-pitched whine of the canoe engine and the silence before me. I yawned loudly and shook my limbs. Feeling cold, I took my sweatshirt out of my pack and put it on, then followed the path lit by a floodlight up a dirt ascent laden with clumps of sparse grass. At the top, the floodlight revealed a white cottage and a long building that resembled a dining hall with another well-sized building next to it and another large building across from them. They were all made of wood and looked soggy like they were sinking into the ground. In the building that sat alone away from the others, a light was on in its screened-in porch. Walking up closer, I could see two white fellows in faux ethnic balloon pants sitting on the floor of the sparse, cavernous room. They were leaning up against a wall, legs straight out, and drinking what appeared to be rum and Cokes; a half-empty rum bottle and an empty liter of Coca-Cola were rolling around on the floor. Happy to see there were people awake, I walked in through the squeaky screen door, put my backpack down, went over to the fellows, and said, "Hello."

"Shh. No noise," said the frizzy blond with a clipped British accent.

"Orphanage, right?" I asked in a low tone.

"Who are you?" the Brit asked, looking at me suspiciously. He had a mischievous half-smile that increased his resemblance to the cartoon character Dennis the Menace, and I assumed him to be as juvenile. His hairdo was so absurd it made me smile. He had placed two ribbons tied into bows to create two well-formed pom-poms out of his kinky hair. When I read his ratty-looking T-shirt, I chuckled. In cursive lettering were the words, 'It's my hair that makes me sexy.' I took him to be around twenty-five.

"My name is Eleanor. I'm a *niñera*."

"Jolly good. Did you hear that Alex? We've got help." They clinked their glasses together and took long, sophomoric slurps. It was tempting to ask them for a drink, but another night. Tonight, I wanted to sleep. In a bed, if there was one, but as noted earlier, I was tired and would take a chair and table or even the floor.

"Where's the bathroom?" I asked.

"We go outside in the bushes," said the other fellow, Alex, who had a thick German accent. It was then that I realized I knew him. His dyed China-red dreads were tied up into knots on his head, atop a moon face with a long, crooked nose. His grin was puckish, and his small, black eyes looked like dots placed by a marker. He still had the same three purple pimples on his soft chin and the same piercings ran up and down his ears, but the nose ring that resembled the kind pigs wear to keep them from rooting was new. The whole quirky mess gave him an unusual appearance. Artistic, as if he were a cubist painting. Strapped with a personality prone to theft and severe jealousy, he was hard to be around. I'd met him in Puerto Escondido months ago. He had stolen my Spanish verb book. He also never cleaned his dishes in the communal kitchen at the rooming house. He constantly insulted everyone. By the time I had left, no one would talk to him except his girlfriend, Milla. And no one understood what she saw in him. I didn't like him there, and I was sure I wouldn't like him here and pretended not to recognize him, and he seemed to do the same with me.

"The bushes are the bathroom?" I questioned, the pinch in my back tightening.

"The boys use the bushes; the girls use the mud," Alex explained without jest.

I wasn't amused and said nothing back.

"The bathroom is through those doors and to the right," the Brit interjected. "The water isn't working. You can't flush."

"Thanks. Is there a place I can sleep?" I said, thinking I was finally making some headway.

"Right on my lap, sweets," Alex goofed while kissing the air.

"Bloody hell, Alex, don't be a wanker," the Brit said, then looked at me. "We're babysitting."

"Yes, babysitting," Alex repeated. "And you need to be quiet." He put his finger up to his lips and looked toward the inner room. "The children are sleeping. Shh."

I rolled my eyes and groaned and went off to the bathroom. The toilets didn't have seats. Filled with piss and crap, the stench was overwhelming. I peed anyway. The toilet wouldn't flush, but then the Brit told me they wouldn't—no running water. There weren't any doors on the bathroom stalls, and the three showers didn't have any curtains. Barebone accommodations, I thought, not particularly caring. I went back and asked if there was drinking water somewhere.

"Drinking water's outside. Two tanks. Drink from the right," said the Brit.

"No, it's the left tank," Alex interjected.

"Right."

"Left."

I went outside and over to the tanks. I tasted the water from both. The right tasted better, so I filled my bottle with the right and went back in and began rearranging several throw pillows to make a bed.

"What are you doing?" asked Alex.

I didn't answer.

"You can't crash our party," Alex said, sitting upright.

I ignored him.

"There is a room," said the Brit. "Go up to the second floor. Go through a door on the left of the hall to the third floor. The room is up there. It has the only free hammock." He then smiled. Alex smiled too. I didn't smile back. There was something not right about the room or they wouldn't be smiling, but I went anyway. Without saying another word, I picked up my pack and went up the stairs.

On the second floor, there was a distinctive thick cedar smell, and I could hear the rhythmic inhaling and exhaling of heavy breathing from down the hall. The place reminded me of every flophouse, hostel, and cheap hotel I had been living in over the past year, making it feel familiar if not nostalgic.

I took the creaky steps to the third floor. Once at the top, I placed my pack down and took my flashlight out because I couldn't find any light switches. The room was small and lined with boxes on one side, which made it even smaller. The walls were the slanted mahogany rafters of the roof, which made it hard to stand up straight. Because the rafters had gaps, the starlight beamed in creating dots and stripes on the walls. Cobwebs entangled with clumps of dead bugs were everywhere. Even the hammock had a web. I hated hammocks because when I slept, I liked to move around. The hammock I was looking at appeared more for a child than an adult, and I didn't even think I could fit in it. The room also had a dusty, baked feeling to it and a fetor that resembled a complex mixture of decomposing organic matter and urine.

Fully dressed in jeans, shirt, sweatshirt, and socks and sneakers to keep crawly things from nibbling at my toes, I delicately crawled into the hammock. It was very unstable and swung back and forth in an unmanageable manner. I immediately fell onto the slimy floor causing a loud clunking noise. Wiping my hands on my pants, I gave it another shot. I flipped out again. Below, I heard someone shout, "What?"

I tried once more, but either the contraption was poorly built, too small, or it was just my lousy hammock skills, I fell out. Dumbfounded, I sat on one of the cardboard boxes to think. It sunk to half its size, almost sinking me to the floor. With my knees bent up to my chin and my butt pressed against something pointy in the box, I reached down and felt the polyester, stringy hair of a barbie doll and pulled it out. Her jointless arms and legs twisted at the hip and shoulder and were pointing at me. I let it drop back into the box as a swell of frustration, heat, and fury crested my neck and brow. I was miserably tired, so tired that my brain felt like lead, and my eyes had mutated into hard marbles.

Sitting like a poorly built pretzel, I slumped over and fell asleep, soundly, until a mosquito dive-bombed my right ear and another bit my hand. Jolting forward and swatting the air, drool matted to my chin and left cheek, I heaved myself up while wiping away the saliva with the back of my hand. When a few more mosquitos buzzed my ears, I mumbled, while peddling the air with my hands, '*Pendejos*,' and my favorite, '*Me cago en todo lo que se menea*'— I shit on everything that moves. Standing up, I picked up my water bottle, tripped over a box full of Lego bricks, and knocked over another box full of Matchbox cars to the floor. From somewhere in the building I heard, "Shut up!"

Fed up, I descended back down to the first floor. The porch lamp was still on, but the idiots were asleep. Great babysitters, I thought. They had their heads tilted to the side and their mouths wide open. It was tempting to be very immature and stuff the grungy, two-day-old socks I had on into their mouths, but I took the high road and kept going, out the screen door and down to the river's edge. The cool air had a dampness to it that bathed my face and lungs. The freshness of my surroundings and the vastness of the river in front of me were joyful and life-giving. I breathed in deeply, calming myself. It will all be fine. I had experienced plenty of first bad days in my travels. I had also found the worse the beginnings were, the better the place often was.

I washed my hands in the water, using the sand to scrub off the grime. Then I walked around in circles before sitting down on a large rock by the dock to stare off across the broad river. I would wait for morning. Once the sun was up and the birds were singing again, I would reintroduce myself to the place. All the wrongs corrected by a new day. I just needed to be patient.

But there was a ghostly fog crawling backward over the dark, flowing waters, waters the color of cobalt blue, thick and blackened with gray. The silence was eerie and deafening in its vacuous state. It brewed a visceral fear in me of what might lurk over yonder in the woods or even within the cool hues of the water. A knocking sound came from the front dock pilings, and I froze. Rising, I quickly walked over, thinking it was better to face my enemy than caught unaware by a surprise attack. It was nothing, just flotsam from the river. This made me laugh. Giddy with exhaustion, I may have even wept a bit. With a sigh, I went back to the rock and sat down again to wait.

The air, chilled and scented with the earth's decomposing matter and water, had me hugging myself to stay warm. I slapped a mosquito flat and gooey against my cheek. And unclipped my hair to let it dangle around my neck and face as a prophylactic against bugs. I hadn't been back to the States for almost a year. It was probably snowing there—that is, if I had my months correct, and it was March. Sinking down onto the ground, I fell asleep.

Chapter 3

Daylight

The world was boiling, and I was right smack in the middle of the combustion, bubbling like a plastic top in the gurgling heat, unable to swim but somehow buoyant. Surfacing, the tiny whispers of ethereal air resounded as it went up and down being played on a piano of clouds. When I reached out to grab one of the notes, I couldn't. Grunting, I tried again, but the notes were quick. I laughed. Such a typical dream—teasing and wouldn't allow me to do what I wanted.

I opened my eyes with sudden fright and abruptly sat up, throwing my torso against a wall of bodies, soft, gushy flesh that smelled like beans and paste. Kids. Little kids and lots of them. A couple had fallen onto their bottoms and looked stunned for a moment, only to scramble up and run. Most had scattered like squealing balloons zigzagging with exaggerated fright, bumping into each other as though not sure where to hide. Others charged into the water, distracted by it, they began splashing each other. For a brief moment, I thought I might still be in a dream; the sun bright and hot, I realized I had too many clothes on and ripped off my sweatshirt. The birds singing out of sync made everything seem like madness, but then blocking the rays of the sun with his pom-poms, spoke the silhouette of the Brit. "When you sat up, you should have growled. Gosh, I would have loved to have seen them run if you'd growled. Spun and tripped all the way back to the *dormitorio,* the little rascals."

"Maybe next time," I said, picking twigs and leaves out of my hair. I also wished a different adult was talking to me instead of the pom-pom jerk. I felt all beaten up and was still so tired that to stand seemed paramount to running a marathon. "Do you ever take out the pom-poms?" I asked for no reason except they were his most prominent feature.

"What pom-poms?"

"Never mind," I said and threw my legs straight out to touch my toes. The stretch was comforting and healing to my back.

The Brit, staring at me, smiled, and said, "Try the doggy down yoga pose. Terrific for the hamstrings. The kids will do it too. *Vengan, niños.*" He then bent over and made his body into a V, but his hands weren't far enough from his legs, causing his bottom to be too far up in the air. It was such a ludicrous position that it made me laugh. It felt good to laugh. It was like the feeling the sun gives off after it has been raining for weeks.

"What's your name?" I asked.

"Gunther. And if my memory serves me correctly, you're Eleanor. Now, Eleanor, it's not right for you to laugh. This is good for you," he said, still upside down. With his voice strained, he added, "*Miren, niños.*"

Several of the little kids came over and tried to copy what he was doing. Their attempts were preposterous and resembled nothing like the downward dog position. One little boy wearing yellow rubber boots and blue-jean overalls with the label Gucci across his chest had his bottom on the sand and his legs kicking in the air. Another little boy who looked to be only a foot and a half tall, thin with delicate, refined features, lay face down on the sand and stayed there, not moving. He was wearing Brooks Brothers plaid shorts and an Izod dark blue shirt, and on his feet were a pair of Doc Martens. How odd, I thought, but as I looked more closely at what the other children were wearing, as the rest were falling into place near Gunther and attempting to do yoga, their outfits also heralded big names such as Burberry, Rodini, Lacoste, and Guess. I had imagined orphans, stereotypically, especially in Central America, to be wearing tattered clothing, but here the children were fashioned in clothing explicitly for those with money. Coupled with the beautiful blue river in the background, the yoga group looked like they were at an exclusive lakeside country club.

"What's with the clothing?" I asked. "It's all designer."

Still, in his incorrect downward dog pose, Gunther grunted. "Nothing but the best for our little tykes."

"But?"

"Donations from the riches of the USA. You are American, aren't you? Or Canadian?" He asked as he stood upright, his face red, with drool on his upper lip.

"American."

"Which state?"

"Massachusetts," I answered.

"Massachusetts. That's Boston?"

"Yes."

"I went there with my parents years ago. Nice enough. I'm now taking my gap year. Anyway, been to New York too. Loved it," he said, shaking out his arms. He then burst out laughing because the children were still on the beach trying to copy him. "*Bueno, niños*. Haha—A bit gormless, aren't they." Then turning to look at me, he said, "You still knackered? I know I am. Babysitting is rough on a person." Then changing the subject. "You need to get up. On a bit of a schedule here. We need to wash their faces." With a burst of energy, he clapped his hands together as though signaling me to stand up and start washing faces.

But I was tired, groggy, and he was too full of himself, and it made me not want to do anything he suggested. Then reluctantly, I got up with the help of a big rock, but instead of kicking my shoes off and rolling my pant legs up to help wash the kids, I went over to two girls wearing bright floral Marimekko sundresses. They were the only two who understood how to do the downward dog pose correctly. "Bravo, girls," I said and joined them. The stretch felt marvelous and made my lower back feel even better. Standing up, my gaze fell upon a house that jutted out into the water. "What's that building?" I asked.

"Little kids' schoolhouse," Gunther answered with a flat tone. His pant legs now rolled up. He had waded into the water.

A canoe with a person at the bow and a man sitting slouched in the stern, hand on the outboard motor's tiller, buzzed by close to the shore. "People go up and down this river all day long," Gunther said, staring after it. "You know why they have motors on their canoes?

"To go fast."

"Funny. Yes and no. Some Yamaha sales guy showed up one day and sold the locals engines. Now they're all in debt. They'd rather fish, the locals that is, but fishing doesn't pay for the motor. Driving a taxi does. Did you see the scowl on the man's face driving the boat? Now quit waffling around and help."

The sun, having risen over the treetops, had begun baking the air. Swimming was tempting, but my tired head seemed too heavy, and I felt I might sink. I was also hungry, and my pits were slimy. My teeth felt rough with sludge, and the taste in my mouth was tinny and sour. I thought of the last place I had lived, a mountainous town called *Corriente* with old Maria in her cement, earthquake-cracked house. The shower only dribbled water, and the toilet didn't have a seat, but the idea of eating her hearty oatmeal breakfast with vanilla twists and cinnamon sticks made my mouth water.

"How many *niñeros* are there?" I asked, picking a washcloth up off the ground.

"Ten of us foreigners here, but two are teachers, Hamit and Harry, and one is a doctor, so seven *niñeros*, but then didn't you say you're a *niñera*? So that makes eight of us. Eight. Such a nice, even number."

"All foreigners here?"

"No, there's other local staff too. Just our little group is foreign. Mind you, we don't normally wash the kids' faces in the river. We don't have any running water right now. This morning we used buckets of water and gave them sponge baths in the showers. Now, are you going to help me or not?"

"What about the water tanks?"

"The pipe to the bathroom broke, so no water in the bathroom."

Squatting down to be eye level with the girls, I asked them their names, but they remained silent, just big brown eyes and dimples looking at me. "Gunther, what are their names?"

"Bernarda is the one with the short, dark, curly hair, and the other with light brown hair is Charlotte. Two little gems. Usually, they opt for shorts, but today they wanted to wear dresses. They must have known we had company." Gunther spoke from the shallows of the water. He was standing ankle-deep with a cloth in his hand, beckoning the little boy with the yellow rubber boots to join him.

"Aren't you charming when you're not drinking," I said, looking over at him.

"Aren't most people?"

"I suppose." Averting my eyes and bringing my attention back to the girls, I sat back down because squatting was too tiring. Gunther was directing a huffing noise at me, his mouth agape, it seemed his patience had worn thin by my lack of help.

"Sitting isn't helping," he said.

"I will. It's just that I feel like a truck ran over me last night. I just need a moment."

"By the way," Gunther said, "I wasn't that pissed last night. Alex was the legless ass. A raspberry tart. Hell, I told you the right water tank to drink out of, didn't I?"

"Which one?"

"Left."

"I thought you said right."

"Maybe it is the right. Anyway. Why did you sleep on the beach?"

"Small hammock."

"True." He had finished washing two other little boys and whistled for Bernarda and Charlotte to join him in the water.

They ignored him. Leaning their bodies against me, they picked the rest of the leaves and twigs out of my hair. Each piece seemed to fascinate them. Bernarda had sparkly eyes and a devil's chin and round cheeks that bunched up when she smiled, exposing little, white Chiclet teeth. She was chunky in the way a baby is plump but not fat, whereas Charlotte had lost her rolls, if she ever had any. She wasn't thin but wiry, strong looking for a youngster. Her small but wide nose sniffed a lot, and her two soft, brown eyes looked like they saw more than what was obvious. They both had bean-goo stuck to their cheeks, and their dresses had a few food remnants on them too. I asked them in the most precise, simple Spanish I could muster if they had just eaten; Charlotte opened her mouth but said nothing, and Bernarda whispered something about my hair being soft. Taking their hands, I led them into the water and started washing their faces.

"Gunther, none of the kids look indigenous. *Mestizos.*"

"I've been told the Mayan don't give their kids up, but a fellow, a priest that came by here, said they were starting to. Too many kids, not enough food. That's why most of them are here. It's like a boarding school for the poor. Most aren't adoptable. They go home for the holidays. Well, not the little ones, but the older kids."

"That's what Lenore told me when she interviewed me for the position."

"She's a gem. We all love Lenore," he quipped chuckling.

"I like her."

"So, do I. We just don't see much of her here."

"Back home I have friends that went to boarding school. Odd ducks, most of them. They have a hard time understanding the average Joe. It's like the masses have cooties or something like that." I was finding it hard to wipe the bean smudges off Charlotte's face. The stuff was like glue.

"Now that's not right. I went to boarding school, and I'm about as good a chap you'll find," he said looking over at me with a stupid dumbfounded expression on his face.

"I think you just proved my point," I remarked, and we both chuckled. Then changing the subject, I said. "This stuff sticks."

"We just ate. Imagine if we left it on," Gunther said. Then pausing, he stood up and scratched his head and added, "Now I wouldn't go sleeping on the beach tonight. They're crocs out there. I know people say manatees are friendly, but I don't trust the little buggers. I think they're mean. You sleep on the beach again they may crawl up and bite you." As he spoke, he was washing the face of a tough-looking square box of a boy. He had a small mouth that Gunther stretched side to side like play-dough.

"This is Frankie; the other little boy with the rubber boots is Raymond," Gunther spoke, drawing my attention back to him. "We think Raymond is something like two and a half, not quite three. You know, too small, needs more help than most." He gave Frankie one last wipe and said, "There we go. All nice and clean." Frankie, with a determined grin, sloshed his way out of the water swinging his arms making bear sounds. Next Gunther beckoned for the tiny boy with the plaid Brooks Brothers shorts to come to him. He had been waiting patiently on the river's edge, watching Frankie's face being washed. His name was Henrik, and Gunther directed him to take his sandals off before walking into the water, but he didn't want to, so he walked away to go play with Raymond by a drooping avocado tree.

"Oh, come on, Henrik. Don't be like that," Gunther pleaded, then gave up and said, "*Venga,* Bernarda." She walked out to him. Gunther continued, "That's Charlotte, the little girl you're taking a hundred years on, doesn't speak. According to Doc, she was found in a shack sitting by the body of her dead grandmother. They think she had been there for days. Doc says her vocal cords are healthy and that not speaking is a choice."

"How sad. Although, it doesn't sound like a choice. I mean, I'm sure she'd like to talk," I replied. Then changing the subject,

I asked, "Do you think I'll be able to get some food?"

"You're not very helpful."

"I'll come back after I change my clothes—Brush my teeth—Maybe get a bite to eat."

He looked up and smiled. "No problem. Here comes help." Looking up the ascent, I could see the rest of the *niñeros* coming down the pathway, a scrappy, bedraggled looking clan.

"Get the bucket by the dock," Gunther said to me in an authoritarian voice. "Fill it and use it to flush the toilet. Leave the bucket in the bathroom. Yup… Someone forgot, and that's why the bucket is down here where it shouldn't be." Shrugging, he shouted to the group, "It's about time. Lots of faces to wash!" Looking at me, he continued, "And so few hands. But I'm just jesting. I don't blame you, Eleanor. My first night here I babysat with Alex. I drank so much I threw up. Spent the night in the kindergarten house and pissed on myself."

"What's the word for 'kindergarten' in Spanish?"

"Kindergarten, only with a Spanish accent."

"That's easy," I said, getting up, then asked, "Does everyone drink a lot here?" I was trying to cut down on my drinking.

"No, only when babysitting. And sometimes when we're not. Okay, most nights, or is that every night?"

I walked over to the dock and retrieved the bucket, filled it with water, and then headed back up toward the buildings, ruminating over my life and wondering what I'd done to it this time.

As I was an only child, with my father dead and my mother in a mental institution, family wasn't an obstacle to my travels. There was no one to worry about me or tell me to come home, to admonish my lack of ambition, wince if I dated a bad boy, suggest I find a better hairdresser, insist I should be working and not roaming the lands of foreign countries, or to impress. I was thirty, an age most people became more serious about their lives as in careers, not jobs, and marriage and babies. But left to impress myself and only myself, I stumbled. Because how does one impress oneself? Especially when one is naturally rebellious, fickle, and unwilling to conform to society's rules and games. But recently, with my Spanish moving along swimmingly well, I'd gained a sense of optimism for my future and almost thought of myself as impressive.

Before leaving on my sojourn, short on university classes for my foreign language requirement to graduate, I'd come up with the idea to spend time in Mexico and various Central American countries to learn Spanish. The idea was to go back and take the exam, pass, and graduate. Even though I had been out of college for several years and working, I felt to have more choices in life—I needed a diploma. In hindsight, I was becoming more serious about my life. Yet, it wasn't the deep-down reason I was traveling. Learning Spanish to get my diploma was the excuse—and an excuse I took seriously. I also took seriously the need to discover more of life. Knock some cobwebs out of the dust in my veins I had collected bemoaning my mother's illness, my father's demise, and working at jobs that gave me only a paycheck in return and little else. I needed something. To find, see, hear new ideas. I was a 'work in progress.'

Chuckling to myself, I climbed the hill to the dormitorio. So far, I'd only spoken a handful of Spanish and a boatload of English at the orphanage. Yet, the place was different and interesting. I would give it a chance. I'd never met an orphan, let alone worked at an orphanage. Then it occurred to me, was I an orphan? Unanchored, adrift in the world, I wasn't sure about much, but giving the place a chance seemed like a good idea. The Mayan belief—life is circular came to mind. Since I was on a new jag, place, I figured I was somewhere in the middle of the circle or starting fresh at the beginnning of the loop. Then the idea of circling around and around like being on a merry-go-round made me dizzy, or maybe my unsteadiness was due to hunger. Putting the bucket down, I wiped my brow. The birds sang and squawked above, and the children's giggles echoed from behind. The place was small and compact, almost like being swaddled, how comforting.

At the top of the incline, I came upon the other *niñeros.* We exchanged a few introductions. They all seemed friendly except for Alex, who refused to even look at me or say hello, but then I didn't say anything to him either. None of us lingered too long because they were in a hurry to help Gunther. Molly and Golly were hefty with large, fleshy arms and heavy, pendulous breasts and mentioned something about snoring at night, which I thought was odd because why would I care? Possibly they were just apologizing in case I cared. They both had brassy red hair pinned back with plastic butterflies. They were hard to tell apart from the back, but luckily their faces were very different. Molly had a thin, sharp nose and glossy, gray eyes surrounded by thick, dark red lashes, and clear facial skin for how many freckles were on her arms. Golly had a piggish-looking snout and tiny eyes made even smaller by her large cheeks, which were covered in pin-pricked freckles. They both, however, had an incomprehensible cockney accent. Their hello sounded like *Ay-O*, like they had dropped something and were in trouble.

A fellow with a long, pointy nose introduced himself as Jack. He asked me if I had been making noises in the attic last night. I said, "no." He grabbed hold of a demure woman's hand and introduced her as his wife, Sarah. Everyone seemed to be more or less around my age except for a very tall, regal-looking woman named Catarina. I put her height around five feet, ten inches, and her age at fifty-something. She was thin, with a youthful appearance and expressive wrinkles around her mouth and eyes. She wore a long, fluffy cotton skirt that swished when she walked. She also told me never to call her Cat.

Once in the compound, I saw to my right, by the dormitorio, a small house painted white with a gray porch. Above the door was a sign that said OFICINA. I was happy to see there was an office, which I took to be a place to find the head of the orphanage or at least some information, but the door was locked, and no one seemed to be around. To my left, by the other large house, a few kids that looked older than the children on the beach, possibly from age six to their mid-teens, were mingling around the doorway of the building. I smiled and said, "*Buenos días.*" They nodded back the way people nod when suspicious of someone. I was glad my assignment was with the little ones.

In the middle of it all, something one might call a quad, were several overturned canoes placed on top of cement blocks. The canoes outlined a giant sandbox containing sand mixed with dirt and a few clumps of grass. In the sand and dirt, someone had built a fort with sticks and piled rocks to look like a pyramid. Beyond the buildings was the jungle, with a pathway going left and another going directly into the woods. The left path had a light blue sign painted with crooked, purple handwriting to read, "CLÍNICA." The other sign, painted in the same colors, read "ESCUELA y BIBLIOTECA" and pointed directly into a thicket of brush.

Looking past the shrubs, I saw a muddy path with boards placed over a stream. The path itself, riddled with muddy dips, roots, and rocks, twisted its way to a grassy knoll with a cement pen with pigs. I could see their pink noses poking over the fencing, and one was trying to crawl out. The blue sky above held fragile clouds hovering over the knoll, creating shadows. It reminded me of a painting, one would see, of New England farms back home in *Yankee* magazine. Slightly below the knoll stood another white building that resembled a giant box, and next to it was a building with a steeple. I assumed the buildings to be a school and the library, but why a steeple when the orphanage was secular?

During my interview with Lenore in her office back in the city, she told me she wanted nothing to do with churches, religion. Lenore was from Honduras and brought up Catholic. She felt the whole shebang of God, obeying, and praying, "Was for the birds, but then the birds are too smart to fall for all that jargon," she had said, adding. "What good does it do for these kids to think god will save them?" Then pausing, I felt for dramatic tension, she looked directly into my eyes, and said, "They need to learn to save themselves. We all do."

A husky woman with thick, curly, black hair and dark eyes that smiled more than her mouth, she told me she liked to go out at night to the discos. She wore a Versace dress that at the time I had thought was a knockoff, but now I knew better. It was a size too small. A dress made for waspy, rich ladies was not going to fit a voluptuous Latina the way it was intended.

Lenore, sitting behind her sparse desk with an old, pink rotary phone at her left elbow and a Smith Corona electric typewriter at her right, asked me questions. I remember I had felt a little intimidated by her because she was the boss. She had done something with her life that seemed worthy and was still young, possibly forty. She had an intelligence unique to people who are doers. When she asked me if I liked children, I answered, "Why, of course," as though it were a silly question. But I could tell she could see right through me. Her eyes, no longer searching mine for truth, had detected a flaw and moved on. The truth was, I didn't know if I liked children or not. I was never around them. Most of my friends back home were just starting to get married and didn't have any babies yet. So, maybe I did like them. It wasn't a lie, just an unschooled supposition.

But it didn't matter. My position was voluntary. I was to receive room and board for my efforts. Either I would work out and stay or I would leave. Or I would do both because everyone did both. When I left her office, I thanked her, but she neither shook my hand nor thanked me. Instead, she walked me to the door and nodded goodbye while handing me a letter of introduction to take to the orphanage. I was under the impression she was slightly jaded about all the people that showed up to volunteer. I gathered all our faces looked alike; our ideals honorable—well, I had said nothing to her about having aspirations of doing good for the world. It was the language I was after and something different to do while pursuing it. But I was sure the foreign body that stepped into her office pontificated about the glory of helping others and the honor it was to do so. Possibly, she may have been wondering why I hadn't. It was very simple; it didn't occur to me.

Walking through the screen door into the interior of the dormitorio, I saw the place was empty of people, tidy and dusted, and made my way to the bathroom.

Chapter 4

Cadmael

The white porcelain rim and bowl of the toilet had been polished. There was not one spot and it glistened. But there was a disinfectant, animal fetor that hung in the air. It was hard to take at first. I gathered it had something to do with having crap in the bowls all night. Before sitting, I lined the rim of the toilet with the pink crepe paper that was hanging off the tiled wall with a wire. It was something I always did because it just seemed more sanitary. As for the constantly missing toilet seats, they are expensive, and for many, redundant.

While sitting I stared at the stall walls. White was a ubiquitous color here. The toilets, the sink, the showers, the walls, and all the exterior wood of the buildings were white, except for the dining hall. If white were to personify cleanliness, which most likely wasn't the case, the paint just cheap, but if it were, I thought, then the dining hall should be white too. Instead, the dining hall, left in its naked origins of wood and palm fronds, made it similar to the jungle surrounding it.

The muggy air that waft in through the window contained the same mold smell that seemed to be everywhere in the compound. The funky odor dropped in and out of my nostrils, and it was offensive. I think it came from the jungle, or maybe it was a product of the standing pools of water littering the ground at the back of the dormitorio. It wasn't the rainy season, but that didn't mean it hadn't rained and wouldn't do it again. Yet, despite my unflattering thoughts, overall, I liked the bathroom. The gray floor had been swept clean and washed. Not a cobweb or bug in sight. But then I saw that under the utility sink in the room's corner, a line of ants making their way up the piping. They were walking fast. I wondered what was in the sink that the ants might want. Suddenly, out of nowhere, two house flies landed on the pink toilet paper by my left knee and started fornicating. Their beady eyes were glaucomatous and unemotional, the sex stilted as they barely moved, and when they did, it was only to twitch.

Ripping a piece of the toilet paper off, it knocked the fucking houseflies to the floor. Searching the floor to find them, they lay by my right foot, still engaged and twitching. I was pleased that I hadn't interrupted them.

Getting up, I took the bucket of water and poured it into the back of the tank and flushed. It wasn't the first time I'd had to flush a toilet in this manner. I'd been in many a village that had questionable water supplies.

At the sink, I fiddled with the faucet knobs to see if possibly there was water, but there was nothing. There weren't any mirrors either. I knew my face had to be filthy, but I supposed if I didn't see it, it wouldn't bother me. I was used to not seeing myself; for the past year, I had barely looked into a mirror. If there was one, it was usually warped, making a person's chin too long and their eyes too big.

Unclipping my barrette, I leaned over, letting the rest of the twigs and leaves Bernarda and Charlotte had missed fall to the ground and ran my fingers like a comb through my thick, tangled hair.

Startlingly me, came the unexpected grunting noises and heavy boots of two workmen shuffling into the bathroom.

"Hola," I said, standing straight, almost at attention and baffled by their presence. They threw me a quick glance, nodding a silent greeting. Their cowboy attire was splattered with mud, and their dark faces looked greasy and hot. I shrugged; anyone could walk into this bathroom. Not a worry, just something noted. The men, fascinated by a pipe that ran the length of the far wall, began poking at it with their index fingers. The older fellow mumbled something in the same language I'd heard last night; French sounding and filled with shushes and upticks. Having had enough of their intrusion, I left.

In the next room, I could see into the area where the kids slept. Several cribs lined the walls beneath expansive windows. Another workman was standing outside by the water tanks with a wrench in his hand. He was looking in at me. I waved, and he waved back with his wrench.

Looking around the room, I noticed it was long with a swept-clean, maroon cement floor, and white walls. There were several plastic baskets full of clothing, blankets, and towels, and under a bench were a couple of pairs of shoes. Curious, I went over to a basket filled with dresses and picked out a few. They were doll-like, and the labels on the back displayed Saks Fifth Avenue and Dolce Gabbana. There was also a half-deflated rubber ball on the floor; three very worn, beige bean bag chairs; and several neatly stacked books placed against a solid wall. The room was lit by windows on both sides, allowing a breeze to come in.

Walking into the next room, I ran my fingers over a row of cribs, inlaid with thick mattresses covered with colorful wool blankets. Again, everything was neat and tidy and clean. The brown cement floor swept and even shined. Looking up, I noticed the maintenance man by the tanks was looking at me again. I waved, and he waved back, resting his eyes upon mine for a few interposing moments before turning away. With his wrench, he banged down hard upon the rusty spigot attached to the left water tank. I hoped whatever he was doing would fix the problem, but then he broke the spigot and water gushed into the tall grasses below. Clean, drinkable water, I thought. I was thirsty. With haste, I rushed outside to nab a few drops before it was all gone.

Kneeling, I cupped my hands to bring the water up to my lips. It was sweet and refreshing, and I gulped it down. I also splashed it all over my face, scrubbing my cheeks, my mouth and forehead. The coolness and the act of washing the crust and sleep away was exhilarating. And then I stopped and stood up because it occurred to me that my actions might look odd, almost crazy to the workman.

Water running down my chin, I smiled at the man while wiping my mouth with the back of my hand. He was looking at me critically, squinting his eyes and nibbling on his lower lip. Unlike the other workmen, he was young with clear, dark eyes. His features, Mayan, he had high cheekbones and a firm chin, and he had a slenderness to his face that alluded to a sensitive nature. Flushed with heat and sweat, his muscles tense and full of energy, he was very handsome, and I believed he was aware of it—not a turn-off, just an observation.

Wiping my hands on my shirt, I introduced myself and shook his hand.

"I'm Cadmael," he said.

When I asked him, what was wrong with the tank, he replied with a glint in his eye and in basic Spanish, that the tank needed cleaning. That there were too many dead things in it. Seeing my worried look, he laughed, adding in English, "A joke."

But the joke had merit. The water which was still flowing

out had leaves and spiders in it. He explained he was draining the tank to fix it which hardly assuaged my feelings of disgust. I spat several times onto the ground.

Then letting my eyes roam from his grinning face to the tank then back to him again, I felt he was waiting for me to either say something or leave, but I did neither because I was still thirsty. Adjusting his stance, he leaned his body against a tree by the tank. The sultry turn of his head, and his nonchalant swag, ruffled me. Looking into his eyes because I felt it was better than staring at his body, I paused longer than I should have. They were a beautiful brown and fluid with specks of green. My face still dripping with water, my thirst still not quenched, I asked about the other tank attempting to ignore his flirtatious manner. He told me it was empty.

"What about drinking water?" I asked in Spanish.

Smiling, he leaned over and tapped my chin lightly with a finger. Then pointed to several large plastic containers, and said, "Water. Fresh."

His body had a carnal haughtiness to it. I knew he was teasing me. Stepping back out of his reach I smiled wondering how many *nineras* he'd slept with over the years. Lightly laughing, I shook my head. What silliness, I thought, averting my eyes to the blue sky, then over to the green canopy that outlined it. Having regained some high ground, I looked at him without fluster, and folded back into the quad and over to the dining hall. I was famished.

Chapter 5

Harry

We began our introductions by staring at each other. There were three of them. They stood behind the buffet counter looking at me with perplexed eyes and tight, disgruntled mouths. My stance solemn but hopeful, I stared back. One woman was short, thin, and young; another was pregnant and a little older; and the third was a middle-aged, humorless woman with broad, set-back shoulders and a chest that reminded me of a puffed hen. She was also chewing bubblegum with a hapless, bovine manner. It made her funny to watch, but I didn't dare smile because I was under the impression she wasn't trying to be amusing. They all were wearing thick Mayan skirts, and for shirts, they had on cotton T-shirts with writing that I could not see due to their white, stained bibs. The orphans get the name brands and the masses get the T-shirts; I mused.

Behind the three women were pots and pans piled neatly on top of a counter; a six-burner cast-iron stove; and a shiny, empty metal sink. It seemed they had cleaned up breakfast and put everything away, but I wasn't going to budge. I was on the brink of collapsing from hunger, and there was still a small pot of beans on the stove and a basket of tortillas on a counter by the back door. I figured if I played it right, the goods could be mine, but my only hand was to be stubborn, and by their expressions, I felt they might be better at this game than I was.

Then luck stepped in. The hefty, ill-humored woman blew an enormous bubble. When it popped, it stuck to her straight, firm nose. This made the pregnant woman next to her laugh. While she laughed, her bib drooped down, and I saw that her T-shirt had dark lettering that said, "What Part of 'No' Didn't You Understand." I chuckled. I am not sure, but possibly this caused the young, thin one to burst out laughing. While laughing, she covered her mouth with a dishrag. The dishrag had a bug on it, and when she saw the bug, a large beetle with hideous horns, she threw the rag and the bug onto the floor and stomped on both, causing a loud crunching noise. This caused us all to cringe and created more laughter from the pregnant woman; the young one was now in uncontrollable, laughing hysteria too. It was all I could do not to plunge into crying laughter because both tears and hilarity were welling up inside of me. But I wanted food most of all, and the bubblegum lady wasn't even smiling. She looked downright mean, but the standoff had been broken.

The two younger ones had peeled away, laughing, to the corners of the kitchen, bent over and with hands over their mouths. The hefty woman was left to face me alone with bubblegum stuck to her nose. A feeling of hope rose up inside me when I saw a glint of mirth enter her narrowed eyes, but I didn't dare smile. The battle was still being played as she seemed to try her best to appear angry. Then she huffed a loud, lazy, humorous huff that had me biting my lower lip in order, again, not to laugh. With my shoulders taut, my breath stuck in my mouth, I waited, listening to the girls wheezing, the birds singing, the humidity rising, and every pore in my body perspiring.

Finally, the older woman shifted, just a small shift, but it gave me great relief and a reason to breathe. She then put her left hand on her hip, cleared her throat, pulled the gum from her nose, and popped it back into her mouth. Sauntering over to the stove, she took a plate from a pile and filled it with a ladle of beans. A thick pile of delicious blackness. She then threw a tortilla the size of a frisbee on top of the beans, and a fork, and when she handed me the plate, she winked. Another humorous act, but I kept my smile tempered, which was hard because her T-shirt read, "My people skills are fine." Thanking them all profusely, my mouth watering, I turned with my plate of food in hand and looked for a place to sit, feeling like the world was truly my oyster.

The dining area was a huge, vacuous space, filled with long, wooden tables and benches set in rows. Above it all, there was a vaulted, thatched ceiling with objects flitting around the wooden rafters, possibly birds or bats. Scrutinizing the tabletops and floor, I was pleased to see there weren't any droppings and settled down at a table near the entrance to eat. Then from somewhere in the back of the room, I heard a person shout, "You're back!"

I looked around but couldn't figure out where the voice came from.

"Behind you!"

In the shadowed lighting toward the right back corner, I could see the silhouette of a man waving a fork in the air.

"Join me!" He yelled in a jovial tone.

I walked over carrying my food.

"Amazing! you got food."

"You have food?" I replied sitting down.

"They always give me food. Esmeralda loves me."

"The bubblegum lady?"

"Yes. Bubblegum is her favorite. I always bring her gifts when I return from the city," he said, putting a spoonful of rice and beans into his mouth. Looking at his rice and the lack of it on my plate, I felt like I had been shortchanged.

"What's your name?" I asked.

"You know who I am."

I didn't say anything. Instead, I remained silent while running my eyes over his face. I had been to so many places and met so many people I might have known him. He was near to my age or a few years older, and he was gorgeous—yes, gorgeous. This stopped me from filing through my memory banks because the more I studied his features, the more I was sure I wouldn't have forgotten this man's face; he was absolutely stunning. No, breathtaking in the way something unique can be, such as a brilliant thought or song or taste, the way their sheer inventiveness renders one speechless. His features angled but not sharp; his nose poignant but not hooked. His eyes were dark and nearly black, only they were blue. His cheeks and chin perfectly formed into masculine strength. I could tell he had just shaved: his pale skin, smooth and unworried, had a nick by his right ear. Even his hair was beautiful. Thick, dark brown tufts piled on top of his head and fell just below his ears. It gave him a messy but endearing quality. His hair also seemed in need of constant attention. Within the few seconds we had been together, he had pushed it away from his forehead twice, and after the second time he mumbled, "Since you left, I've had no one to cut my hair." His voice was deep with an accent that touched of Oxford English along with hints of some other foreign entity.

"I think you have mistaken me for someone else," I said, taking a bite of food. It was a tasteless, bland clump of beans, and the tortilla wasn't much better. It resembled soft, slightly undercooked plastic corn.

He had stopped eating to rub his chin and touch his tongue to his well-formed upper lip to say, "You're Maddy. I'd know you anywhere."

"My name's Eleanor."

"No. that can't be right."

"I think I know my name," I said, putting my fork down.

"Come to think of it, Maddy has blonde hair." He then paused and looked over at a tree. When he came back to the conversation, he said, "Or was that Phoebe? Anyway, it doesn't matter." But apparently, it did. After tapping his fork several times upon the table, he eyed me critically and asked, "Are you sure?"

"Yes!"

"Okay, well, I don't suppose you cut hair?"

"I can, but I doubt you'll like the results."

This made him laugh, a deep baritone guffaw. When he finally stopped, we continued eating in silence. It seemed everything was all messed up now because I wasn't who he thought I was, which made me feel awkward, but I didn't want to get up and leave as that would have been even stranger. Staying put, I ate my food, filling but tasteless and very unsatisfying. Looking over at his plate for no particular reason except boredom, I noticed there were blobs of red flecks all over his food.

"Do you have salsa?" I inquired. When he hesitated to answer, I got up. "I gather it's in the kitchen?"

"Stay. No. Now you know better than that, you have to bring your own," he admonished.

Settling back down, I said, "I don't know better about anything. I'm new."

"You didn't say you were new."

"Well, I am. Now I don't have any salsa, but I bet you do."

He leaned back, cleared his throat, and eyed me suspiciously. "You don't ask people to share their salsa here—it's rude." His dark blue eyes, the color of a New England ocean on a clear, crisp day, danced about in the morning light with such mischievousness that I figured he had to be joking.

"Rude?" I questioned.

"Rude." He ate again without looking at me, and I thought he wasn't handsome anymore.

After a few moments I said with annoyance, "So, you're not sharing?"

"No. No sharing," he said, looking up quickly to give me a pigheaded stare, then averted his eyes once more to chow down.

"Does sharing only apply to salsa or is there a 'no sharing' rule for everything? Like, oh, I don't know—let's say I wanted to use the pencil you have by your book?" I asked.

He had a book by his plate that said *Historia de Central America* across the cover, and beside the book a notepad and a pencil. He had stopped eating to stare at them as though pondering which item he liked the least. Finally, he looked at me and said, "I might let you read the book. Can you read Spanish?"

"Working on it."

"Okay, you can borrow the book."

"But I want the pencil."

"No, only the book," he said, raising his eyebrows to punctuate the 'no.'

"Let's go back to the salsa. That's what I really want."

"We don't share condiments," he said with a stern voice while pushing the book towards me.

"Keep your book," I said, still adamant that this was all just a preposterous joke.

"Are you sure?" he said, pushing the book toward me.

"I don't want it," I said, pushing it back toward him. "I want the salsa."

"Seems someone is on a rude jag," he said, pursing his lips, lips I no longer found enticing. Then smacking them, he opened his mouth and smiled. "You must be an American."

"Whatever," I said, feeling tired. "And what frosty European country do you come from?"

He laughed again, another great, big, hearty laugh. When he stopped, he placed both hands on the table and leaned forward as though he wanted to tell me a secret. Then, speaking in a hushed voice, he said, "Salsa and other stuff like ketchup, mustard, are sacred, but then who wants to put mustard on beans?"

"Or ketchup," I said, taking another bland bite, then changing my mind, "I'd put mustard or ketchup on these beans without hesitation."

"Yes, could be tasty. Now, how do I explain? Put it this way. If you left money lying on the ground, and next to it a bottle of—." He took out a small bottle of red *salsa picante* from his pants pocket, flicked it near my face, then snapped it away, and quickly stuffed it back out of sight. "—The money would be left, and the bottle would be gone." He then threw me a look as though what he had said made perfect sense. I said nothing back; I wasn't going to agree with such nonsense, even if it was true.

"Gobs and gobs of bland food," he rambled on, his voice becoming more and more lively. "Too much salt added to overcome the blandness. But you won't puff up. You'll sweat the salt off by midday, just in time for your next infusion at lunch. The food here never changes." Then, abruptly, he changed the subject as something at the water tanks caught his attention. "There's no water right now. The fellows know what it is, but they need to go into town, someone needs to drive them. But it won't be today. Look at them just sweating and standing around. Lots of sweating and standing around." I looked over at the workmen; they were standing beside the water tanks, chatting.

"Remember to drink out of the left tank. The right is river water," he said, leaning in again.

"Are you sure?"

"No."

Sitting back, he continued with his monologue. "We always have eggs in the morning, but they always run out, which is why we aren't eating any now. Sometimes we have cabbage; they even put some sort of sweet, creamy stuff on it. I think it's the powdered milk combined with sugar. And occasionally, we have a pig. In fact, I think we're due for a pig. But then maybe not. Speaking of pigs, you have mud on your face. Around your nose and eyes. Green—your eyes, they're green; green's a pretty color."

Instead of thanking him for what seemed like a half-baked compliment, I changed the subject, feeling more exhausted than ever. I was tired of talking about food. "Who runs this place? I mean, who do I talk to about sleeping arrangements because I won't sleep in the attic room, and I heard the beach isn't too safe either—crocs, possibly nasty manatee?"

"Manatee? I suppose there could be a mean one. Well, Lenore runs the place, rarely visits. But sometimes her niece shows up. Her nickname is Blue-Eyes. She helps out, or I think she does. Not sure."

"Is she here?"

"No, she's never here. What's your job?"

"*Niñera.*"

"Most new people are. Maadddy—"

"Eleanor," I corrected him.

"Eleanor. You could drive the workmen into town tomorrow and buy some salsa," he said, looking at me with a smile.

"I could use some today."

Ignoring me, he said, "I'm the history teacher here. I'm Dutch. So, yes, I do come from a frosty European country." He then stopped talking to look at me skeptically. I could tell something was churning in his mind. "The People's Republic of Dormitorio," he finally said, adding, "they figure out who sleeps where. It's more like what's available. Those who have been here the longest get the better sleeping arrangements. Jack and Sarah have a room to themselves, but then they have been here almost as long as I have."

"Which is?"

"A little over a year. Then again. Has it been that long?" He then counted the months on his fingers. Stopped, shook his head, and said, "Less than a year, I think. So, you don't smell like this all the time, or do you?"

"It's been a rough couple of days. Slept on the beach last night."

"That was you? Interesting. Do you have a sleeping bag?"

"No."

"Mosquito net?"

"No."

"A blow-up raft?"

"No."

"A change of underwear?"

"Yes, well, I need to do laundry," I said, laughing.

"Have you been traveling around?"

"Yes, but not camping."

"Yeah, I know what you mean. Okay, my roommate just left, and well…"

"What was your roommate's name?" I asked, curious.

He paused for a reflective moment, then said, "Maddy, but I won't call you Maddy. I'll call you by your real name?"

"That would be nice. It's Eleanor."

"Yes, Eleanor. I have a huge room, and I am not always there because I have a fiancé." He paused and looked at me with those penetrating, deep blue eyes as though wondering if I was listening correctly.

"I'm practicing abstinence." As though that was a reason to not worry. What I said was also only a half-truth. After imagining having sex with the Swiss, I had decided to not be so rigid with myself as deprivation could lead to bad choices, but I wasn't going to tell this fellow my troubles.

Sitting in silence, I stuffed my mouth with beans. For some reason, he was looking at me with a peculiar expression.

"Why would anybody practice abstinence? Odd, but, well, good," he finally said, then rubbed his chin and continued with a troubled tone. "Alex has been wanting to sleep in my room, and I don't want him as a roommate. He's nice enough, but I, well, I like it when there is another person in the room, but not Alex. Nothing wrong with him. No, I take that back. There is plenty wrong with him, but then there is usually something wrong with people." He paused here to raise an eyebrow at me, then continued. "Look, I like having another person in the room because, well, it's comforting."

"Comforting?"

"Yes, comforting. Like having a pet."

"A pet?"

"I go away most weekends, and I'm out a lot." And then he paused to fiddle with his history book as though not knowing how to phrase what he wanted to say, but he finally managed to just say it. "So, if you want?" He leaned in, latching his eyes onto mine. "I'll give you a corner of my room?" And then he smiled, adding, "Seems I can share."

"Not bad."

"Is that a yes or a no?"

"I guess a yes."

"I think I detect rudeness again."

"Thank you." It was very hard to say 'thank you' to him. All I could think was, 'What a strange fellow,' and, 'If I had salsa, would he kill me in my sleep to get it?' But then again, the arrangement couldn't be better. He said he would rarely be there. After a few moments of readjusting my attitude, I added, "Excellent. We're roommates. How wonderful. But I have a question."

"What?" he asked, ripping a piece of paper from his notepad. Not waiting for my question, he said, "Tomorrow, drive the workmen into town. Buy yourself a sleeping bag, et cetera, et cetera." Then, to help me out, he wrote down on the paper a list of things I needed to buy and handed it to me, saying, "I don't think I forgot anything. And while you're there, have a nice meal." It was as though all the nonsense from before had disappeared.

"Thank you." I meant it this time. He was kind. I then asked something that had been bothering me. "What's your name?"

"Harry. Harry Van Cleef," he said, standing up.

"Cleef? I've heard that name before."

"It's a famous name. I like it." A very unusual response to one's last name, I thought. It was as though he had chosen it.

Gathering his book, pad, and pencil, he cleared his plate by bringing it over to a bucket, his sandaled feet snapping along the cement. Before walking out, he turned and said, "You should swim. It's the best bathtub we have."

"Yes. But stop." I remembered where I had heard his name. "Yena. Yena wants to see you."

Looking at Harry, I saw his face had darkened, and his eyes grown steely and chilled, then flat, as though his mind had wandered off someplace, to a thought he had misplaced or didn't want to remember. I kept my gaze locked on his unforced stare, watching it transform from vacant to suspicious. I was baffled at how the name had affected him.

It took a few moments, but he finally wandered back into the man I had first met, jovial and somewhat bizarre. Smiling, he said, "Great, how nice. How do you know her?"

"I met her last night, briefly."

He nodded, then turned to leave again. Stepping into the open doorway, he stretched his arms up over his head, exposing a flat, slightly tanned tummy, and yawned. Glancing over the quad, possibly to regain a sense of equilibrium, he gripped his book, pencil, and notepad against his right palm and chest; fished around in his pockets with his left and pulled out a pair of sunglasses. Placing them on his face, he breathed in deeply and stepped down onto the dirt below. Taking off with a brisk stride, shoulders rolled forward, he went towards the sign that said, LA CLÍNICA. His worn khaki pants and light blue Lacoste short-sleeve shirt were an endemic fashion here. I watched him disappear into the woods. Feeling content, well-fed, and with a place to sleep—my stay at the orphanage was looking promising.

To the right of the building, I could still see four older kids hanging outside their dorm. They were old only compared to the three- and four-year-old children. They were most likely eight or ten. There were two girls and two boys. They were kicking dirt at each other by roughing up the ground and then giving the soft, powdered earth a good wallop with their feet. It caused the girls to squeal and the boys to grunt and laugh.

Looking sideways through the opening in the back of the dining room, I could see the group from the beach lazily strolling up the embankment. Tall Catarina; pom-pom Gunther; bitter Alex; pointy Jack and his demure wife, Sarah; the brassy redheads, Molly and Golly; and the children. The adults swayed their arms in idle inertia as they waited for their zigzagging charges to catch up to them. Kids picking at the grass, tossing sticks with random movements, a clump of them protesting the act of leaving the beach. It occurred to me that if school started at nine, then it wasn't even nine, possibly not even eight o'clock in the morning. I couldn't help but think of what an abominably early hour it still was, and how it already felt like I'd lived a whole day. Mustering up some strength, I bused my plate and went out to greet them.

Chapter 6

Hamit

Directly across from the orphanage was a fancy boat club. Through the binoculars that I had discovered hanging from a hook at the end of the dock, I could clearly see the place. A one-story building on pilings jutting out over the river. Its roof thatched and brightly lit by the sun, and it had an open-air dining area with waist-high, wooden railings. Attached to the front of the dock in large, in black lettering, was the club's markedly unimaginative name: "CLUB DE BOTE."

The place exuded an esoteric wealth that piqued my interest. Not that I cared for or sought opulence, it was more that it looked comfortable, and I had slept on a beach last night.

Scoping out the boats, I counted ten Bertrams lined neatly along a dock that hugged the shore. These boats seemed to be favored by the rich. In Boston, the expensive vessels lined the piers too. Next to their behemoth bloated bellies, resembling errant sidekicks, were several smaller motorboats with glinting outboards. In the lagoon to the right of the building, windless and dark, stood sleek sailboats. Their hulls were mainly white, but some displayed blue, green, and red bottoms. Possibly, I thought, their owners drank more than most and needed something else besides the odd throw pillow to know which boat was theirs. These boats embedded in the windless cove were silent and picturesque, sails down and booms draped with drying towels and clothes, whereas, farther out into the river, a small schooner and a sloop were fighting the currents. Their bodies twisted and bucked like snared, giant, angry birds, and their dinghies jerked and floundered at the sterns.

The whole shebang—the club and the canopy of paurotis palms, giant kapoks, and corkwood trees looming in the background with birds gliding in and out—was fascinating to look at. The echoing of laughter and clinking of glasses, a flaunting of a fairytale world beyond the hopes and dreams of many. I imagined the patrons were eating Waldorf salads with sweet apples, walnuts, and cherries or burgers piled high with fresh lettuce and juicy tomatoes. I hadn't even brushed my teeth yet, and the thought of a sweet and crisp meal to cleanse my palate seemed glorious. Sighing, I laughed at my self-imposed poverty. It wasn't so bad, except I itched, and my pits stunk.

Putting the binoculars back, I jumped off the low end of the dock into the shallow waters. The water rippling against my knees was cool and languid. 'Yes, the best bathtub,' I thought. I could hear the kids singing a nursery rhyme inside the kindergarten building. It was off tune and involved clapping. Then lots of laughter.

The river lay flat in our little nook, allowing for safe swimming, but the middle of the river, with its tremendous surge going north, imparted an unnerving quality. It was the push from the freshwater lake, Lago de Cho, to the hungry, salty Caribbean Sea. I doubted the motorized canoes had much trouble going north—but going south would be difficult unless they hugged the shore.

"A couple of weeks ago, they found a guy with *ceeement* tied to his feet, clunking around the mangrove roots up yonder," said a voice with a southern drawl. "Cost only one dollar to kill someone here. They forget that the damn cement is porous, makes the corpses float." He then chuckled, a deep, phlegm-filled sound that caused him to wheeze and cough.

Turning my head around, I saw a stout man with a bulging belly standing on the beach by the dock. His cotton, short-sleeve shirt wrinkled, with sweat stains on his belly was half-tucked into his extra-large, orange cargo shorts. He had the face of a duck. His nose protruded out and up, and his thick lips seemed to be reaching for his nose. His white, thinning hair looked matted down with some sort of grease, but was unkempt in the back, causing white strands to stand up, giving him a cowlick. His skin, paper white with blotches of red. Unattractive at first glance, there was something about him that seemed untamed and very humorous which added desirability, but not much. He held, with both his hands, fat hands with thick fingers, a mug with a neon pink picture of a naked lady sitting under a black umbrella. When he took a sip from the mug, he slurped. I could smell the enticing aroma of coffee and wondered if he had more. He wasn't looking at me but gazing out over the water.

"We're on the wrong side of the pond," he said after a moment of silence. Slurping again, he looked over at me, his eyes folded into the fat of his brow, and asked, "Do you have the time?"

"No."

"They're supposed to be coming today, but maybe it's *tomorra.*"

"Who?"

"Why, my wife 'n' kid," he said, taking another loud slurp, his gaze perusing the river. He looked over at me again. "You new?"

"Yup."

Looking back over the river, he changed the subject. "The president flies in on weekends. He swoops down in his Bell 212 helicopter. I knows my aircrafts 'cause I was stationed in Da Nang during 'Nam. You know that war was never declared a war, just a *confleet.* Hell—lost half my skull over there for that *confleet.* Got a titanium plate in its place." He coughed and wheezed, his spasms causing him to spill his coffee on his hand. He shook his hand dry and said, "Guess what my head can do now?"

"What?"

"I receive radio transmissions. Want to know the weather?"

"Hot," I said.

"Sunny and hot. Real hot. Hotter than a witch's brass tit in a desert—it's so hot." He then looked back over toward me and down at the water. "Anything nibbling at your toes?"

"No."

"I don't like swimming. Grew up in Alabama by a swamp. Lost an earlobe to a snapper." He gazed back over to the club while he scratched his heavy middle. Then huffing, he blurted out, "That man is bad. Full of maleficence."

For a moment I had to think about who he was talking about. "The president?"

"Yup."

Months ago, I had read an article in *La Noticia* that had shed light on how the president thought. During a balcony speech to the people, he had expressed his displeasure of being a leader of a country full of 'Indians.' He felt he was better than that. "If he doesn't like the indigenous people, I wonder why he ran? Why he even lives here," I said rhetorically.

"Enough of his own kind here." He then paused, shushing

me. "Do you hear a boat?"

A water taxi whizzed by, carrying a load of boxes.

"Nope—anyway, I'm Hamit."

"Eleanor."

"Well, Eleanor, if that man comes over here, I'll make a point to step on his arches, enjoying the sound of their crunch." He took another long, loud slurp from his mug, then snorting he turned his entire body toward me, wide and boxy, and said, "Now my wife is small and pretty; my son takes after me. If they show up, I'll be at the steeple schoolhouse."

He then turned around, giving me a full view of his flat, giant orange bottom. He walked away up the embankment by kicking one foot out in front of the other with his body leaning backward. He was very awkward and peculiar. "What a cast of characters at this place," I chuckled.

Splashing water onto my arms and legs, I used the sandy bottom as grit to scrub the muck and grime off my skin. The river smelled like wet wood, its texture soft and cleansing. Mangrove thickets hugged the sides of the beach and were filled with birds. Inside the mangrove's spidery roots were hairy, brown coconuts bouncing rhythmically back and forth. I imagined a body with cement blocks attached to its feet being caught up in the entangled roots and felt ill.

To wipe the image from my mind, I walked deeper into the water, then dove in headfirst down to the bottom and back up, swimming into the darker blue areas. A glorious serenity swept over me. The celebratory act of being filthy was to become clean again, I thought, lying on my back looking up at the blue sky, its depths limitless, its blueness sublime. Suspended and feeling weightless, I rolled back onto my stomach, taking a few more strong pulls toward the current, then stopped. The water gurgling in front of me, its grab inches away, I rolled back onto my stomach and kicked with lazy, frog-like strokes along its periphery.

A few days ago, while in the bus station on my way to the orphanage, I had traded a Spaniard my book *El Viejo y El Mar* by Ernest Hemingway for a book whose cover was torn and the name unknown, but it was in Spanish, and it was hard to find books in Spanish that weren't biblical, so I took it. Glad to have a book, I wondered whether there would be time to read it here.

Flicking the water into the air with my hand, I kicked my feet, fluttering around the top, rolling over, and diving deep but veering away from the slimy bottom. It was only the shallows that were sandy. When I came back up, I could hear someone shouting my name.

"Eleanor!"

It was Gunther. He was standing on the beach waving me in with his hands. He had a bunch of the little kids standing by his side, and they started waving too. "You can't drown; we need help. The children need you."

"I can swim," I said.

"Good for you," he said, standing now with his hands on his hips. "Now come on back. It's snack time."

I splashed back onto solid ground. "I don't have a towel. Everything I have smells like bat piss from that damn attic," I added, standing in front of Gunther, dripping wet.

"I hope you're not a whiner," he blurted out, then asked, peering down at my bottom. "Are those lilies on your suit or petunias?"

"Roses."

"Lovely. After snack time, I'll show you where the washbasin is located. To wash your clothes."

Over by the school, Catarina and Alex were marching the children up into the quad. Charlotte, Bernarda, and another little girl who told me her name was Penelope came over to me.

Penelope put her soft, small hand into mine and then stood without moving. She had big, round, light brown eyes lined with thick, black lashes, a small nose, and a little mouth that she pressed down on with her upper lip as though she were thinking about something puzzling. She had on purple jellies and a green-and-black striped Benetton shirt and yellow Perry Ellis leggings. With her long, black hair she looked rather chic.

Charlotte and Bernarda fought over my other hand. Not wanting to cause problems, I let Penelope's hand go, ruffled the hair of all three, and suggesting we walk hand free. It made me realize why Catarina had the kids holding onto her skirt. She was up at the top of the embankment with five kids attached to her. The girls and I walked by Raymond and Henrik, who were quietly sitting on two rocks under a withered tree.

Raymond, in a tiny voice, said he was very, very tired. I suggested we all walk over to the quad together, but the boys didn't move. Instead, the three girls sat down on the dirt beside the boys. Then the one called Frankie stormed over like he owned the world. He was wearing a purple, button-down Galliano shirt and blue Prada jean shorts. His fists were tight, his mouth pursed, his arms swaying. He was almost as small as Henrik, only much beefier and bellowing defiance. His eyes, full of mischief, sparkled in the sunlight. He told me several times, in squeaky Spanish, that he wasn't going to spend the rest of the morning in school but would prefer to swim. He wanted to put his bathing suit on and would I come with him to get it.

"No," I replied. He stormed off and found Molly and Golly, who were walking down the embankment. The girls shook their heads 'no' at him. This caused him to kick a clump of grass repeatedly until Alex slinked by and tapped him on the shoulder. He stopped, looked at Alex, and smiled, and they walked off together up the short hill. 'At least Alex was good for something,' I thought.

We all sat on rocks and a couple of large logs in the quad sipping on a beverage called 'the green drink.' No one knew what was in it, but we felt it was a kind of horchata—rice, milk, and then the green part was questionable, but cacti seemed probable. I found the drink to be very tasty. Everyone drank it up, and before marching back down to school, we had to wipe the children's faces as they all had green mustaches. While we had been sitting around drinking, a boy named Albert came over and sat by me. He had a soft, oval face with dreamy, dark eyes that twinkled when he spoke of the colors red and yellow. He, too, had a button-down shirt on, a generic make, and I couldn't help but wonder how a non-designer shirt had gotten mixed up in the donations. Albert's shirt with a floral pattern filled with pinks and greens, clashed with his plaid Brooks Brothers shorts. He gave me one of the yellow flowers he had picked that grew in clumps around the grounds. He then asked me if he could have my bathing suit because he was fond of roses.

Chapter 7

Sarah and Jack

In the back of the dormitorio, there was a cement washbasin that had a spigot with a pump. At first, I wondered why they weren't using the water from the spigot to wash the kids' faces, but understood when I had to walk over the spongy, wet ground that sucked at my flip-flops, ripping them off more than once. I was glad to see the cement basin was on a mound of dry dirt.

Shaded by a mango tree that had littered the surrounding terrain with rotting fruit, I pumped away with one hand while kneading a pair of my soapy shorts with the other. It felt good to be doing this simple task. It was straightforward and relaxing, as it called for repetitive motions and no thinking. I watched several salamanders scurry over and around the basin. Frogs and lots of other squiggling things plopped and swished around in the mucky puddles.

The mosquitoes that buzzed in never landed. I had sprayed myself, after swimming, with the DEET I found near the screen door. It smelled like creamy caramel, and I delighted in its scent.

After a piece of clothing was washed, I took a few wet steps over to a clothesline that someone had strung between a low-lying juniper tree to an orange, blossoming jacaranda. Then clipped it with the plastic clothespins snapped onto the line. At one point, while scrubbing, I looked up to rub my nose and saw Jack standing only a few feet away from me. It was as though he had appeared out of nowhere, and I found his presence peculiar. I stopped scrubbing and waited for him to say something. I figured he must have something important to say or why else would he walk through the sloshy, wet grasses to see me.

His feet had sunk deep into the soggy ground, and on his right ankle clung a black caterpillar arching its head and sniffing around. Jack had on knee-length, beige shorts, and the skin on his calves was ghostly white, which made the caterpillar and the pink bug bites on his legs more noticeable. The fresh bites he had scratched and many had scabbed and were painful to look at. I was glad to see his arms, lightly tanned, were unmarred. His button-down, short-sleeve cotton shirt, which was only buttoned halfway up, exposed a very white, pasty, concave chest with a few curly, black hairs sprinkled across it. He was very thin and slight. His narrow shoulder width and the fact that he was short made his head look too big, but he wasn't unattractive. He had an oddball attractiveness to him that, depending on his personality, could have been enticing or a huge turnoff. Presently, he was being somewhat ugly.

He was staring at my breast with his large, pointy nose and his two small eyes, resembling a big-headed rat, if rats had big heads. He also had an unhinged drool to his lower lip that made him grotesquely infantile, like a big-headed rat waiting to be fed. I couldn't help but wonder if his mother had given him breast milk or just threw him a bottle and shut the door. I would have just shut the door.

However, I knew that I had a nice set of boobs. Round, cheery, and not too big or too small. Recognized by me as my best feature. They made up for other structural deficits that are not worth talking about. I also liked to play up their seductive abilities and had picked up an erroneous, provocative habit while washing my clothes in front of a male housemate back in Corriente. When kneading my clothing in the sudsy basin located in the household's courtyard, a young French boy, who lived in the house, too, liked to come out and sit in a chair in front of me to chat. I would purposely press my breasts together with my arms and pop them out the top of my V-neck T-shirt, then drop them back in with each release. It did take some dexterity to keep the nipples from being exposed, but sometimes I would let them jump out, just to see his eyes grow bigger.

Looking at Jack's hungry expression, I realized I was most likely washing my clothes in such a manner. I was also still wearing my bathing suit, which was loose and droopy around my breasts. Jack must have seen my bouncing boobs from afar, and like the sirens they are, they compelled him to come over to get a closer look. Standing up straight, I picked up the miserable pair of white ankle socks I was washing, stained with holes in the heel and big toe, and brought them up to my chest to cover my naughty breasts. I didn't know Jack and teasing him was probably not a good idea.

A dense silence thickened the already soupy air, and we both watched a leaf flutter down between us. I waited for Jack to explain his presence, but he seemed tongue-tied, or maybe I just assumed he was. Then something else piqued my interest. On the high ground, behind Jack, was Sarah. She was on all fours, looking like a cat stretching out its front legs while digging around in the earth. Jack followed my line of vision and turned to look at his wife. He paused for a moment, then turned back, his expression somber.

"Sarah's an entomologist," he said, his tone hinting at regret. He then made a noise through his long nose, then proceeded in crisp, monotone words to tell me about himself and his wife. His eyes now looked at my forehead or the tree behind me, but never directly at me. He also turned from appearing vermin-like to someone I imagined read lots of books, preferring them to people. Possibly people were too annoying for him. It had something to do with his energy level and his inability—or maybe it was a refusal—to smile.

Sarah and Jack were from Wisconsin. They had been working at the orphanage for nearly a year, but then he thought it could be only three months. He was working on getting a doctorate in child psychology, and Sarah was studying the bug life of a rainforest. Jack's doctoral dissertation was on 'children with or without parents coupled with commune living.'

"Commune living?" I questioned.

"Why yes, I lived in one once. This place reminds me of it. Only we don't have to do dishes."

I'd never lived in a commune before but thought possibly he could be right.

"This orphanage is a perfect setting for gathering corroborating evidence," he continued while finally picking off the black caterpillar from his leg. Tossing it a few feet away, he continued, "My hypothesis? To prove that this place, right here, these kids are a model for how a child should be raised. One size can fit all. Most parental units or individuals are ill-equipped to raise humans properly. Overwhelmed, self-indulgent creatures that either overshadow a child's growth with their own insecurities or don't bother with being around at all. It's the actual cause of socioeconomic injustice, and it's just not fair. Children would be better off raised by others that know better." His tone was flat and snooty, full of academic condescension.

"What's unfair?" I asked, wringing out a pair of shorts, disgusted by the hole near the crotch.

"What?"

"Seems unnatural? People like having parents. Come to think of it, I think parents like their children more than the kids like their parents," I said, inspecting a pair of chinos with a stuck zipper. "I don't think it would work—that is, not allowing parents to raise their kids. I don't think the point is fairness."

"Then what is it?" he snapped.

"I have no idea," I said, suddenly confused because all my clothes had become dysfunctional—and when did that happen?

"Then you shouldn't be voicing any kind of opinion if you have no ideas. Leave it to the experts."

"I suppose that's you?" I said not thinking Jack was an actual expert, but a wannabe expert, then added, "If I were writing a dissertation on kids, the title would be 'Looking for Approval Ruins People's Lives.'"

"People who do not seek approval are poor employees," he fumed. His expression sour. His shoulders stooped so low that he looked like a question mark, indicating a possible malfunctioning spine.

"Are you going to have religion in your commune?" I asked while pulling a shirt out of my pile of rags in nearly perfect condition. "I can't believe it, one good shirt," I mumbled.

"Religion? There will be no religion!" He snapped.

Looking up at him, I smiled. "What if one of the little kids comes up with one? I've heard little kids are good at creating imaginary characters. I had a friend who had one, took up half the back seat when we carpooled to elementary school. Yup, three of us had to push over, almost sit on each other's laps so this made-up friend had enough space."

"Odd. What for? Never mind—please don't answer or say anything else. Anyway, I am the go-to guy here," he said, changing the subject while flicking an insect off his arm. We both watched in silence as the bug sailed over to Sarah and landed on her bottom. She didn't notice. She seemed to be too preoccupied with whatever was lurking in the grasses.

"Go-to guy?" I questioned, bringing my attention back to Jack.

"Yes, if you need anything, let me know."

"Nothing, but I am going into town tomorrow and—"

"I know. Gunther's going too."

"How did you know?"

"How could I not know? Now listen, we have meetings every night. We talk about what worked and what didn't during the day. We have different chores that we divvy up each evening for the next day, so no one gets stuck doing the same thing all the time. We get up at five o'clock; breakfast is at six-thirty; school is at nine; recess is at ten; lunch is at noon; playtime, which is clean up and free time, too, is the entire afternoon. Dinner is at six o'clock. Nothing changes. It's perfect. Structure and consistency to help them develop properly."

"Define 'properly?'" I asked, knowing I was being a touch obnoxious, but so was he.

"Why don't you?" He said with one raised eyebrow. "I'm curious to see what you would say. I might even put it in my dissertation."

Stumped, I folded my arms across my chest, then quickly unfolded them because I realized I'd pushed them up. "I have no idea how to raise a kid properly," I muttered.

"So why did you bring it up?"

"I didn't; you did. Anyway, when is bedtime?" I did think I would have enjoyed growing up in a rainforest with a river to swim in, but I didn't think I would have liked Jack as one of my fathers. He was too uptight, not much fun, a giant pissant.

"Bedtime. Bedtime. We're working on it. Should be early, but it's always late."

A bird chirped while another sang an upward-down tune. I slapped a mosquito that had been resting on my ankle, sucking blood. Even the DEET had issues here. Most likely watered down by the humidity. The bite immediately itched.

In our silence, we both looked over at Sarah again. She was upright, sitting back on her calves. Her sundress bunched around her thighs, exposing smooth, white skin, her knees smudged with grass and dirt. She was looking at a bug that was running around in circles in the palm of her hand.

"There are over six hundred thousand species of ants in a rainforest," she said, her voice ethereal and shaky as though she were about to cry. "But that number is being whittled down." Then looking over at us with two large, glassy blue eyes that seemed too big for her very white, oval face, she added, "The habitat is shrinking. Before we know it, poof... Gone." And then she cried, making small gasps. She looked and sounded very, very sad, with tears dripping down her cheeks into her mouth and off her chin. She made me sad, too, and tears started to well up in my eyes, but then a mosquito bit the top of my head. Irritated, I caught the blood-sucking jerk. Then with an angry vengeance, smashed it between my fingers and wiped its seeping carcass onto the cement basin, shredding it into unrecognizable pieces. Looking over at Sarah, I was glad to see she was too enmeshed in her weeping to have noticed the brutal killing.

Jack, who seemed lost in thought, awoke from whatever he was thinking about and walked over to Sarah. He gently helped her up off the ground. Brushing the insect out of her hand, he squeezed her waist lovingly and wiped her tears away. "Don't cry, honey; we have plenty of bugs here," he said, his voice soft and cooing. Holding Sarah against his body, he turned toward me and said, "Lunch is in about twenty."

They walked away arm in arm, Sarah resting her head upon Jack's shoulder, and Jack's head resting down upon hers like puzzle pieces that fit perfectly.

Jack was right about one thing: 'I'm a terrible employee.' Before heading off to go traveling, I had been a secretary that took too many coffee breaks and often let my boss answer the phone. Hell, it was for him anyway. A job and not a career. Humph. I wondered if I hadn't been an only child, and if my father hadn't died when I was ten, and if my mother wasn't in a mental institution, delusional and paranoid, possibly I may have more thoughts on what to do with myself. I wondered if maybe Jack was on to something. And that possibly having more than two parents or parents that weren't parents, but people schooled in raising kids was a good idea. But then again, his theory was organically wrong. It also occurred to me that Jack would like my mother, and she him.

Across the quad, I could see the older kids coming back from school. There were a lot of them, and not one had a backpack or even a pencil or pad in their hands. Did they not have homework? They also were causing a dust storm with their shuffling feet and grabbing hands. They pushed at each other, pulled at each other's hair. Then a scuffle between three boys broke out. They looked like mad dogs fighting.

Back in the city, while talking with Lenore, she in her tight, faded Versace dress, voice sultry, lipstick a flashy red, boobs lifting and resting with every breath upon her cold, gray metal desk told me that the kids needed to leave the orphanage once they turned fifteen.

"A wonderful age to get a job," she had said, then added in stuff about their duty to help their families out. If they had one. "We aren't in the business of making babies," she had continued. "We're in the business of saving babies. Teenagers and idle time are a terrible mix." Watching the kids kick and punch each other, I thought, anything above four seemed like a terrible mix. Unclipping a light cotton shift from the clothesline, the thinness of the material allowing it to dry quickly, I slipped it on over my bathing suit. It hung like a sack of potatoes to my knees, which was perfect. Driblets of sweat were beading under my eyes, fogging my vision. I wiped the sweat away with the back of my hand and walked over the waterlogged ground to the dormitorio.

Chapter 8

Lunch

Everyone was there; the niñeros and the little kids. They were having a hoot playing, running around the screened-in porch, which I discovered was called the great room. The kids screamed and giggled pretending to be scared, or found something funny, even though it wasn't.

I went over to Bernarda, Charlotte, Penelope, and two other girls named Annabelle and Rosamond. The girls were building a fort out of cardboard. The five of them were pensive and quiet in their deliberations. Their serenity, a bastion of peace. I helped them angle the cardboard into a giant box big enough for all six of us to crawl into. We sat knee to knee and played Patty-Cake. Only Penelope knew the words. Bernarda shouted out the words she knew the best like, "PATTY! BAKER! OVEN!" Charlotte just grinned, and Annabelle and Rosamond hummed.

From across the way, one of the kitchen ladies banged on a pot and shouted, "*¡A comer!*" It was time for lunch. No one even blinked an eye. They kept wanting to play, ignoring the clanging as though it didn't exist.

It was hard to get the kids to stop playing and go to lunch. Helter-skelter, they ran from us and hid behind doors. "Playing is just too much fun," Catarina had said to me as she pulled a kid named Otto out from under the throw pillows.

"Lunch is an issue," Jack said, standing next to me and holding on to the three girls so they wouldn't run away. He then asked me to do him a favor. "I think I saw three kids, Wooter, Greggo, and Earl—possibly a fourth, Frankie, that little devil. They went down to the water. Could you get them?"

As I dashed out the door, Jack shouted, "Tell them they can swim later, after lunch."

"Don't they always swim after lunch?"

"Yes, yes, yes, but they forget—and then again, they never forget."

As I crested the hill, I spotted all four. Frankie, the only one I knew, was kicking a mound of dirt like a ruffian, grunting with each kick. He was concentrating too hard to pay any attention to me. He had sweat running down the sides of his cheeks, his arms swinging, and his right leg kicking and kicking while puffs of dirt exploded into the air. Since I figured he wasn't going anywhere, I went to get the others.

They were walking around the kindergarten building's one-foot-wide dock that didn't have a railing. Young children in the States would have already jumped, fallen, and drowned, but these three didn't seem eager to get into the water. They seemed sure-footed, chatting among each other. When I walked up to the water's edge, they looked over at me but then went back to chatting about something they saw in the water.

"*Muchos peces*," I said, assuming they were looking at fish.

A kid with spiky black hair glanced over at me and nodded.

"Lunch!" I said in Spanish. Weren't the kids hungry? Didn't they want lunch?

Nothing. They didn't even look at me.

Behind the boys on a post, a pelican flapped and stretched its wings. A smaller, very thin boy with a rectangular face and a crew cut blurted out, "*Pelícano.*" They were looking at the prehistoric bird just as it stretched its broad, bat-like wings and bobbed its cup-like beak up and down. They giggled at it, but nothing more.

"It's time for lunch," I said in Spanish. I didn't blame them for not wanting to leave as there was nothing interesting about black beans and rice, again. They turned back around to look at me again. I could hear their breathy sighs over the lapping of the water and Frankie's kicking and grunting. Time passed. "*¿Quién es Wooter?*" I asked, thinking if I got to know them, they might listen to me better.

"*Sí,*" said the kid with the spiky hair.

"Earl?"

"*Me llamo Earl,*" said the kid with the rectangular face. He then nudged the boy next to him, who hadn't said his name. "*Este es Greggo.*" Greggo and Earl seemed to be twins—same height, same face, same skinny bodies.

I imagined going onto the dock to make my presence known more forcefully. And then I imagined them running away, falling into the water, splashing around, and possibly drowning because I was too tired and slow to fetch them out in time. It could happen. I picked up a stone and threw it into the water. The splash set the pelican into flight. It flew up over the mangroves and soared low, skimming the river; then it flew up and back down, diving deep into the water. The kids looked spellbound as they watched the bird appear back on the surface with a fish in its beak, throwing its head back to gobble the food down.

"It's time for lunch," I said again in Spanish. "*Como el pelícano.*" The pelican is eating, didn't they want to eat too?

They moved off the dock. "*Que bueno,*" I said as they nonchalantly walked down the narrow wooden plank to solid ground. Standing next to me, we stood for a few minutes looking at each other. They wore Brooks Brothers shorts and shirts, and I whistled, thinking how nicely dressed they were. They tried to whistle back. It was comical. Pointing to the cafeteria, they walked away with little enthusiasm, up the incline, zigzagging through the bushy, dried grasses.

"Frankie, ¡venga!" He was still kicking even though the mound was gone. Then suddenly he stopped, jumped up three times into the air, and charged up the hill, taking bold, muscled steps, stopping two or three times to kick something or tug on a piece of grass.

"Now, that wasn't too hard was it, Eleanor?" I said to myself, watching the little fellows melt into the rest of the kids on their way into the hall.

"It's a mere two-minute walk from the dormitorio to the cafeteria on a good day," I heard Jack huff, joining the group.

"I think we will beat our fifteen-minute handicap," Gunther bragged. Then turning to me he said, "Yup, we need to get into the caf before the big kids, or, well, what a mess. Hard to get them to focus once the big kids get into the line." He then poked my arm gently. "You're not going to leave us now? They're really a good lot."

"No reason to leave yet," I said, smiling.

"What does that mean?"

"I'm not leaving."

"Everything is a test. Isn't it?" Gunther said, lightly nudging my shoulder.

"I suppose," I replied, lightly laughing and nudging his shoulder back.

"They were on the school dock, weren't they?" Jack questioned me as we moved the children into the buffet line. "Some of these kids were shining shoes before they arrived. Others selling Chiclets on the streets. All by themselves! They'd never fall in."

"They could slip; anyone could slip," Sarah said in her melancholy voice. "I could slip."

"But you're not going to, honey," Jack said kindly. He threw his hand out to touch her but missed.

"A bit of bollocks them acting this way, but don't worry. Once they start eating, they are perfect." Gunther's tone was solid and knowledgeable.

Getting the kids to line up by the buffet counter in an orderly fashion took another ridiculous five minutes. Absurdly distracted by the enormity of the room, some sought out dents on the cement floor, chased little bugs, and wandered around in circles while others just stared, moping about something in their head. And then there were the few who knew exactly what they wanted. Kids whose names I hadn't learned yet. They rushed into line, grabbed their plastic plates, and held them high over their heads as though food would drop from the air at any moment, but when it didn't, they grew bored and walked away, hitting each other with their plates, crying, and then tattling on each other. All of it was sheer nonsense until they finally gave up their foolishness and stood in line as though nothing out of the ordinary had taken place. Poof! All spastic outbursts, gone.

Esmerelda was especially gentle with the kids. She even smiled. She had three gold teeth. The kids on their tiptoes would peer up at her from below the counter, eyes wondrous. But as though we were a rogue dark cloud, when she looked at us, the volunteers, she frowned, clamping her mouth shut.

Before we arrived in the dining room, Catarina had placed the children's forks on the tables along with plates and filled all their cups with milk.

"The more organized we are, the more organized they are," Jack lectured me.

We allowed the kids to carry their plates of food to the table. They were good at it, tiptoeing or shuffling along, making sure not to dribble a drop, and dodging the older kids who came piling in like a swarm of vermin. Only Henrik and Raymond had trouble, so I carried their plates to the table for them.

The benches, low, and the tables high, Henrik and Raymond stood when they ate, as did many others, or they kneeled. The children were slow, distracted eaters, putting little bits of food on their forks or picking a bean up with their fingers and placing it in their mouths, then forgetting they were even eating. Several made nasal sounds like they had stuffy noses and 'nom-nom' sounds. The entire ordeal of eating was exhausting just to watch.

"What time is it?" I asked Catarina, who was the only one of us that wore a watch.

"Noon. It's always noon when we eat."

"Right. I just feel like I've lived a lifetime already today. Time seems to stand still here."

"It's comforting. Especially when you're my age. At home, I get up, eat breakfast, and then it's dinner." She laughed and said, "You'll get used to it."

Chapter 9

Still Lunch

Lunch revealed to me what appeared to be everyone at the orphanage, an eclectic assembly of orphans, toilers, and wayfarers. There were the workmen, laundry ladies, and maids eating at a long table in the back of the kitchen. The kitchen women toiled away at serving, heads down, eyes focused, with pots and pans filled with food steaming around them. There were our twenty-four youngsters, toddlers, and those a touch older, and over a hundred or more other children ranging in ages from five to fifteen, along with the five people that looked after them.

The older kids sat toward the back of the cafeteria while our little band sat in the front by the kitchen. I was glad the big kids didn't sit with us because they were unnerving. Upright and loud, they exuded an undisciplined air like they were up to no good, as though at any moment they might throw milk on me or kick my shins. They tossed the Frisbee-size tortillas back and forth, twirling them on their fingers like pizza dough or misshaped basketballs. A group of boys had smashed black beans all over each other's faces. A girl with her hair pulled neatly back with a pink ribbon was using her fork as a catapult to lob food over the tables, randomly hitting unsuspecting kids. Everyone was talking at once, and no one seemed to be listening. When I paid attention to their cacophony, it gave me the feeling of drowning in a noisy pool.

Feral, I thought while helping Henrik off the table to go visiting. "Who are you visiting, Henrik?" But he wouldn't answer, just wandered off. As I watched him, he went to see Esmeralda, who gave him something from her pocket. When he came back, he had a piece of soft candy in his hand. I helped him back up onto the bench, and he stood beside me, popped the piece into this mouth, and began chewing and chewing and chewing. I thought how cute he was and how little, and how much I preferred our three tables of youngsters to the wild-eyed youth behind us.

The grown-ups with the robust older bunch seemed indifferent to the barbaric mayhem. There were two men and three women, nonindigenous and possibly from the city. One of the men was tall with a pencil-thin build and a massive head of black hair. Standing, he made theatrical gestures at a group of boys who had put something down his back.

The three women, who didn't appear over thirty, were slim-limbed with thick middles. Their jawlines constantly moved like spastic pistons because they, too, were talking, which meant they couldn't possibly be listening. They also laughed a lot. One of them, who had big, round ghost eyes and fat squirrel cheeks, caught me staring. She locked her eyes onto mine, projecting mean little rays of hostility. I waved. Her reaction was to point at me with her chin while babbling to the other women. It was obvious she was talking about me. Especially when they all looked my way like curious cows in a field. I gave another limp wave; they nodded back, with lips turned down and nostrils flared.

Looking away, I lazily placed a spoon of rice and beans into my mouth, and said to Gunther, who was sitting across from me, "The women over there are giving me foul looks."

Gunther laughed and rolled his eyes.

"What's so funny?" I asked.

"Nothing. Well, they don't like us—that's all."

"Why?"

"Lenore, a very shrewd woman, mind you, gave paying jobs away to non-paid foreigners—us." He then clarified his remarks by saying, "Lenore wanted foreigners—Europeans, Americans, Canadians—raising the little tikes. She can get them for free. She also prefers how we raise kids. Teaching them, instead of doing everything for them." His lilting tone was delicate and pleasant to listen to. His words, baffling.

"So, what are we teaching these kids?" I asked, thinking I hadn't seen us teach a thing.

"I don't know."

"Interesting."

"Yes, it is interesting."

"Luis and Umberto," Gunther said, pointing them out to me. "Look after the boys." Umberto was the black-haired, tall man, and was now sitting and laughing with a group of kids. Louis, much shorter and stocky, was by the milk barrel trying to get several children, who were chatting and drinking milk, to sit back down. "They're super," Gunther continued, "but the only person Louis and Umberto talk to is Harry. Harry pays them to be his substitute—here and there. The women are good with the girls. Don't know them at all, though. They leave us alone. I'm also not going to call it envy, even dislike for us, but I think it is more of an angry sadness they feel, for themselves. You know, we're working for free to help the kids. They are grateful. But these were jobs. Paying jobs." Gunther took a bite of his meal and chewed slowly, seeming caught up in a thought he wasn't sure how to express. Greggo and Earl, who were standing on the bench next to him, were eating by using Gunther as a crutch. Each had one hand on Gunther's shoulder and a fork in the other. With each scoop of food, they leaned into him and spilled more of their food than they ate, on to the floor, and their clothing.

Then abruptly Gunther waved his spoon at me, almost knocking the two boys off the bench. Their eyes wide and black beans flying through the air, they managed to re-steady themselves. Gunther caught up in his thoughts, didn't notice, and blurted out, "Luck, it's all about luck. Not being hit by a stray bullet."

"That's random," I replied.

"Luck certainly is," he adamantly said.

"What about common sense?" I threw in.

"Well, if you don't have luck, common sense won't help you."

"With common sense, a person would know not to walk into a dark cave that says, 'Caution, monsters live here,' making luck obsolete."

"But if you don't have any luck, it's most likely the creatures aren't in the cave. They're at your house eating your flatmates, who had the common sense to stay home, but lacked luck. And because you don't have any luck, you go home before the vile creatures are finished, and they eat you too." We both laughed, a lighthearted pealing that felt refreshing.

Wooter, who was sitting next to Greggo, took his cup and scrambled down off the bench. Watching him amble over to one of the older kids who was standing by the milk barrel, I saw him pull on the kid's shorts to get his attention. Something passed between them, and the older boy picked up the milk ladle and gave Wooter a generous pour. Bernarda and two other little girls in lovely Lilly Pulitzer dresses, were over by the milk barrel with cups in their hands too. They pulled on the same older kid's shorts. He ladled more milk out for the girls. Over by the buffet, I saw Albert, and a kid named Mouse, getting seconds from Esmeralda.

Mouse then came over with his full plate, shoved it on top of the table, and climbed up next to Alex, who to my chagrin, was sitting with me at the table. I don't think he meant to. He was preoccupied with the children when he sat down. When he finally noticed me, he frowned and so did I. Mouse put a mouthful of beans in his mouth, swished them around, then opened his mouth wide to show us the partially masticated food. When we made faces, he fake-laughed loudly and then he shut his mouth, puffing up his cheeks and popping them, splattering food all over the table and everyone's plates.

Alex then did something that astonished me because it seemed out of character. He gently placed his hand on Mouse's back, and in Spanish, with a thick German accent he said, "Now, now… food is to be eaten, not spit out." He wiped Mouse's face off, using his own spit on the stubborn, sticky beans stuck to Mouse's face, ruffled his hair, and firmly, but with care, took Mouse's fork from him. Mouse leaned into Alex and remained at his side, quietly, as Alex ate what remained of his own meal. It was an endearing sight to see and almost had me think better of Alex. He also must have noticed I was watching him because he looked over at me and said, "I know you from Escondido."

"Right." He had finally decided to remember me; what a shame.

"You knew my girlfriend, Milla. She's coming tomorrow." His expression wooden and hard to read, but he couldn't hide the embedded acridness he held for me. It wasn't as though I had been singled out. In Escondido, at the rooming house on the beach, I watched Alex trip people when they walked by, I saw him take their items when they weren't looking, like shirts, books, and sunglasses. He was rude and not funny at all. I had been puzzled, at the time, that Milla, who was good-natured, someone who laughed easily and never said anything mean about anything or anybody, even the rat that plagued the communal kitchen, liked someone as twisted as Alex. But then what did I know? As I thought of the past men in my life; some were wonderful, and some were drug dealers, drunks, womanizers, and narcissistic. All in good fun, though—most of the time.

Licking his puckish lips, Alex leaned back and with a haughty tone said, "I need Harry's room."

I remained silent, astounded at how fast information circulated in this place.

"Now be a good girl. Let Milla and me move in."

"It's not mine to give," I replied.

"*Dummer Arsch.*" It was one of his favorite insults and meant 'stupid ass.'

Mouse, who had snuggled in against Alex's stomach, had fallen asleep. Alex had his arm around him like a cradle. It was a sweet sight. So, what if he was kind to children (although a very good attribute to have at an orphanage) overall, he was a jerk. His face was repugnant and currently gloating with smugness. I said, "I don't want to talk to you." Wanting nothing more to do with him because I certainly wasn't going to give up the room, I picked up my plate and moved over to the table behind us.

"*Mein kleiner Dieb,*" he said, barking another snide remark at my back. One I had heard him say before but didn't know.

"Yup, there always has to be one rotten apple in the pack," I mumbled, sitting next to Jack.

"You mean 'barrel,'" Jack corrected me.

"Right. Enjoying your meal?" I noticed he had red dots on the side of his plate.

"Why not," he replied.

I looked around to see if I saw any more red dots. Sarah's plate had green dots. Molly and Golly had wiped their plates clean, leaving no signs of any colored dots. Catarina, Hamit, and Harry were sitting at the third table. I knew Harry had salsa but wondered about the other two. Chuckling, I thought, *Of course, they do,* then proceeded to remove Mouse's spit pieces from my food and noshed down a bland pile of rice and beans.

Jack stuffed the last bits of his tortilla into his mouth. "Gotta go," he said standing up. Then putting a hand on my shoulder, he remarked, "We like the kids to bus their plates, but they need guidance. They're bad at it." This caused me to wonder if the previously paid staff had made the children bus their plates. Then I thought most likely not if they did everything for them, and certainly not, if the kids were 'bad at it'—so much easier to just do it for them. "So, we are teaching them something," I said to no one in particular.

The high carb meal had me feeling weighted down, or was it, Alex's ugly remarks? Whatever it was, it occurred to me that I had a room, but not a bed. Not even a blanket. The thought of not sleeping well again caused me to feel even heavier. Putting my fork down to ponder over my 'not so ideal circumstances,' I noticed Sarah, who was sitting across from me, mewing and fidgeting while looking around the room as though she had lost something. I began to look around the room to see what it might be. I noticed when she spotted Jack at the exit, she jumped up, cleared her plate, and ran after him.

"Them's two—sex addicts," Golly said, looking at me with an amused, judgmental expression. Twisting her mouth around, she sucked on her teeth like she had food stuck in them. We watched Sarah and Jack slip into the dormitorio. Then Molly, while picking at a molar, added, "*Awright geeezzaa*! I hope one day I *'ave* a relationship like *'em. Sorted, mate.*"

"What?" I questioned.

"They got a nice relationship," Golly replied, slowly enunciating each word.

Chapter 10

Molly and Golly

The afternoon was a high-wire act of buzzing beetles filling the air with electrifying amps and white moths dancing in the sun's rays. Some of the kids wanted to play in the quad, Bernarda, Charlotte, and Penelope being three of them, and two others were the twins, Earl and Greggo. Then Raymond and Henrik and a hefty, square backed boy with a wide middle and tall for his age, came to play too.

The kids didn't have any modern or conventional toys. They played with sticks and stones, made dirt rivers and leaf boats, and built mountains with bramble and castles with pebbles and mud. They were content playing with each other and the earth. It was all very symbiotic. Henrik dug a small ditch. Charlotte made it bigger. Penelope pushed a leaf boat through the ditch, and Bernarda constructed a stick house along its banks. Albert, who came up from the river with a handful of flowers, smelling and caressing them, gave Molly, Golly, and me each one before tucking the rest into his Jam'n Bermuda pockets. He had changed out of his previous shorts. No one knew why he had done this. He just did it. Albert picked up a piece of bark and made farting motor noises while pushing it through the ditch. At one point, he found a bigger piece of bark and left us to play with it at the beach.

The kids were quiet and diligent as there were more actions than words. They seemed to solve their dilemmas by adjusting the method or tool. They had time to think. The creations were their own, which wasn't to say I didn't want to play, too, but it didn't seem necessary. Besides, the tranquil serenity of playtime had my body folding in and head nodding, begging me to sleep. The humidity was at its height; the beetles buzzed insanely, and puddles of sweat pooled below my eyes. Slumping down onto the ground, I leaned against the log I had been sitting on and dozed. A languid, dreamy sleep. Only to be snapped awake by Molly and Golly's high-pitched laughter.

"What? Who?" I said, stumbling to sit up. Molly and Golly were next to me, sitting on the log. Catching sight of their legs, I saw they had oodles of bug bites.

"The bugs like you," I said, looking up at them, my head heavy and sluggish.

"*Fuck'n* bugs love me legs. Given me pizza legs," Molly said, scratching a raw-looking lump of flesh just above her ankle.

"*Lor' luv* a duck! Don' scratch, you'll make it worse. Know what I mean," Golly remarked, tugging on Molly's arm. "You know, the *dustbin lid* over there," she continued, changing the subject, and pointing at Greggo. "And his twin." She pointed at Earl. "They're Lenore's *Li'l Tom tits*."

"What?" I mumbled. Their cockney accents were so thick it was making me want to go back to sleep. Their lack of consonants was too much, and the '*Aaa*' sound was excruciating on the ear. I wished I'd stayed down by the river with the rest of the crew. But then I asked, "What are Tom tits?"

"Babies. Lenore's kids, dustbin lids," Molly clarified. "And the *faaat* one." She pointed at the square-backed boy. He used his weight to push his fellow orphans around. Motoring his leaf boat up the canals with a bullying, clumsy manner, he stepped on everyone's boat, such as Charlotte's twig-boat, which made her frown. Charlotte, unable to talk, had a quiet, hidden personality. Without fussing, she went over to an unused area and made another river. Penelope and Bernarda followed her, leaving the large boy to play by himself. I felt bad for him. His body was too big for his age.

"*Oi,* the big guy. We can never teach *'im* a thing," Molly continued, then whispered, "He's Hamit's kid. His name's El Gordo." Molly then laughed a horrible-sounding laugh. It was a sound a poodle would make if it were a deranged human.

"El Gordo?" I said, then asked. "What's his real name?" El Gordo meant 'the fat one.' Who would name their kid that? By saying his name, his head popped up, and I quickly replied, "*Nada.*" He was wearing navy blue, baggy gym shorts, and a T-shirt with a growling tiger on it.

"Hamit named him," Molly giggled. "Hamit's kid. Looks *like'm* too."

"Did you just say he's Hamit's kid?" I remarked, asking for clarification. "And the twins are Lenore's?"

"What do *yah* think?" Golly piped in. Her deadpan expression gave nothing away.

"I don't know," I said, leaning back against the log and shutting my eyes again. I felt a deep wave of paralyzing sleep enwrapping my brain. The heat was like a sedative. Their game, confusing. Golly nudged me awake, and said, "Bernarda. She's a real pistol, *innit.*" She scratched a puss-filled sore on her fleshy calf. "Why she's... she's Jeje's kid."

"Who's Jeje?" I asked, stretching my limbs to help ward off

sleep. Then sat up straight.

"Young kitchen girl."

I chuckled while moving away from Golly's gross legs. Their accents were becoming normalized to me as the ebb and flow of rarely using K's, swallowing their L's, inflaming A's, never using H's, and replacing the 'th' sound with an F somehow made sense. Feeling peppier, I wanted to hear more about their odd matchmaking, I said, "Go on, who else?"

The two of them began looking around, their minds churning. Then Golly squealed, causing all the kids' heads to pop up. Hushing her voice, she said, "Raymond and Henrik."

"And?"

"Manolo. You know, the launch driver. They're his kids." She thought her declaration to be very funny. Covering her mouth, she rocked back and forth on the log, laughing, and Molly joined her. Once again, the kids' heads popped up.

Molly and Golly's flaming copper hair, cinched back with butterfly clips, caused them to look as juvenile as they were acting. I liked them though, and their game. Matching the kids with the adults added intrigue to sitting in the sand and dirt and watching the kids. But I was curious about Molly and Golly. They seemed an unlikely duo to have volunteered to work at an orphanage in the middle of a rainforest in Central America, I asked, "How did you two, end up here?"

"*Blimey*! It's somethin' people do in England, *befawer* becoming serious. They travel. *Nuff* said, yeah?" Molly yapped, then added, "We not twins, you know."

"I didn't think you were," I said, wondering why she thought I thought they were twins.

"*Wee* best friends," Golly clarified.

Then Molly randomly said, changing the subject, "*Wee* don't have any nappies."

"*Cou'd* use a sheet'," Golly remarked.

"The kids don't look like they need diapers," I said.

"Some do when they sleep," Golly continued.

"Wooter needs a giant nappy." Molly squealed.

"Yes, yes, a giant nappy," Golly said excitedly, repeating the word 'nappy' again and again.

The word 'nappy' had an annoying sound, again, due to the emphasis on the A. They also seemed to love saying the word; possibly the A sound had a favorable ring to them, like the sound of an uncontrollable chihuahua they once had. Or the screech of metal on metal as a train went around a bend when they were traveling somewhere. Or maybe it just had them thinking of their mothers, fathers, and friends at an amusement park, riding a rollercoaster.

Charlotte and Bernarda, who were to my left, perked up and smiled every time they heard the word 'nappy.' Their heads would cock to the side, and I was certain their ears moved. Penelope, standing with her boat stick in her hand, and her face punched up into a snarl, pointed her stick at Molly and Golly, and said, "Stop."

"What!" Molly said, looking at her.

"STOP," she repeated, seeming angry.

"Cheeky, aren't you," Molly pounced.

"She knows some English," I said, amused.

"She's annoying. She's Alex's kid," Golly said, looking grumpy, her shoulders pulled in and her jaw slack. So, she finds Alex irritating too.

Molly and Golly, having been shut down by Penelope, didn't want to talk anymore, so they sat in silence, digging their sandaled toes into the dirt and pouting. It was as though shutting a door to a noisy room; the quiet was delightful.

Picking up a small pebble, I crawled over to where Henrik and Raymond were piling up rocks and tossed it on top. They took it off. Henrik handed it back to me. Wiping the sweat from my brow, I sat on the ground cross-legged, watching them. Their rock placement was very methodical, and I gathered I'd disturbed their organization. The afternoon, although tranquil, had a fervor to it, as though the world around us was chaotic and humming, but unable to touch us. The river with its motors, shouts, and surging waters was another world seeming far away from this nano slab of dirt and sand.

A colorful macaw, striped red and blue, perched in a linden tree by one of the upside-down canoes, fluttered its wings and squawked. I watched it until it flew away. Letting my gaze roam, I caught the eyes of the workman, Aapo. He had been asleep underneath the shadows of the middle canoe, while Eadrich, the oldest workman, had the canoe to the left, and Cadmael, the youngest, was to the right. Aapo, middle-aged, with creased, hard features, was staring at me. His face was muddy and streaked with sweat, and the whites of his eyes were prominent. He looked menacing. He wasn't blinking, so I thought he might still be asleep, dreaming with his eyes open. But then he turned his head away to look up into the belly of the canoe. Awake, how strange, I thought. There had been something about Aapo's stare. His eyes and expression that reminded me of the women who earlier, at lunch, had been sneering at me. Gunther had called it 'an angry sadness, not a dislike.' I felt it was both a festering bitterness and self-pity. I'd seen the same discordant expressions on a few of my Spanish teachers back in the city, in Corriente, in Mexico. They became bandy and argumentive over my ability to travel in their country, but they couldn't travel in mine. The exchange rate, unequal. This rambling discourse, which often took place, brought up the issues of failing monetary systems in countries that borrowed too heavily and forfeited their bill-paying by cheating their citizens. Their index fingers pointing at me, to unscrupulous foreign companies refusing to pay taxes and stealing their land, and the abuses, the list unconscionable. It also made me tired. Our worlds were as different as the moon and the sun, yet in the same galaxy; we wanted the same thing. It was in their eyes, their speech, their actions. 'A never-ending search, battle,' I would say to my teachers if I could get a word in. Met with laughter and a nod and convinced that in America money fell out of the sky. "Why, of course," I would reply—it was a matter of perspective.

Leaning back against the log, I watched Golly and Molly pull themselves out of their pout by pushing each other back and forth until they laughed.

Then Golly turned to me and said, "I have an idea. Why don't you babysit tonight? Ya don't have a bed, so why not? *Nuff* said, yeah?"

"Babysit, sure." What a great idea. I imagined the throw pillows and what a nice bed they would make. Then Raymond came over and sat in my lap, flopping down onto me like I was a chair. I laughed and said in English, "What are you going to be like when you grow up?"

Golly giggled, replying, "Why, he'll be president of the country. Won't you, Raymond?"

The funny kid nodded. 'Yes.'

Chapter 11

Catarina

Dinner over, and the quad and path to the river partially lit by the compound's two floodlights, I made my way down to the water with a bucket. I was in no rush and took slow, short strides. The tape that had been put in the boombox in the great room was ranchero music. The lyrics weaved a twisted tale of sweaty love making. The tune was eerie and seemingly inappropriate for kids, but I doubted they listened or even heard the words. It was the rhythm, the beat of the bass that drew them in. Their eyes lighting up, they danced. The young ladies from the kitchen and a few of the older children had come bounding through the screen door to join the rumble too. It was an unexpected sight, but welcomed, their hips gyrating, their faces glowing in the dull twenty-watt bulb. I could feel the thumping beat under my feet and the words as I walked. With each step, the sound faded, like a motorboat making its way north or south on the water.

Descending the grassy embankment, I heard rustling from behind a bush to my right. My mind raced to thoughts of danger. 'What evil lurked so early in the evening?' I thought, shrugging away fear and replacing it with something concrete like a bird or an iguana tucking itself in for the night. When I walked over to the bush, swinging the bucket by my side and snapping twigs under my feet, the rustling stopped, causing me to pause and hold my breath. The only sounds were the lapping waves at the shore and the distant melody and vibrations of the music.

Then without warning, a boy and a girl scrambled out from the underbelly of the bush, with giggles and small cries. Their sudden appearance gave me a chill, then a calming sigh of laughter. They were around fourteen years old and running while holding hands to the big kids' dorm. Their clothing was disarrayed, and the girl's hair was full of bramble. Having regained my composure, I thought about what Lenore had said, "Teenagers and boredom are a bad mix."

Once at the river's edge, I sat down on a rock and put my bucket on the ground. The bugs were noisy, buzzing near my ears and doing their best to bite my ankles; I picked up a fallen branch with thick leaves on it and began swatting my legs and head to keep the bugs at bay. The flow of the river was felt more than seen. I had been at the same spot this morning. The same unnerving tug of the water rumbled beneath my feet, as though at any moment it would grab up a foot or an arm and drag me in. The morning light-years away, and yet, only hours had passed. Slow measured hours filled with seconds and minutes that took their time.

After dinner, a nightly meeting had taken place. It had been amusing—that was until it lagged, and we all grew bored. It started with everyone sitting in the great room on throw pillows in a circle. Jack stood in the middle of us all. The kids, nestled around us, were quietly reading to themselves, although most weren't really reading, just looking at pictures.

Jack, bent and pointy, was doing a huffing thing that made his nostrils flare while twisting his hips one way, then another. It made his question-mark stance look goofier, and as though he was a contortionist that didn't know what he was doing. Catarina whispered into my ear, "It's Jack's method of loosening up before diving into a lecture."

Once ready, he orated the hazards of putting clothing in the wrong bins because it made dressing the children frustrating and time-consuming, and something about causing cross-dressing since the children picked out their own clothing. If the dresses were mixed with shorts and pants, well, 'What kind of message is that sending?' he asked. People snickered.

He then went into playtime.

"I like playtime," Alex said. Alex was lying on his back, spitting foam into the air, and when it fell back down, he would catch it with his tongue, or it would land directly back into his mouth. It was disgusting to watch.

"Of course, you do, Alex," Jack said, sneering at him, cringing at the foam-eating. "Now I have an experiment. We have boxes of toys up in the attic. Let's bring them down."

"Toys? I don't think they have ever played with conventional toys," Gunther remarked.

"That's why it's an experiment," Jack said.

"What are you going to call this one?" Gunther blurted out.

"The title to the chapter will come to me when we see their reactions," Jack replied.

"We? What do you mean by 'we'?" asked Gunther.

"I meant me," Jack corrected himself.

"Why not we?" Gunther asked.

"Because the dissertation is about me, and my thoughts."

"So finally, you admit you're a madman using all of us as your guinea pigs. And taking all our good thoughts to be yours," Gunther said, proud of himself.

Jack huffed, paused, stared at the floor, shook his index finger at Gunther, and said, "Not a madman Gunther. An intellectual." This made us all giggle, which caused Jack to huff again. Then he changed the subject back to clothing. Disturbed over the shabby condition of it all, he held up a lovely, turquoise Donna Karan dress. Its' hem had frayed. Gritting his teeth, he threw the tattered clothing onto the floor and made an ugh noise. Catarina picked the dress up and tossed it to Alex, who wrapped it around his dreads as a headdress. Everyone thought, except Jack, the color complimented his red hair. I kept quiet. If I was going to speak to Alex, it wouldn't be with a compliment.

Jack then shifted into being optimistic about our little people's wardrobe. He liked the fact that we probably had the best-dressed orphans in the world. I liked that idea too. We all did, and there were a lot of 'hip, hip, hoorays' over dressing well. Enlivened by our nonsense, Jack became more animated and threw his right arm into the air, pointing to the ceiling as though whoever lived above in the rafters or the sky should be listening to him, and broke into a sermon. "If the clothing was washed on the gentle cycle or even on 'normal' in a modern-day washing machine, it would last, keep its color, never get a hole." He shouted the last few words, which caused the kids to glance up from their books.

"The clothes," he continued, arms reaching. "Could be hand-me-downs for generations. But that is not the case here. Here, the cement washboard rules. Here, these busty, thick-armed women scrub the threads into indiscernible, infinitesimal dust."

"Could we call it thread-barren instead?" Gunther interjected.

"What? Sure," Jack mumbled, then added, "Yes, thread-barren, Christ! Threadbare spots and a lot of discoloration."

"My pants used to be white," Gunther again interjected. It was obvious he was making fun of Jack, but Jack didn't notice or didn't care. Gunther's balloon pants were red and brown and always had been red and brown. Looking around the room to see if anyone else thought this meeting was odd, I noticed Catarina was busy picking the crud out of under her nails. Molly and Golly were asleep, lumped together like chunks of cold lard. Alex was playing with Frankie. Gunther and I were the only ones looking at Jack acting like we were paying attention.

"Lenore should be visiting soon," Jack continued, ignoring Gunther's remarks about his pants. Then with his mouth open, a word on the tip of his tongue, he abruptly stopped talking to concentrate on something outside the window by the cafeteria. This caused Catarina to look up and say, "She's bringing more clothing, I assume."

"More what?" Jack asked, puzzled, walking over to the window.

"Clothing," Catarina stated, annoyed.

"Why?" Jack said, scratching his chin, still peering out the window. Sitting up, I could see Sarah was trying to catch the bugs and moths that were swarming around the light by the cafeteria entrance. She had an open mason jar and was sweeping it through the air.

"Don't bring any of those things into the dorm! We have enough creepy things crawling around in here!" Jack shouted at her. The little kids looked up again. Raymond and Henrik took the opportunity to become very vocal. The little boys were not only making up a story to go with the pictures but were adding words such as 'goo-goo, boo-boo, eek,' and 'wee-kee.' Curious to see what book they were reading, I crawled over. It was *Green Eggs and Ham.*

"Now, where were we?" Jack said, walking back into the middle of the circle, keeping an eye on his wife. No one said anything. Jack huffed, pointing his large proboscis around the room, he noticed people weren't listening anymore, except for Gunther. Bunching his mouth, he held his chin in his hands and pouted.

Catarina rose, straightened out her skirt, and said, "I have stuff to do." She walked out of the room. In the silence, we could hear her sandaled feet clapping along the cement floor all the way to the bathroom.

Then Molly and Golly woke up. Sitting up, they rubbed their eyes, looking sweaty and disheveled. They rolled their bodies over to a group of kids that were reading the book *Are You My Mother?* Molly pointed to something in the book that made her burst into a high-pitched giggle. The kids laughed too.

Only Gunther looked ready for more lecturing, but Jack was done. He was at the door helping Sarah with her jar of bugs. Jack was kind and caressing as he took the bottle out of her hand and placed it back outside the door. Returning, he folded Sarah into his arms, and they headed up the stairs. Molly and Golly once again commented on them being sex addicts. Then, someone, I don't know who, put a cassette in the boombox. All the kids dropped what they were doing and jumped up to dance. Downtime had ended, and so had the nightly meeting.

Now at the river's edge, self-flagellating with a branch clustered with leaves, I breathed in the cool air, coupled with a feeling of contentment. Away from the need to talk and be part of something bigger than myself, I was enjoying the alone time. As my eyes adjusted to the dark, I could see the outline of the trees on the other side of the river and the single bulbs from the various houses. They looked like fireflies permanently on. The club's yellow and multicolored Christmas lights were soothing and nostalgic. I had spent Christmas on a beach in La Playa, Mexico with friends from language school. It had been raining.

We sat under palm fronds at a bar with swinging seats drinking margaritas. There were green blinking lights and Rubin the bartender wore a Santa Claus hat. I remembered laughing a lot and then smashing open a piñata filled with McDonald's happy meal toys.

"Fancy seeing you down here." It was Catarina. She had a bucket with her. It was the black bucket that had a crack in the bottom and leaked. She put her bucket down and pulled on my shirt to follow her onto the dock. "I think he's here," she said.

"Who?"

"Him."

Slapping a mosquito, she dug into her skirt pocket and pulled out a pack of cigarettes and quickly lit one. Taking a long drag, she blew the smoke out all around us, then offered me one. I took a cigarette, lighting it off hers. I wasn't a regular smoker. More like a social smoker, or someone who smoked when the need for smoking was necessary as in to stave off bugs. They were Gitanes, short, stumpy French cigarettes, and made me lightheaded. But they did the trick because the bugs disappeared.

"You must have brought them from Montreal," I said, tossing my branch aside while exhaling the smoke all over my arms and legs.

"Yeah, I only have a few packs left." She said, peering out over the water. "Do you see the sailboat?" she asked.

"Where?"

"There," she said, pointing to a boat sitting around a hundred yards out. The mast light flickered as the boat rocked. It also blended in with the Christmas lights. But as we studied the outline, slowly the whole boat appeared. Then another light flicked on, illuminating the boat's sails and the outline of a person sitting in the cockpit. Whoever it was stood up, fiddled with something, and then sat back down.

"I think it's him," she mumbled.

"Who?" I asked again.

"Harry's friend."

"Dutch?" I don't know why I said that. Harry was friends with Umberto, and he wasn't Dutch.

"Not sure. Why did you say Dutch?"

"Harry's Dutch."

"No, he's not."

"He told me he's Dutch."

"He likes Dutch people, or no, it's the licorice he likes. I don't know how it gets here. Sent, maybe. It's sweet and strong-flavored."

"Yum."

"He doesn't like sharing it." She then began looking around and asked, "Where are those binoculars?"

"At the end of the dock."

I followed Catarina as she walked down the dock. I wasn't fond of licorice, but sweet sounded good. I imagined Harry munching on it in the room and not sharing, and me not giving a damn except that maybe I would want to lick the sweet from it.

Catarina placed the binoculars up to her face and narrated to me what the man was doing: "He's going down below." I could see he had left because the light in the cabin allowed for the detection of movement, but I didn't tell her that because it would spoil her narration.

"Now he's coming back up. He has coffee or something.

He's pouring from a glass bottle into it. I bet its booze. He's sitting back down. He's lighting a pipe." When he lit a match, it illuminated his face briefly, but not long enough to know what he looked like. I saw he had a white face and maybe a long nose.

"So, where's he from?" I said, standing off to the side to let Catarina position herself better. Fish were jumping in our cove, drawing my attention away.

"I don't know, I think America."

"I meant Harry," I said, looking back at her. "If he's not Dutch, where's he from?"

"I don't know. Come to think of it, his mother may have Dutch ties. Oh, my—I love the way he puffs on his pipe. The smell is dreamy."

A fish popped up and swam around in circles, making a whirlpool. The moon only a sliver made it hard to see, but there seemed to be some phosphorescence in the water causing the combustion to sparkle. I wished I could use the binoculars so I could see the fish better, but I supposed her man was more important than my fish. Taking a drag from the cigarette, I blew more billowing puffs around us.

"He's just sitting and drinking—and smoking. I saw him with Harry a month back. He's handsome, dreamy handsome." I stared at her face, half-hidden behind the binoculars. In the blue darkness, Catarina looked young. It took her wrinkles away and made her thick, strawberry-blonde hair the color of fall corn. Standing there, she had an energy about her that felt wild and possessed. It seemed to be due to the man on the boat, I said, "You should get Harry to introduce you."

She laughed, then sighed. Resting the binoculars on her chest, she gazed back out over the river, and said, "Now my sailor man, if it's him, is American." She said American with a John Wayne accent, and I laughed.

"American," I repeated, using the same vernacular. Taking a quick drag and blowing the smoke around us, I asked, "Can I have a look?" She handed me the binoculars.

I saw that he was hunched over, reading a book by the light of a small hand lantern. "He could be cute. It's hard to tell, but his face looks—well, I think he's older," I remarked, forgetting that Catarina was much older than me. "He constantly puffs on his pipe. Good thing you like the smell."

"He looks like The Marlboro Man. You remember that commercial." She then giggled and asked, "Do you think I could swim out there?"

"Now?"

"Tomorrow, if he is still there, or the next day." She rubbed her chin and continued. "At lunch, Harry told me you were driving into town in the morning."

"People don't keep much to themselves here."

"Why would they? This place is the size of my pinky. Anyway, he thought, I might want to ask you to get me something. And I do. See if you can get me a bathing cap." Then she laughed. "I hate the idea of climbing out of the water looking like a drowned rat."

"I've a better idea. Why don't we shout to him? Have him come over." His boat was anchored in the heaviest part of the currents.

"And ruin the surprise?" She then laughed again, a deep throaty guffaw.

"I gather you swim well. But look, those currents hit right around where his boat is anchored," I said, trying to discourage her.

"I'm a fantastic swimmer." Taking the binoculars from me,

she took one last look before placing them back on the dock's hook. We snubbed our spent cigarettes out, and Catarina stuffed the butts into her pack as not to litter. Hurrying, we dashed off the dock because the mosquitoes were coming in from all angles. Remembering the buckets, we filled them and sloshed water on to the ground with every step taken.

The party was still going strong. The one ranchero song, to be played over and over again until ten or maybe it was eleven. Getting the kids to brush their teeth was easy; they liked it. They used Crest bubblegum flavored toothpaste, which I tried because I had the region's chalky, only hinting of peppermint-flavor, toothpaste in my bag. Overly sweet, I opted to continue with the bland chalk. They fell right to sleep. Golly had mumbled something about putting them to bed earlier. Gunther countered, "But then they would be fussy."

Since I was the babysitter, I re-arranged a pile of throw pillows outside the crib room, took a seat, and opened my book.

Chapter 12

The letter

I read while listening to the hushed breathing of the children asleep in the next room. A twisted, bent, plastic lamp illuminated my little corner with a muddled, yellow bulb. The lumens weren't great, but it was never great trying to read anywhere in this country. The wattage low, and the light never near a bed or a chair.

The whole compound was strangely quiet as the birds, the bugs, and the river were asleep. It left me wanting for company. I needed something other than the taxing prose of my book as the Spanish words and unfamiliar syntax were causing me to nod off. It was my first night with the group and knocking off one of the kids because I didn't hear them choking or crying would be a giant screw-up, not to mention, tragic. Standing, I crept into the crib room to inspect my charges. Sound asleep. I went back and sat down.

'Siempre he econtrado que el amor no es Seguro. Las personas, nada más que animales esponjosos, piensan que están por encima de sus instin-

tos básicos, lo que causa víctimas—¿Quién es su víctima.' I was having trouble understanding what the psychiatrist in the story was trying to say. Although the words were simple, the multiplex concept was not, and because it seemed to be a revealing statement about the main character's personality, I was keen on interpreting the text correctly. My mind slow, the sentence reminded me of a word jumble.

The issue with difficult Spanish structures had to do with my thought process. I was literally translating the words, but what I needed to do was think of what it all meant. My beginner Spanish teacher in the mountains of Mexico had taught us all a bunch of *maldiciones*, bad words, and phrases, to keep us interested in the language. *Maldiciones para los calles*, street language, it was called: *pinche pendejo*, fucking idiot; *cabrón*, asshole; *no me jodas*, don't fuck with me; *chingar*, fuck; and one of my favorites, although I enjoyed using them all, *me cago en todo lo que se menea*, I shit on everything that moves. For the next couple of days during the morning breaks, when everyone else in the school would chat about what their host families were like or verbs, my classmates and I were swearing at each other and laughing. Now my grammar and ability to translate a poetic verse, suffered. Or, rather, that is what I told myself.

"*Pinche pendejo*," I mumbled to the book. Then speaking out loud, but low, I read the translation I had written down, 'love and victim.' Needing more words in the sentence I scribbled, 'I have always loved and then I became a victim?' Whoa, not right. My head started to hurt with too much thinking. Speaking out loud again, I whispered, "I am loved, but too many victims." Possibly?

Stumped, I put the book down and leaned back to rest, only to pick it back up again to write in the margins the *present de indicative* Spanish verb conjugations for love: *amo, amas, ama, amamos, aman.* Yet most Spanish speakers don't say, '*te amo*' they say, '*te quiero*' — I want you, not I love you.

As the hours ticked by, and they did very slowly, I fell asleep periodically, only to be jolted awake due to the book slamming to the floor or my lower back sliding onto the cold cement. It was like a brainwashing torture and it made me miserable and grumbly. The night continued in this manner until, blasting into the silent night, El Gordo began screaming like a blaring car horn. The abrupt noise bounced me to my feet.

El Gordo was sleeping on a cot across from me, in a corner by the clothing bins because he was too big for a crib. He slept with his eyes open. Although his corner was dark, all night long I could see him staring at me as the lamplight reflected off his glassy eyeballs. It was eerie. I tried my best not to look at him because he reminded me of some nocturnal, creepy carnivore, but whenever I looked up from my reading, I couldn't help but glance his way.

The sound he was making was horrible. Loud and inflammatory. My book having fallen to the floor, the lamp tipped over, my blood chilled by the sudden sound of his honking, I went over to him. He needed to stop, but he was stuck in some crazed, honking jag. Looking into the crib room, no one seemed to be moving or up—yet.

El Gordo, quivering, laid prone on the cot, while his mouth remained wide open, honking. I put my hand on his arm and whispered, "El Gordo, El Gordo, wake up." But it did nothing.

I gently tried to shake him awake, but still, nothing changed.

"El Gordo!" I said louder and with more insistent shaking, but he didn't respond. Retrieving the flashlight that was over by the shelving I turned it on and directed the light into his face to get a better look. "For Christ's sake! What is wrong with you?" From the crib room, a small cry broke out, and something fell to the floor from above. He was waking everyone up. Then as abruptly as he had started, he stopped.

His mouth open, the light exposing his back molars and

deep into his throat. I could see his tonsils and wondered if they were the problem. He didn't brush well; there were still black bean bits stuck along the rim of his upper teeth. His cheeks were glistening, revealing that he had been crying. The stillness of his body unnerved me as his chest ceased to move up and down. I wondered if he was having some psychotic breakdown. My only dealings with psychotic breakdowns were with my mother. They were easy to deal with because I just ran out the door to a friend's house, but I couldn't do that here. He then exhaled, making a deflating, squeaky balloon noise. His breathing grew relaxed and steady, and the tension filling his rigid body unwound. His eyes, after so many hours of being open, finally shut. But was he asleep? I stood for what seemed like a long time, staring down at him, keeping the flashlight beam directed on his face.

Going back over to my pillows, I sat down and shut the flashlight off. He immediately began to honk... honk... honk once again. And once again the jarring sound caused me to jump up, grab the flashlight and turn it back on. With the light shining on his face, he stopped honking, his eyes that had re-opened, shut. His dark hair framing his sweaty face, and his chubby body was calm. Under my breath, I cursed my fellow volunteers for not telling me about El Gordo's sleeping issues.

Not daring to take the light off him, I rearranged my pillows into a comfortable bed with one hand, while keeping the flashlight on him with the other. Sitting back down, we looked at each other. El Gordo who had open his eyes was staring at me with white, ghoulish pupils. Glancing out the window at the sky and the moon sliver that had sunk low, it seemed daylight would be arriving soon.

It wasn't long afterward that I heard footsteps coming down the stairs. It was Catarina. She came padding into the room wearing a nightshirt and flattened slippers, looking half-asleep. My first thought was that it was time to get up, which was an exhilarating idea. But when she stopped at El Gordo's cot and said in a hushed voice, "Damn kid wakes me up all the time," I knew it wasn't but asked anyway.

"Is it time to get up?"

"No."

She went into the bathroom and came out minutes later. "You know, without the running water, we don't flush at night."

"Of course." The toilets were a mess and smelled.

She looked at the flashlight and El Gordo. "What's with the flashlight?"

"He likes it."

"That's new."

I watched her shuffle back up the stairs.

A few minutes later, Jack came into the room. His presence woke me up because I had fallen into a semi-unconscious state. Not wanting to talk to him, I kept my eyes half-shut and watched him slink by. He was wearing boxers and no shirt. His chest was hairy and concave. He looked sickly. He also seemed to be still asleep. Walking in a rhythmic downward trod, he neither looked left nor right. He went into the bathroom where he was loud and splashy. When near completion, he belched the names '*Raaaaaalph*' and '*Aaaaaart.*' Then he whistled like he had made a big mess and was proud of it. When he came back into the room, he paused and looked at El Gordo and said, "Odd kid," then left.

Sarah passed Jack as he was going up and she was coming down. She had on a pair of boxers and no top. She was flat-chested and looked like a teenage boy, her hair cropped, her long bangs dangled in front of her face. I was amazed at how she walked, loud and pigeon-toed. Unlike her husband, her peeing was silent, almost non-existent. She came back out and left without saying a word.

Then Molly and Golly came into the room. I clamped my eyes shut again. They were talking in their quiet voices, which was a normal loud voice, and they were exceptionally galling. They were pissing me off, but I didn't want to tell them to shut up, because then they would have stopped to talk to me. Which they tried to do anyway.

Feeling them standing in front of me, I heard one of them say, "She asleep?" This caused me to press my eyes as tightly together as possible.

"*Ew*, her eyes are twitching."

"*'Ook*, Golly, El Gordo's *lookin* at us."

"*Ew*."

"*Ew*."

They went into the bathroom and made all sorts of noises and sounds indicating the bathroom grossed them out. Then they started talking about a boy back home who had perpetual snot dripping out of his nose. 'What the hell?' When they went to leave, they stopped in front of me and stared at me for a good minute. Then, sounding like elephants with all left feet, they lumbered up the stairs. I couldn't believe the little kids were still asleep.

A few minutes after they left, Harry stormed in.

"Christ! Grand Central Station," I mumbled to myself.

"What?" Harry asked walking over to me.

"The children are sleeping—Shhhh." I was in a panic.

"It's around five. They get up. You get up, the whole lot of you get up at five. I'm going to bed."

"Why do you get to go to bed?" I asked.

"Because I can." Harry seemed out of sorts, almost furious over something. His clothing was wet, and his boots were thick with mud.

"What happened?" I asked, sitting up.

"Nothing. Nothing I can't fix—I think?" He said, breathing in to let out a sigh, then asked. "What's with the flashlight?" He was speaking loudly, almost shouting. El Gordo sat up, putting his hands over his eyes to shield them from the light. He then looked under the cot. He pulled out a worn, beaten-up teddy bear and hugged it, and went back to bed with it tucked into his arms and fell asleep with his eyes shut.

"A bear. All he needed was his bear."

"That kid. He always sleeps with a bear. Everyone knows it," Harry said, dripping in front of me, adding. "I have a list of stuff I want you to get for me in town." As I was shining the light on Harry now, I could see his eyes were dark and seeded with something burning inside him. The intensity was fascinating to look at. His emotions swinging from trying to be in control to sad to happy within seconds. He was a lot more mercurial and affecting than he'd been in the cafeteria. What an interesting fellow, came to mind.

"You better write it down," I said, wanting to get all the items straight. Everyone had asked me to buy them something. Jack wanted more salsa; Sara wanted a small net; Molly and Golly wanted candy; Catarina a bathing cap; Alex, he wasn't talking to me, so I didn't have to get him anything, and Gunther was coming with me.

He left and went upstairs. A few minutes later he came back down with just a towel wrapped around his waist and an envelope in his left hand. He seemed calmer. His feet were bare, and he stood in the puddle he had just made. His body looked stronger than it did when clothed. My gaze stumbling around his midriff caused him to look at me, puzzled. Nonchalantly, I rolled my eyes up to meet his. He was to be married—what a shame. But then, I wasn't looking for a liaison, especially with my roommate.

He handed me the envelope with a piece of paper inside and a handful of money, and said, "Give it to the owner of the hardware store. The money is a down payment. Get a receipt."

I stuffed it into my pants pocket, and said, "Will you help me with something? A brief translation." I picked up the book and flipped through the pages until I spotted where I had left off. "'*Siempre he econtrado que el amor no es Seguro. Las personas, nada más que animals esponjosos, piensan que están por encima de sus instintos básicos, lo que causa víctimas—quién es su víctima?*' Could you repeat it back in English? Verbatim, if possible?"

Without hesitation, he said, "I have always found love to be unsafe. People, nothing but fluffed up animals, think they are above their basic instincts. This causes victims—Who are your victims?" And then he began to laugh, a big, loud, boisterous laugh that I found obnoxious because who could sleep through boisterous? Even if it was time to get up. And to think, hysterical El Gordo had just fallen asleep with his bear. I also felt he hadn't translated the words correctly, because 'fluffed up animals' seemed stupid to me.

Stifling his laughter. Still full of mirth, he looked down at me, his intense stare unsettling, and asked, "Who's your victim, Eleanor?"

"No one. I don't believe in victims."

"I don't believe your book agrees with you," he said in a very low voice while keeping his gaze tightly locked onto mine.

He then stormed off into the bathroom not waiting for a reply, but disgusted by the stench, he stormed back out and stopped once more in front of me. "I forgot to tell you. I noticed your clothes hanging on the line. Rather beaten up, don't you think? Well, while in town you might want to buy a few things, something nice. The owners of the Club de Bote told me they're thinking of throwing us a 'thank-you party' soon—for helping the orphans. They're good that way. Oodles of tasty food."

"Now who's being rude?" I said, irritated about the clothing comment. But he ignored my snap or didn't hear as he was staring out the window and at the sky, and said, "I believe the party will be during the Rabbit Moon phase—how unfortunate."

"What's a Rabbit Moon?" I asked, but he had dashed off, out the screen door, slamming it behind him, which was puzzling because I wondered where he would be going with just a towel, in the wee hours of the morning. And went back to my first impression of him, odd and irritating.

From the crib room, a child coughed, and another stirred. Then little voices began to speak back and forth. The children were awake. I lazily got up and went into the crib room. Most of them were standing in their cribs with their hands on the top bar. They looked like lemmings searching for danger, only they were cuter with big, round faces and big, round eyes.

A little confused at what I should do with them, I began making the same sounds I make with the neighborhood dogs back home. "*Looky* at all of you, big boys and girls. Did we sleep well?" Only I said it in Spanish.

Directly above me, while I was steeped in this saccharine behavior, I could hear the adults upstairs fumbling with their garments and shoes. Swear words were floating in and out of their rumblings, a glass broke, and someone stubbed their toe.

Starting with Charlotte because she was closest to me, I took her out of her crib. Charlotte was heavier than I thought she would be. A solid child. She wrapped her arms around my neck and snuggled. When I went to put her down, she clung, but everyone wanted out and there wasn't any time for long hugs. I apologized, ruffling her hair. Once on the floor, she followed me around the room.

All the kids had the scent of urine on them. Wooter, whom I held away from me, had a backside full of crap, and Bernarda wasn't any better. Once on the floor, they all ran into the bathroom, except for Charlotte who stayed glued to my side. Her need for me was precious, and I felt endeared to her. While I had walked around the room, I narrated to her what I was doing. This seemed to make her happy, which made me happy too.

The morning, quiet except for a few birds and the slapping of small feet running on the cement, until someone put a tape into the boombox. It was a hip-hop Latino song. A nasal, raspy voice sang, "*Muévelo—Bebé.*" The volume was high, and the sound chaotic. When Jack and Sarah stepped into the crib room, they were dressed and looked half-asleep, and Jack shouted at me over the music, "We need to take them to the river to wash. But you and Gunther need to leave. I heard the launch pull up to the dock."

"What's with the music?" I shouted back.

"What?"

"Nothing."

Wanting to change into something clean, I ran out through the screen door and over the sloppy backyard to the linden and jacaranda trees. Perusing my clothing, I saw what Harry had meant. The whole lot of it was embarrassing, but so what? I hadn't met a traveler yet whose clothing didn't have holes or a tear.

Sensing that someone had followed me, and I turned around. It was Charlotte. She was standing on a mound of dry land. I told her to stay put, but she didn't listen and walked through the soup to me. She wanted to help. I gave her my shorts to hold. Then I grabbed the rest of the clothes, and we walked back into the dorm. When Catarina appeared with several other children holding onto the folds of her skirt, she winked at me and told Charlotte to hold on to her skirt too. Watching them head down to the river, I thought of Old Mother Hubbard, although no one held onto Mother Hubbard's skirt in the nursery rhyme.

Dressing in the fouled bathroom, trying my best not to breathe, made me sweat. Grabbing my daypack and water bottle, I burst out into the quad and ran down to the dock. It was a muted gray dawn, and I found myself stumbling over bramble as I made my way to the water's edge. Passing the *oficina*, I saw a woman I hadn't seen before standing in the doorway. She had a flashlight in her hand and shone the light on me. She asked me who I was in Spanish. I stopped and told her. I could see she had dark skin and light blue eyes. 'Blue-Eyes,' I thought. Digging into my daypack, I pulled out the letter of introduction that Lenore had given me. I handed it to Blue-eyes. She thanked me, and I went on my way.

At the beach, the kids were wading in the water naked, their faces being washed, water being splashed on their limbs. I could see the sun was still resting below the tree line, the drowsy light weaving golden streaks with orange hues into the indifferent flutes of the river. The sailboat was still present, dark and solitary. I thought of the man below the deck in a cozy bed, asleep. It was a lovely thought as the morning fog drifted in, like translucent cotton filled with mystery and serenity. Looking left toward the dock, Gunther, Aapo, Cadmael, and Eadrich were waiting for me. I picked up my step; I was going into town.

Chapter 13
Manolo

Manolo was slick-looking. His pressed, navy-blue cotton pants and white-collared shirt were spotless, except for the tiny Polo emblem over his left breast. His loafers, dark leather, unmarred and buffed, a novelty that helped give him the mythical lore of wealth, something unconscionable for a poor, indigenous boy from the north. He had come down to the river with his humble parents for land, according to Golly and Molly. They had said, "his *fadher* was foreign." A rich wolf who had seduced his mother while her husband was working in the maize fields in the west. Undoubtedly, this was another fanciful tale by the girls to bide their time while watching the kids. But then again, Manolo had the air of an aristocratic hound. Taller than the average local, his brown skin glowed with snooty aplomb. He seemed like a real poser standing relaxed behind the wheel of the launch, a Boston Whaler fit with two seventy-five-horsepower motors. Enough moxie to power us anywhere in seconds.

"A lady's man, that one is," Gunther said, leaning into me.

"Don't think he can't tell that you think he's cute. My advice is not to look at him. He's the dog's bollocks in these parts. He'll diddle you while fondling another."

I laughed and took a sip of water. I hadn't had time to brush my teeth. The taste in my mouth was stale, but the water was cleansing, and the crisp, morning air felt good on my cheeks. Sitting by the stern in front of the giant bobblehead engines were Aapo, Eardrich, and Cadmael. They were huddled together, hunched over with brown jackets wrapped tight, hats pushed down, only chins exposed. I wondered where they had come from; possibly they had houses in the back recesses of the jungle behind the orphanage. Leaning against the hard fiberglass siding of the boat, I imagined drinking coffee and thought about how wonderful an infusion of caffeine would feel.

"And another thing," Gunther said, leaning into me again. "Manolo's not only our ticket out of this muddy mound of earth, but more importantly, he buys our booze."

"What do you mean?"

"Give him money, and he delivers the rum. Now, remember, in his world women treat him like a god. So, don't get cheeky."

"I'm not cheeky," I said, knowing damn well I was often cheeky. I took another sip of water, and my empty stomach growled. "Maybe we should eat first, before doing anything else, when we get into town."

"I'm game. Now, everyone has the ability to be cheeky with a pillock like him." He threw his eyes towards Manolo. I wanted to ask him what 'pillock' meant but felt I didn't need another English word to hamper my Spanish.

Gunther, being a chatty fellow, continued talking. "Now, I need my rum." He said these words with an alcoholic's sincerity, making it impossible not to chuckle.

"You shouldn't laugh; this is serious business."

"Don't worry," I said. "I won't mess with your supply guy."

"Yours too."

Dribbling past the 'no-wake zone' sign, I saw that the words were hand-painted in black with uneven lines. Underneath the black print, someone wrote with even sloppier lettering '*peligroso*' in red. The morning mist floated around the edges of the river, transforming what was once serene into something spooky.

"One would think of monsters and cryptic thoughts looking at that sign," Gunther said, leaning in again, the warmth of his body not offensive.

"It's beautiful here," I said. The sharpened foliage in the light of the rising sun and the flurry of bird activity spellbinding.

"The mornings are the best before all the river wankers wake and the duffer clods are still asleep. But we don't normally see it because we're bathing the kids. Then breakfast. Bloody hell, I could use a big, fat tortilla right about now." Sitting back, he tucked himself down into his seat and shut his eyes and muttered, "Could be all ruined soon."

"Breakfast?"

"No, the jungle. The river. All of it. Poof! Gone," he said, keeping his eyes shut.

"How?"

"They discovered oil in Lago de Cho." He then opened his eyes and looked directly into mine. I was under the impression he was trying to read my thoughts. His irises a deep, glassy blue, his pupils enlarged, and his skin puffy around them, with darkened shadows beneath.

"You look tired," I said, wondering what this was all about. I felt he wanted to tell me something but wasn't sure if he should.

"So do you," he said back, adding. "I was up all night."

"So was I." I frowned.

Gunther then let out a big, windy sigh and said, "Lago de Cho. It's the lake that feeds the river. The banks are blooming with flowers and all sorts of vegetation. Howler monkeys swinging from tree to tree. A damn pity to ruin it. Hell, lots of buggering and destruction going on around here because of that oil."

"That's depressing." The image of the river's waters awash in slimy, black crud, and the foliage beat down with machetes, bulldozers and modernization was heart-wrenching.

"Land grabbing," he whispered, his eyes closed again.

"I think I read something about land deeds being changed or counterfeited by some government guy—The Minister of Interior. A murder, too. A boy. Anyway, I thought the land had been given to the people that lived in the mountains. When the fighting ended."

"Yeah, some moved here. But mountain people like mountains." Pausing, he continued. "Isn't that the way? The government, the rich, discover something valuable, and they want it. Even if it means going back on their word or counterfeiting land deeds. A real web of deceit and greed creating another sad tale. For instance, that boy that was killed. Harry knew him. First time I ever saw Harry get angry. I mean really angry. Stormed around, broke a few things, went into the big city, and came back with a black-eye." Gunther cleared his throat, then changed the subject. "You know, the manatee can be nice. I've seen them bobbing along in the water. Disturbing they will get all gunked up." Gunther stretched his arms to the sky and bent down to touch his toes.

"Doggy down again?" I questioned with a smile, although saddened by the manatee and their future.

"Gosh, I'm miserable this morning," Gunther grunted while reaching for the sky again. "Golly went on like a bloody codswallop last night, keeping me up. Her snoring could win an award. A cup of coffee would be just right."

"In town?"

"Doubt it. Nothing but the dodgy stuff from the floor. They export the good stuff. I suppose I'll take the dodgy bits, though."

"I'll take the dodgy bits," I said, repeating his vernacular. "I'll take the dodgy Nescafé." Gunther, then seeming too tired to make any more conversation, slid farther down, resting his feet on the bench across from us and, without further notice, fell asleep.

Looking around for something to entertain me, I shot a glance toward the workmen and saw they, too, were asleep. I pondered the oil issue while picking out the stains on the workmen's clothing. It looked like they had been painting, along with working with grease. Cadmael was the best dressed. He wore jeans that looked new. His shirt pressed with few splotches. The older men's hands looked too big for their bodies, callused and scarred. I gathered they knew what was taking place on the river. If I knew, and I had only been in the area for a day and two nights, how could anyone else not know?

I then thought about eating a muffin. I don't know why I was so keen on eating a muffin, especially one with fruit in it, like blueberries or raspberries. The problem was that they didn't make muffins in this country, that I knew of. In the big cities, I'd found bakeries that made cookies and loaves of bread. The bread, made with bleached flour and salt, resembled unsweetened cotton candy. The cookies were an amalgamation of bleached flour, fat, and water. Dense, lard-filled products with little or no sugar. Tooth-breaking crisps. Nevertheless, I sat in the boat with my mouth watering, thinking about eating a muffin, but then I would take a cookie, possibly two, with a cup of café con leche made with powdered milk and Nescafé.

Manolo shifted the throttle forward, kicking the launch into a faster gear and sliding me into Gunther. He didn't wake up. Inching away, I gave Gunther a nudge as I wanted to discuss more politics with him. He was out cold and didn't even respond to my nudge with a whimper or an annoyed shrug. Exhaust plumed up from the back of the launch, and oil splatters made slimy rainbow trails in our wake. I was sullen about the manatee, the fish, and the birds, and how much I liked to swim. It saddened me to think it might all disappear one day. Fouled, future waters with bubbling oil pouring into the river from the lake was upsetting. Everyone was asleep, except for the taciturn Manolo, I had no one to complain to. Huffing, I chewed on my lower lip and turned toward Manolo. 'Why not ask him what he thought of the discovery of oil?' Which was when I noticed we had slowed down. Manolo was concentrating on something on the shore and began to inch us toward a patch of mangroves. When I asked him where we were going, he waved my words away like I was some kind of pest. Not wanting to be cheeky I kept quiet, but searched the shore, too, trying to see what he was after.

Then out of the thicket walked a petite girl in a tight, black cotton skirt, wearing a pink, puffy-sleeved blouse with a low neckline. I threw Manolo an exasperated look. Pit stops to flirt with little girls weren't something I thought we had time for. Again, I refrained from commenting. His little girl giggled with her hand up to her mouth, swaying back and forth, so happy to see him.

Her round face was accentuated by small, plump breasts; she couldn't have been more than fifteen. Standing by a twisted patch of mangroves with thick, green leaves dripping water, she was now waving with a gleeful, enthusiastic grin on her face. He waved back, his expression placid, his eyes churlish and alive.

The skiff chugging, he throttled back the motors, and we idled, drifting lazily toward the shore.

"This is going to be a long morning," I mumbled to myself.

The girl, nearing hysteria in her anticipation, gave several demanding waves for Manolo to come closer, quicker. I gathered she wanted to come aboard, but right before the boat slid into a cluster of roots, Manolo kicked the engine into reverse, propelling us gently backward. This caused the girl's face to droop with disappointment and her waving to become more frantic. Manolo was quick to insert damage control. With his eyes sparkling, he told her in florid Spanish that she looked beautiful. She ate it up, standing motionless and smiling, her body language exuding contentment.

Manolo asked her to wait for him, that he would be back after he got rid of his cargo, which was us. She giggled a reply I could not understand, her Spanish incomprehensible as it was high-pitched and mixed with Mayan words. Her incessant giggling was too much. Manolo gave her a two-fingered wave goodbye. Cupping her hands over her mouth, her eyes sparkling, she waved goodbye with a shake of her head. The mist engulfed her body, and the birds cackled above. I wondered if she would remain that way until he came back. 'How tiring,' I thought while picking at my crusty teeth.

Gunning the outboards, we charged backward only a foot before jerking to a stop. This flipped me back into Gunther. He didn't wake up and nor did the workmen. Their ability to stay asleep, astounding. Turning my attention back to Manolo and the boat, it was obvious what had happened: the blades had snagged a root. If he were nicer, I would have jumped up to help; although I wasn't sure what I would do. Instead, I sat, unslaked and hunched, studying his face and waiting for his next move.

Sucking on his teeth, he bunched his lips together and began looking around the water and shore as though the answer was out there. The birds, small and large in the trees, were chatting up a storm, and the little girl was belly laughing. This made me laugh too. Loudly, like stuck air bursting through a funnel. Manolo snapped his eyes around and threw me a very damning glance.

"What a nasty fellow," I mumbled in English. But I found myself smiling again as the little girl had grown bolder and her laughter, louder, overshadowed the birds. It was like peals and peals of tinkling, clanging bells.

Her laughter had Manolo standing still. He gazed at her with an expression of disbelief. I thought he should be doing something other than just standing and staring at what I presumed to be his girlfriend. It was downright irritating to watch. Then suddenly, Manolo awoke from whatever was bothering him, turned the idling outboards off, and began sifting through boxes underneath the steering wheel. Finding a machete, he moved to the back of the boat, climbed over the sleeping workmen, and leaning over the transom, he began hacking at the water, grunting. The splashing was tremendous.

After a few minutes, he stopped and looked up, possibly looking for help. Not paying attention to him and frustrated by the situation because I was incredibly hungry, I mumbled, "Me cago todo lo que se menea." It was bad timing. Once again, he threw me a mean look. I gave him back the best sneer I could muster. Standing up, machete by his side, his shirt sopping wet to reveal a hairless chest and cold, distracting nipples, I could see his pants had ripped on something, and he had cut his right hand as it dripped blood. His perfectly coiffed hair was loose and blinding him, and everything was quiet, with only the sound of the little girl laughing.

"Manolo," I said, continuing in Spanish, "Can I help? Could I get you a bandage?"

It seems the little girl heard what I said because her face grew grave and she said something that sounded like, "If you had come to shore and gotten me, this never would have happened," which was silly and cute, and made me smile at her.

"Manolo," I said again, refocusing on him. "Why don't you raise the motors?"

I could tell he wasn't happy that I had said this. It was something he knew and should have done. Jumping over the workmen and back to the wheel, he raised the outboards out of the water, then went back and sliced a vine the size of an adult's arm off the blades and tossed it near the shore. Returning to the wheel, he took off his shirt, tossing it aside. This action made the little girl's eyes grow big. He then found a small towel and wrapped it around his injured hand. Taking another towel from a box, he wiped down his sweaty face and chest. Both the girl and I watched him do this, and I believe he was aware he had an audience because I saw a slight grin. He was good-looking and lovely to watch. Finished, he started up the outboards and sped off toward El Puente, leaving the little girl standing alone, a still, silent figure by the mangroves. 'Rather gruff,' I thought. 'Not even another goodbye.'

As we whizzed down the river, my hair flying free, I saw Manolo take a third towel from a box and again wipe his sweaty, wet, taut body. I looked around to see if anyone had woken up. What a scene he was making with the towels! But everyone was still asleep. It wasn't until we reached the dock at El Puente that the rest opened their eyes as though an alarm had gone off. Bam, they were all awake.

"Ick, I've been drooling," Gunther said, wiping the spittle from his cheeks. "Why's Manolo half-naked?"

"I don't know?" I replied not wanting to get into it.

"Manolo," Gunther said, getting out of the boat, "where'd your shirt go?" But Manolo was not in the mood to talk.

"What did you do?" Gunther asked me while watching Manolo drive off in a fury.

"Nothing," I replied, walking away to scout out the town.

"I know you did something," Gunther said, chasing after me.

"The guy's a bit of an ass."

"No one cares because that's not the point."

Again, not wanting to get into it because it was a long story, and I was hungry, and I wasn't sure if the story would incriminate me or not, I walked away to find some food.

El Puente had the same ghostlike appearance it had emanated the night I arrived. In the light of day, the chipped, stucco walls and overflowing garbage were more apparent. As it was morning, I hoped a store would be open, but no luck, not even a hapless vendor with a bucket of soggy tamales floating in tepid water. Pausing, I couldn't quite figure out which house had been Yena's. Not that it mattered, but I was curious about my whereabouts the night before last. Possibly I had dreamed it all because it seemed so long ago and unfathomable with the drunk man and nutty woman.

As there was nothing to the town, I went back and followed Gunther and the workmen behind a building. The car was parked half on a rutty road and half in a ditch in front of a pink cement structure. It was the place, I thought; the door looked like the same wooden door where I had been struggling whether to go in or out.

"Yena's house," I said to Gunther while walking over to the car.

"Yes, Yena's place. Strange woman. But rich. She owns houses here and lots of land in El Pueblito. Friend of Harry's. He's helping her sell most of it. I guess there have been some issues. It was her son that was killed and the government has been trying to take her land," Gunther stated. Then his tone grew suspicious and condemning. "So, what did you do?"

Ignoring Gunther's question, I said, "The Minister of Interior. It must be her land he's been fooling with," I said with a knowing smile, happy I could contribute to the gossip. Then added, "This car works? It looks like it should be in a junkyard."

Gunther was glaring at me, uptight and with his mouth balled. For a brief moment I stopped to think about his temperament, persnickety but amusing, I supposed. His garrulous chatter was easy on the ear because it was easy to filter out; he was like a well-worded butterfly dashing in between bushes. A new friend, possibly? But one that was upset with me.

"I've a mind to not talk to you anymore," he snapped.

"Manolo screwed up; that's all. He was trying to impress some girl and made a mess of it," I finally said, diverting my attention to the car. It was a blue Chevy Impala, low to the ground, and leaning to the left because it was half-way in a ditch. Parked three feet away from Yena's house and under the auspices of several windows, it looked like someone had been peeing on it from above. The hood paint was sparse and chipping and yellowy with thick glop puddled in the indents that produced a urine odor.

"Pitiful. Maybe we should take the bus," I said, sniffing the air.

"The car will work. Give it a try," Gunther remarked, then still not convinced I was innocent. "If Manolo no longer gets me rum, I will—well, I don't know what I'll do, but something."

Ignoring him, I gave the driver's side door a couple of hefty tugs. It creaked, lurched, then opened. The whine of the old hinges reverberated throughout the empty streets and beyond. A sleeping dog by a bucket of trash woke up and scratched his ears while licking his sandpaper-dry mouth. A couple of unkempt children appeared from behind a rusty steel barrel. I waved to them, and they ran away squealing only to come back and peek around the corner. They had big, brown eyes, and they clung to each other's shoulders, creating one body and three heads. We pretended not to see them, and they came over and stood by us.

"I sell you car?" the tallest kid said in broken English. He was skinny and looked to be about five years old. "Fifty bucks," he said, grinning.

I held the key up and said back in Spanish, "I already own the car, but thanks."

The two smaller kids ran away.

"Not yours," the tall boy said, standing his ground.

"Not yours either," I said back in English, adding, "*Este es del orfanato*."

He shrugged and walked away, joining the two other boys standing behind the rusty barrel and the sleepy dog.

Gunther, during my quibbling with the kids, had gotten into the car. He was sitting in the front passenger seat, drumming his fingers impatiently on the dashboard; his mouth relaxed, his eyes distant and intense. The workmen were still milling around, griping to each other about the back seat; it was full of tears and rogue springs. I was at a loss as to what to do about it, but then Aapo went over to the trash bin and pulled out a couple of cardboard pieces. They lined the seat with the cardboard and got in. Wondering why one of them wasn't the driver, I asked them if they could drive.

"No."

Then to Gunther, I mumbled, "When did that ever stop anybody around here from driving? I don't think anyone wants to drive this heap of crap. That's why no one cared that I'm new and driving into town."

"Now, now, don't be like that. I'm here, aren't I?"

"Why?"

"Why not? Okay, I want a tasty meal."

"You'd risk death for a tasty meal?"

"Wouldn't you?"

We both laughed because it was true.

The ignition was worn and chipped like someone had been starting it with a screwdriver or a knife. The key drooped loosely from it, making me think a screwdriver or a knife might work better. The shift gizmo was missing, which added to my growing anxiety about driving the car. "Now, how am I going to know what gear we're in?" I complained. The clutch was almost rock solid, stuck, and I had flip-flops on. There was also a powerful mildew smell, and I believed vermin were using the vehicle as their home. I didn't want to touch anything, but if I didn't, how would we get anywhere?

Resigning myself to fate, I turned the key and pumped the gas. After a few gallops and oil-fueled puffs of exhaust into the air, the car started up, purring and hiccupping. Putting my arm over the seat rest, I looked into the back seat; the workmen had the windows rolled down and were chewing on toothpicks. Pressing the clutch down, I played with the directionless stick until I figured out where reverse might be and hit the gas pedal hard.

The car leaped forward, almost ramming us into the cement wall in front of us. Thankfully, I hit the brake in time. Once again, I fiddled with the naked gear stick and bucked us backward into a small ravine. Then I shifted us forward over a few large rocks, knocking over the rusty bin and scaring away the dog and the kids, and drove out onto the main road. The speed was excessive for the terrain, but not because I had a heavy foot on the gas pedal. The car just seemed to have a mind of its own.

Jumping in and out of potholes at a dangerously high speed, I could see in the mirror the workmen swinging back and forth, still picking their teeth as though we were on a peaceful Sunday drive.

When we barreled up over a gnarly hill at a great speed, the bumps knocked the key onto the floor. It didn't matter; the car kept going. At one point, I ran over an empty wooden crate in the road that attached itself to the chassis. We dragged it until the car splashed through what appeared to be a gray-colored stream. The stench was overbearing, and we left the box and the stream behind us. Good riddance.

After a good half hour, the road flattened out and the pavement became more regular. We passed by swaths of banana groves and rows and rows of pineapple plants. The sweet scent was thick and syrupy; the pungent, sugary air caused the mold smell to become even more nauseating. To our right, a fenced-off golf course presented itself. It belonged to the large fruit company that operated in the region.

The golfers, dressed incongruously for the area, were not unlike our orphans; plaid and collared, short-sleeve shirts, and khakis. They glanced over at us as we drove by. We waved. They didn't wave back, most likely because we looked like the help.

El Pueblito was a typical dusty, blight-ridden town. One-story cement buildings painted half blue, with the rest white or the solid colors of beige, pink, or a dull yellow. Rebar twisted and flayed at the tops of structures as construction had been halted for whatever reason. I'd seen hundreds of these towns; it was hard to tell them apart, but each one had something unique. This town held the headquarters of a profitable fruit company. As we drove into the center of the town, the disparity of wealth gave off a disreputable flavor.

"Who works the fields here?"

"Locals. Some migrants. I think it's a dollar-a-day job," Gunther remarked. "When they're not well, some take the bus to go see Doc."

"Doc?"

"Our clinic, doctor. It's free."

We drove along looking for a restaurant. We passed a path to the lake, and I could see hints of a vast stretch of water. There were shops to get hats and brooms, and a hotel called the *La Vista*, which Gunther commented on. "I'd say a lot of hanky-panky goes on in that hotel. Plush. The only place to sleep beside the dollar-night bordello. Harry likes the *Vista*."

"He stays there?" I asked, wondering where a good restaurant might be.

"That gobsmack has the life, I tell you. He plays golf with the fruit people and eats at their headquarters. He's a nice fellow too."

I slammed my foot down hard on the brakes so as not to hit a dog sleeping in the middle of the road. The car stalled, sputtered, and died. The key still on the floor, I reinserted it and managed to get the car going enough to pull it over to the side of the road.

"Yeah, better to go on foot," Gunther commented.

"So, I gather the oil company is buying the land he's selling," I said to Gunther as we walked down the street. Not that I cared what Harry was up to, but it bothered me to think he was helping kill off the local wildlife.

"No, I don't think he is—that's why it's taking so damn long to sell it all off, or at least, he said he was trying not to. But he also said something about everything being twisted, all screwed up, especially with the death of the kid. They have to sell quickly and leave. That is, Yena, and her family." Gunther had once again fallen back into a judgmental mood, raised his right eyebrow, and said, "I don't think it was the girl that pissed Manolo off. What did you say to him?"

I gave him a teasing smile and crossed the street. The workmen were walking fast toward a place called *Maria y Joaquin's Café*, and I was following them.

"No more gossip for you then!" he shouted to my back from the sidewalk. "Keeping it all to myself now!"

I turned to look at him. His infantile behavior was comical. Joining in, I said, "Yeah, you think? You know what? I'll give you—I give you five minutes. And that's generous. We'll see if you can keep gossip to yourself."

He put two fingers up to his mouth and made the imaginary gesture of locking his lips. I laughed and continued walking to the restaurant.

Chapter 14

El Pueblito

There was a payphone right outside the restaurant. It cost a few cents for a local call, but an overseas call was difficult to calculate. I made a point to always call collect, not that it mattered. Since my mother had moved to the mental institution, my uncle Phil was staying at her house. It was a big house with large couches and my father's wonderful paintings on the walls. Uncle Phil felt someone should live in the place to protect it. The truth was, he was going through a divorce. I didn't mind him living in the house. I was glad he was there. He was the only family member I had besides my mother. He didn't even have any children, so no cousins. A couple of times I called him during my travels to give him an update and to receive one, but after our last chat a few months back, he told me not to call anymore because he had decided phones were evil, disruptive, and demanding things, just like his wife, and he wasn't picking up anymore. Uncle Phil was my mother's brother. My mother also refused to receive phone calls at the institution. The one day she had accepted my call, which was before I left, she told me she didn't have any children.

They had all died a mysterious death, and she was glad they had all gotten their comeuppance because they had ruined her figure. For some people, parenthood is a scam.

As I stared at the payphone, I could feel the heat of the day wrapping its clammy claws around my neck. A bead of sweat ran down in between my breasts. I had a great urge to call someone and tell them about my life, where I was, and what I was doing. I thought it was swell of me to be working with orphans and not just concentrating on myself, although it was still exactly what I was still doing—working on myself. But it didn't sound that way. I thought of calling a friend, but then my friends weren't keen on me calling collect, and the number of coins it took for a conversation was ridiculous. Besides, the receiver looked banged-up, as though someone had been smashing it against the metal parts of the wall, and there was gum stuck to the mouthpiece.

"Calling someone?" Gunther asked, walking up to me, his tone and mood placated by a cigarette he was puffing on. He was also munching on a cookie from a packet he had tucked into the waist of his balloon pants.

"No," I replied, amused by his gluttony.

Smacking his lips together, he opened the door to the restaurant and in a joyous tone, said, "Age before beauty." Then continued, "Right smart, this restaurant. I've eaten here a few times. The *carne asada*'s scrummy."

I walked in through the open door. I had been dreaming of something sweet, but the mere mention of pounded, thin, salty beef did seem "scrummy."

The restaurant had a cheery brightness to it. Lots of windows, white walls, and sizzling smells. A plump woman bundled up in indigenous clothing was sweeping in a far corner, and a gruff, ponderous man with a stained white bib stood staring at us by the kitchen door. We walked over to where the workmen were seated. They had already ordered Coca-Colas and were sipping on them. Gunther ordered Cokes for the both of us by merely pointing at the Coca-Colas on the table and nodding to the man with the bib.

Delighted to be sitting in a restaurant, we all smiled at each other. Gunther then began babbling to the workmen in half-English and half-Spanish about the disgusting smell of *Brillo* in the room. I didn't like it either, but it wasn't worth making a whole morning's worth of conversation about. Besides, it was good to know the place was clean even if the cleaning product was overused.

Letting go of the *Brillo* irritant, Gunther started in on the "deplorable little black flies" that were nibbling at the spilled pieces of rice on the table. Something about their presence ruining his appetite. His babbling was incessant, and I distracted myself by playing with the two plastic purple flowers placed into a Mickey Mouse vase that was on the table. Mickey Mouse had his gloved finger up to his lips as though he was telling us to be quiet. I turned Mickey's hushing finger toward Gunther. He looked at Mickey and at first seemed offended, then laughed, saying, "Jolly good, jolly good."

We ordered our food, everyone getting the *carne asada.* The waiter noticed our attempts to slap away the flies, but they wouldn't go away. He brought a fan over, directing it at the table and turning it on high, which made all the flies go away. Relaxed, we waited for our food. Gunther, finally exhausted by all his annoyances, had stopped talking. The silence allowed me to ask the workmen a few questions about themselves.

Eadrich was from an indigenous village located in the northern mountains. He had left due to the government's conscription policies to fill up the ranks of their army. Cadmael was his son, and he didn't want him to be forced to join, nor did he want to either. He called the government and their cronies criminals and wanted no part of them. Eadrich's wife was the kitchen lady, Esmeralda. Aapo was his cousin.

"Tidy little family thing they have going on," Gunther remarked.

"Isn't that normal? I mean, tidy little family things?" I said.

"Why yes, England is filled with them."

I told a story to the workmen about my time in the north of the country, about soaking in the hot springs, and how I loved the plentiful eucalyptus trees as their scent was very calming. When I was through, Gunther told me I sounded privileged because he doubted any of them had ever had the free time to soak in the hot springs. He also, while I was speaking, pointed out my grammatical mistakes at every chance he could. He explained to me that even though he didn't speak Spanish beyond a child's ability, he knew his grammar.

"I took French in school, but before coming here, I memorized a Spanish grammar book," he said, adding. "Although I never quite cracked it—the speaking part, that is, I do know what is right and what is wrong. And I'll tell you one thing: these boys here don't speak well at all." When he spoke, he was crunching a cookie, flaking bits of it everywhere. He had been trying to sneak pieces from his pants' waistline without anybody noticing.

"I understand them," I said back. "Speaking of right and wrong, you should share your cookies. Not nice to eat in front of hungry people."

"What cookies?" He asked without a smirk.

"Never mind. Anyway. Listen—about my ability to speak Spanish. At least I can form sentences. And most of them are correct. But all you do is say one Spanish word and fill in the blanks with English."

"I beg your pardon—" But before he could go on, the food arrived.

Four plates piled with rice, black beans, a long piece of

pounded steak, and a vegetable medley of tomatoes and zucchini were put down on the table. Placed in the middle, was a large basket with a cloth covering a stack of tortillas. As we all dug in with zeal the only sounds to be heard were the whirring of the fan, the scraping of plastic knives and forks on ceramic, and melodious ranchero music resonating from a small speaker by the kitchen door.

Just as we were finishing up, another group entered, two fat kids, a stout woman, and a thin, withered man with a cowboy hat on. Locals. The fan was moved to their table, allowing the flies to pour over our empty, food-splattered plates. The flies, unable to distinguish between our flesh and cooked food, flitted with warp speed around our ears and arms too. We slapped the air with no results, quickly paid, and left.

The town seemed dustier and more stripped of color than earlier. Thin dogs milling around boarded-up buildings added to the decayed, dystopian appearance. I noticed the La Vista Hotel resided next to a cement block structure; a small box of a building with metal bars for a front wall as though a cage. The locked cage-like door had a small opening to pass liquor through. Inside was a refrigerator filled with cold beers for sale. The man inside the cage was drunk and dancing to static ranchero, rap music. He was twisting around and banging into the walls like a real kook. When he saw us walking by, he stuck his tongue out and rubbed his crotch, then licked his lips. No one made eye contact for fear he might spit or call one of us out. On the scruffy sidewalk below the window, were two men asleep against the wall and a cat lapping up spilled beer. It was a miserable testament to the degradation of drinking, yet not a complete turnoff. On the list in my pocket of items to buy were several bottles of rum, and one of the bottles was for me.

As we ambled our way down the dusty street, I saw an unpaved road that led to the fenced-off headquarters of the fruit company. It was a clean building with a solid, white cement fence around it with barbed wire running along the top. Several Mercedes were parked behind a chain-link fence guarded by a well-armed attendant. Wealth and poverty living side-by-side and feeding off each other, I supposed.

Walking down a few more blocks we found the hardware store, but it wasn't open, which made us all grumble with disappointment. It had to be past nine o'clock, but no one had a watch. To bide our time, we slogged our stuffed, tired bodies over to the park to wait. The workmen peed by a tree. Lucky them. I went back to the restaurant and used their bathroom, a dingy room with a clean bowl but no toilet seat. The flies were nearly unbearable.

Back at the park, I saw there were several iron benches. The ground was nothing but erratic clumps of grass that were high and short, plus some trampled dirt. The large jacaranda trees were gorgeous and made up for the missing grass. Bristling in the light morning breeze, they sounded like paper being folded repeatedly. I claimed the bench under one of the trees. Gunther took a bench by me, whereas the workmen stretched out on the ground, placing their cowboy hats over their faces. Putting my sweatshirt under my head, I wrapped one of the sleeves around my eyes to block out the sun. It didn't take long to fall asleep. It was like falling off a cliff onto a downy pillow.

I woke up twice before getting up. The first time I awoke, my eyes opened like lead levers. It was hard to keep them from shutting again, but after a couple of shuts and opens, I was able to keep them focused and peered out from my sleeve to look around. For a brief second, I thought I was back at the orphanage, waking up on the beach again, and a dull sensation of regret swept over me. I fell back to sleep. The second time I woke up, it was because I heard people chatting. Turning my head, I saw Gunther was awake and sitting with Harry on his bench. The sun was directly behind their backs, and it painted an oddly shadowed picture of smoke swirling in contorted coils around them, their hair genuflecting and prancing like wood nymphs in the morning breeze.

They were talking about someone called The Scott. There was something about him living on a boat and that he was broke and needed money. I wanted to get up and ask if he was the fellow that had anchored his sailboat in front of the orphanage, but I couldn't raise my head and before I knew it, I had fallen back to sleep. When I did finally sit up, stretch, and regain my bearings, the sun was tilted towards the west, and the morning scorch had given way to a dimmer afternoon as though the sun would be setting soon. Gunther was on his bench, smoking a cigarette and reading a book. He was reading *Wuthering Heights*.

"Girl book," I said, teasing him while stretching my arms above my head.

"Boy book now," he replied. "Did you sleep well?"

"Yeah, I feel great." And I did. For the first time in days, I felt rested. Noticing the workmen had disappeared I inquired, "Where's everyone?"

"Visiting relatives."

"Was that Harry I saw earlier?"

"Yup, the wanker's playing hooky again."

"I need some supplies," I sputtered getting up. My neck was stiff, and my hand had fallen asleep. Shaking my limbs, I left Gunther on the bench to read and walked down the street to the hardware store. I couldn't help but wonder why Harry had given me a list of stuff to get him when he was planning to be in town. Possibly he just wanted me to earn my keep.

A few cars rumbled by on the road; their lack of catalytic converters caused the exhaust to spew thick, noxious fumes, and I quickly covered my nose and mouth with my hand. I often mused about staying and living somewhere in Mexico or Central

America, but then the lack of catalytic converters on the cars always brought me back to reality. Besides I wasn't sure how I would make a living.

The hardware store was a typical tienda. It had a few straw baskets and brooms, along with plastic items out front, coupled with a metal tire rim, oil cans for sale, and a mangled-looking Weedwacker. There was no door to the store, so I just walked in, stopped, and looked around. The man behind the counter was counting the money in the cash drawer. He had heavy tufts of thick, gray hair and a face that looked like a folded piece of thick, brown, coffee-stained paper, and a ball-size belly. The lettering on his T-shirt, stretched tight, read, 'I'm silently correcting your grammar.' 'Great, not another one,' I thought.

I went over to the man and read him the list of items that I needed.

"*Muchas cosas*," he said, giving me a burlap bag and indicating it wasn't free by showing me the price. He then pointed to the shelves lining a far wall, suggesting I would find everything there. I nonchalantly walked over, eyeing the cookies and Clorets. I nabbed a couple packets of both and two small bottles of Coca-Cola, which I promised to return for the deposit. The back shelves were dusty and scarce. I counted three boxes of laundry detergent and various canned goods, but not one of them was the same. I found the salsa and threw several bottles into the bag. There were four different local rums; I grabbed the biggest and the cheapest. A bathing cap with colorful flowers all over it had been randomly placed next to an orange sponge that looked used, I took the bathing cap. Mosquito netting, sheets, a blanket, a pillow, a rubber raft, and a few other knick-knacks like pencils and pens I tucked into my bag too. My list completed, I walked back and gave the man Harry's list, which was still inside the envelope. The man's nubby fingers had a hard time opening it. His brow sweating and his armpits, damp, had made wet circles on his shirt. He smelled of booze. The paper in his hands looked too delicate. He was better suited for counting money, I thought. Squinting his eyes, he read Harry's list.

"*No entiendo*," he said, handing me back the paper. The note only had one line written on it and a signature. It was the letter from Lenore that stated I was to be a niñera at the orphanage.

I looked in my daypack for the correct envelope, but then remembered I had given it to the woman outside the oficina before getting on the launch this morning. She must have wondered about its contents. Embarrassed, I tried to explain the mistake, but he didn't seem interested.

I paid, stuffed as many items as I could into my daypack because I didn't want to buy his bag, but had to buy it anyway. My daypack was just too small. Turning to leave I was stopped by the sight of a large, brown rat sniffing and nibbling at the black beans in a bin, by two other bins filled with corn and rice. I froze, thinking if I moved it might chase me. The man saw the rat too. He growled the word "pendejo" and threw a hammer at it. His aim was too high, and he broke the foggy, smudged window above the bin. The rat, seemingly unfazed, merely looked at the man. 'What a cheeky rat,' I thought. The man, angrier now, charged the rat with all of his hefty weight, and the rat jumped off and scurried behind the cans of paint on the floor. The flurry of activity scared me, and I took several steps backward, knocking over a bunch of buckets. My biggest fear was that the rat would come out of its hiding place and run toward me and possibly climb up my leg, which would have been horrifying.

The man brushing his greasy hair away from his face, stood motionless, staring down at the cans of paint, and so did I. After a few minutes, when the rat didn't come back, the man shrugged, and went back to counting his money.

Once again, I turned to leave, but the waft of fresh air filtering into the room from the broken windowpane caught my attention, along with the echoing sounds of someone slapping something. Bending down, I leveled my eyes with the opening and saw a woman sitting on a stool by a smoking fire. She was kneading and patting tortilla dough. She was round and looked very serious about her task. Then she glanced over at the window. She must have sensed someone was peering out. I could tell she saw me. She stopped working and cocked her head to the side and said something to someone hidden behind a tree in front of her. Shifting my position, I saw it was Harry. He was chewing on something he had in his hands, a tortilla most likely. Briefly, our eyes met, causing him to flinch and step farther behind the tree, leaving only a foot and a knee for me to see. Turning back toward the woman, her gaze directed at me, I saw it was Yena. She had the face of a hag and saint all wrapped up in one, I thought, as she most likely saved my life the other night. The wee hours of the morning are when the drunks wake up, the thieves start to roam, and the hungry packs of dogs come out to forage and hunt. "Thank you, Yena," I mumbled.

Averting my eyes, I walked out of the store and turned to go say hello, but then stopped. It was strange that Harry had stepped out of sight. Why would he hide from me? I had seen him earlier, so what was different now? Once again, I thought, what an odd fellow. Continuing my walk back to the park, I stopped again. I wanted to tell him I could not give the man the list, and this way he could go tell the man himself. But my feet knew better and took me toward the park. I mindlessly continued down the street, ignoring the catcalls from the kook in the cage. But then I stopped in mid-step again because I truly felt stupid. My mind wouldn't stop perseverating on how disappointed Harry might be with me. It was such a simple task to give someone a piece of paper, and because he gave me a place to sleep, I wanted to do something for him; I wanted to be grateful, not indifferent. Twiddling my thumbs and sniffing the air, I thought about how good I was at indifference and how bad I was at grateful. I wanted to work on being grateful. The Spanish translation, *De corazón Bueno,* meaning, *of good heart.* Then I laughed at myself and how silly I was acting. "Eh, pendejo," I grumbled and started walking back to the hardware store to Harry and Yena.

Someone tapped me on the shoulder from behind. I jumped, thinking it was the kook having escaped his cage. To my relief, it was Cadmael. His lips were pursed, his eyes concerned. He told me we needed to leave immediately because it was dangerous to drive at night. I knew what he meant. At dusk, it wasn't the banditos that caused accidents. It was the loose cows and horses. For some reason, they liked to walk out into the road once the sunset. Escaping under the cloak of darkness, I supposed. They were the number one cause of accidents in the region, next to not knowing how to drive, drunks, and bad roads.

I followed Cadmael back to the park. His steps were fast and with purpose, and it was hard to keep pace with him as my flip-flops were meant for strolling. Still torn about the letter and Harry, I finally shrugged, letting it go. Besides, wouldn't he go into the store and check with the fat man about his goods?

The drive back was the same as the drive there: horrible. When we arrived in El Puente, the sky was pitch black. Manolo and his little girl were waiting by a crooked lamp post. The light was on; it illuminated their feet, alluding to the existence of their presence but not fully disclosing them. When they walked out to say hello, Manolo's hair was tousled, and his shirt was untucked on one side. The little girl had lost her bow.

Manolo was also in a good mood. He winked at me. I winked back. All was well.

It was late, so we bought hot dogs from a man with a cart for dinner, and we each drank a beer, except for the little girl who had an orange soda. Standing around eating, Manolo kept poking and playing with the girl's hair, which made us all roll our eyes at each other. When we finally motored back, no one spoke, although we grumbled when Manolo took his time dropping the girl off.

The low gurgle of the motors' slumberous droll had Gunther and me yawning. As we slid into the dock of the orphanage, Gunther and I smiled at the sound of the ranchero song with its singer's raspy voice and the heavy base bellowing down upon us from the dormitorio. We had missed the nightly meeting and the kids were dancing. Poking Gunther, I grinned, "I've got a bed, and a room to put it in."

"Now don't go bragging," he teased, and we both laughed. It had been a good day.

Chapter 15

The Room

The hall was dark and musty like it was filled with cobwebs, although I didn't see any. At the end of the hall, a light was on in the hammock room. Slanted, oily-looking rafters and loping hammocks made me want to scratch my skin even though it didn't itch. The silhouettes of Catarina's slim build, and Alex's stooped body, were milling around and shifting through their backpacks. They were having a conversation. Alex was better with Catarina, I thought. Kinder.

"You're back," Catarina said, looking up. She hurried into the hall. Reaching into my bag, I pulled out the bathing cap and tossed it to her, along with her change. She threw me a kiss; I smiled back and waved goodnight. I wanted nothing more than to set up my new bed and luxuriate in it.

Opening the door to Harry's room, now mine, too, I flicked the light switch on by the door. The bulb was the same single twenty-watt do-nothing that made everything everywhere have a fuzzy, dingy hue to it. But I had no real complaints. The room was fantastic; big, clean, and there were two windows with screens.

Harry's side, which was to the left, looked like a setup for a king. I don't know where he found a rubber raft that big. It was two of mine put together, no three. His sheets were rumpled, but the bed was made, and his mosquito netting was tucked tight around the bed edging. At the foot of his bed, against the wall, was a small dresser with a mirror and toiletries aligned in rows. He had a comb, nail clippers, a plastic container of toothpicks, and a gray bag that I gathered had all his other stuff in it, like shampoo and a toothbrush. I noticed he wore Old Spice deodorant, which accounted for the frankincense-and-myrrh scent in the room. Mixed with the cedar rafters, the air had a lovely perfumery flavor. Harry was neat, which I liked. My housekeeping abilities were unarguably undesirable, but I was sure we could find a happy medium.

My first order of business was to give Harry back his money. I put it on his table next to his toilet kit. The next task was to inflate the raft I bought. It was blue with colorful fish all over it and came with a built-in pillow. It was going to be a tiresome job, so I took a plastic cup out of my backpack and poured rum and Coca-Cola into it. It was sweet and yummy. I gulped half of it down before attempting to blow up the raft. After a few moments, I realized that drinking while blowing was making me drunk and laughed while pouring myself a little more.

Once the raft was nice and firm, I tucked it into my corner, a dusty but otherwise clean-looking space. I put a thin, wool blanket over the raft and the sheets over the blanket. It had been Harry's idea to make the bed this way in order not to sweat at night because rubber, heat, and skin create puddling.

My new pillow along with the built-in pillow caused the incline to be too high, but great for reading. I then secured the mosquito netting. The netting was a little tricky due to the nature of the material; clingy and it tangled easily. Luckily, there were nails on the slanted roof, which I could hook it onto. When I finished, I stood back and examined my work. It wasn't as impressive as Harry's corner, but it had a delectable coziness to it.

Changing into a clean T-shirt and leggings, I took my flashlight out of my pack, turned off the overhead light, and crawled into bed to read more of my book with a newly bought pen to take notes. The raft made a squeaking sound as the rubber muddled against the floor and kept squeaking every time I moved—an annoying sound, but I gathered I'd get used to it. Delighted to have privacy and be lying completely flat, except for the lift of the pillow, I opened up my book and peeled through the pages until I found where I had left off. Taking another sip of my drink, I read, "*Tenía la cara de valles, montañas y caminos que se cruzaban sin ir a ninguna parte.*" Interpreting it, I wrote in the margins: *He had the face of valleys and mountains and pathways that crisscrossed going nowhere.* Eadrich's face was worn away with weather and patience, I reflected, and then somewhere between remembering his face and the words, I fell asleep.

It was still dark out when I awoke. The room was shadowed and streaked with the color of tarnished pewter due to the low-lying moonlight filtering into the room. Once again, at waking, I was confused about where I might be, but then felt the netting and remembered. As my eyes began to adjust to the lighting, I could see my tossed-off clothing folded upon the floor by my bag. Next to the clothing was my book and turned-off flashlight. I thought hard about whether I would have done any of those things. No. I glanced over at Harry's bed. He was there.

He slept naked and was curled up into a crescent, his back to the wall and his face turned toward me. His body was ashen, soft, and warm-looking. His dark brow resembled a child's ink drawing. His massive head of hair was dark and cupped his face. I marveled at the peace he had in sleep and found solace in just looking at him. Slinking down into my sheets, I listened to him breathe. It was light and barely audible.

Then out of the blue, I heard a clunking sound come from the hammock room. In the room next to ours, I heard bare feet walking around. Someone else came down the hall past the door. The moon having slid off somewhere, had caused the room to become dark. The wee hours of the morning, I thought. When everything shuts down, turned itself off, but not us. It was time to get up.

Throwing the netting to the side, I crawled out and over to my flashlight and turned it on, setting it against the wall, as not to bother Harry, but producing enough light so that I could see.

With little care, I changed my clothes, brushed my hair with a few strokes, and then clipped it up. Taking a sip of water from my water bottle, I swished the liquid around in my mouth, then drank the rest. Fumbling in my bag for a toothbrush and paste, I slid into my flip-flops and reached down to turn the flashlight off, but before doing so, I glanced momentarily at Harry. He was looking right at me, which caused me to pause. His sheet was pulled up around his body like a cocoon, his face immobile, and stunted like a birthing butterfly.

"You're awake?" I said. A feeling of foolishness swept over me. My underwear had two holes, one for each cheek. All my underwear had holes, and Harry knew all my clothing had holes. I had also forgotten to buy anything new, but then why should I listen to him? My clothing, my life. But damn those cement washboards and damn the harsh soaps.

"Do you have any aspirin?" His eyes were steady and unblinking.

Reaching into my toilet kit, I found a bottle of Bayer and threw it to him. He put his hand out through the netting and caught it.

"Water?"

"Gone."

He dry-swallowed the pills. I wanted to ask him when he had come in and what made him want to fold my clothes. But the phrase *de corazón bueno* ran through my head, so I said, "Thank you for folding my clothes." Followed up with, "See you later," while reaching for the door, then turned back to say, "I never delivered your list to the man yesterday."

"I know."

"The money you gave me is by your toilet kit." Then, because there was a bigger issue that had been bothering me, I asked, "Why did you hide from me?"

A noticeable silence stiffened the air between us. The question had sounded like an accusation, which was not what I wanted, but the words were already said. It made me uncomfortable, and I looked down at the floor. "I don't care. It just seemed strange," I said, latching onto my indifference and looking him in the eye.

"I wasn't hiding from you," he said, his tone low, gravelly from sleep. "I didn't want the man in the store to see me." He cleared his throat, then continued. "If you had called out my name, he would have come over, and, well, he wants something from me, and I don't want to give it to him. It's not an issue. I can get the goods in the city. I'm building a garden for the clinic."

I took what he said to be the truth. Although, I did find it strange that all of this secretive business was over a garden. What other explanation could he have? I was neither friend nor foe, so why lie? I went to shut the flashlight off in preparation to leave.

"Eleanor?" he said, stopping me.

I glanced back at him.

"I won't be here for the next couple of days. I'm going to the city. You know it's a holiday."

"What holiday?"

"Not sure, it just is one. A lot of the older kids will go home for the weekend. No school on Monday."

"What day is it," I asked.

"Friday. It will be quieter here. But the little kids go to school all the time. What else are they going to do?"

"Does your fiancé live in the city?" The question came out before I could edit it. It sounded peculiar to me, like I might be jealous. I knew it was all in my head, but at the moment, standing there in the room looking at him, there was something about Harry that was causing me to feel off-balance—like I was being drawn into a cave to be devoured. Twisting and turning in my head by the door, I chuckled at myself, shaking the feeling away. The room full of morning sleep, the scene reminded me of saying 'adieu' to a lover, not a roommate.

"Yes, I will be seeing her," He said. His answer brought our world back to where it should be, at least for me. He had a fiancé. He was just my roommate. Nothing more, nothing less.

"What her name?" I asked thinking I should know, especially since we, or maybe just Harry, would talk about her.

"Jacquelina."

"Pretty name."

"It is."

"Have a great time." And I meant it and turned to leave once again.

"Sure, it would be a shame not to."

I laughed lightly; I could still feel his gaze upon me and

looked back at him. Once again, I felt girlish and off-kilter. His presence like a whisper calling in the dark. I wanted to say something witty back, but I didn't have a thing. Then up through the floorboards came the nasal twang of the singer: "Muévelo—Bebé—Muévelo—Bebé"

"Get used to it," Harry replied over the muffled din. Reaching under his pillow, he retrieved what I gathered to be earplugs. Placing one in each ear, he rolled over to face the wall. Turning the flashlight off, I tucked it by the door and left, the words of the song translating in my head: *Move it, baby—Move it, baby—Move it fast—*

Chapter 16

Catarina and The Sailor

That morning was the first time I had been a true member of the wash team. The early hour had an opaque blackness to it as we stood on the beach fumbling with the kids' soiled clothing. The children, still confused at why they were washing in the river, whined about having to go into the water. Someone mentioned crocodiles. Another manatee. Neither comment was helpful. The weak blues and pinks peeked over the distant forest canopy, followed by a blazing ball of solid yellow. It washed the river in color. It was a sight out of a future world. I envisioned Mars and spaceships. The kids fretting, brandishing messy behinds brought the beauty into perspective; we were nannies and our duties were to the children, not our meandering minds, but then, who can stop a meandering mind? Onesies made by Gucci and Gloria Vanderbilt defiled with urine and poo, we piled by a budding aloe plant. Someone brought up midnight bathroom runs for the kids, but it went nowhere because it wasn't as though the kids woke up when they had to go.

The adults, still half-asleep, the kids dazed and naked in the cool morning air; we pushed them with irresolute kindness into the water. They pushed our hands away; we pushed back. They needed to rinse off. Once in, we couldn't get them out.

Certain children like Wooter and Raymond had large bowel movements stuck to their legs and backsides, along with my darling Bernarda. It was apparent they didn't digest the black beans well. Beans came out in the same form that they went in—whole. The beans made a mess of the shore. The river wake pushed them onto the sand, creating a suspicious black line.

Once back in the dormitorio, the children fussed over clothing because they didn't like rips or stains. Jack had been right. We needed a new infusion of donations. Their shoes mangled, but solid and mainly sandals, were in disarray, having been haphazardly tossed by the bins and under a bench; we lined them up, and they felt better as they scrambled to pick their footwear out. No one minded sharing clothing, but shoes were sacred and only had one owner. By the time the gong for breakfast resounded like a city crier selling goods, they all had shiny faces and their designer-labeled attire looked smashing, if not a little torn, but the attitudes were bad. They preferred playing, not eating. I didn't blame them; rice and beans, although nutritional, were boring. It made the time between the gong and sitting down to breakfast, long and interminably exhausting.

After breakfast, once again we marched our charges down to the river to clean their faces. When it came time to bring them back up to the dormitory to play before school, Catarina and I stayed by the river's edge. We had a bucket and a hoe. Our task, to clean up the shoreline of undigested black beans. Still early, but late enough for the sun to have baked the dampness in the air into desolate mugginess. With the heat and the morning still new, in came the mosquitoes. We sprayed ourselves with DEET, which made our old bites sting.

"Do we ever spray the kids?" I asked while scraping the

hoe along the sand, collecting the beans.

"No, it makes them sick. Doesn't matter anyway, they've been bitten so many times they've grown immune."

"I've read about that. Didn't think it worked," I said, stopping my work to watch two black beans float out into the shallows.

Catarina wasn't helping; instead, she was standing on the dock holding the binoculars up to her face, smoking a cigarette. Her strawberry-wheat hair loosely hung around her shoulders. Her white cotton blouse billowed in the fluttering breeze. Above her, on the overhanging branch of a sapodilla tree, a blue parrot preened itself and screeched. Taking the cigarette out of her mouth, Catarina said, "Tell it to go away. If it poops on me, I'll be mad."

"What do you see?" I asked, looking out at the sailboat.

"He's eating. I think it's toast. I bet he has butter. I bet the toast has gobs of butter and jam on it. Blackberry jam. No, I bet it's marmalade or peach jam; I love peaches." She took a long drag and let the smoke float out gradually. "He's making me hungry."

"For him or the food?" I asked, chuckling while walking up beside her. Even though we had just eaten, I knew what she meant. She was hungry for the taste; that was all. "Yesterday, while in town, I think I heard Harry talking about the man out there," I said, staring off at the boat. "If his name's 'The Scott,' he's broke."

"It's not money I'm looking for. I've got plenty." She giggled. She put the binoculars down on the dock and looked at me. Her expression sober, her eyes flecked with a quiet coquetry. "That is his name, The Scott," she said, smiling.

"How did you know?"

"Talked to Harry last night." She put her cigarette out with her fingers, tucking the extinguished butt into her skirt pocket. "Can't have butts lying around. Bad for kids and the environment." Then she laughed, pulled out the floral bathing cap I had gotten for her, from her other pocket, and put it on. She tucked her thick curls up into it, running her hand along her neck so as not to have missed a strand. Facing me, she asked, "How do I Look?"

"Unique. Fun. A little like my mother." The flowers were spectacular but old fashion.

"You should have stopped at unique and fun," she said, with a light laugh.

Taking off her shirt and skirt, she handed them to me. Underneath she wore a turquoise one-piece bathing suit with spaghetti straps. Her arms were thinner than I had thought. She looked older, smaller all around, and I wondered if she had the strength to swim out to the boat?

"You came prepared," I said, keeping my apprehension to myself.

"You bet I did. Now wish me luck."

"Good luck," I reluctantly said. It troubled me that I might be the last person to see her alive.

Without hesitation, she dove in. A solid, straight dive. When she came back up, her stroke was all wrong. There was too much thrashing, causing her to exert misspent energy. Looking around for anything that might float, I saw the bumpers along the docking side of the pier were lifesaver rings. Untying one, I yelled, "Hey, turn around," and threw it to her. She hadn't gone very far, and it landed next to her. Grabbing it, she used the ring as a kickboard. The going was slow. The man in the sailboat was watching too. He was standing up in the boat with one hand on his hip and the other holding a pipe. He looked tall and wore a fedora. Something about him hit a familiar chord.

Feeling a presence to my right, I glanced over to the shoreline. I don't know when he had shown up. It was Harry, standing on the beach by my abandoned hoe. He was gazing out over the river, watching Catarina along with the rest of us, solemn and with the intensity of a ship's captain. He had on a black bathing suit. A suit style that is often seen on Hollywood actors in the fifties. It was slim-fitting and rested just under his belly button, the length down a few inches on his thigh. Sean Connery in *Goldfinger* came to mind, along with William Holden in *Sunset Boulevard*, but Harry looked better than both of them. He looked good. Not too fat, not too thin, and in shape. His legs were long and sinewy, his stomach flat. He glanced over toward me and waved. I waved back, quickly averting my eyes back to Catarina. If she went under or was carried away, I wasn't sure what I would do. I was a capable swimmer, but I'd never saved anybody from drowning before.

Just as I had figured, when she reached the deep blue color, the gurgling thrust of waters snagged her slim body and dragged her north. It gave me a queasy, jumpy feeling. I unhooked another lifesaver, thinking I should go after her because the man on the boat seemed to be too busy watching and smoking his pipe. 'What a dud,' I thought.

Then I heard Harry clear his throat. Looking over at him, I saw that he was rubbing the top of his head the way someone does when they have resigned themselves to do something they hadn't planned on. He took three or four steps into the water, and without further delay, he dove in. When he reappeared, he was ten feet from his entry. He broke into a crawl, his strokes long and powerful, his kicks unabashed and straightforward, and he easily caught up to her. Catarina, surprised at Harry's sudden appearance, laughed, a high-pitched lilt that resonated across the surface like bell skidding over ice. Harry, holding on to the lifesaver ring, laughed too, a deep guffaw with a light, enchanting fullness that seemed to drag me further into his world. Then with powerful pulls with his free hand, he kicked and swam them over to the boat. Impressed by his chivalry, for a very fleeting moment, I thought about having sex with him. Then spastically, I shook my head, *no* to shake sense into it. Not only was he to be married, I remembered him saying that I was a pet—something to come home to. Company when his wife-to-be wasn't around. I didn't like the idea of becoming involved with someone who looked at me as a pet.

Having shrugged off my brief insanity, I refocused my sight and thoughts on both Catarina and Harry. Grabbing the binoculars, I twisted the lenses until I saw their smiling faces. They were having fun. The man on the boat, his hat angled down over his left eye, had finally put his pipe down and flung a ladder over the side of the boat. Catarina climbed up, and he helped her by taking hold of her rump and giving her a heave into his arms, where she remained longer than what seemed necessary. Parting, he handed her a towel. Harry followed close behind. When he was finally on board too, the men shook hands and Harry went down below as though he knew the boat well.

Feeling a great sigh of relief that they were safe, I rubbed my eyes, stretched, then went back to see what the three of them were up to. I was hoping they would be eating bread with jam. And to see some coffee being poured. Sometimes, when it's the only thing to do, living vicariously was better than not living at all.

Harry, having come back on deck with a towel, began to dry his hair, creating a big mop like mess on top of his head. He then sat back to sun himself on the deck. Catarina was chatting with the man. They weren't even eating. What a rude man, not offering food. Before putting the binoculars back down, I went back to get one last look at Harry. He was still lying back against the gunwale, talking with his eyes shut and laughing. I could hear him from where I was standing. The distance muffled his voice, but his laughter was delightful. Then they all laughed, which meant he must have said something funny. I shrugged it off again, the emphatic notion of him and me, together. But the more I gazed over at his stomach, arms, and legs, and watched how he held himself with confidence and poise, the more unruffled my self-proclaimed chastity became. Removing the binoculars from my eyes, it had become obvious to me that having Harry as a roommate would be like an alcoholic who's on the wagon, living in a liquor store. The alcoholic being me.

I put the binoculars back on their hook, the sounds of their laughter still trickling through the air. Picking up Catarina's clothing, I went back down to the beach to finish my job of dredging the shore of edible waste. Repeating in my head, one day at a time, one day at a time.

Chapter 17

Doc and Albert's Flowers

Halfway up the path, carrying my hoe and Catarina's rake, and a bucket full of crappy black beans, I saw a woman ambling her way toward me. Each step looked as though it were painful. Swaying, she stopped to take a deep breath. She was tall and full-figured, the color of darkened walnuts and pecans. Her clothing was too big for her. Gym pants ripped at the knees, a faded green shirt loose and billowing; her face sublime in the subtle fashion a person without make-up or glitter at first seems plain, then stunning. Her hair was down; it was a massive, unbrushed tangle, long, wavy, and thick. On her face she wore sunglasses, and her full lips looked nibbled and chafed.

"Yah, the new *gurl*—Eleanor," she said, sitting down. Her long legs wrapped and crisscrossed on the ground.

"Yes," I replied, not sure what to think because she was all mottled with sweat. Her energy level, cumbersome and ailing. It was like a sick but beautiful animal had just crawled out of the jungle.

"I'm Doc," she said, her voice tired and almost a whisper. Before I could respond she added, "Harry out in *dah boo't?*" Her accent was Caribbean or possibly Belizean since the country was nearby.

"Do you need help?" Her head was now resting in her hands.

"*Ya* and no. *Fook'n* malaria. Hell, the walk from *dah* clinic was too much for me."

"Malaria?" I had been out and about for so long that I didn't even think to take a malaria prophylactic. Malaria, dengue, and a few other insect-borne diseases were never on my mind. Most travelers ingested amoebas, which ravaged them with long bouts of diarrhea, but that was where it ended. Yet I had met a fellow while in San Jose that had bugs living inside him. They were crawling through his veins and making their way to his brain. No one would sit next to him in the bars. He left one day. I have no idea what happened to him.

Doc must have seen the worried expression on my face. "Don't worry," she said. "I come here *wit* it. But some mosquitoes here do carry it. A low-grade type."

I was about to say—but couldn't we contract the bad type from you? Meaning, a mosquito bites Doc, then me, and well? But I let it go because I didn't see the point. Besides, no one else seemed to have it. Looking up, I saw Esmeralda by the door near the kitchen's outside wash area. She had on a white apron smeared with the morning's meal. Her expression was flat and unemotional, but that was normal. She waved me over. I walked up to her, and she silently handed me a wet rag while giving me a shove to take it back over to Doc.

"*Tank* you," Doc said when I handed her the rag. She rubbed the cloth over her face, leaving it resting on top of her head.

"Can I get you some water?" I asked.

"*Nah*, I just need to sit for a minute."

It was almost time for school, and the kids would need assistance walking down. Over the soft, humid wind I could hear the squeals of laughter coming from the great room. Glancing towards the dormitorio door, I saw Jack and Sarah talking together, standing halfway in the open door. Sarah had the jar from last night's meeting in her hand, and it looked as though she wanted to bring it inside, but Jack wouldn't let her. I was tempted to leave Doc. Then the kids came walking out. Their temperament was nonchalant—as they chatted and walked to school. Incapable of walking in a straight line, they meandered from one fallen stick to a bush, to a tree, to a piece of grass down the path. Frankie, Raymond, and Henrik were goose-stepping; I stereotypically assumed Alex had taught them to do that. Mouse had run over to Esmeralda. She took something out of her pocket and gave it to him. A candy. He put it in his mouth and ran down to the schoolhouse, skirting the older kids' dorm, around the back of the cafeteria, and through a clump of gnarly bushes.

Doc grunted, and I looked at her. She was getting back up. I went to help, but she waved me away. "I'm fine," she said, and wobbled toward the path that had the sign for the clinic. Her legs twisted in, her head giving way to a slight wag. She turned back and shouted, "Eleanor!"

"Yeah!" I said, not having moved.

"Tell Harry I won't be *goin'* to town. Tell'm don't forget the medical supplies."

"What if I don't see him?" I didn't want to commit to something I might not be able to do. Lesson learned from yesterday.

"Oh, well." She went back to walking.

Cadmael, who was working with Aapo and Eadrich by the water tanks, snapped his head up at the sound of Doc's voice. Throwing his wrench down, he raced over to her. She was taller than he was, but not by much. When he grabbed hold of her waist, he leaned down and planted his face against her breasts. Doc in return leaned into him like a crutch and played with his hair, twisting small clumps in her fingers the way lovers might do while strolling in a park. Knowing that Cadmael was Esmeralda's son, I glanced over at Esmeralda to see her reaction. She was smiling, something I didn't expect, the emotion became her. It lit up her face.

I then glanced over at Eadrich and Aapo as they were family members, too. I wondered if their expressions would be as delighted as Esmeralda's. Fixated on their work, hammering away on the piping, they were too busy to notice.

Fluffing my shirt to let some air in, I turned to go down to the school. Having not seen Albert at my heels, I almost fell into him. He had enchanting mauve and vermillion flowers in his hands.

"*Flor*," he said to me while smelling them. "*Huele hermoso.*"

"*Sí, huele hermoso*," I repeated, crouching down to smell them. I saw his eyes were glistening and his cheeks were rosy and full of levity. It was touching that he had such fine taste for nature's delicacies, and at such a young age.

The scent of the flowers was hypnotic; I kept going back for more. They contrasted with the ill jungle odors that were so prevalent. Offensive malodors that frequently caught me off guard only to haunt me for hours, leave, and come back again. Decay, not just of wood and leaves, but of animals and waste and mildew. The shadows along the muddy pathways, the grounds around the cement washing area, under the schoolhouse, by the outside walls of the dormitorio, at the foot of a tree. Harsh odors that were constant reminders that what lives dies, and when it dies, it smells.

I asked Albert where he had found the beautiful flowers. Instead of telling me where, he looked away, sighed, and kicked the dirt with his sandaled feet. He became enthralled by the little clouds of dirt he was creating with each kick, but then stopped to pick up a pebble. I didn't think he was really interested in the dirt or the pebble. He was stalling for time. I saw the kids were already walking into the schoolhouse and suggested he go to school, but he pretended not to hear me. So, I asked him again about the purple and vermillion beauties because it would be nice to make a bouquet out of them and put them in my room. It would be pretty. I would set them down by my bed and smell them at my leisure. But Albert just shrugged and turned his back to me. This made me think he wanted the flowers to be his and only his. I didn't blame him; they were precious like finding a ruby or sapphire in the middle of a rock pile.

"They're your flowers," I said. I figured I could find my own, the place being small. "Now you need to go to school."

He turned toward me smiling, his cheeks rosy and dimpled. He wanted me to smell the flowers again, which I gladly did. The floral aroma made me think of perfume and how nice it would be to have some. Nothing cheap, but something expensive that mimicked nature.

I also sensed Albert didn't want to go to school.

I suggested we go down to the school together and look at flowers another day. This confused him because we had never decided to look for flowers together. Scrunching up his nose and upper lip, he mumbled something about his flowers not liking school and wanted me to hold them for him. "Thank you," I said. But just when he was about to give them to me, he recanted, pulling them away.

"Albert," I said, thinking what a wily child, "Let's you and I walk to school."

As I was looking down, a pair of large, wet, sandy feet appeared by Albert's. "Hello, Harry," I said looking up. "Did you have a pleasant swim?"

"Biggest tub we have." The saying was becoming old, but I laughed anyway. Harry's hair was slicked back, his body bathed in river water, glistening in the sunshine. He had his sandals, and a shirt bunched up in his right hand and seemed in a very chipper mood. I found myself staring at his handsome face far too long. He had morning stubble on his jaw and chin. He held his head at a slight tilt to the left in a relaxed manner. On his left cheek, he had a small mole—a beauty mark, I assumed. Since we were standing in silence, my gaze fixated upon him, he turned from looking off into the jungle toward me. For about five seconds, we had a staring contest, even though it wasn't meant to be one. I smiled and averted my eyes toward Albert and his flowers, and the dilemma of school. But all I could think of was what Gunther had said about Manolo, "Don't think he doesn't realize you think he's cute." It made me feel foolish because I didn't want Harry to think I thought he was cute. I also wondered why he was still standing in front of me, looking at me. Glancing at him again, he had a puzzled expression on his face. Needing something to say, I said, "Albert doesn't want to go to school."

"He never does," Harry answered, then placed his hand on Albert's shoulder. Turning Albert toward him, he ruffled his hair, while in a gentle tone telling Albert to go to school, and he did. Just like that.

"Seems you have a magic touch," I said, which made me smile because I took what I said to be a double entendre.

Harry not noticing my silliness, had a paternal expression on his face as he watched Albert reluctantly, but dutifully with his flowers held in front of him and smelling them frequently, walk down the embankment. Satisfied, Albert would make it to the school, he glanced over at me, and said, "What do you think? A poet in the making?" He then paused to make sure, once again, that Albert was going into the school, which he was. "Watch him, he likes to play hooky," Harry Spoke, adding. "Wanders off into the woods, the mangroves. I've caught him roaming over by the pigpen the other day." Sighing, he smoothed his hair back with his free hand, and continued, "Cat will be back before lunch. The Scott will motor her over."

"Ah—they're getting along." And then, as though an afterthought, "I don't suppose those red and purple flowers grow up by the pigpen?"

"Never seen them there. Don't know where those grow."

"Doc. I met Doc," I blurted out.

"You did," he said, his brow knitting together while his eyes took on a curious twinkle.

"Her malaria is back. She won't be going into town with you—but don't forget the medical supplies."

The message seemed to have caught him off guard, and the twinkle in his eyes disappeared. Standing, dripping little streams of water, and looking disheveled, he kept his gaze upon me, as if trying to figure out what I had just said. I also had the feeling he wanted to say something, but then thought it best not to. Putting his hand up to his mouth, he rubbed his lower lip and let his eyes roam from the dormitorio to the clinic path. Suddenly, with swift movements, he placed his leather sandals on his messy feet and his shirt on his wet body. Then, with brisk, determined strides, he dashed off towards the path.

I watched him disappear, branches flipping up as he barreled his way into the jungle. Another act of chivalry, I thought. Off to save Doc, too. Shrugging, I turned back around and picked up my bucket and hoe. I tossed the black beans in the woods, looking around to see if there were any red and purple flowers, but only yellow ones. I put the hoe against the building and walked down to the river to fill the bucket back up with water. The rest of the group was down there wetting their toes. We all walked back up together discussing our children. Telling stories about Frankie splashing water on Penelope, and Penelope splashing back only more furious and so on, and so forth. And how we all would like to go swimming because the sun's heat was already oppressive, but it was chore time. We went into the dormitorio and began picking up the great room. Scattered on the floor were throw pillows, books, clothing, and cardboard for building forts. It was all very peaceful, as there were a lot of hands, and we were all content to have something to do.

Chapter 18

Peeing Outside

As the afternoon waned, the lack of running water became more of an issue. We were eating a high-fiber diet. I wasn't sure, but it tasted like the tortillas may have even had sand in them. The green drink alone could cause a sudden, giant bowel movement. As a result, we were spending most of our time lugging heavy, leaky buckets of water from the river to the bathroom. The beating tropical sun made excessive lifting torturous. The task, sloppy. We all complained, and I suspected that anybody who went swimming urinated in the river.

Understandably, the older kids were seen periodically peeing in the woods, the girls squatting and the boys splattering the low-lying leaves. This caused Jack to bristle. "What if our little ones see them?"

'So what?' I thought. It hadn't even occurred to me to let the kids pee outside, but now that a few were, it seemed a perfect solution to such a tedious situation. Besides, going to the bathroom outside would only be temporary—until the workmen fixed the pipe. But then, what did I know about bad habits and good habits? About how easy it was to break a good habit, exchanging it for a bad habit, and never being able to retrieve the good one again. So, when I said, "Come on Jack, why not?" I was truly in the dark about the 'why we shouldn't.'

Gunther, too, thought it was a splendid idea to let the kids pee outside. But Gunther, who I was getting to know, did not believe in common sense at all, as he had argued the day before, and reminded me, while we stood outside by the washbasin, that, "It's *luck* that is the balls." So, when he let Wooter and Albert urinate into a puddle of muddy water by the basin, and I scolded him for doing so because it wasn't sanitary—he matter-of-factly snapped back, "Bloody hell, do you not listen? Luck will prevent you from coming down with a disease. Besides, this stuff is ammonia. You're better off walking through the peed in puddles than the non-peed in." Then he suggested that during my next trip to El Pueblito, because I had become the orphanage's driver, which I didn't mind because it allowed me a tasty meal once a week, that I should look into some pharmaceuticals to "foster a more positive outlook on life."

"Whatever," I remarked, not wanting to argue because his remark was stupid.

But as luck would have it, Jack, who had been leaning against a corner of the dormitorio with his chin in his hands, a pose he often took whether thinking or not, had heard Gunther tell Wooter and Albert to pee in the puddle. Jack wasn't quick enough. Before he could storm over, the boys were finished. Catching his wide-eyed look and gaping mouth, I smiled. This should be interesting.

"Christ! Hell! Shit!" Jack snapped. His sandals slapping through the wet ground.

Prompting me to mumble, "¡Me cago en todo lo que se menea!"

"What?" Jack fumed.

"Nothing," I replied, stepping aside. Since it wasn't my idea to let the boys pee there, I wanted out of the line of fire.

Jack's hyper, angry presence caused Albert and Wooter to start peeing again. Nervous reaction, I thought, but then they were smiling, almost challenging each other to pee the most. I wondered how they were able to do that? Pee on-demand, and with gusto. Gunther told them to stop and tidy up, but they ignored him. Jack's face became pointier. His fists clenched, his knuckles white, his teeth bared. I had the feeling he didn't want to shout, but holding it back seemed agonizing to him. During breakfast, Jack had been discussing a chapter in his dissertation on the importance of "parenting calmly." Which was also the name he gave the chapter. It would have been a shame for him not to follow his own lesson.

"Bloody hell, Jack," Gunther scoffed. "You'd think the sky was falling in."

"Don't say bloody hell in front of the kids."

"You just did," Gunther said, his voice slightly louder than normal. "Look here, Jack, it's only natural to pee outside. Porcelain toilets are a modern-day phenomenon. Something to be proud of, but not necessary."

"Are you kidding me?" Jack said, circling in front of Gunther, looking like a tailless dog. "The kids now know the freedom of outdoor peeing! They'll never stop!" Then Jack crossed his arms, and asked, "Have you ever read Hobbes?"

"Now don't go judging my education," Gunther said, arms down by his side, his shoulders relaxed, taking the chafing in stride. "And, yes, I know Hobbes."

"He was British."

"So are a lot of people," Gunther said with a tone of annoyance.

"Hobbes was brilliant: 'Life without rules'—people become 'nasty and brutish.' Is that what you want for these kids?"

"A bit excessive, Jack," Gunther said, laughing.

While they talked, the boys, who had run out of pee, were now searching for rocks and sticks. Finding a bunch, they tossed them into the soiled puddle. Each time a rock or stick plopped into the water; they gave little jumps of glee. I suppose, if I weren't so amused by the scene, I would have taken them away from the area and down to the river to make sandcastles or look for flowers.

When the sound of peeing into the puddle rose again, we all turned and saw that Mouse had joined in the fun. This caused Albert and Wooter to throw down their sticks and rocks and begin to try to pee again. Both Jack and Gunther snapped at the boys.

"What happened to 'parenting calmly?'" I asked with a straight face.

"What?" Jack barked at me, adding. "Not now."

I wanted to say—then when? But let it go.

Gunther and Jack with controlled tempers demanded the children put their penises back into their shorts. Gunther, seeming anxious now that Jack's Hobbesian thoughts could be right, told the three boys, "There will be no more peeing outdoors. We have rules to follow."

Wooter, Albert, and Mouse pretended not to hear by continuing with their fake peeing stance.

"How's luck working out for you now?" I mumbled to Gunther, then added. "I think this is where common sense is needed." He responded by ignoring me, or should I say, pretending not to hear me.

Gunther once again told the boys to zip up. This time they dismissed his words by chatting with each other. "To think they're only three," I said.

"Could be four; we're not sure," Gunther remarked.

"They're already experts at getting under one's skin," I said, watching them.

Then Jack and Gunther went into a full-frontal assault of nagging the boys into putting their penises away. They also wanted them to go down to the river and play. I gather, unable to take the demanding barrage of 'don'ts' and 'no's,' they finally complied by zipping up and heading off to the beach, but not before throwing a few sticks into the muck.

Mouse, perpetually excited, ran around in circles like a maniac picking up everything in sight. When he chunked a thick, short log into the mix, the backsplash hit both Jack and Gunther's shins and feet.

"Yuck!" Jack wailed, which made Gunther laugh. Jack flummoxed and incensed stared at his shins with I imagined steam coming out of his ears. Then he stormed away, slapping his sandals in swishing motions through the spongy ground. Gunther and I silently watched Jack head to the river. He was taking exaggerated strides, which made his short body with its long legs, stretched to capacity, resemble a cartoon character.

"Seems you've caused a mess," I said, adding. "I think Jack is right. The boys aren't going to stop."

"Now, negativity never helps anyone. Positivity," he remarked and headed off to the beach too.

I left too. I had a bucket of water in my arms and it had grown heavier. Dumping some onto the ground, I emptied out, too much. Now the joke was on me, I thought and chided myself for laughing at Jack and Gunther. But then Jack and Gunther were funny, so I decided I could laugh at them all I wanted, and they could laugh at me, and I wouldn't become mad at all because why should I?

Chapter 19

Peeing Faux Pas

By late afternoon, the outdoor peeing situation had taken a more obsessive turn. We, the niñeros, began to realize that the boys—Wooter, Albert, and Mouse—had had no intention of forsaking the mud puddle for indoor toilets. It didn't matter what they might be doing, swimming in the river, building a sandcastle, or just sitting around. Without so much as a sound, they would just walk off together as though they had created some secret society. All it required only a look or a head nod to mean it was time to go behind the dormitorio and pee.

We took turns following them, to keep them away from their target, but sometimes we didn't catch their disappearing acts. Once at the puddle, a place they never went alone, they would pull out their penises and either pee or pretend to pee or throw rocks and sticks at the muck. Catarina, who had come back beaming from her visit with The Scott, couldn't stop saying the word 'delicious' to describe him. She also felt it was fine that the boys peed outside, but suggested, "We should steer them towards the woods."

Molly and Golly, seeing Mouse finally having some friends, both commented, "Fu'ck a duck, why it's not so bad if they pee'n outside in the muck." Mouse being an erratic, impulsive child often annoyed the other kids. His jerky movements caused him to ruin sandcastles instead of building them. He twisted cardboard instead of molding it. When he threw rocks, he often hit people in the knees and sometimes their faces. Peeing outdoors was a sport anyone could do. The messier it was, the more fun they seemed to have. It was the perfect activity for Mouse, and he was finally accepted by a few of his peers.

It didn't take long before Albert, Wooter, and Mouse had gathered up more of the boys, such as Earl, Otto, Frankie, and even El Gordo, to pee with them. Quiet and secretive about it all, they were constantly whispering to each other. They had also grown bored with the puddle by the washbasin and were now peeing everywhere and on anything. There also seemed to be an understanding that the girls weren't capable of standing and peeing. This caused the boys to become arrogant and haughty when they walked by them. They boasted to the girls about being able to move objects. They showed off their new powers by making stones and twigs roll fast and sometimes slowly, depending on how much they had to pee.

Bernarda, Charlotte, and Penelope had become puzzled by this urinating turn of events and their inability to join in the fun with the boys. Their faces twisted and their lower lips pushed out, they stared and frowned at the boys until they came up with a solution. They found plump little sticks and stuffed them into their underwear. Penelope, who had on leggings, looked like some miniature, skinny, pervert; the stick was obvious and ran from her crotch to her belly button. When the girls wanted to urinate like the boys, they pulled out their sticks and went, "Yeeee," and "Weeee," while pretending to pee. No one knew where they got those sounds from. We tried to tell them it was all right not to have a penis, but our psychology was lacking, and our words only made their pouts more exaggerated.

Later in the day, I saw the girls pretending to pee on a thorn bush. While they stood with sticks in their hands, they were watching, with contorted faces, Henrik, Raymond, and Mouse peeing on a log in the quad. The boys were trying to knock a caterpillar off it. When I went over to tell them to leave the poor thing alone, they turned and peed on my foot. This made them laugh. Yes, they had become 'brutish and nasty.'

And Jack? Jack, who had been angry to the point of near-spontaneous combustion, was now thrilled, walking around whistling the "Doodle Dandy" tune. It was irritating. He was knee-slapping happy because he had been right. He also declared he would dedicate a chapter of his dissertation to what it means when your child will only urinate outdoors. He would call it "The Peeing Faux Pas."

A notebook in his hand, his nose pointing up toward the trees exposing large, ovular nostrils, he continued, "I want to share a few thoughts with all of you." And began to read. "Once a child discovers the freedom of peeing outside, it becomes one of the first steps of rebellion toward adult control. It manifests itself as a pulling away from their primary authority figures (the parents or people who act like their parents). Since birth, they have needed the help of adults to be cleaned after the expulsion of waste. It starts with the diaper. Then the hand up to the toilet. Once they accomplish going to the bathroom themselves, they are free from having to ask permission for the rudimentary and frequent task of urination and defecation. It instills a sense of freedom and independence." He then scratched the top of his head and added, "The theory's good. Possibly needs some rewriting."

"Well, I hope you are putting me in your acknowledgments," Gunther quipped at Jack.

"Possibly," Jack replied.

"Sounds doubtful," I said while wondering if my three girls, Charlotte, Bernarda, and Penelope, would recover from this day.

"Wanker," Gunther had sniped at Jack, walking over to a hairy cedar to pee.

"So, you're advocating for them to pee outside now," Catarina said.

"No! Not at all. Turn the place into a sewer. If it isn't already," Jack replied with his fists balled. He seemed to be the type of fellow whose temper waxed and waned like waves on a choppy ocean.

"All the more reason to build the little boxes so they can step on them to sit on the toilet. All by themselves. Independence. I like independence," Catarina stated, smiling.

"We did talk about that, didn't we?" Jack said, once again calm.

"And it was my idea, those boxes. You wouldn't have the peeing faux pas crap either if it weren't for me. Gosh, I'm just full of ideas, but does anyone give me acknowledgment?" Gunther said coming back from the tree still griping. "You just can't steal people's ideas."

"No," Jack said.

"No, yes? Or no, no."

"No."

"No, what?"

"NO."

"Christ—never mind," Gunther said, sitting down to pout.

"A bunch of wildpinklers," Alex said, nodding his head

toward Raymond and Henrik, who were peeing on each other's feet by the schoolhouse. Henrik's urine was splattering all over Raymond's yellow rubber boots, and Raymond's urine was drenching Henrik's, Doc Martens. The boys were in hysterics; their bodies were jiggling with laughter.

"Wildpinklers," Jack repeated, writing it down.

"Do you even know what the word means?" Alex asked.

"Sounds good," Jack replied.

"Dudelsack that dissertation," Alex said, then continued, "I'm with Gunther. Acknowledgments are nice."

But Jack wasn't listening. He was too busy writing and pausing to think. Alex had Mouse and Frankie sitting next to him on the ground. They had been going nonstop all day and were now trying to keep their eyes open.

Jack, looking up from his notebook, said, "We have wood and hammers and saws, but we need nails."

"Shouldn't the workmen have nails?" I said, thinking I may have seen one hammering a board.

"They use a lot of glue," Catarina remarked.

"On what?" Jack asked.

"I just see them using glue," she said back.

"There's a box of rusty nails on the shelf in the great room," Gunther said, finalizing the conversation. He then walked away from us toward Henrik and Raymond. He told the boys to wash their feet off in the water. The boys listened and followed the request without being stubborn. "They must be tired," I said.

It was almost time for dinner, so we counted all the kids in front of us because we didn't want to leave one behind. As it turned out, one was missing. It was Albert. We all agreed he wasn't going to the bathroom because he didn't do that alone. No one panicked. Everyone knew Albert was a wanderer.

Catarina was about to leave to go check the pigpen when out from behind the schoolhouse sauntered Albert with a bunch of white flowers with red pistils. He came over and sat down on a rock, showing us what he had while rambling on and on about how nice they looked and smelled. They weren't half as nice smelling as the purple and red flowers. Which got me, once again, looking around the compound, wondering where he may have picked them from. I even asked the group if they had seen any red and purple flowers, but the only ones they had seen were the flowers Albert had given to Esmeralda at lunch. Catarina brushed Albert's hair back and told him his flowers were wonderful. Catarina was the only one amongst us who had children. Two boys and a girl, now healthy adults with good jobs and "tolerable relationships." Her husband had died three years ago. I trusted her judgment on how to deal with the kids and saw others asking her for advice too. Even if Jack would have liked us to think otherwise.

With the sun rapidly setting in front of us, we got off the ground we were sitting on and called the kids over. We needed to get them out of their bathing suits and put them into dry clothes. But then the dinner gong reverberated down the slope and throughout the cooling evening air, and we all realized we had messed up on the timing. It pained Jack to think we had miscalculated dinner. He then smiled and said, "there must be a reason for our misstep."

Chuckling, I asked, "And what will you call this chapter?"

With a furrowed brow, he rubbed his chin, and replied, "Lack of Attention to Detail Causes Ineptness."

"Or Ineptness Causes Lack of Detail," I remarked back.

"I hope you're not thinking of writing anything serious. You're not very good at it," he said with a straight face, then turned abruptly and walked away.

Under my breath, I mumbled, "Inept Jerk causes Orphans to Miss Dinner."

Gunther, who was standing next to me, said, "Wanker Starves Toddlers."

"Pendejo Ruins Evening—" I added.

We laughed. Then continued laughing as we created new chapter titles, all the way to the dormitorio.

Chapter 20

Toys

A few days later, we built the boxes for the bathroom toilets. They were a minor success with the kids. With one step up, they could either sit on the toilet or stand. The dilemma? When sitting without help, they often fell in. And without our help, they couldn't get out. To remedy this issue, we began giving toilet sitting lessons. The children seemed to enjoy these lessons so much that they began holding their own classes. It wasn't unusual to walk into the bathroom and see three or four of them taking turns, practicing sitting on the toilet with their clothes on. Proud of ourselves and the kids for putting their best efforts into the task, we praised ourselves and the children at nightly meetings. But even though the boxes were a step in the right direction, the enjoyment of peeing outside seemed impossible to curb. Yet we felt, given time, the boxes and the toilets could win out—or just mere wishful thinking.

Harry still in the city, I had the room to myself. I liked the space, and without Harry to garble my libido, I felt freer. Since the kids usually went to bed around ten o'clock, I would have a nightcap with Catarina and Gunther. We would hang out in the great room and then head down to the dock for a smoke. It was at the dock where Catarina would leave us. With a flashlight from her pocket, she would signal The Scott to come get her. Once back in my room and in bed, I would read until one or two in the morning. Since Harry was away, I left the overhead light on. I didn't bother to fold my clothes or pick up the mess of cookie wrappers and beverages by my bed. On the third day, I picked up because I thought he was coming back. But he didn't, and I thought, what a waste of effort since it took a lot of effort for me to be neat.

During our nightly meeting on the third day, Molly and Golly wanted to know when the party would take place at Club de Bote. No one knew, but Alex grumbled something about the *sitzpinklers* would probably have it during the full moon because they were the type of people that liked full moons for parties. No one was sure what he meant by that. When I piped in suggesting that a lot of people liked full moons for parties because it made them more fun, my comment received several, "rights" and "yes, yes'."

"But what is a Rabbit Moon?" I asked.

"Mayan," Jack replied. He then scratched his head and looked at Sarah. "Probably has something to do with fertility."

"I like *'abbits*," Golly said.

"I *don'*," Molly said.

Changing the subject, Catarina brought up the toys "just rotting away" in the attic room.

"Legos and Barbies," I added.

"Let's bring them down tomorrow," Jack suggested, then looking at his notepad he asked, "What do you all think of the chapter title "Plastic vs. Organic Toys?"

Catarina wanted to know if she would get an acknowledgment in his paper because she suggested we get the toys. Not this again, I thought.

"You didn't suggest it, I brought the toys up the other day," Jack corrected her. Which was true. Not that it mattered, because Jack and the rest of us had forgotten about the toys.

"Maybe she should get an acknowledgment for reminding you," Gunther said. This caused everyone to snicker.

"Milla is coming tomorrow," Alex said, changing the subject again. "It's too bad we have selfish people in this group." When he said this, he was looking at me, then continued, "I will be in El Puente tomorrow morning greeting her. Do what you want with the toys. I'm all for the organic play, not plastic fake shit. Anybody have a tent?"

"Use the attic," Gunther said.

There was a moment of silence followed by giggles.

The next morning, when the kids were in school, Gunther and I lugged the boxes down from the attic. It was a smelly job that made my arms itch, and we both spat a lot. Once all the toys were outside, Golly, Molly, Gunther, and I stood by them examining the goods. There was a positive suppleness to the air, not a cloud in the sky, the blues palpable and the leaves shimmering like glinting fans. Although the offensive gases emitting from the boxes made us cringe, we were, as Gunther put it, "Chuffed to bits over the act of giving."

"What joy they'll *aav*," Molly said, admiring the baking oven.

"I wish I had a *cam'ra* to take their pictures," Golly mewled while snuffling the hair of a blonde Barbie. "She smells like the backside of a dog." She tossed it back in, wiping her hands on her oversized T-shirt.

There was also a sewage scent in the air. At first, we thought it was due to the boys peeing outside, but then Cadmael, who walked by us and stopped to admire the toys, corrected our theory. He told us, in part Spanish and English, and using a few Mayan words, that the pipe carrying water from the river had cracked and upset the septic. In the same breath, he said, "But the water tanks are fixed and now we have running water in the bathrooms."

"But not if the river water isn't coming in," Gunther said.

Cadmael had a shovel in his hand. We watched him walk into the back of the dormitorio where Eadrich and Aap were digging a hole behind the washbasin.

"I always thought they piped all the waste into the river," I remarked while wondering if we should deal with the toys another day. We wanted to wash them off, but the washbasin seemed off-limits now.

"They do upriver. You know, use the river as their toilet," Gunther yawned, forgetting to cover his mouth; all his back molars had fillings.

The four of us stood in silence for a few minutes. It was something we did before embarking on a new subject or project or thinking of more ideas about the old ones. Someone sighed, and another made a strange yo-yo sound with their mouth. It was Golly. It was her warning signal that she had something brewing inside her that wanted to come out, but she wasn't sure how to voice it. We all stared at her, waiting for her to stop making yo-yo sounds. When she did, she made a declaration that the kids wouldn't care about the toys. This speculation opened up a whole new point of view about "the plastic bits," which was how Golly now referred to the toys.

"It's because of what Jack said," Golly said, fumbling with

her lower lip with her tongue. She had a bug bite there, and it was bothering her.

"What did Jack say?" I asked, standing as still as possible so as not to sweat excessively.

"What doesn't he say," Molly jumped in.

"What did Jack say?" I asked again for no particular reason.

"I can't remember," Golly pouted.

"Well, I don't care what Jack said," Gunther remarked, his voice testy as he tossed as many toys as he could into a wheelbarrow he'd borrowed from the workmen. He was still miffed at Jack for not giving him 'acknowledgment' for his ideas. Bristling with irritation, he barked, "Come on, we need to wash the toys." He had long, squiggly dribbles of water running down his face as the day was exceptionally hot.

"Testy today," Molly said with perfect diction, causing us all to look at her.

"No, well, yes. I want to give the kids the toys," Gunther said. His tone, sincere.

"Fine," we all said.

Tossing more toys into the wheelbarrow until it was full, we strolled over the squishy ground to the washbasin. The smell of feces became stronger, which made us look at each other and frown. I had a small kids' wheelbarrow which I had put the Barbies and G.I. Joes in and began putting the plastic dolls into the sink. Molly and Golly each had a box full of Legos that made them cough and hack.

The workmen had already dug a hole as deep as they were tall; all of them were inside of it. We listened to them chat in their native tongue, trying to understand what they were saying. Gunther thought they were talking about us. I felt they were talking about back home in the mountains because I kept hearing a word that sounded similar to 'mountain.' Molly and Golly said they were gossiping about girls' tits. Then we forgot about the men and watched the older kids walking up from the dock to their dorm. They were carrying knapsacks and pillowcases full of clothes as they had used them as suitcases for their trip home. As usual, they were joking and poking each other. "Back to boarding school from being home for the holiday weekend," Gunther mumbled.

"I don't like them," Golly said.

A bird above the cafeteria screeched, and we stared at it waiting for it to make another noise.

We then discussed our made-up history of the youngsters. One day they would be the older kids, which seemed hard to fathom. "*Bu' wha' were 'hey lives befaw comin' o'he awphanage*?" Molly rhetorically said. Gunther and I stood perplexed, trying to figure out what she had just said. Even Golly looked stumped. When no one said anything back, Molly repeated it with better diction, "What were their lives like before coming to the orphanage?"

We determined that our children's first few months of life were most likely riddled with very dubious relationships or catastrophic endings like Charlotte's. After all, they were orphans. Their present life, we agreed, was solid and predictable. They walked the radius of what resembled a lumpy, non-regulated soccer field day after day, eating the same food morning, noon, and night, the weather hot and wet, humid-hot and not-so-wet, hottest and hotter, and constantly wet and humid. Nothing changed more than a nano-inch except for us. We were the only things that changed. We figured it was the reason the children's eyes appeared distant at times, which we diagnosed as tragic.

"But then whose life isn't tragic?" Golly lamented while pulling her oversized shorts out of her butt-crack.

"Queen of England's life isn't tragic," Molly said with a

look of triumph.

"Possibly if we talked to her, she would say it is—all those teas and the bloody hand wavings," Gunther replied while studying a toy cash machine, then added, "My life wasn't and isn't tragic at all. My parents are divorced, but they're happier. My mother has remarried three times. Drippy men with small wankers. My mother's swell, though, and I love her, especially her kidney pie. My father, his name's Pete. Pete's a fantastic fellow."

"Me mums makes meat pies that taste like paste; me dad's a truck driver. '*Hey r'* all right," Molly said.

"I don't much like them," Golly said.

"I thought you said you weren't related," I remarked.

"Any idiot would know we are. Of course, we *aav* the same parents; we *wins*," Golly said, making the yo-yo sounds again. "But not identical. I'm prettier."

"Eleanor?" Gunther asked, then added. "What about your folks?"

"They're fine. Normal," I said.

"I don't think that's possible," Gunther remarked with a sigh.

"You're right, but why talk about it," I said.

"*Cuz* it's good to talk about things," Molly said, nudging me.

"These *oiys* are making me sad," Golly said, picking up a truck and deciding to wash it.

Sarah and Jack, spotting us from the quad area, came over. Sarah was upset that all the toys looked like humans or were replicas of human inventions. She wanted a bug doll. Jack was bowed and circumspect. He had a few titles that he threw out at us: "Is Plastic Necessary?" and "Modernization and the Imagination: What to Make of It?"

He said the gist of his "toy chapter" for his dissertation would be filled with defamatory examples of bad biological parenting and how playing with fake stuff makes one greedy. More pertinent to this section of his dissertation would be a look at "how the modern world is destroying free will with cheap thrills," a substructure to his substructures.

Jack also appeared more jubilant than anyone so far about the toys. I assumed his constant jumping up and down and frantic touching of each object were because of his dedication to his work; the information he would glean from the subject of children and toys. Molly and Golly were convinced he wanted to play with the stuff and that was the reason behind his recent, constant smiling. They had seen him tuck a navy-blue Matchbox car, a Charlie Mack 1960 Corvette, into his pocket while sifting through the boxes. When Sarah and Jack walked away, Molly immediately said, "What kind of parents did he *aav*?"

"Unfit," Gunther answered, "if they are anything like him."

"I can't believe he pinched a toy," Golly piped in, hands on her big hips.

Alex and Milla came over and rummaged through the pile of toys. Alex was in a good mood due to Milla's early morning arrival. I was elated to see Milla, too, and she, me, until Alex kept whispering in her ear not very nice stuff about me. His whispers being loud, I could hear everything he was saying. He said I was a hoggish slut with tendencies to laugh at inappropriate times. I took offense because I wasn't hoggish, but then possibly he had meant selfish, and yes, I could be selfish. Slut? Not for a year, and laughter was healthy. It was one of Jack's four tenets for raising children in what he called his "Third Book" even though he did not have a first or second book. He just liked the sound of 'third book.'

The other three tenets were:

- Agree to disagree. (A difficult concept with three- and four-year-old children.)

- Avoid harsh discipline. (We did this by not particularly disciplining at all.)

- Adults should be examples by keeping their behaviors normalized. (The problem was the word 'normalized.' No one could come up with a good example.)

The word 'normal' frequently came up and discussed ad nauseam. For example, during snack time, the word 'normal' was brought up because of Alex and Milla's earlier behaviors. Alex had somehow gotten the key to the oficina. When he arrived back from El Puente with Milla, they spent their first two hours of togetherness in the little white building fornicating. When walking by, one could hear them panting and thumping. None of us thought highly of their choice of place to have sex. We were trying to get the older kids not to have sex, and the younger kids didn't need to know about it yet. Also, the building's backside was a favorite peeing place for several of the boys.

At one point, Milla and Alex were having a particularly loud spate of sex while little Henrik and Raymond were letting loose by the building. Before I could get to the boys and lead them away, they had already peed all over each other with wide eyes and open mouths, as the howling inside the oficina resembled the skinning of a live cat.

Alex and Milla's behavior was so absurd that the rest of us were rendered speechless at first. When we, meaning Gunther, Molly, Golly, Catarina, and myself, finally regained our composure, we agreed it was normal behavior because sex was a very normal act.

"All animals do it," Gunther had reminded us.

"Some animals shouldn't," Golly had pointed out. But we all agreed the place they had chosen wasn't normal or appropriate, even if the act bordered on normal.

Jack's response was to mutter, "What noise?" Golly seemed to think Jack, being a sex addict, rather liked the smutty noises.

At lunch, Alex and Milla were met with mumblings from the group such as "Maybe you could keep it down," and "I think there's a shed in the jungle that would be better." Alex snorted at our remarks and thought people were jealous. Alex's mouth was swollen from use; he fiddled with Milla's pink spandex tank top, her breasts and shoulders seeming of great interest to him. Occasionally he wandered down to her crotch and backside. Milla, cheeks flushed and her neck sporting a large red hickey, we were convinced, had been screwed stupid. I had known her as a gregarious, kind, intelligent person, but at lunch, she giggled at our remarks, ignored our suggestions, and fanned herself with the scarf she had worn to cover the hickey. It was only when Mouse appeared at Alex's side that reality sank in.

Mouse, having grown sullen from the lack of attention from Alex, drew Alex away from Milla long enough to convince him that show-off sex wasn't popular with the kids. It wasn't anything that he said. It was merely his presence. We could see it in Alex's eyes. Mouse reminded Alex that he had a purpose here. And his purpose was to look after the children, especially Mouse. For the first time since I'd known Alex, he appeared sheepish and even blushed. Then coughing because fake coughing can give a person time to think, he came up with a solution. Alex proposed a compromise. If he and Milla could move into the oficina, they wouldn't make any noise. "Silent sex."

"Really?" Jack inquired, looking dismayed and grossing us all out.

"*Ja, ja,*" Alex said.

"What about the woman who works in the office?" I asked. "The woman with very dark-skin and light blue eyes."

"You mean, the young girl with the tight jeans. Striped black-and-white tank top with the exposed lace bra and the remarkably small stomach?" Jack asked.

"I hadn't noticed," I remarked, adding. "But—yeah."

"She doesn't work here. No, I take that back. She pretends to work here. She's Esmeralda's daughter or niece. Lives in a small northern village in the mountains. Visiting, that's all."

"She took my letter?"

"Why not?" Jack replied, stuffing his tortilla filled with rice and beans into his mouth.

"Why?"

"What?"

"Stop."

"You stop."

I got up and bussed my plate, helping Wooter and Bernarda with theirs. We hadn't washed the toys yet because we had procrastinated too much. I thought I'd go out and get a head start.

Chapter 21

Body Parts

Gunther followed me out of the cafeteria. "Let's get these babies washed," he said, saddling up to my side and poking my arm. He was the type of person who liked to touch; pull hair, nudge, poke, and hug. Being less demonstrative, but someone who liked to play, I lightly pushed him. He almost tumbled into the pee mud. He laughed while I stood aghast at the near-miss of grossness. But this wasn't a time for more procrastination. We needed to hurry. We wanted the kids to have the toys for their afternoon playtime. Dumping the contents of my child's wheelbarrow into the washbasin, we doused the Barbies and G.I. Joes with the cheaply made, watery dishwashing liquid we'd borrowed from the kitchen, and scrubbed. Gunther, not able to resist bubbles, blew a clump at my face. I blew a clump into his. Our silliness made us laugh so hard we cried tears of laughter and gasped for air. When we finally regained control of our senses, there was a silence so quiet that I could hear myself breathing. Looking at Gunther, I wondered why I didn't have a crush on him. He was fun, and I knew he liked me. But then, maybe our relationship wouldn't be the same. Its carefreeness gone. The fun turned into something more demanding. Thus, I thought, the wily nature of romance, and began scrubbing the toys with enthusiasm. Gunther wiped the wheelbarrow out with a towel from the dormitorio's towel stash. He then dried the toys. Watching him, I realized he was like having a fun brother. If I had a brother. It was a wonderful feeling to have toward someone. Just like I didn't mind, although it worried me some, my obsession with Harry because it was fun to have a romantic interest even if it were to remain unrequited. Then, by accident, I splashed water on Gunther, waking me up from my thoughts. He splashed back. At the end of our water fight, we were drenched, and we still had a box and the large wheelbarrow of toys to wash.

Finally, finished with our task, we dumped the clean toys into the middle of the quad's play area: Trucks, tugboats, motorboats, a play phone, Lego bricks, Matchbox cars, a toy hoe and rake, and a little oven for baking. I also placed the child's red wheelbarrow, filled with the washed Barbies and G.I. Joes, in the middle of the area so the kids could, at will, pick through its contents.

Frankie, the twins, and Mouse wanted nothing to do with the pile of toys. It was as though we had told them to play with garbage. They put their suits on, and Sarah volunteered to swim with them. Before departing for the beach, Sarah had also glared at the pile of toys with an expression of deep offense, her brow crossed, eyes dark. Lecturing us, in her lilting voice that often bordered on the sound of crying and joy wrapped into one, she said, "Bugs can't eat plastic. Nothing can eat it. It's like a pile of rocks. Only rocks are pretty, and when they disintegrate, they make sand. Ants love sand." She dramatized her last words by letting out a wail of despair, clenched her hands into fists, and shook them.

"Go on," Golly said, picking at a scabbed bug bite on her left thigh. "Git—" Sarah didn't take offense to Golly. She was happy to leave with Frankie, the twins, and Mouse.

Wooter, Albert, Charlotte, Penelope, Bernarda, El Gordo, Rosamond, and several others, whose names I had yet to learn, walked over to the pile of toys and began picking through. There wasn't any running or whooping. They did it because we told them to. El Gordo poked and prodded the orange, fake phone with his fingers before selecting it. He immediately pulled the receiver off, tossing the dial aside. As he was walking toward the beach with the receiver, I asked him where he was going. He told me he was taking his boat to the *rio.*

"Boat?" I said, nudging Milla who was sitting next to me. "El Gordo thinks the phone is a boat."

Milla had decided to be friends with me since Alex and she had a place to *fuck*—her word, not mine. Only she pronounced fuck *frook*. She was Swedish or maybe it was Norwegian, but then she was a Laplander, which made her possibly Finnish. She spoke English with a corny, heavy-tongued accent. When describing her homeland, she would say *tune-draw* instead of tundra, and she liked to have a good sweat in the *sownas*. When I pointed out the crumpled flower Albert had stuffed in his back pocket, she said, "*Bowtiful floower*." It made me depressed to think not only was I not speaking much Spanish but that my English was being shortchanged too. I'd already picked up a little cockney and would say stuff like, "Me bottom is wet from the blimey humidity," and I referred to the kids at times as "Tom tits."

Albert had zeroed in on the red wheelbarrow full of Barbies and G.I. Joes. He wheeled them over to Esmeralda, who was standing by the outside wash area of the kitchen, watching us—it was something she liked to do in the afternoons. When she grew tired of standing, she would sit in a dented, lopsided wrought-iron chair in front of the sink. The pregnant kitchen lady was with her too. Looking over the dolls Albert had in his wheelbarrow, they each took one, tucking it into their skirts. Only the dolls didn't fit. Their heads and hands could be seen sticking out. Albert then took his goods around the quad, walking in circles, visiting trees to pee on, and stopping to pick a few of the yellow flowers that were scattered around the grounds.

Bernarda, Penelope, and Charlotte were playing with the cars and trucks, but not in the manner one would think. They were throwing them at the dirt, picking them up and chucking them again and again, creating billowing dust. Molly went over and showed them another way to play with the cars and trucks, which was to move them over like boats over the earth. Molly made motor noises and honked a few times. The girls stuck their tongues out while running the cars all over the place, spitting and drooling, trying to make motor noises.

Wooter and Rosamond were constructing a building with Gunther using the Lego bricks. It had lots of twists and turns that didn't make any sense.

Henrik and Raymond grabbed the tugboat and a speed boat and went to the beach.

It was all very amicable and placid. There wasn't any fretting like when they went to eat their meals. It seemed the same as when they played with rocks and sticks. The kids were content.

Jack, who was sitting with his notepad observing the children, hadn't written much. His jaw and mouth were tightly pressed together. He looked frustrated. Eventually, he put his pen and notepad down and went over to the girls, Bernarda, Charlotte, and Penelope, who were over by the path that went to the pigs and the big kids' school. There were long planks that crossed over mud at the beginning of the path. The girls were pushing their cars along the planks. Jack joined them and took his navy-blue Matchbox car out of his pocket. He had the girls tilt the boards up, and they began racing their cars into a puddle. I looked over at the open page of Jack's notes; it said: "If I never have any time to play, I don't want to live."

I showed the page to Milla, and she said, "Jack's okay, he *spocks* directly from the liver." Alex, who had just walked up from the beach to retrieve Milla because he wanted help with the little ones' swimming, corrected Milla's idiomatic expression by saying, "Jack's a *sitzpinkler*."

Gunther chimed in, "I think he could be a nancy."

"I knew it," Golly said, glancing up. "I knew *eeeh* never played as a child."

I kept my remarks to myself as I was very busy. I'd gone and gotten a bucket of water, using a toy bucket, and was building a sculpted mud road along a high mountaintop made of mud and sticks with Wooter and Rosamond. They had grown bored playing with the Lego bricks and left Gunther to build his mangled fort by himself. Another little girl named Luna joined us, too. Luna had wispy, thin black hair, and was missing a front tooth. She was very good at packing the mud along the mountain walls for reinforcement. Her little hands scooped up the wet dirt and patted the sides with gentle swipes and patience. Rosamond was using tiny pebbles to decorate the side of the road. Wooter was making a moat.

We made a great team. We also were creating guardrails with Maya nuts; small, round, hardshell orbs. If the construction worked, I figured it would be fun, even thrilling, to see the 1947, purple Roadster and the 1965, yellow Citroën Matchbox cars I had put aside, flying down our mountain.

Birds sang, a light breeze was present, soft, and ethereal. The afternoon heat folded around us like a thick, wet glove. The slightest movement caused profuse sweating. The kids' cheeks, flushed and wet with perspiration, were a signal that we needed a break. Molly had already fallen asleep with four kids pressed into her voluminous flesh. My three workmates eventually joined them. Under the upside-down canoes, the workmen were snoring. There seemed to be little choice in the matter. It was like a field of Wizard of Oz poppy dust had fallen upon us. Leaning up against the log, I dropped off too. Napping, I was happy to learn, was something we did every afternoon. It made getting up at five and going to bed at midnight or later, workable.

When I awoke, Albert had re-appeared with his wheelbarrow. He had come back into the circle. Somewhere between giving away a few dolls and picking flowers, all the arms, heads, and legs of the Barbies and G.I. Joes had been dismembered. Ripped from their torsos. Golly and I looked at each other, astounded. Why would he do that?

Gunther yawned, stretched, and stood up. Picking through the broken dolls, he asked Albert what he planned to do with the mess. He said he wanted to sell them. This made us laugh.

"I bet he was a Chicle' vendor," Golly said, adding, "Blimey!"

"Brilliant. A true entrepreneur. From Chiclet seller to body part peddler," Gunther said.

"Sick in the *'ead*," Molly interjected.

"It's *wha'* happens when you *don'* have *paren's*," Golly remarked.

It was a long, hot afternoon. We beat the subject of selling body parts up into a pulp. It eventually became a moral mess. Similar to the game of Telephone, our imaginations took words and replaced them with thoughts best left untouched. By dinner, we were talking about the orphanage's side business of selling body parts by harvesting them from the young bodies of its clientele. Because it wasn't true, and because it was so ill-minded, we thought it was funny. We talked about fattening the kids up. I even overheard Milla say to Esmeralda, "*Lootz* of *froood* for the kids. We're rendering *laaard*."

The rest of the local staffers—workmen, the snippy women who looked after the older girls, and even Hamit's wife, who had arrived with their fat son that resembled El Gordo, causing me to think there was some truth in El Gordo being Hamit's son—tilted their heads and peer at us, puzzled. There was an uncertainty in their eyes and the way they held their mouths, agape, flabbergasted at what they were hearing. But we were having fun and didn't have a clue that our fun was unsavory.

Chapter 22

Russian Bank

Harry arrived back, late, possibly midnight, from the city, a week, and a day after he had left. When he walked through the door, I was settled in bed with the overhead light on, along with my flashlight, clothing unfolded and thrown on the floor, drinking a rum and coke, and reading. I was shocked to see him and a little embarrassed.

"Welcome back," I said, putting the book aside while running my eyes over the room and the mess.

He looked at me and the surrounding area and puckered his lips. I felt he wanted to comment on my slovenly housekeeping skills but stopped himself. Instead, he sighed and smiled. Not wanting to seem too pathetic, I scrambled out of bed, gathered up my clothing and wet towel, and put it all in a pillowcase I was using for dirty laundry, although it had nothing in it. Mumbling, I said, "I thought you were coming back a few days ago, but you didn't and well—" I paused to look at him. "I'm only neat if I have to be." This made him chuckle. I felt better.

He had a bag of food with him. He walked over to me and asked, "Hungry? If you are? Pick one." There was an orchard of various fruits: apples, pears, oranges; and several packages of cookies. Shocked that he was willing to share his food, I said, "So, I guess it's just salsa and pencils you don't share." He laughed and nudged the bag toward me. I took an apple. I hadn't had an apple since leaving the States; even though apples grew in certain areas of the region, I never saw them. Also, we never had fruit at the orphanage, which I found odd since there was plenty of fruit in the area, along with a fruit company near us. I took a bite; it was crisp, the snap and sweetness like candy and autumn.

From the florid beam of the overhead light, I saw he was wearing a tie with little dogs that appeared to be terriers. His Old Spice deodorant, light, yet distinctive and appealing. "You're so dressed up," I commented.

"I had a meeting. An important meeting," he remarked while looking at my T-shirt. "Is that Tinker Bell?" He then read the words under her feet out loud. "Faith, Lust, and Pixie Dust."

"Variation of the Peter Pan saying," I said, then added. "I didn't buy it. When I was in Mexico, I had my laundry done in a group wash area. Somehow, I ended up with this T-shirt. It's good for sleeping in." Long, it fell to my knees. The neck was loose, the armpits had holes; soft and worn, I liked it. I also wouldn't have worn it if I knew Harry was coming back. Tinker Bell had big boobs and lips.

He went over to his side and changed in the shadows of the rafters, and I crawled back into bed. He did the same. His mattress squeaked. Once settled, the two of us prone under our mosquito netting, munched on our apples in silence.

"Eleanor," he said. I loved the way he said my name. It resembled the serious note of an exotic trombone, and I wanted him to say it again, so I didn't respond.

"Eleanor," he said, saying my name louder, but the tone

still exotic.

"Yes," I finally responded.

"I'm going to be home more. I know I told you otherwise. Just a few nights I might not be here."

"Why would I mind," I remarked. "It's your room too." I wasn't sure what I thought of him being around all the time. I knew I was going to have to be neater.

He said the corruption in the city, with its poorly paid police force and greedy government officials, was unbearable. When he finished his apple, he put the core in a plastic bag outside of his netting. I tossed him mine to dispose of it too. The last thing we wanted was more bugs. He talked for a little while longer, telling me about the indigenous people protesting in the streets. "It's always about land. But the lack of humanity is probably the biggest issue," he said. When he spoke, he seemed preoccupied with an oval, gold locket that he had around his neck. It was attached to a thin, gold chain. He kept rubbing the flat sides as if it were a good luck charm. At one point, he went to take it off but then hesitated, patted it, and settled into sleep. I wondered if he noticed how much I was watching him.

"Can you not sleep?" he asked.

The overhead light had been turned off, but I still had my book on my lap and the flashlight on. "Does the light bother you?"

"No, but I'm, well, I'm not tired. I know it's late, but well, maybe I'll read too." He had a book under his pillow and a flashlight. When I inquired about the book, he told me the name: *Ardiente Paciencia*, or *Burning Patience*. A Chilean writer named Antonio Skármeta, who was of Croatian descent, was the author. Harry went on to tell me the story. "It's about a poor postman in Isla Negra who befriends Pablo Neruda. He asks for his help writing poems to the woman of his dreams."

Harry's words made me pause. "How romantic," I said, adding. "Do you like poetry?"

"It can be useful." I thought of Jacquelina and what a lucky girl she was to have someone as adorable as Harry sending her love poems—or so I imagined he did.

That night, if only one of us had been a good sleeper, we never would have gotten to know each other. But as it went, Harry nor I could find much solace in our respective beds or our books. I don't know if it was a restlessness brought on by darkness. Or a love of life that demanded staying awake? Or our DNA was just never that tired. Whatever the cause of our insomnia, it didn't matter; we made good use of it. I don't mean by reading or other nonsense—but by talking and then by playing cards. It started with a very simple, unimaginative question.

"What's your favorite color?"

He said it was green.

I told him green was everywhere in the jungle; didn't he have another, more intriguing color?

"No, and lucky for me I don't have to go searching for it," he had chuckled and then said, "Your turn."

I replied, "blue." Which wasn't any better.

I asked him about Holland and his childhood. At first, he stumbled, then he told a story. When he was a boy, he had a songbird the primary color of yellow. The bird had arrived as a gift from his grandmother. He called her Luri because the name meant 'all good things.' Luri being confined to a shoebox with holes, and his mother not allowing the bird to fly around the house, he built a cage at school during woodworking class and made it one hundred and fifty-two centimeters high, out of tall grasses and pine. "It was like a basket, only with lots of holes. The cage was big enough for me to sit in. I sat with Luri and read," he said, his voice calm and reflective. "But she died one day. Just fell off her perch onto my lap." The story seemed to make him sad; I felt sad for him too.

As the night carried on, instead of lying in bed staring at the ceiling and talking, when Harry mentioned having a deck of cards, I told him I had a deck too. Which was perfect to play the game Russian Bank as it required two decks. It was a game of deceit and guile for which one needed a quick eye. We were well matched. He had a keen eye for treachery; I was well aware of beguilement.

The idea was to catch the other person cheating. We brought the crooked lamp up from the kids' dressing room for better vision and used a small fan to keep us cool. His stealth moves and covert duplicity were inanely obvious at times. My obsession with staring at his beautiful face, a downfall. We ate the fruit he had brought and sipped from juice glasses I found in the great room, the tepid rum I had, with a splash of coke. We kept having to have rematches. The hours ticked by without notice. We were both confused when up through the floorboards came the hip-hop song telling me to 'move it, baby—move it.'

"The night went quick," I said.

"Leave the cards where they are. No touching, no tripping, and scattering them. We'll continue tonight after I return from El Puente," he said with a crafty glint in his eye. Looking back at the cards, I wondered what he saw that I didn't. Feeling too rushed to count what was there and what might be missing, I shook his hand in agreement. I was needed downstairs.

Harry went to bed with his earplugs, and I went to peel soiled onesies off toddlers. Tired, and a little tipsy, I figured naptime was just around the corner.

"Are you drunk?" Catarina asked as she watched me walk down the stairs.

"Possibly, but nothing poo and urine can't cure," I replied, gulping down what was left in my water bottle.

Catarina had just walked in the door from spending the night with her yachtsman. The Scott having grown tired of motoring her back and forth, had shown her how to start and stop the motor on the dinghy, now she used it, with its three-horsepower outboard, to putter to and from his boat. Her feet and long skirt wet from disembarking, she'd tottered around the great room picking up a Matchbox car and a couple of beheaded, legless, armless Barbies. She made puddles whenever she paused.

"You take the kids out of their cribs, I'll undress them," she said. All the pipes finally fixed; we could bathe the kids in the showers. Over the past week, Catarina and I had been taking turns setting the kids free of their cribs and ridding them of their nightly clothing in the mornings. We never said much to each other during these wee hours, but at night, after dinner, when it was time for her to return to The Scott, I would walk with her down to the beach to send her off. We'd smoke cigarettes and talked about, mainly, her relationship. She would convey certain ideas about The Scott, speaking in terms a person would use when describing food— "buns to die for" or else "scrumptious nuts to nibble on." She felt "poached" or "roasted" after sex, sometimes even "fried." She loved chewing on his mouth, equating it to a "platter of exquisite morsels." "Yummy," she often said. Her words always made me hungry.

She also said "yummy" during the day when looking after the kids. It would just pop out of her mouth, even if what she was looking at was disgusting, like someone's messy behind. She made me laugh. She was insanely smitten with The Scott. Not only did they "eat each other up," but his pantry was filled with sumptuous canned goods like sardines, pickles, asparagus, and Chef Boyardee ravioli. Her descriptions of these foods: "rich and saucy like him."

This morning, standing halfway down the steps looking at her yawning and dripping on the floor, I wanted to tell her about how much fun I'd had with Harry playing cards. I wanted to tell her about the yellow songbird he had as a child, and that he liked the color green. But I didn't. And I didn't tell her after dinner down by the docks either. Instead, I just wished her luck and sent her on her way. The dinghy swaying under her weight. The putt-putt sound disappearing into the dark, the moon hidden below the canopy. I liked the orphanage. I liked the kids. The group of niñeros were funny. I liked playing cards with Harry. My life was simple and uncomplicated, and I wanted to keep it that way.

Chapter 23

Time Warp

As the days passed by, the daytime hours, minutes, and seconds seemed caught in a circular, repetitive motion of perpetual sameness. Even my nights playing cards with Harry, although splendid and no matter how tired I was, I made myself stay up, had a sameness to them. Either he won or I won. It made it hard to distinguish one day from another. It caused me, all of us, to believe we'd been at the orphanage longer than we had. This aberrance of repetition, deformed time. A minute was more like an hour, an hour an entire day, and a day a whole week, a week a month, and so on. It didn't mean life was boring, just predictable, and unremarkable. I didn't mind it. My life was lasting longer than if I'd never arrived. I was thinking this is how the world should be. No rushing. Working together within the confines of a remote space filled with overgrown trees, water, sand, and the laughter of children. It was calming and pleasant. I also, finally, understood my mother's contentment with her institutional living. Never a day out of place; bingo mid-day; scrabble after dinner. Meals served at the same time. The menu predictable and with only slight variations.

We had a variation in our diet. The workmen killed a pig. A giant, pink pig that fed us large luscious chunks of pork until it became thin pieces of strapping. We also received a donation of cabbage. We had cabbage with our pork. But these fluctuations in our diet didn't seem to mark time, any more than Wooter losing a tooth or Penelope learning the doggy paddle. Mere memories, but when did they happen? Entry and exit points to the day always being the same. Did an incident happen a week ago or a month ago, if the sun was always bright and the birds constantly singing? None of us knew.

While sitting next to Jack on a log during snack time, I mentioned the disorientation of time at the orphanage.

He replied, "Einstein. I gather you've heard of him?"

"Of course," I replied, ignoring his derogatory insinuation. It was the only way to deal with Jack. He was socially inept, and we, the group, for the most part, forgave him for it.

He then pulled a notepad from his back pocket and scribbled down a few sentences. Looked up at me, then wrote some more, and finally said, "Has to do with Einstein's Special Relativity. Time speeds up or slows down depending on how fast a person moves. We move very slowly here and therefore, so does time." He then scratched his chest and said, "Excellent. Raising children and time warp. I can use that."

I smiled because I thought of asking him for an acknowledgment. Instead, I said, "I have no idea how long I've been here."

"No one does," He remarked, looking around for his wife. She was by a puddle that had been heavily peed into. It looked like she was collecting water bugs. Agitated by her activity, he left to bring her into the dormitorio.

Later that night, I told Harry about Einstein and time warp. He agreed, time was strange here, but he also had a watch that told him the day, and he also left the place frequently. But he still couldn't tell me how long he'd been in the country, let alone working at the orphanage.

"Maybe it's a country issue," I said, tongue and cheek.

"A Central American time warp," he joked. We both laughed, and since he was distracted, I flipped a card, threw another down, and won the game.

"I don't like cheats," Harry barked, taking a sip of his rum with a splash of coke.

"Harry, this entire game is about cheating," I said, pouring myself another beverage.

While dealing out the cards for another game, I told Harry about Jack's hypothetical theory on child-rearing. "He likens this place to a commune. Doesn't approve of parents, especially biological parents. Thinks their dodo brains." Then seeing Harry trying to cheat, I remarked. "You can't make that move."

"Yes, I can."

"No, you can't."

"You're right."

"Now back to Jack," I said, watching Harry move a few cards around. Continuing, I said, "He has this dissertation he's writing. For instance, Chapter Twelve, 'Routine and Consistency.' The thing is—the orphanage has already been set up as a model for this equation. But we have reinforced it with other stuff."

"Really? Like what?" Harry asked, leaning back with his drink in his hand, waiting for me to make a move. His eyes were steamy from the heat and the booze. Their intensity caused me to stumble just for a moment as the blueness briefly took my breath away. Taking a sip from my cup, I put an ace of diamonds by a queen of spades.

"I don't think so. Nice try," he said, raising his left eyebrow.

I took the card back and threw another that worked, but if caught again, I'd lose. Continuing my line of thought, I said, "As I mentioned before, the orphanage is pretty much a straight line from the dorm to the caf, to the school, to the quad, to the—"

"I get it."

"Yup, everything is routine and consistent. But we've added stuff like—we don't keep the clothes in the bins anymore. We've divvied them up and gave each kid a cubby hole. Henrik and Raymond's cubby holes are at the bottom of the rung so they can easily get to their clothing. Shoes are put on the floor under a bench for safekeeping. We insist the children fold their clothing when it returns from the laundry and that they neatly put it away. Dirty clothes are put into a hamper, no throwing them onto the floor anymore. What we're doing is taking routine and consistency and coupling it with gradual responsibility."

"You haven't been doing this all along?" he asked, with a smirk.

"Kind-of, but not consistently. Why are you smirking?"

"Nothing. I mean, it's just that. Have you thought of applying, what is it? Routine and Consistency in this room?"

"Funny," I said and laughed. "Now there is nothing wrong with my side of the room." And there wasn't. All my clothes were folded and neatly placed on the floor. Dirty clothes were in the pillowcase. Although out of the corner of my eye, I saw a rogue sock. It had a hole, and the bottom of it was black-gray.

"I'm just playing," he said, his tone sincere. After a minute's pause, he said. "It's hard to always keep everything in order.

All it takes is one day. An hour of something going wrong and poof." I felt he was talking about something that may have happened recently and waited for him to continue with the thread, but he stopped talking. A shadow had swept over his face. He seemed lost in some distant thought.

Changing the subject, I asked, "How's El Puente and all those dinners you have there?"

Glancing up from the cards, his expression hard to read, he asked, ignoring my question, "What did you get your diploma in?"

I smiled. He didn't want to talk about his present life. He never did, except for Jacquelina. He brought her up whimsically almost every night, like a note on a calendar to remind me she existed.

"Political Science," I said, half lying. I hadn't graduated yet. But I would graduate once I arrived back home again and took the language test. Something I felt that wasn't going to happen for a while. I began rearranging my cards, placing them strategically down. Harry didn't need to know I hadn't graduated, and that my need to know Spanish was also a need to understand who I was, and what I wanted out of life. He didn't seem like the type of person who had the need or even the desire to spend time figuring himself out. At thirty-five, he had an air of wisdom, as though he had been born knowing more than most. Yes, an old soul, I thought. My soul felt immature and silly around his, but I wasn't going to let him know that either.

As the night grew into the early morning hours, and Harry talked about his childhood. I felt that Catarina had been correct in saying Harry wasn't Dutch. He did like licorice, and smoked Gouda was his favorite cheese, but that's like saying I like apple pie, so I must be an American. Although the songbird was a pleasant story, most of his childhood had been spent in a place of unrest. He had to leave school when he was seven for an entire year because the entrance to the building had been bombed. He made toys out of shrapnel and once stole a gun from a sleeping rebel.

"I didn't know Holland had rebels?"

He said there were a lot of bad rules in his "village," which he corrected to "town." As a youth, he spent most of his time stealing gum and cigarettes from kiosks in a square that had several abandoned buildings, too many pigeons, and old ladies wearing colorful hats and shawls. "Harry, it doesn't sound like Holland to me," I would say. "Who was bombing the people? What rules didn't you like?"

"Did I say bombings? Strange. I didn't mean that at all. Oh, and rules? Like many, as a child, rules were to be challenged." I knew it was the rum making him slip up. His stories were half-truths because when he strayed too far, he brought up The Hague or getting high in Amsterdam, clichés he could have left alone as they were a dead giveaway to his ruse. At times, his stories were also strange and creepy, like the rat that lived in his house when he was five and pissed on all the flour. Or the one-armed maid from the mountains with a big nose and a sloppy lower lip that wiggled when she became angry. Then there was the boarding school he was sent away to, due to, troubled times. "I also wasn't behaving the way my parents thought I should. I had an unhealthy intelligence."

"What does that mean?"

"It was something my father used to say. They sent me to Spain during my teenage years, and then I went to England for more schooling."

"Yes, you use *vosotros*, and your accent is British, and well, something else too." I was beginning to see Harry as a complicated man as none of his youth was ordinary. But no matter what was fact or fiction, I found him fascinating. I knew my stories didn't quite have the same flare. I grew up as an only child in a country that, although at battle with a Far East nation, Vietnam, it wasn't the one being bombed.

We had lived in the woods in a house that had ten rooms. We weren't rich, but we weren't poor either. No rats, but we had mice. We had money for basics and comfortable furniture. My father painted, my mother knitted and made delicious soups. During the ages of four and five, I pretended to be a woodland elf. I called myself Siofra and wouldn't answer to any other name.

"The woods are a perfect place for fantasies," Harry had said while peeling an orange, several locks of his hair coming loose and falling over his eyes, a common occurrence which always gave me pause. It took a lot of restraint not to push it back for him.

"Look out the window at the moon. It's pretty, like a painting by Manuel De la Cruz," he said.

"Who?"

"He's a Spanish painter, gothic, old."

We were in the middle of a very intense game and one I was winning. But I got up anyway to look at the moon. Behind my back, I could hear him shifting his cards. "What are you doing?" I said, glancing back around.

"Nothing," he chuckled. A smart player got away with it, but he was clumsy and noisy. I waved my index finger at him letting him know I was on to his tricks.

Standing at the window, breathing in the damp night air, I looked at the moon keeping one eye on the game, and said, "It's half its size, but bright." Surrounding its curves were deep blacks matted with stars. It rested in the middle of a tree nook. It looked like something out of a fairytale. A big grin in the sky.

"When you arrived there wasn't a moon, just the shadow

of one."

"How do you know?" It puzzled me that he would even remember that night.

"I was up most of that night conducting business in El Pueblito. When I arrived back, the sun was just below the canopy. I saw you on the beach."

"You did?" I said, turning around and looking at him. He was sitting cross-legged, resting his elbows on his knees, staring at the cards. No doubt trying to think of a winning move while my back was turned.

"Your thick hair," he said, rearranging the cards, not noticing I was watching him. "Dark and wavy. It was framing your face. A face that looked like a porcelain doll in the dim light of the rising sun." His words caused him to glance up at me. Our eyes caught together and rested. Caught up in his mythical sounding tale of 'Eleanor' on the beach, I listened intensely to each consonant and vowel as his voice grew distant, hesitant, and soft while keeping my gaze steady upon his. "There was a nest of sand and leaves around you like you'd made a bed. You were sleeping so soundly and not moving that, I thought, maybe you were a doll, but then you stirred."

"Did I wake up?"

"No, you looked peaceful. I left."

"Don't you think you should have woken me up?"

"Why?"

"I don't know, the crocodiles and the manatee." For some reason this made us laugh. It was the type of laughter that made us laugh more like it had poked our silly bone or was tickling our ribs. Still standing by the window, unwilling to pull my gaze away from his. His eyes alive, swimming in heat and rum, I wanted to kiss him. Just like that, I wanted to walk over and take his face into my hands and kiss him. Then, without warning, an uneasiness crept over me. My thoughts of kissing him were out of place. But I imagined he, too, was pondering sex. I could see it in his expression. But no. Looking away, I sat back down. Then sobering up my lustful thoughts, I said, "Now let's see how you have cheated."

But as I was having a hard time focusing, and to put things right, I asked, "How did you meet Jacquelina?" Not that I cared. I was becoming a little annoyed that she even existed. But she did exist.

As it went, he spent the next half hour talking about her, and I won the game. Small victories, I thought.

Chapter 24

Gossip

Enhanced 'routine and consistency,' had us, the niñeros, realizing that what we had earlier perceived as subdued tranquility, was merely a lack of knowing the various levels of contentment. This had Jack pondering a thought, "What you don't see, you don't know."

Gunther pointed out that the expression wasn't new. And Jack had it wrong. "It's what you don't know you have to live with," Gunther corrected.

Alex said, "No, it's nur bahnhof verstehen."

"In English, please," Catarina stated.

"Absolutely, no clue," Alex translated.

"*Inn'it wha' ew don' know won' hur' yah,*" Golly said.

Whatever it was? Life was better, easier. The children truly seemed happier, so how could we not think our world had improved. The marches over to meals were much more pleasant. Going to school became less whiny. The boxes we built for independence in the bathroom had finally, curbed the peeing outside. Only Henrik and Raymond remained stubborn about this, randomly peeing on ants, beetles, and worms. The kids were also learning how to balance themselves on the toilets, and there was less falling in.

At night, the children all knew to put their shoes in a row under the bench. Even tough guy Frankie, who was used to throwing his shoes into a corner, now laid them nicely down to rest at night. Crazy Mouse followed through too. Mouse, who found it hard to pay attention, rarely knew what he should be doing. When we, more like Alex, got him to stop shaking, he would look around, smile, and nod, then mimic his fellow orphans. It helped that it was a group task.

"Individuality can produce a persecuted feeling," Jack liked to toss in here and there, his hollow eyes revealing a tortured soul.

"*Don* worry Jack, we like *ya*," Golly would say when she saw he looked blue. We were convinced Jack had been bullied as a kid.

The conventional toys, lost or broken, were also no longer used. The jungle elements such as twigs, mud, and rocks had regained status, capturing once again an organic element to their playtime. Albert had grown bored with his ruined dolls; the arms, legs, heads, and bodies of the Barbies and G.I. Joes. He had abandoned them to the small wheelbarrow which he had left by the trash bin near the backdoor of the kitchen. He went back to solely looking for flowers.

At night, we still danced but shooed everyone out early—that is, the kitchen ladies and the older kids—in order to read to our little ones, which allowed them to fall asleep early without a fuss. During our nightly meetings, we congratulated ourselves on doing a good job. They were learning. We were proud.

Yet there was something unsettling or, should I say, brewing among the adults. It was hard to put my finger on it, but the signs were there.

It was as though we couldn't take the silence, the lack of conflict. Possibly it was a malignant pathos within us. An eruption of a dominant gene that opposed calm. With our minds and bodies relaxed, our fight-or-flight instinct annihilated by harmony and serenity. We needed an outlet. Our need for disruption was like a primordial hubris—subtle and nondescript in its vagaries, had appeared like a faucet drip growing louder and louder. In other words, the adults began to unravel. Slowly, like the warped time, we were living in.

It was our gossip. It was getting worse. And we couldn't seem to shut up. Somewhat of a moot issue when hanging around young children who barely spoke their own language, let alone English. As for the local staff, we weren't sure what they understood. Cadmael knew some English. Possibly the others, too. But since speaking a foreign language is more difficult than understanding it. Except for Cadmael's sparse attempts now and then, no one else said a word, but that didn't mean they weren't listening. Hearing what we said and gleaning bits and pieces and folding it together, with their imaginations, into a story. We felt they were on to us, but then, "So, what?"

One day, while I was talking to Milla about selling the children's body parts and wondering what other countries took place in such a diabolical deed, I caught the workmen staring at me, wide-eyed, resting under the canoes. It wasn't that they didn't watch us from their lairs daily; it was their expressions this time. They looked horrified.

Another time, when the subject of body parts came up, I was with Molly and Golly. They wanted new stomachs. They felt if they could replace their bad metabolism with a fast metabolism, life would be grand. They giggled like misfit hyenas over having the stomach of a three-year-old. During this conversation, Esmeralda and the two other kitchen ladies had inched their ratty-looking, wrought-iron and plastic chairs over to us from their normal perch by the outdoor kitchen sink. I assumed they were trying to understand what we were saying.

"They *caan't* understand us," Molly said.

"Don't be so sure," I said back, then added. "Language is not just words, its expressions, and tones that are the dead give-away. Well, that's what I read somewhere." While I spoke, the ladies shuffled their chairs back to the sink. "Interesting," I whispered. "I bet they know more than they let on. I mean, they hear English all the time. For Christ's sake, they're linguist! They already speak two or three languages."

"I *don'* know their language. Not one word," Molly said.

"Do you ever listen to it?" Golly asked, nudging Molly like she was a dummy.

"No *blimey, no.*" Her answer, dramatic, as though we were trying to get her to eat a worm.

"I bet," I said, still speaking in a hushed tone. "They're picking up words here and there. Piecing them together. Bodies, parts, children."

"I *be'* they *aav* good imaginations," Golly giggled, adding. "*Tink* we evil."

Then we all laughed because it sounded sinister, and sinister seemed funny.

Molly's mood darkening, she said, "I *tink* they're evil."

"Nonsense," I said.

"They could be evil," Golly said.

"Maybe," I remarked. We remained in silence for a good minute. The kids playing while a light breeze fluffed at their matted, damp hair. It was insufferably hot. I wiped my face with my shirt, yawned because it was almost nap time, and said, "So what do you think the kitchen ladies do when they go home?"

Golly made up a story. It was a perverse, mischievous account of warlocks and witches. When I turned my head to see if the workmen were still awake under the canoes. All three had their eyes wide open. They then crawled out and walked briskly away. Witches were real in this country. *La Noticia* printed daily stories of people putting spells on their neighbors for revenge. It was a jailable offense. Could even get one stoned to death.

Golly's imagination didn't end with *brujas and brujos*. Watching Eadrich, Aapo and Cadmael run off into the jungle, she insinuated they were savages living wild, naked lives full of debauchery in the backwoods. It was a dark tale of sex, sodomy and bestiality. Her cockney accent, uneven tone, and timing made the story captivating. "*Mu'ating* crops like legumes and grains to 'leggrain.' And making *loda* babies."

When Gunther joined us, he corrected the story and said, "The men aren't warlocks, but guerrillas. Using the orphanage as a cover-up."

"Yes, I see it," I said. We all agreed that the staff, if they could get away with it, would chop us up with machetes. Which made us laugh. The stories were fun.

As the days passed, we added more details to the business of selling body parts, babies, *bruja*s and *bruj*os, guerrillas undercover, and unquenchable sexual appetites. We also began to believe what we said. And felt the locals were talking about us too.

When Hamit, who liked to come into the dormitorio before breakfast to tell us the news, said his head, that received radio frequencies, told him that the guerrillas in the north were thinking of coming south, we told him they were already here.

He didn't even blink an eye. Just grumbled, "That's too bad." When he told us, El Gordo was an undercover dwarf to spy on us. We agreed. Hamit said, "You all better keep an eye on him. Don't let him near a machete." We shook with fear and disgust. "What a horrible way to die," someone said, but then we all laughed. When Hamit said, "Esmeralda has put a spell on my wife to make her mean." We said, "So that's what's wrong with her." No one liked her. No one liked Hamit's wife. She was a skinny, straight-backed, stuffy woman from Panama City who wore pencil skirts and cotton blouses she buttoned to her neck. Her hair, cropped short and slicked down on top of her head, made it look painted on. Now since Hamit was talking about her, we added her to our afternoon fables; Hamit's wife had become reptilian. We needed to keep the youngsters away from her or she'd eat them.

And more absurdly, when a group of outsiders arrived—a tour boat with a shallow draft going up and down the shores of the river visiting different sights—lunch at Club de Bote, tortilla making at an authentic Mayan village, and bird watching.

They pulled right up to our beach and threw down a gangplank. They brought platters of brownies for the kids. It was a humanitarian visit; they told us. They wore floppy hats and white deck shoes. Their shorts and shirts were the colors of peppermint and pistachio ice cream. Their visit caused a few of the older kids to revert to their days on the streets. They stood before our rich boating guests looking depraved and sad. They told them they were parentless and poor, and that we mistreated them. "I need money for food. We must buy food. We starve."

It didn't help when Milla thanked them for the brownies, adding, "We're fattening them up to make lard." Nor that Molly and Golly showed a group of stout ladies, with sunglasses on to prevent glaucoma, the broken doll parts, and said, "We're selling body parts. Need any?"

Or when I said, "These kids are the biological children of

the president of the country."

When they finally walked back up the gangplank, pockets empty of money and shaking their heads, we could hear them muttering stuff like, "Odd group. Do you think the kids don't have food?" Which made us laugh. They also gave us something new to talk about for days. We talked about their dour mouths and untarnished sneakers and started rumors that they had stolen a few kids.

Chapter 25

Love

I don't know how many drives to El Pueblito I had made before deciding I didn't want to do it anymore. It unnerved me. My emotions made little sense because the week before I had enjoyed the trip. Gunther had gone with us, never one to miss a tasty meal. We ate *carne asada* again and napped in the park while waiting for parts for the launch engine to arrive from a neighboring town. It all had been pleasant. Gunther and I had had great fun teasing each other over nothing, just nit-picking at our foibles and shortcomings.

But then, suddenly, I dreaded having to drive the beaten up, stinky car. The pressure of keeping it on the road and everyone safe, I thought. Possibly the result of my easy living. "I think being here is making me soft and nervous," I complained to Harry while playing cards.

"You don't seem it," he said, adding. "Your nerve at playing this game—is like steel."

"Before coming here I'd been very free and fluid. Riding buses, hitting various cities, and staying a while, then leaving," I said, sitting back on my heels and squeezing a juicy lime into a half-filled glass of rum. Continuing, I added. "When I was in *San Cristobal de las Casas,* I rode horses every day. Up to *Chamula* and over to the river with crocodiles. In *Lago Atitlan*, I walked on hot coals and fought off banditos by telling them I was a *bruja.* In Oaxaca, I spent my days weathering the doldrums of language school by going to the ruins in the afternoon. I hung out with the women, the *Zapotec* vendors. I liked talking to them. They swore a lot. When the *turistas* didn't buy anything, we would say, '*por que estos pendejas turistas no compran, lo por que son mierde!*' I also ran up and down the ruins like a Billy goat. The women kept saying I would fall, but I never did." Tucking a clump of hair behind my right ear, I added. "What's happened to me? Now I don't even want to go into El Pueblito."

"I don't blame you. The town's a flea-bitten scare."

"I don't even think I can speak Spanish anymore. My mind has become mush." I was rambling. It caused me to throw the wrong card down, but he didn't notice.

"Do you want to leave?" He asked, his voice thin like something had been ripped from it.

Looking up at him, I thought, no, I can't. I'm in love with you. But said, "I could. It would be better for my Spanish. But not yet, I like it here. Why leave a place I like?"

"Why don't we speak Spanish together," he said. His face brightening.

"Yes, we should. I haven't been speaking very much Spanish lately. I'm rusty."

My mind felt slow. My retention watered down with drink. Unexercised reflexes, I thought. It was as though I had been lapping up warm milk with sedatives, and I stumbled around with even the most rudimentary words. I couldn't even remember the name of the book I was reading—but then, I laughed to myself because the book didn't have a name.

Harry rattled off a series of stories in crisp, rapid Spanish about his father, Don Ricardo Unia, and one about a sister named Soledad. He gave them Spanish names. He was slipping again because shouldn't the names be Dutch? But his voice clear and smooth was a delight to listen to. His accent a mystery. He wasn't a foreigner speaking an unfamiliar language, but a native. He neither spoke like a Spaniard nor anyone local. What country was he from?

"Are you really Dutch?" I asked him. "I've heard Dutch people speak Spanish. You don't have a Dutch accent."

"Remember, I lived in Spain."

I stopped questioning him about it. He didn't want me to know.

At one point, he began a story about Jacquelina eating with her at a restaurant in the city, but then stopped. He said he didn't want to tell that story anymore. He looked sad.

"What's wrong Harry?" I asked in English. Everything I said to him was in English because it was too tiring to think about how to speak in Spanish.

"You're not trying."

"It's too late. Not tonight." Feeling embarrassed, I poured myself another drink. "They don't use *vosotros* here. It confuses me," I said, adding. "Why don't you live with Jacquelina?"

Most nights, I tempered my drinking. Nursing a beverage, and only having two or three, but the last drink I had poured was my fifth. It made me braver and pushy. Since he wasn't answering me, I added. "You seem to love her a lot. Why are you here Harry? At the orphanage? You seem too talented to be living such an obscure life."

"Why not?" He said, looking like he wanted to laugh. To wipe the seriousness of my words away, I assumed. Glancing at his glass, I noticed he too was drinking more than usual. His mouth wet, his eyes shiny, he continued. "One job is as good as another."

Then staying stuck on being nosy, I asked coyly, "Is it a front to allow you to do other stuff? To stay in the country to buy and sell land?" It wasn't exactly what Gunther had told me, but I had a hunch.

My explanation of what he was up to had him looking at me strangely. His brow twisted inward, his mouth opening and shutting a few times without sound. Leaning back onto his hands, his legs bent to the side to allow for the card game, he gave me an amused, penetrating stare. I could see the moon had leveled itself and was peering in through the window like a meddlesome neighbor catching wind of something good. The bad lighting gave a sultry film noir effect to the room. Harry's silence caused the whirring of the fan to become louder. I would wait for a reply before saying another word. Scooping the cards up, I shuffled.

"We weren't done with that game," he said.

"We weren't?"

Then Harry laughed.

"What's so funny?"

"You." But his bewilderment was palpable. Possibly laughing was the only answer he could give me. Handing me a packet of cookies he said, "Here, munch on these. And please tell me, what is this all about?"

"It's time for me to go to bed," I said, stuffing a cookie into my mouth. "How about an orange too? Toss me one, please."

Instead of tossing me the orange, he handed it to me by taking hold of my hand and placing the orange in it. Leaning in close, his breath colored with rum, frankincense, and myrrh, he said, "Don't go to bed yet."

I said nothing back. His touch melting my obstinance and need to know. I weakened and let him cradle my hand in his. He then pushed my hair away from my face with his free hand and said, "Eleanor, you're right. I am selling land. It's complicated. I do like teaching—"

"You rarely teach," I interrupted, laughing, adding. "Didn't you go sailing with The Scott today?"

He laughed too. "True."

Sobering up some, I said, "I don't care what you do, Harry. It's your life." Groaning, I stumbled to get up, "I've had too much to drink." I tried to pull my hand away from his, but he held it tightly.

"Sit."

"I should go to bed," I said, sitting back down, roaming his face for clues, wondering why he was still holding my hand. Here we were in a room lit by a soggy lamp and a busybody moon. It was warm and sultry with only a light breeze from the fan which brushed us gently. We were drunk, inches away from each other. An ambiance made for a romance novel. But I wasn't drunk enough to be fooled by it, not when there was an elephant in the room, especially when there were two of them. Jacquelina being one, and my fear of kissing him, the other. I was already crazy about him. If I kissed him? If I slept with him? Nothing would be the same. Being Harry's hapless lap dog—concubine—wasn't the issue anymore, I had resigned myself to the possibility. But it seemed inevitable that it wouldn't end well. So, I smiled. Not tonight, I said in my head. It pleased me that I could be so mature. Maybe I was growing up? "Harry," I said while giving him a sheepish tilt of the head, "What about your fiancé? You haven't told me why you live apart."

Letting my hand go, he replied, eyes downcast, voice a touch mottled. "It's better we don't live together. She has her life; I have mine. Eventually, we'll join." He didn't look at me the way he usually did when speaking of the river, the sun, books, and tales of his youth. He looked confused, downtrodden. Hemmed in as though masking some regret—Or maybe it was just wishful thinking on my part. Stuffing orange pieces into my mouth, I once again got up to go to bed.

"Stay for another game," he asked, changing the subject and once again appearing happy.

The cards shuffled but undealt, and with a wave of tiredness sweeping over me, I replied, "Tomorrow, Harry." And stumbled off to bed, alone.

Chapter 26

The Monkey

The next day, I had a hangover. The morning hours were dreadful. During snack time, I added a three-count pour of rum into my green drink. It was delicious and helped my equilibrium. After lunch, the dull throb in my head finally disappeared. I spent most of the afternoon playtime in the water with the five-to eight-year-old kids. They loved it when I tossed them from my knees over my head into the deeper waters. Most of them could swim to stay afloat by either using the doggy paddle, breaststroke, or a mangled crawl. Occasionally I threw a kid behind into the dark blue, and they would sink. Nothing too worrisome. I would just strut over, reach down, pull them up, and bring them over to where their feet could touch. What always surprised me was how they wanted to be tossed again. Brave? Foolish souls? I couldn't decide.

Another week went by, then came the day before we were all to go to the Club de Bote for the party. I awoke, gasping for air. It was as though I'd been holding my breath. Taking in big gulps of air, I soon calmed down, but then an eerie, perplexing wave of fear crept in, feeling like a cold fog sneaking through my veins. I'm not sure the cause of what I deemed a panic attack. I had no recollection of dreaming. But I must have been. The taste in my mouth, bitter. Sipping on the water I had by my bed, I turned to look at Harry.

Although dark, I could usually make out the form of his body. And if I quieted my heart and breath, I could hear his. But he wasn't there. Turning my flashlight on, I threw the beam over his bed and to his corner of stuff. Was he dressing? No, he's gone off somewhere, which I found strange. He had been in the room last night. We had played cards and bickered over a rule that allowed for a second chance; he wanted one, but I didn't because I didn't need it that night. It put him in a foul mood, and he went to bed shortly after our disagreement. But then, I think he had begun the night ill-tempered because he wasn't laughing a lot, and Harry was the type of person who laughed easily.

Since he never got up before me, the only explanation was that he didn't feel well. I quickly got up, dressed, and went downstairs to see if he was in the bathroom. He wasn't there. I shrugged, let it go, and went into the nursery to take the kids out of their cribs. He was a man of mystery.

While showering the kids, Mouse ate some soap and threw up. Albert declared flowers were evil because one had pricked him. He got over it. Penelope and Bernard had decided they preferred being naked to wearing clothes. We finally got them dressed.

When Hamit came into the dormitorio to tell us the morning news, we smiled. His comical reporting and cynical nature made him funny. This morning he looked unhappy, which made us feel unhappy too. He had crumbs on his chin, and a white film on his lips as though he had been eating toothpaste. He looked frumpier than usual. The handle on his neon pink lady coffee mug had broken off. He belched waving the efflume away as though an annoying bug. Standing with the sun to his back, his cowlick looked like feathers, and his wide girth flat, like a wilted sheet.

"The rainy season's here. And the moon will be full *toomorra.* Rabbit Moon," he announced, slurping his coffee, then looking up into the sky as though the radio waves were speaking to him. His dejected mood ruining the godly effect. He let his arms drop with a thump to his side. His attempts at smiling fake. He had all of our attention.

I had been reading *The Gashlycrumb Tinies* to Bernarda and Penelope. Looking at Hamit, I mumbled, "H is for Hamit hoodwinked by hooligans."

"Yup, rained last night. And that's about right—a full moon—making my bug bites itch. What again is a Rabbit Moon? Never mind, I don't care," Gunther remarked, standing by a wall fiddling with his nose. "What else you got?"

Hamit puckered out his lower lip while playing with the broken edges of his mug and said, "Guerrillas blew up the utilities north of here. And—and my wife is leaving—to go live with her sister in *Houndurass.*"

Since no one liked Hamit's wife there wasn't any remorse in the room, except exuded by Hamit. Then someone whispered, "Good riddance." She liked to try to get me to carry her things around, especially this one beaten-up piece of luggage. I supposed she was always looking for an escape route.

Hamit babbled on about heading out for a few days to wipe the "stench of despair away" in *Puerto Punto* along *La Callejón de Putas.* It was a whore town. The streets were lined with kiosks filled with made-up ladies wearing spandex and stiletto heels—very inappropriate footwear because the streets were often muddy. No one discouraged him. He looked like the kind of guy that had to pay for it. Quite a few of us felt bad for him. During breakfast, he became a topic of conversation, "Poor *'amit,*" Golly said, slopping up her rice and beans with pieces of tortilla. Only Alex and Jack seemed to think he was a lucky guy.

At snack time, we had another unforeseeable occurrence. Alex and Milla were in their house, the oficina. The door was open. They were naked and arguing. It was very wrong of them to have the door open because we could see them clearly: white skin pocked with bug bites and thick, black pubic hair that was much too long. They were yelling at each other in their native tongues. "An argument truly going nowhere," Gunther had commented. Molly went over and shut the door, but not before a backpack went flying out.

Milla was leaving too.

"Oh, good. I get my drinking buddy back," Gunther remarked while staring at the fuming Alex standing in the oficina's doorway. Lips swallowed up by anger, he was giving Milla the finger. She was dressing in front of everyone. Once she slipped her sandals on, she ran off to the dock to wave down a water taxi since Manolo wasn't around. Not even a goodbye.

"Rude," Molly said.

"Their scene was rude," Catarina said.

"Speaking of rude—there goes Alex's good mood," I said, flicking a beetle off my arm. He had been almost pleasant since she arrived.

The worst of the day happened during afternoon playtime. I missed my nap because Albert had quietly slipped away from the group. He went into the trees to the south side of the dock. But before doing so, he had looked around the way a person does when they don't want anybody following them. I was sure he was going to get one of his sweet-smelling red and purple flowers. I had had my eye on him for weeks just waiting for this moment, and his covert turn of the head was my cue to move. Forcing myself up off the ground, with stealth, I maneuvered my way toward the dock, hiding behind thickets and trees. The river bristling with sunshine caught my attention for a brief moment. Continuing in a hunched, serpentine walk, I reached the dock. Standing upright near the edge of the mangroves Albert had walked into, I could see him. He was several yards away studying two large, brown birds that were picking at something.

I walked a few feet across the thick roots of the mangrove trees. A waft of soupy, fouled air struck me. It was the smell of a rotting animal. I put my shirt up over my mouth and nose, and said, "Albert, *venga*." He needed to get away from whatever it was.

Albert looked over at me, then back to the birds. A blackbird with a red-striped beak joined them. I walked nearer. "Albert, *por favor*." But whatever it was, fascinated him. His arms by his side, his hands were bent and reaching out, his mouth edged open. He was wearing bright plaid shorts and a striped, collared Guess shirt, and his hair was slicked back. An impressive looking little boy.

One of the brown birds hopped up and jumped onto the dead thing. Its head bounced up. It was a small skull with sunken eyes and a jaw with several long, oily teeth. The face was half-eaten and had chunks of hair and skin hanging from it. "Dammit, Albert!" I was angry that he wouldn't listen as danger seemed imminent and present.

Squinting, with my hand over my nose and mouth, I saw it was a dead monkey. And then it occurred to me that Albert couldn't move. He was stuck in place, frozen by the vileness of the image. Making my way over the thick roots, gagging with every breath, I reached Albert, picked him up, and carried him back to the group. He was surprisingly quiet when I put him down. He stayed by my side for the rest of the afternoon. It was the first time he ever wanted to be by anyone. He was a loner, who occasionally played with Wooter. Most of the time he wandered searching for pretty flowers by himself.

Chapter 27

Doc

The day of the party everyone: staff, kids, niñeros, workmen, the birds, and the bugs, all seemed out of sorts like a catastrophic storm was brewing on the horizon, and we had neglected to batten down the shutters. The party had us all buzzing, but I felt it was something else, something beyond the excitement of tasty, free food and booze. To the unobservant or unfamiliar eye, not a hair looked out of place. I couldn't help but think, whatever was amiss, was in us, hiding—and it would not take much to unleash it.

Harry still hadn't come back, but that wasn't unusual according to my source, Catarina. She said he often disappeared. It had me chewing on the side of my mouth and pouting. I had imagined us together, eating and drinking at the club similar to a date. Then it occurred to me that he may have disappeared to fetch his fiancé, to take her to the party. This realization crushed my fanciful dream, and now I didn't want to go.

"But you have to. If you don't, you'll feel left out because we will tell stories about the scrummy food forever," Gunther said, poking me. Then nudging. Then trying to hug me.

"Eleanor—earth to Eleanor." I looked over at Doc. She was waving me over. It was mid-morning during snack time, and I was helping her with her rounds. Her malaria, dormant, she had been walking up to the main compound periodically from the clínica to inspect the kids for lice, worms, and overall health. Usually, Catarina or Alex helped her, but Catarina had gone into El Pueblito with The Scott to buy a non-gunked up shirt and wouldn't be back until after lunch. Alex, after Milla had left, went down to the clínica, and volunteered to help Doc as he needed something to do with his free time. She deputized him as her assistant, which made him responsible for cleaning up spit cups and bloody snot-gauze and keeping the place in order when she wasn't there. Golly, Molly, and I felt it was an excellent distraction for him. He had become *kuddelmuddel* and didn't want to be *kummerspeck*. After Milla's water taxi swept her away, we all felt too, that what he really was, was a giant *pendejo* because he couldn't stop with the insults, such as "*Backpfeifengesicht* and *weichei*." According to Golly, who somehow knew German, or at least claimed to know German, Alex was calling us slappable idiots. To counter, she called him a "*James Blunt*." A cockney slang that caused her and Molly to giggle.

Now in the quad with all twenty-four kids. They were talking and drinking their green drink while waiting for their turn to see Doc. They were used to the inspections. Some even made up maladies just for attention. Doc was good with them. She would pat the ones with the dramatized symptoms on the head and say, "All better now," even though she did nothing except touch them. Often that was all they needed.

"*Dhat* dead monkey *be* more likely to produce salmonella or trichinosis, not cholera," Doc clarified for me. "The toxigenic bacterium serogroup *Vibrio cholerae* has contaminated *dah* river," she continued as she meandered, stopping at each child with me at her heels. "But it *be* farther up where the population is dense and many of the outhouses are directly over *dah* water. The river runs north, *thanx* god." Glancing at me, she paused for a moment, then looked away to rustle through her worn, leather bag that I was holding. She pulled out a brown bottle of deworming medicine, mebendazole. The bottle had a skull with crossbones; beneath the warning label it read, "Candy-flavored."

"*Mon*, cholera is a diarrheal illness caused by infection of *dah* intestine." She continued to prattle on as though talking about a warm summer breeze. She pulled on kids' ears, put drops on their tongues, and shuffled through their hair looking for lice.

"It *be* a horrible death. It's like your body is melting and coming out your ass. Some people have just mild symptoms, but most have *dah* blue skin, sunken eyes, lots of watery diarrhea, vomiting, and leg cramps. Rapid loss of body fluids causes dehydration and shock. Without treatment, death can occur within hours. We had one case here a couple of months ago. Make sure you drink from *dah* left tank, not *dah* right."

I looked over at the water tanks; I had been drinking from the right tank because it tasted better. "Maybe the tanks should be marked," I commented.

"Threadworms, hookworms, tapeworms, roundworms," she said, ignoring my comment. The nasty worm names sounded like a grocery list. "The kids *dayh* eat the dirt, *dayh* drink the river water when *dayh* swim, *dayh* poop in their bedding, which is washed with cold water, not hot. These worms are everywhere. We can never really rid them of the parasites because *dayh* constantly re-infect themselves. It's what makes *dayh* stomachs puffy."

Most of the kids had the type of stomach seen on thin, old men who drank too much beer. I had thought their round bellies were due to them being kids. Malnutrition had occurred to me, but they were well fed. So, it was worms.

Standing next to her with her bag cradled in my arms, I couldn't help but wonder about my gastrointestinal tract and the ugly possibilities of what might be there. "What about us? The adults?"

"It's *dah* principal reason why life expectancy on *dah* river is only forty years. Worms don't kill immediately. It's a slow death. Do you bite your nails?"

When she said this, I was in mid-bite.

"Well, don't."

In her bag, she also had some fizzy tablets for giardia, paregoric for diarrhea, cream for scabies, and a bottle of Pedialyte for cholera. By a warped-looking mahogany tree, she had placed a giant bottle of lice prevention shampoo. At swim time today, she told us to shampoo the kids' hair with the stuff.

Dabbing Charlotte's bug bites with Tiger Balm, Doc sighed. "The jungle is a tough place to raise kids, but also a fun place. *Dayh* swim, *dayh* play. *Buiti*—all good."

I dug my fingernails into my scalp because it itched, and then I handed her the bottle of mebendazole. She put a couple of drops on Charlotte's extended tongue. Charlotte smacked her lips and made an 'Umm' noise.

Then out of the blue Doc asked, "How's living with Harry?"

Not giving me time to answer, she continued. "Harry's smooth, you know. A real Casanova. Watch yourself." Her melodious accent had an edge to it. I wondered if she liked him, but then she was with Cadmael. Or so I assumed.

She leaned down and sifted through El Gordo's thick, black hair. "*Mon*, he got loads of them eating away at his scalp."

She cupped his cheeks in her hands and cooed, "My poor baby. We'll wash your hair good and clean today."

"He's got a fiancé," I said, taking the empty bottle of worm killer out of her hand and giving her a new one.

"Harry has a fiancé?"

"Yeah," I said staring at the bottle of lice shampoo thinking I would like to use it today too.

"*Yah*, he does," she said, smiling without showing teeth.

"So, that's that," I said, staring at her back, feeling depressed over the reality of it.

Doc was crouched down, looking at a cut on Frankie's right pinky. "Just a scratch," she said. He then stuck out his tongue, and she gave him a few candied drops. "He likes the stuff," she mused.

"They burned the dead monkey," I said, changing the subject.

"Good thing."

A few clouds had moved in, blocking the sun, and the birds momentarily stopped singing. The small voices of the kids chatting, broken up by laughter, became louder, then quieted down too. Finishing up, Doc turned toward me, standing very close. Her heavy-lidded eyes moved slyly around and latched onto mine. Reaching over, she pinched my arm hard. I flinched. She had long nails and had pierced the skin.

"Oh, sorry, you had a bug, but I got your skin," she said, the corners of her mouth turned up into a smile.

I didn't buy her line. Staring at her for a few minutes trying to think what might have come over her, blood dripping down from the cut, I handed her back her bag and walked over to the dormitorio. I needed a Band-Aid. One of my own Band-Aids from my own kit, not from hers.

The dormitorio was free of people and silent. A light fluttering of leaves from a jacaranda tree brushed the screens of the far windows. Warm air blew in lazily, flapping the pages of the books that were open and lying on the great room's floor. It was calming, and my anger subsided, but not my disbelief.

Walking into my room, I saw Harry sitting on the floor by his bed. My first reaction, to run over and hug him. But I went with the second thought. "Harry, where have you been?" I said matter-of-factly and went over to my backpack. Then because he said nothing back, I added, "Did you hear about the monkey?" He let me reiterate the events that had taken place in the past few days without interrupting. Talking and digging into my bag, I finally found some Bacitracin and a Band-Aid and doctored my cut. I was happy to be talking to him again. But he stopped me when I ragged on Doc.

"She did what?"

I walked over and showed him the growing blue bruise and the small, but deep slice. That's when I noticed Harry was filthy. There was dirt all over his clothing, and his bare feet were chafed and smeared with mud. Glancing up at his face, I saw that he had a puffy, red lump on the left side of his forehead. His hair was out of sorts and wet, his blue eyes the color of gray, his olive skin pasty.

"Mangroves can be tricky," he said, his tone fragile, something new in his repertoire of emotions. But then he laughed, grabbed my hand, and asked me to get a pot of boiling water from Esmeralda. He wanted to boil the germs out of his damaged forehead.

"What happened, Harry?" I asked, adding. "Which mangroves?"

"I—don't——can't. Not now. Please, just get me some water." I did what he said. He was a mess, and it tore at my heart.

I went to the back kitchen of the Cafeteria to avoid Doc. She was still in the quad. Molly had her bag in her arms. I could hear them chatting about the kids. Esmeralda was happy to boil water for Harry. She grumbled at me, along with shooting a suspicious glance. She also pushed the knives out of my reach. Whatever, I thought. Walking back into the dormitorio with the hot water, I could hear Harry singing in the shower. The song had a lovely, sonorous tune; he was singing in Spanish. It was a song about mountains and love. Heading toward the melody, I hummed the tune. My mood buoyant and my gait light. In the bathroom, the humid air was flushed with the scent of minty soap. He was in the second stall, naked and all lathered with foam. I had seen Harry naked in glimpses as he slept. I rarely saw him dress, and when I did, he was shy and turned away from me as I looked the other way too. We always tried to be respectful of each other's space, but we lived together, which made it difficult. As it went, privacy was impossible at the orphanage. Since the kids showered in the morning, we all had to shower later. There weren't any curtains. We all had seen each other naked washing. We all had seen each other on the toilet. We talked to each other about our day sitting on the toilet and in the shower. The kids came in while we were sitting on the toilet. They were always curious if we were peeing or pooping. It was all very natural and open. It would have been impossible to have it any other way.

"Harry, you have a lovely singing voice," I said, adding, "I'll leave the pot on the counter by the sinks."

"Thank you," he said, then blurted out. "Wait! I want to tell you something."

I leaned up against the wall by the sinks and waited. He finally came over with a terry cloth towel wrapped around his waist. He looked scrubbed and healthy, although the knock on his head was an awful color of red, blue, and purple. I could see scratches on his legs and arms too. I handed him the cloth I had gotten from Esmeralda for him. Then leaned back again and waited for him to speak. He had a minty scent emanating from his tan, firm body, and the small, curly black hairs on his chest were pleasant to look at. In silence, I watched him dip the cloth into the pot and place it on his forehead.

"While I was in the shower, I was thinking about everything that's been happening here. You know, about the excessive gossiping and people seeming itchy for some excitement. And the monkey, and Hamit's wife, and Milla leaving. Now, don't think I'm foolish." Harry said, wincing when he pressed too hard on the gash on his forehead.

"A little late for that," I teased.

"It's the moon," he said, glancing at me briefly to catch my reaction.

"It's always the moon," I said. Then sighing, I added. "Hamit said it's your Rabbit Moon tonight."

"Not my moon, but yup, the Rabbit Moon begins tonight," He said.

"I guess it has to do with fertility. Mayan."

"Fertility. No, that's not it. The locals were discussing it this week," he said, continuing, "I don't think much about hocus pocus, but I had a terrible morning and the week has been nothing to brag about either. And, well, I think this moon is making everything worse. According to the locals—"

"—According to legend," I laughed, adding. "Is this going to be a creepy campfire story?"

He laughed too. It made me smile to see him happy. Not thinking, I blurted out, "I love the way you laugh, Harry."

This caused him to pause and study my face for a moment,

then he smiled and said, "Thank you, but you still have to listen to my boogie-moon tale. Now the locals in El Pueblito said—this moon—this Rabbit Moon, so craven and disastrous; so disruptive and insane that darkness will fall upon those who have fallen into bad ways."

"Is that you, Harry?" I interrupted.

"No, now listen. No one's safe. It's mischievous and mean. Aapo is leaving to go protect his relatives in the north. It's got everyone jumpy."

I laughed. "I'm not jumpy."

"The words of the locals," he remarked.

"I know," I said, chuckling, then added. "This seems so unlike you. They're so many moons. So many to choose from: Wolf moons, Super moons, Blue moons, Pink moons, Harvest moons, Half-moons, now Rabbit moons. Rabbits and moons—makes a good title for a children's book."

Laughing again, he said, "Well, this children's book isn't cute, more like a Brothers Grimm fairy tale. When the moon appears tonight, it will unleash tiny little rabbits, if it hasn't already. These rabbits will run around the earth, causing chaos for a month."

"Wonderful. I don't suppose the rabbits have names like Frankie, Penelope, Wooter—" I said laughing again.

"—Sounds about right."

We both then quieted our silliness. Looking me in the eye, I looked back at him. We just stood there in silence for a few moments, listening to the rustling of the trees. He leaned in and gently drew my pinched arm toward him. Then taking my hand into his, he held it tenderly, weaving his fingers into mine. I let him do this. I had missed him the way a flower would miss its petals and the ocean its water. From some inner sounding board, from the look in his eye, the tone of his voice, he missed me too. He kept looking at me as though I might leave. Checking to see if I was still there.

"Are you going to the party at the club tonight?" He asked still holding my hand, but when I didn't answer him immediately, he lightly squeezed my fingers, played with the palm of my hand, and released it. Yet, kept his gaze on me for a few more seconds waiting, waiting for an answer.

Leaning coyly against the wall, I watched him wring out the cloth and dip it once again into the hot water. Studying him, I wondered who this Harry Van Cleef really was? The answer not simple, possibly unobtainable. I finally said, "Wouldn't miss it." Yes, I was going to go. It seemed absurd not to. But there was something different about Harry this bright, sunny morning. It was the first time he had held my hand during the day. Possibly the bump on his head had caused him to forget he was attached to another. A giddiness rose up inside of me as the thought of a date, a quasi-date, but a date with Harry, a reality, and I smiled. But unlike Ulysses and his sirens, I didn't have a rope—

"—Good—good," he said, his demeanor appearing more upbeat. "The owners do this every so often. I think it makes them feel better since they usually cater to the rich."

As he spoke, Bernarda, Charlotte, and Penelope came into the bathroom and wrapped their arms around my legs. Hugging me, they asked if I would come to help them with the fort we were building in the great room. We had been working on it forever because it was always being wrecked by too much roughhousing. We had gotten the cardboard from the shipment of cabbage that had come in eons ago.

I left with the girls. Harry began singing again, the same beautiful tune. I thought about the Mayan's and their Rabbit moon and an entire month of devastation. Then chuckled. The Mayans had many gods with undesirable characters that ate up crops and made life miserable. The Rabbit moon was another one of their tales to explain bad-behaving people by making them into naughty rabbits. Then looking out the window, I saw everyone had left the quad. It occurred to me that after snack time, the kids went back to school. Ruffling Charlotte's hair and looking at all three of them, I said, "Sly *pequeñas conejas*? You're supposed to be in school."

They smiled, twisting their bodies around into knots. Then followed me out the door and down to the schoolhouse.

Chapter 28

The Moon

Henrik, who had been sick most of the day, had thrown up on me three times. I'd tossed almost all of my clothing outside in a bin to be washed. Beside the trashy Tinker Bell shirt, nothing else was clean. It was a dilemma. I wanted to look better than I normally did for the party. An impossible feat, I thought. What a shame. My hair, smelly, was a clotted-up mess.

The laundry ladies, barely five feet tall and almost as wide, were the babysitters. Their arrival allowed us to get ready for the party, spiff ourselves up. The best I could do was take a shower, and if she didn't mind, borrow some clothes from Catarina. Clinging to me, because of his health, I handed Henrik over to the babysitters when they walked in. He made a weak crying noise, then dropped the idea and smiled at the high-breasted woman that held him. With gusto, I ran toward the bathroom.

Catarina, who disliked showering on The Scott's boat because the head smelled like dead mice and there was no room to turn around in the shower, was already soaping up. I jumped into the stall next to her. The cold water was always an issue at first, for everyone. In the mornings we had to fool the kids to get them to shower. We did this by having a group of seven or eight children step into a stall, then turned the water on. They would wail and stamp their feet. Some might say this was cruel, but they wouldn't get in if the water was on. There were always a few attempts to bolt. We met this rebellion by blocking the exit with our bodies and arms. Trapped under the cold spray, the briskness eventually turning tepid and enjoyable. Their transition from horrified to contentment was visible in their faces. Lots of smiles and laughter. When we handed them washcloths and soap, they giggled, splashing their feet in the puddled water. They liked to wash the stall walls and each other. When it came time to get them out, we had to turn the water off. This was just as upsetting as turning it on, but otherwise, they would have stayed. We had a routine to follow.

"These kids and their lice," Catarina muttered. We were both using the delousing shampoo. The warning label said overuse could cause neurological damage.

"I wonder if it's better to just be bald," I replied. The shampoo smelled like cookie dough, which, mixed with the throw-up effluvium, was nauseating. "Did you bring your Dr. Bronner's Lavender with you?"

"Here." She reached around and handed it to me. Her nails filed and polished.

"Fuchsia, nice," I commented.

"I want you to check my hair," Catarina said. Standing in front of me naked, she bent down so I could see her hair and scalp. The bad lighting made her strawberry blonde hair blur into a mesh of tangles. I saw a few twitching things that looked like tiny pieces of paper. "You might want to use the nit comb," I said.

"I've got them?"

"I don't know. Maybe."

Dismissing the inconvenience of having "freeloaders" in her hair as part of jungle living, we went back upstairs. She lent me a billowy white cotton blouse speckled with pink roses and green leaves, and she gave me a pair of blue jeans she said she didn't like. For herself, she put on a floor-length sundress and motored off to The Scott's boat. She was all full of bubbles and lustful thoughts, and kept saying the word "yummy;" I was sure if The Scott cared for her as much as she cared for him, a couple of hungry lice would be of little consequence.

Outside in the quad, under the rays of the cafeteria floodlight, the group waited. We all looked touched up, but that was all. Sarah had on an adult size Lilly Pulitzer sundress that had ended up in a delivery of clothing for the kids. With her flat, short hair pulled off her face by a bumblebee clip, her thin, shapeless body standing motionless, and eyes bouncing along the ground looking for bugs, she was a larger version of our children. Her knees were dirty, too, because she had been looking for dung beetles earlier in the day. Jack had pants on, khakis with a frayed hem. They were too big around the waist. He was using a purple bandana as a belt. His shirt was missing a button, but his hair was combed. We all thought he may have washed it. Alex had the same thin pair of striped balloon pants on that let his penis wobble across his upper thighs. He swore they were new. He had braided his flaming red hair instead of tying it in a knot on top of his head. The braids made him look like a spooked girl, though this was more due to his pinprick, black eyes.

Gunther looked rosy, but that was because the sun had burned his cheeks earlier in the day. He was wearing his hair in pigtails instead of pom-poms, but no one could see the difference. Molly and Golly had on matching yellow and orange floral dresses that buttoned down their fronts; the orange matched their hair. They must have gained weight since buying the dresses because the strained buttons exposed lumps of white, bulging flesh around their midriffs and heavy, freckled cleavage. All it would take was one button to pop, and everything would burst out. As for myself? The borrowed blouse was more like a short dress, the blue jeans more like blue leggings, they were tight, but the material being stretchy, made them comfortable. I felt different in the clothes. Somewhat more sophisticated, even fashionable since everything I had was threadbare and loose. My hair was clean, fluffy, and heavy. I had rolled it into a French knot and secured it with a stick.

We walked down to the dock where Manolo was waiting for us with the launch. We were seven people who most likely back in our hometowns would have had nothing to do with each other. But with ease, we made light chatter about the children and the day, then squabbled over seating and foot placement when we got into the launch. I ended up sitting in between Molly and Golly, which was not my first choice. But because one of my flip-flops' toeholds had snapped, delaying me, I lost the seat by Gunther to Alex. Sitting in between the girls was like being squashed between two sweaty cushions. Leaning forward, resting my elbows on my knees, allowed me to breathe. The two of them used my back as an armrest.

Kicking the launch into gear, Manolo headed swiftly across the river. Spray spit up into our faces, and the multicolored lights emanating from the club drew us in like a beacon of civility. I noticed The Scott's boat was dark except for a lone light over the bulkhead. One of Catarina's skirts was hanging from the boom, drying. Then I looked at the moon. It was full and bright, a giant sphere of marigolds and apricots. Resting mere inches above the rainforest canopy, its magnetic powers alluring.

"Heaven's best jewel," Gunther said. Then added with a snicker, "Does anyone see the big rabbit ears?"

We had been talking about the Mayan myth earlier in the day and decided anything that went wrong we would blame on the Rabbit moon and the unleashing of the little rabbits. At least for a month. Then we realized we might not know when the month was up, so Molly put a notch on one of the wooden sides of the cubbyholes, declaring, "Day one." We found the solution very satisfying and, once again, proud of our resourcefulness.

"I see its' sniffing nose and unblinking eyes," Jack mused.

"*Ew*, it's looking right at us. Bad rabbit. Go away." Golly fussed, waving her fist at it while digging her resting elbow into my back.

Haphazardly listening to my cohorts, I found myself glued to the moon. Whether it was because of its rich colors or a desire to see something fantastical, I saw the image of a giant hare sitting with its legs crossed, smoking a cigar, and he or she was staring right at me. It was smiling a devilish grin, as though to say, "I've got you now. Just try to escape." I knew it couldn't be real. I was hungry. For the second day in a row, I'd missed my nap by the dugout canoes. Henrik being ill; the day before it was Albert and the monkey. Possibly I was hallucinating. But when I blinked, the image didn't go away. Sitting up, I poked Gunther's back as he was sitting in front of me, and said, "That damn rabbit is up there."

"Gone daffy on us. Well, nothing a good drink can't cure," he remarked, tweaking my chin. Then he turned back around. The engine cut out; we were gliding into the club's dock.

Standing up, once again we all fussed with each other about who would get out first and shouldn't someone grab the rope and why wasn't the dock higher. Golly and Molly both ripped a hole in a back seam. They didn't care. We didn't care. I was also told by Manolo, in a sharp tone, that if I didn't take my broken flipflops with me, I wouldn't be allowed back in the boat.

Chapter 29

The Party

It was a party for the club's boaters too. I overheard someone say they had to pay to attend. Tall and skinny, fat and round, cocktail guzzlers full of high-seas hyperbole, the air was thick with smoke and gin. The crowd, already drunk, waved cigarettes and spilled their drinks when they spoke. It was apparent they spent too much time in the sun; unhealthy complexions, wrinkled, and red. This group of outsiders gave us pause at the entrance. The outside world of money and small talk seemed deformed and unfamiliar. Letting our eyes dance around the room, we caught sight of the buffet table. My jaw dropped, my eyes widened, I said, "We've gone to heaven." A whole pig, grouper, potato salad, slabs of beef, ribs, sandwiches, tamales, pizza, soup, bread, watermelon, even asparagus, we became like bumper cars and pushed and shoved our way through the crowd, tactless and determined.

Hearing Catarina shout my name, I stopped inches away from a ham and cheese sandwich and glanced around. She was at the bar with whom I assumed to be her man. She had one arm around his neck and was waving to me with the other. He was a handsome fellow with thinning hair and an angled, rugged face. When he placed his hat on, a beige fedora that he pulled down to dip over his left eye; eyes the color of a coral blue sea and as penetrating as daggers, I stepped back, appalled. According to the paper *las Noticias*, his name wasn't The Scott, but Dan Scotchwick and he was from Indiana, USA. I remembered these details because the killing of Yenara Pinola Alvares' grandson had taken place in El Puente, a town I had grown familiar with. I thought of my conversation with Hamit, so long ago. "*Ceeement* blocks float," he had said. I was sure the body he had mentioned floating into the mangroves was Alvares' grandson. Fumbling with my footing, not knowing whether to walk over or not, I waved back and smiled.

"Come say hello!" Catarina shouted, waving. And now, Dan Scotchwick was waving me over too.

"I want to eat! I'll come over later!" I picked up the ham sandwich and took a bite. I couldn't help but wonder why someone hadn't taken him out. How could he be here again without being killed? Families sought revenge for their loved ones in these parts, and with impunity. Grabbing a plate to put the ham sandwich on it, I went down the line of food, piling big chunks of everything onto the plate. I figured Mr. Scotchwick, the murderer, didn't recognize me. Over the din, a male voice shouted my name. It was gruff, filled with booze and smoke. Looking over at Scotchwick, I saw he was insisting I join them with his coral blues. Again, I shouted, "I want to eat! I'll come over later!" They were drinking and looked half in the bag. I figured they'd be blind drunk soon and forget about me, or at least hoped.

Golly was sitting at a back table with a mound of food in front of her. Beside her was Hamit, and saddled up beside him was a boxy, big-eyed woman. She looked worn out and had too much makeup on and wore spandex that was too small for her busty figure. I gathered she was a souvenir from his trip to *la callejón de putas*. I joined them. Hamit made introductions. Her name was Matilda. Every time Hamit squeezed her thick waist, which was often, she laughed, showing a mouth missing two front teeth and back molars encased in gold. Hamit, who was sweating in his leisure suit, kept leaning in to smell her hair and neck until they finally got up and left. They were staying at the club. Hamit wasn't sure if he wanted to come back to the orphanage—"too many memories," he had said. I thought they made a pleasant couple. But before they walked away, I asked, "Who's going to teach the kids English?"

"One of the hag dorm biddies," he growled.

"They don't speak English."

"You don't have to."

"What about the news?" I blurted.

"Easy, never changes."

"Yes, it does. It's raining. It didn't rain when I first got here."

"Rain and hot. Hot and rain. No big *dif*—"

So that was that—no big *dif*. But I was going to miss our morning news briefs. Golly thought it was better he left, "*Hee* a bit *David*."

"What?"

"Crazy."

When the waiter came by, I ordered a fruit punch and so did Golly. We ate in silence. I ate most of the sandwich, then went on to the pizza, ribs, fish, salad, and mushroom caps until there were only a few bites of tamale left. My drink now placed in front of me was a bright orange-red concoction with an umbrella. I drank the whole thing and ordered another. It was sweet, like having dessert. Then, for better comfort, I undid the buttons at my waist. Leaning back, the chair against the rail, stuffed and relaxed, I played with the umbrella in my half-empty glass and looked around wondering where Harry might be. He was late. It also bothered me that he was friends with Dan Scotchwick. I was hoping there would be a reasonable explanation. But then if there wasn't one? Did I care? I wasn't sure.

To my left, two tables away, I caught sight of Molly and Gunther sitting almost on top of each other. Molly was feeding Gunther with her fingers. She would dip a piece of something into his mouth and rapidly pull it away before he could get a bite. Until finally she would let him eat it.

"That's disturbing," I said to Golly.

"She's besotted with him," Golly said, giggling while putting her putty fingers over her tittering, red mouth.

"Golly, you have lipstick on."

"Found it in me pocket," she giggled.

"What's so funny?" She wouldn't stop giggling. "Golly, how can you be drunk already? You just got here."

"I *don' 'old* me liquor well," she said, breaking out into a hyena-hysteria, then snorting.

Out of the crowd, Doc swayed toward us with a plate of food and a drink. She sat down with a thud, spilling a little of everything. I hadn't spoken to her since she pinched me.

"Sorry," she said, her jaw slack. "I *dint* mean it. *Dah* bug I killed on your arm. I hurt you." Wearing a tight yellow shirt, which accentuated her large breasts and small waist, she looked like a poster pinup slated for a male locker room. Even with her drooling drunk mouth and lopsided eyes, she was a babe. Sitting next to her, I felt like a child, or more like my body had forgotten it was supposed to be female. "Sorry I hurt you," she slurred, again and again, then leaned in and kissed me on the cheek, hugging and smothering me into her flesh and exhaling stale, boozy breath.

"It's okay," I said, pushing her away. She started eating but didn't seem to get much food into her mouth. Her ability to chew was off balance. Frustrated, she slid her head down on top of her breasts and went to sleep.

"Doc been here all afternoon," Golly said, still giggling.

"I can tell."

I belched and immediately felt better, so I put the last few pieces of the tamale into my mouth. I realized I was eating for taste more than need. Crunching down on the food, I tongued something hard and undesirable in the tamale and immediately spat it out over the railing, into the water. Golly and I watched in silence as giant carp rose up from the murky depths with puckering mouths. They fought unmercifully over the small morsel. Once devoured, they slunk back into the deep, tails first, their eyes staring at us as they disappeared.

"Don't *wanna* fall in *'ere*. Stodgy fish— may *ea'* me. Yoo-hoo... Yoo-hoo, look at *meee*!" Golly shouted, waving to the fish, and snorting so hard she forced mucus out of her nose. Then calming herself, she began stuffing a ham and cheese sandwich into her mouth.

"You know, Golly," I said, watching her. "When you travel, you represent your country."

Swallowing her food, she looked at me and said, "Yeah, Americans are a bunch of Neanderthal cunts." Then burst into a fresh round of giggles and snorts while trying to take another bite of the sandwich. I was shocked by how clearly, she pronounced "Neanderthal."

Wiping my mouth, I took a long swig off of Doc's fruity

drink since mine was empty and Doc was snoring. Her head snuggled on top of her breasts, her plate of food pushed aside, she looked at peace. It occurred to me to pinch her, but what if she woke up? Looking at Golly, I gave her a deadpan stare and let out a burp that turned a few heads. It was one of those belches that came from down deep in the belly and felt great. And as not to seem unrefined to the aghast stares of the boaters and boozers, I pointed at Golly. Golly began swallowing air to retaliate. When she finally burped, it was a tiny little hiccup, but she grinned as though it were a masterpiece. Picking up one of Doc's chips, I dipped it into the guacamole on her plate, crunched down on it, and chewed extra loudly, exposing the masticated food. Golly took the chips and began chewing loudly with her mouth open. Tired of eating, we tossed a few chips into the water and waited for the carp to reappear. They came in wiggling their tails and nabbed the food. We threw a few more pieces at them. They ate and left. Golly and I belched again. Then boredom set in. Sitting back, we looked over the crowd.

"He looks lonely," Golly said, nodding toward Alex who was sitting at the bar downing shots of rum. She rose to join him, knocking her chair over. Her dress bunched, was stuck in the crack of her bottom, and I noticed the seam on her left shoulder displayed another tear. Golly took unsteady steps over to Alex. At her arrival, she poked him on the shoulder. He looked delighted to see her and put his hand on her rump. Golly showed her appreciation by wiggling her rear around in snug circles. When did they start getting along? I wondered.

Remaining in the seat by the railing with Doc snoring beside me, I felt like I had been stood up. Disappointed? Or was it more like disenchanted? I ordered another punch. Harry had said he would be here, but he wasn't. Through the haze of smoke and bodies, I could see Catarina and her man, Danny boy the killer, smooching at the bar. Gunther and Molly were still playing games with their food. Gunther nibbling and biting at the air as Molly teased him with pieces of pizza. Golly and Alex had disappeared somewhere. The image of Golly making out with Alex, nauseating. Finishing my third or was it my fourth drink, I ordered another. The beverage was just the right mixture of sweet and sour; the toxicity bordering on flammable. Glancing across the oily inlet at several Bertrams and a sailboat lined up along the dock by the shore, I gazed for a while at the flames of the tiki torches illuminating it all. Then a man came into view. He was walking toward the sailboat and walked onto it. I watched him take a beverage out of a box on the deck. Standing at the stern of the boat, he lit a cigarette and stood sipping his drink. We made eye contact. Blond, he looked in decent shape and around my age. He waved at me. I waved back. He then waved for me to come over, but I shook my head no.

Interrupting my exchange with the blond, a man standing next to me, introduced himself as Rubin. He sat down at my table without asking. Bald with a pug nose, he owned one of the Bertrams, along with a sesame seed farm in Chile. His friend Enrique joined us too. Enrique had a patch over his eye and a mustache with a slice through the upper right half. The men were older, possibly sixty. Gray and weathered, they smoked cigars and drank Bourbon on the rocks with their pinkies extended. They also salaciously licked the booze off their lips with each sip. Rubin told me, in English, that he and Enrique were vacationing at the club, and that they planned to go fishing. "Would you like to join us?" He asked.

"No, thanks. I'm busy," I said. When another man came over, the men mumbled something to each other, shook my hand, and left. The man that had shooed the men away introduced himself as the Minister of the Interior. I was about to tell him to go talk to The Scott because he was a criminal too, but he was called away by a thin brunette wearing lots of jewelry.

Having imbibed what seemed like a gallon of booze, I got up to go to the bathroom. It was then that I realized I'd overdone the drinking. Drunk but not wanting to appear it, I steadied myself while re-buttoning my pants. The action caused me to sway, but that didn't deter me from picking up my replenished drink from the table. A roady, I thought. A sign by the shore entrance had an arrow pointing to the mainland, and said, '*Banos.*'

Holding the railing, I wobbled down the ramp to the dock. My world was spinning, so I shut one eye. "Bad me," I mumbled to myself, thinking life was going to be hell with the kids tomorrow. I also found the green Christmas lights wrapped around the pilings at the end of the ramp, mesmerizing, and stared at them for a while. Feeling queasy, I was happy to see a water bubbler at the base of the steps going up to the bathroom. Before making the ascent, I stood by the bubbler filling and refilling a Dixie cup over and over again with water. The chatter and laughter from the party were dreamlike and made me want to throw-up. Then another sound appeared, a low moan like someone hurt was trying to speak but couldn't. Queasy more than having to go to the bathroom, I dismissed both, thinking someone might need help. I took a right down the dock that went to the lagoon, the low, rhythmic groan acting like a string, pulling me along.

Chapter 30

The Blond

The dock I was walking along jetted out into the middle of the club's lagoon. With my drink in hand, I reached the end of the dock. Standing under the lights hanging from two pilings, I believed the sound was coming from the shore, across the green, soupy water. Water illuminated by the lights was attracting small and big fish. They were popping up and making splashing sounds. Ignoring them, I tried my best to concentrate on the moaning. As I was at the backside of the club, the forest surrounding the cove was black with only a few shiny leaves flickering in the moonlight. A thick white line glistened down the middle of the river. The scene was beautiful and eerie, and my drunken state added a surrealness to it. Then suddenly life grew dark. A cloud had moved across the moon, and it began to rain, light sprinkles that thickened, then disappeared. "Hamit and his rainy season," I mumbled, adding. "And rain is definitely different than hot." Using my shirt to wipe the raindrops from my face, it did occur to me that I used my shirt to wipe away sweat too.

Watching the cloud gradually float away. I sighed and took a sip of my drink. The moon, having returned, burnished the earth with its ashen colors. I could see a strip of land across from me. It was light gray where it met the dark river. "Hello!" I yelled, thinking I saw movement. There was no response, but the moaning had multiplied, or possibly my drunkenness had enhanced it because it had turned into two low moans. Squinting, but unable at first to believe my eyes, I saw a couple of large, white maggots slithering around on top of each other in the mud under a loping, demented-looking tree. I rubbed my eyes and blinked a few times, but just like the hare staring at me from the moon, nothing changed.

"Gross. Maggots," I mumbled to myself. It was also creepy to think that maggots moaned. On top of it all, the queasiness that had been bothering me was now hitting my upper gut. It was edging toward my esophagus. I breathed in deep, trying to keep it all down while fixated on the slimy movements of the larvae. They were making sucking, muddy sounds coupled with low grunts. It was all fantastically disgusting. Then a maggot laughed. A salient and cuspate chortle. It was Jack. What the—?

Sitting down to help my weakening knees and gurgling stomach, I made out Jack's pointy nose bobbing up and down. His legs erect, his feet leveraged against a rock, he was pounding down hard on the maggot under him whose legs were flapping in the air. I had been wondering where they had gone off to. Yup, sex addicts, I thought, chuckling.

Then, with no more warning, I threw everything up. My dinner came out like a blasting firehose. My entire meal was heaving itself into the river with such tremendous force that I had to hold on to the clapboards as not to fall in. On my knees in the child's pose, staring down at the fish, blurry-eyed, gasping for air, retching sounds echoing, I thought it would never end. When it briefly subsided, it was my turn to moan. I wiped my runny nose and gooey mouth, only to fall forward and vomit the last of the pink, projectile froth into the greedy mouths of the fish. "Dear God!" I said to the sky. Feeling the worst was over, I lay down on my back, the cup of punch upright and full by my head. I closed my eyes and went to sleep.

"*Estás bien*?"

Confused, I snapped my eyes open. A man was staring down at me a few feet away from my face, nose exaggerated, the cheeks pushing his mouth into a puckered circle. I looked him over. It was the blond fellow I had been flirting with earlier. He was lithe, tan, and wore cargo shorts that fit him well. "Thanks, I'm fine," I said, shutting my eyes again and willing him to go away.

"Are there people over there?" He asked. Opening my eyes, I saw he was standing straight, his nose in the air, looking off toward the muddy beach.

"Maggots," I said, sitting up, my head throbbing. Taking a sip of my drink helped. It also washed away the hideous taste I had in my mouth.

Glancing up at the blond, I watched his expression as he was trying to make out what was going on in the mud. Chuckling, he said, "That's not very sanitary."

I laughed.

"Spank me again! Harder!" It was Jack's voice. A resounding slap, then another—slap-slap-slap.

"That's new," I commented.

The blond gave me his hand to help me up, and I took it. I was better, much better, but possibly still a little drunk.

"You do realize feeding the wildlife isn't a good idea," he teased, looking down at the water.

"Funny... American?" I could tell my words weren't coming

out as smoothly as I wished.

"Canadian—Halifax."

"Nev—never been. I was on my way to the bath—room," I said, picking the hair off my clammy, damp face. I smelled of booze and soaked garbage and wondered if I would throw-up again, but then thought not.

"The club dumps their sewage in this lagoon," he said.

"That's *groooss*," I replied, shaking my head, but stopped because the movement was making it hurt.

He waved his hand for me to follow him. His steps, however, were too energetic and long for me. Stopping, he turned to wait. I was feeling dizzy.

"Maybe you should leave the drink?"

I took a sip and poured the rest into the water.

"I'll carry you?" Before I could protest, he bent down and picked me up. I didn't mind. I was very tired and wanted to go back to sleep. I even rested my head on his shoulder. It was much better than walking.

"Raspberries? All that mess, and you smell like raspberries?"

"Amazing." I felt he had to be joking.

"I'm Dorian. Dorian Titlemen. And you are?"

"Eleanor. Elle… an… or."

"Eleanor, Elle… anor?"

"Yes, Eleanor."

"So, your first and last are the same?"

"No, Ele—anor Abernath—y from Boston." I needed water, and badly. I let him carry me down the dock to the bubbler where we stopped. I drank half the container. When I finished, he picked me back up, which I found funny, and continued carrying me up the steep ascent to the bathroom. It was made of uneven rocks, which he stepped upon with ease. Once there, he gently put me down and said, "I'll wait for you."

"No. Thank you, but I'll be fine," I said, then added. "Thank you for your help."

"My pleasure. All right, Eleanor Abernathy. Come see me afterward. I'll be at my sailboat." He pointed to his boat, pausing I believe for me to comment on its size or something like that, but I said nothing, so he turned and made his way down the steps. I watched him go, thinking it was too bad I didn't care for sailboats.

The water had made me feel much better and nearly sober. Standing outside the bathrooms, I looked at the two doors. The door to the women's bathroom had a picture of a chicken. Its breasts were exaggerated and held up by a lacy brassiere; it seemed tacky for such a fancy place. When I flipped the light on in the bathroom, several geckos ran for cover; a cockroach was crawling up the wall by a cobalt blue sink. The light, a dim, singular bulb hanging from a wire, was directly over my head. It looked as though it may, at one time, have been encased in a decorative lamp, but someone had helped themselves to it. The shellacked tile floor was swept clean, and to my delight, there was a toilet seat and toilet paper. The hand soap was in a bottle labeled "chamomile-citrus." I picked it up and smelled it. Delightful.

Sitting down on the toilet, I luxuriated in the seat's thoughtful curves long enough to create dents in my thighs. Splashing around in the sink, I washed my face, armpits, and legs. Luckily, I was able to scrub the pink splatters out of Catarina's blouse. There were paper hand towels piled up on a little table that also had a bottle of jasmine-scented lotion. I couldn't stop smelling the lotion and was tempted to take it but didn't. I used more than half of it on my face, neck, arms, and legs, then immediately regretted my overindulgence because the bugs seemed to be attracted to the scent too. Again, I doused myself with water, splashing around, and wiped off as much of the lotion as I could. Then, I once again dried off with the paper hand towels, using them all up. Feeling refreshed, I walked out, sat down on the steps, leaned into the wall, and took a nap.

When I awoke, a breeze was lapping my face like the fur of a soft puppy, and I was feeling exceptionally well for losing my dinner. I didn't even think I was drunk anymore. As I walked back down the hill, I could hear the melodious ranchero music playing from the restaurant. The earlier mayhem seemed to have scattered somewhere into the night. I sensed the party was over except for this last attempt at keeping it going with music. The words to the song, "Your love is bursting in my veins," or something to that effect.

Glancing over toward Dorian's boat, I saw that he had a light on in his cabin and was standing next to a flickering tiki torch, smoking a cigarette. He waved. I waved back but immediately regretted it as I saw him move down the dock toward me. I knew he wanted something from me that I had no desire to give. He met me at the bottom of the steps. He had a pleasant, almost beautiful face, like one of those Roman statues in a museum, only with eyes that moved, and he was bronzed from the sun. I'd been traveling long enough to know northern girls from the western hemisphere were rare and hard to grab hold of down in these parts. Here, I was a novelty; nothing more, nothing less. I didn't take his persistence and advances as a monumental compliment. Yet, if I wasn't so hung up on Harry, I may have found him 'scrummy' or 'yummy.'

"Can I buy you a drink?" he asked, his voice smooth and direct.

"No, but you've been sweet." My words sounded stupid,

canned. If he had said them to me, I'd know he was just playing me. I thanked him again and went to leave. He touched my arm, then held it. His hands were rough and firm, but gentle. I affably removed his hand and gave it back to him. "Bye, Dorian from Halifax." He took a drag from his cigarette, blowing the blue cloud out in a straight line that hinted of frustration. As I walked down the ramp, I felt his eyes following me. I had a feeling I would hear from him again. I hadn't mentioned the orphanage, but he seemed like the type of guy who could figure it out.

Back inside the restaurant, I saw the place had cleared out. The bar seats were empty, and the table occupants had thinned down to only a passed out drunk, and in a corner table, sat a man and woman, yachters, talking closely. There was a faded, relaxed hue within the restaurant's emptiness. Dumbfounded about how I was going to get back to the orphanage, I went over to the bar and sat down on a stool. I asked the bartender when the party had ended. He told me an hour ago. His name was Max. Max poured me a gin and tonic with lime and placed a bowl of chips on the counter.

"I don't suppose there are any water taxis at this hour?" I inquired.

"Where have you been?" A voice boomed from the river entrance to the restaurant.

"Harry," I said, beaming. It was on the tip of my tongue to tell him he'd just made my night, but instead, I said. "How unexpected."

Walking over, he sat down next to me. He had a scowl plastered across his face. Grabbing hold of my shoulders, he benignly turned me toward him and looked into my eyes, and over my face as if to make sure I was alright. "You had the whole place looking for you," he said.

"Who's everyone, Harry?" I asked, thrilled he'd been worried, then added. "I have a feeling all my peeps were too drunk to know I wasn't present."

He smelled like cigars and whiskey. I wanted to kiss him and give him a great big hug, but instead, I sat sheepishly staring back at him as he continued reprimanding me. "Going off without telling people—well, you had us—Golly was beside herself. She thought the fish ate you."

I laughed lightly. Then leaned in toward him, and said, "You must have arrived late." He had on a button-down white shirt that he had rolled up at the sleeves and had untucked from his dark green cargo pants. He looked lovely. Unable to resist touching him, I pushed his hair away from his face and studied his forehead, "It doesn't look good. How do you feel?" His bump had turned an ugly purple and the gash had scabbed over, black, and brutal.

"Fine. I forget it's there unless I rub my head."

"How come you arrived so late?" I asked, nudging his wet sneakers. "Your feet are sopping wet. Splashing in water again?"

This made him laugh, then clearing his throat he said, "I was sitting in the dinghy out on the dock when I heard your voice, I stumbled a little trying to get out."

His words made me smile. Not knowing how to respond because I found it adorable that I had made him stumble, and it wouldn't have been a nice thing to brag about, I remained silent, staring at his face letting him talk. "I arrived late to avoid a government official," he said, then asked Max for a neat whiskey.

"I think I met your government official. Minister of the Interior."

"Yeah, crooked as the day is long." Max delivered his drink, and Harry gulped half it down. Turning toward me, he said, "Okay, your turn. Explain yourself."

"Bathroom."

"What?"

"I took a nap on the steps."

He chuckled. He seemed in good spirits and told a funny story about his day. He'd had lunch with a fellow from Chile, and another man who when he took his patch off his eye to rub his brow, his glass eye fell out onto the floor causing a ruckus in the restaurant. "Scared the staff stiff." Before I could tell Harry, I had met those men, Rubin, and Enrique earlier, Harry blurted out. "It seems everything is coming to an end."

The phrase hit me wrong. It didn't sound right; it had no future. "What does that mean? Coming to an end?" I asked.

"I don't know," he said, cupping his hand to my cheek and looking me in the eye. "I don't know," he repeated, removing his hand to put a chip in his mouth, along with ordering another drink.

Our date, or rather, my made-up-date, had become too serious. I didn't want to be too serious because I felt that would be a terrible way to be on a date, fake or not. Besides, if I became too sad about him going away, which I wasn't too sure he was, I might cry, so I nudged his knee with mine and told him a few stories of my own such as Hamit not wanting to teach anymore, and Molly and Gunther's food teasing. Harry didn't think Hamit was serious, and as for Molly and Gunther, he was glad he missed the show.

Max, who had been putting glassware and condiments away, was now leaning against the back wall of the bar with his arms folded, looking like he wanted to go home.

"We should get going," Harry said.

"I gather we're taking your dinghy?" I said. Then turned to Max, I asked him for two bottles of water and a bag of chips to go.

"Yeah, The Scott's skiff."

Hearing The Scott's name, I drummed the counter with my left index finger, wondering if I should say anything. It had been wonderful sitting at the bar with Harry, and I had no desire to ruin the rest of the evening by bringing up an uncomfortable situation. Even if Harry was a criminal, I wasn't sure if I wanted to know. I wanted to kiss him, to hold him in my arms. It was already bad enough that he had a fiancé. As it went, morality wasn't on my side, and as for Harry, I wasn't sure if it ever had been. But then, I said, because I couldn't help myself, "Dan Scotchwick. I read about him. Months ago. Big article in La Noticia."

Harry shifted in his seat and looked at me with that peculiar way he has when trying to read my mind. His eyes, the color of the ocean on a cold winter's day.

"We shouldn't talk about him here," he said, finishing his drink. But then added. "I don't like the man. In fact—hate him. The whole issue is complicated on so many levels that—" He stopped talking and stared at his empty drink. It wasn't like Harry to say he hated anything. I kept silent because the issue seemed too tangled, too disruptive. However, curious about the fate of my friend Catarina's heart, I asked, "What about Catarina?"

"I warned her."

He then sat up straight and snapped out of whatever had overcome him. Smiling, along with having a bewildered look on his face, he leaned into me and pulled a clump of something indescribable from my hair while saying, "What's this? Why do you smell like raspberries and jasmine, or is it chamomile?" Getting up, he tossed the gooey pink clump into the water and came back over. The abrupt movement jarred the locket he had hidden in his shirt to appear.

"Don't know what that was—pizza possibly," I said, then changed the subject. "What's in the locket?"

"My parents."

"How precious." I was glad he didn't say, fiancé.

He showed me their picture. A handsome couple. He looked like his father.

"Shall we go?" He asked touching my arm.

"Sure, Harry, let's go."

When we stood up to leave, he looked me up and down. "You're all wet. But you look different. You bought clothes."

"Borrowed."

This made him laugh. He then pulled my broken flip-flops from his back pocket. "They were on the dock. I thought you might have swum back to the orphanage." He handed them to Max, and Max threw them out.

My mood blithe, a wave of giddiness filled my throat and heart because what fun it was to be with Harry. Tossing a water bottle over to him, I unscrewed the top of the other and drank a hefty swig before walking out into the late evening air.

Chapter 31

The River

It was the same skiff Catarina took to and from The Scott's. The diminutive size made it look more like a child's toy than a practical, usable boat. The motor appeared weak; a tiny turtle's head stuck to a stick. Harry's broadness and height even dwarfed it more.

Hesitant to get in, I untied the boat and stood on the dock with the boat line in my hand, wondering if it would be better if I just stayed the night at the club. He was pulling on the engine cord and with each pull, the boat violently rocked. When the engine started, it made putt-putt noises, and oily smoke roiled up into a noxious fervor behind Harry's head. It was a disquieting display of bluster, like a sick dog having a fit.

"Come on, get in," he said, waving his hand impatiently.

What the hell, I thought. If Harry made it here okay, the two of us should be able to make it back. I slid in, keeping my weight centered in the middle.

"Why are you facing me?" he asked, as I settled in on the seat in front of him.

"It seemed like a good place to sit. We can talk this way," I said, pushing us away from the dock with an oar.

"I don't have any legroom."

"Well, I don't either. Move your legs left, and I'll go right." Instead, we weaved our legs together, our inner thighs touching each other's knees. It was cozy. The heat emerging from his body, comforting since the night air had chilled, and I was damp from my soiree in the bathroom. The moon was blue and crisp, and I could see that the rabbit, or had it been a hare? Had snuggled into a curl with its eyes open. 'What an eerie sight,' I said.

"What? The moon?" Harry questioned.

I was about to tell him about the hare-rabbit but thought better of it and looked to the left of his head, watching the club shut itself down. First, the lights above the tables went off; then bar lights disappeared. The tiki torches snuffed out, and the green Christmas lights darkened. Only the lights at the end of each dock were left on. Dorian's cabin light was off and the Bertram next to him, gone. Avoiding the moon, I looked up at the stars.

"It's pretty out," I said. He said nothing back, just smiled.

Neither one of us talkative, we sat in silence as we wended our way across the vast river. The current tugged us north, a cinching pull that had small waves lapping with eager jabs at the sides of the boat. Harry diverged south, toward the *peligroso* sign, so as not to overrun the beach.

"Jack and Sarah were on the mud beach," I muttered to Harry, breaking our silence.

I told him how I had thought they were maggots, "White, slimy maggots acting like horny bunnies under the rays of the

Rabbit Moon." My story made him laugh and laugh, a deep, light laugh that sounded like walking on silky sand. When he stopped laughing, we both remained quiet, listening to the sound of the gurgling engine. At one point, Harry knocked my knee with his; our eyes met, then floated away again.

When we hit the middle of the river where the currents pulled the strongest, the boat began rearing up as eddies and churning waters batted its sides. I thought the worst of it was over because we were on the verge of cutting out into calmer waters, but then something large clunked into the side of the boat. I assumed it was a log. Harry swore it was a "damn dead animal." Whatever it was? It caused me to lurch forward into Harry while letting out a sound similar to a muted yelp. Harry grabbed me with his free hand. Holding my waist while grasping the tiller with the other, he tried to keep the course. "Get back on the seat," he kept insisting. "immediately!"

The stern was taking on water. Buckets of it. The gravity of the situation dire. But my legs had fallen under his seat, and my knees were stuck. Twisting my body, trying to pull one leg out at a time, tipped the boat even more. The water damage was irreparable. The boat had become swamped and was sinking. Floating out of the boat, Harry gripping my arms to make sure I came free, we both watched stupefied as the craft disappeared into blackness.

Treading water, we looked over at each other. The situation dicey as the current's overpowering strength had our bodies floating and bouncing north. Yet, when our eyes met, we each gave a comical smirk. I'm not sure why we found it funny. Maybe we thought it stupid? Because how pathetic to have sunk the boat?

"Can you swim well?" Harry said, reaching over and tugging my arm.

"Yes, Harry, I can swim well." I'd been swimming all my

life. I competed in high school. Nothing fantastic, but good enough.

We swam toward the shore using the breaststroke. Harry stopped to kick his sneakers off, saying something about them dragging him down. His feet free, we began again, this time swimming the crawl. We swam across the current and not against it, and since we had been dumped on the south side of the orphanage shore near the *peligroso* sign, by the time we broke through into placid waters, we were only off track by about a hundred feet to the north.

Angling back, we touched ground on the slimy, leaf-rotting river floor by the mangroves next to the schoolhouse. Then, with a little more effort, we lugged our exhausted bodies up onto the sandy orphanage's beach. We flopped ourselves down and giggled at our success.

We lay in silence for a while. To catch our breath, I supposed, along with amazed that we made it. Looking up into the sky, listening to the lapping of the wake upon the shore, I stared at the stars catching a few blinking. But once the chilled night air ate through the sweat of exhaustion, I began to shiver. Harry reached over and put his arm on my back and hugged me against him, his chin resting on the top of my head. For a few brief seconds, I thought there was no better feeling in the world.

"I'm famished," he said. His voice breaking the silence.

"I can't believe the boat sank," I replied, pressing my face closer to his chest, his dampness giving him a steamy warmth.

He sucked in some air and blew it out. "I know." He then rolled over and got up. "I'm going to go get our towels. Meet me in the bathroom. And an apple. I think I have an apple. Banana, too, and an orange—which would you like?"

As my mindset was always a little off-balance around Harry, I thought asking for the banana would be too presumptuous, so I said, "Apple."

"Apple it is." He took off up the hill.

I lay there for a few moments breathing and listening to the river. Jumping up, I too ran up the hill to the dormitorio as though I were in a race, a race with myself to the bathroom.

Chapter 32
The Shower

The dormitory was quiet, except for a few grumblings made by the children in their cribs. The two laundry ladies were asleep on the floor, huddled together like pudgy balls of colorful cloth and loosely bound hair. They had children's books scattered by their sides. I gathered they had been reading them when they fell asleep. With care, I tiptoed into the bathroom. Harry was by the sink, naked, except for a towel wrapped around his waist, eating a freshly peeled orange; he handed me the apple. The overhead light was off; Harry had my flashlight lit and resting on the top of the middle shower stall. It was pointing up. It gave the room a soft, yellow hue instead of its usual gray, fuzzy haze. Shadows dark and light molded our bodies, presenting an intangible yet romantic aura. We stood together eating for a while, munching, and looking at the floor with an occasional glance toward each other. Harry had brought water, too, which we drank.

It was awkward to have him with me in the bathroom. I never felt shy around him before, or for that matter, anyone at the orphanage; out of place, questionable parenting skills, poor word choices, but never shy like I did standing there with him. I found myself second-guessing not only my movements but my thoughts. I couldn't decide if I should just whip my clothes off in front of him and get into the shower—or wait for him to get into the shower first. He didn't seem to be in any rush. I then decided it was better to clean the sand off my backside and the river from my body (although the shower water was river water) than be bashful. Picking up the generic minty soap he had brought down, I walked to the farthest shower from the door, and turned the water on, and got in with my clothes on. It was perfect; I was washing my clothes and myself at the same time. First, I took my blouse off and scrubbed it, then went down the line.

Harry got into the shower next to the one I was in. He turned the water on and began humming a light, fanciful tune. There it is, settled. Nothing but good friends, I thought.

Then Harry stopped humming to say, "Can you hand me the soap?" He was looking over the stall at me. He was tall enough that his eyes were a good few inches above the rim. I didn't think it was very good of him to be standing there staring at me with only my underpants on.

"Why do you have your underwear on?" He asked.

"I'm washing my clothes. I haven't gotten to them yet."

I handed him the soap, then took my underwear off and threw them on top of the rest of the wet clothes, waiting for Harry to hand me back the soap. Humming his merry tune, he stopped and asked, "Could you wash my back? I can never reach my back, and I think it must need cleaning very badly."

His request gave me pause at first because I knew it to be a dangerous presumption on his part to think I could just wash his back touching no other part of his body. But then I thought, 'Of course I can behave,' and walked over into his stall, took the soap out of his hand, and began making small, foamy circles all over his very firm, strong back. "Harry," I said. "You have two moles along your vertebrae and another below your left shoulder. Have you ever had them checked out?" With my fingers, I made circles from one small mole to the next one.

"Moles? Let's see what's on your back." I turned around, and he inspected my back by taking his fingers and drawing lines across my shoulder blades and above my bottom. "I see bathing suit marks. One across your rib cage and the other just above—"

I laughed, muffling the sound as not to wake the laundry ladies. Turning around, I leaned against the stall wall facing him. "That tickles."

The water was splashing off his shoulders and in between us. I thought what a silly game it was we were playing. Then suddenly the goofiness was gone. Looking up at his handsome face, his hair wet, slicked back and slightly sudsy, a profound seriousness swept over me, and I believe over Harry too. The coloring in his face flushed, his eyes dazzled with a subtle yet acute torment. I'd seen that look on his face before, when we laughed too hard over a joke or had the same sentiments about a peculiar idea, or when we touched each other by accident because I had grabbed a card he wanted, or when one was going left and I was going right when in actuality we were going the same way so we bumped into each other.

This seriousness that had come over us struck a note in me that was both fearful and rhapsodic. I had a great urge to cry, but not because I was sad. All my pent-up desires, which I had so dutifully kept at bay, had become unhinged. Gone without even a whisper. The present world surrounding this small shower stall, empty; there was only Harry and me, and no one else. Staring at each other in silence, Harry reached over and put his hand on my cheek, splintering the barriers that had been dividing us. Drawing my face into his, he placed his lips directly on mine. They were smooth, wet, and soft. I kissed him back, a long kiss. He tasted like fruit and whiskey and sweet water.

Leaning into him, he lifted me up; I wrapped my legs around his waist, the cold, smooth tile at my back, the heat of his chest enveloping me. We hit a symbiotic note, and for a few abandoned moments, we were both rendered unearthly, supernal in our need to touch each other. Mad for the exhalation it gave us. Satiated by its depth. The water cascading in rivulets down our arms and legs. Each moment envious of the other. Then something was wrong.

There was a squawking sound like a crazed bird stuck inside the room. Wherever it was, it was very, very angry.

"*Ehebrecher! Ehebrecher!*"

The noise grew louder until it was in the shower with us. Pulling away from Harry's delicious lips, I looked to the right of his head. My vision was blurred by the dancing water on his back, my body still rhythmically heaving up and down. Blinking, I opened only my right eye. I saw Alex's angry face twisted into a snarl barely a foot away. His fist was shaking. I winked at him and went back to kissing Harry. Then panicked at my audacity and dropped to the shower floor. Harry let out a groan.

Alex yelling all sorts of stuff in German. I kept catching the word *Schlampe!*

Harry heard the words this time and looked down at me, his expression frozen, lost in a distant thought. He then looked up at the ceiling, biting his lower lip as though cursing the gods. Turning around, keeping me behind his back, his tone calm and exhausted, he said, "Stop it, Alex."

But Alex kept yelling, "Schlampe!" I had heard Alex say this word before. It meant 'fuck'? No, it meant 'slut!' It was one of those words. His voice cracking from abuse, he abruptly stopped shouting and ran out of the room, his bare feet slapping against the cement floor. The sound of the screen door slamming against the wooden sides of the building shook the foundation.

"Where's he going?" I said, my voice raspy. The water, still splattering down upon our startled, quieted bodies, seemed cold and pointless. The deadweight of fatigue swept over us like some verve-eating succubus. And to make matters even worse, our morning wake-up song was blasting, "Muévelo—Bebé" into the hollow crevices of inopportuneness.

Flashing each other a panicked look, we grabbed our towels and swiftly made our way through the downstairs to the second-floor steps. The laundry ladies were up and patting down their skirts. They didn't seem to notice. Molly and Gunther were on their way down the stairs as we were going up. Sleepy and entangled in their need to study their footing, they both mumbled, "Good morning." I had left my clothes and flashlight in the bathroom. A feeling of dread seeped into my mind. It was a botched crime with irrefutable evidence left behind. Then came the awareness of there being no return; life as I had known it had changed. It wasn't remorse I felt, but I did almost prefer the unobtained prize than losing a friend to the insanity of sex. But what was done, was done. My steps became small, and I fell behind. Why rush? Harry didn't seem to notice and plowed into the room with his beautiful body and strutting confidence. His inner pool of mystical strength producing in me a sudden weakness; the fleeting moment of doubt.

I walked into the room and shut the door. Harry had turned the overhead light on and was standing in the middle of the room with his towel still wrapped around his waist. His hands were on his hips, his head tilted sideways, his eyes dark and unreadable. My hair felt wet and heavy upon my shoulders. I pushed it back and met his stare and smiled. Letting go of the apprehension of losing myself to another, I stifled the need to laugh. I was giddy. Giddy with my life. Nothing mattered but this moment and at this moment life was perfect.

Harry threw me the same comical smirk he expressed when the tiny toy boat had sunk. With my eyes attached to his, I turned the light off and made my way over to him in the dark. Tripping on his toes, I wrapped my arms around his waist. We crawled under the mosquito netting of his king-size bed. The rubber squeaked, so we moved to the floor.

Chapter 33

The Aftermath

Joining the morning washing of the kids late, I noticed not one adult was smiling, expressions flat, and cadaverous from too much booze and not enough sleep. But we had a routine to follow, which we did, quietly and with some embarrassment. No one speaking much except to comment on a child or directly to the children. No one was sure what the other might know. Catarina did hand me my clothes with an expression on her face that said, "Really? You devil, you." Golly mentioned the Rabbit Moon at snack time, reminding us that the craziness of the night was the "Rabbit's fault." The casting off of blame helped all our spirits and by dinner, we were joking about the night. Light-hearted and, at times, splitting over with laughter.

As the days rolled on, it was apparent that the fallout from the party had some residual effects. Molly and Gunther had become an item. An annoyingly loving item. Gunther nicknamed Molly "Minnie"; when scolding, "Minnie Mouse"; and sometimes just, "Mouse." Which confused our littlest Mouse. Molly called Gunther "Gunthy" and occasionally while licking her lips, "Gun Boy." When sitting with them during meals and play-time, I found their references to wedding plans to be "flapdoodle," to use one of Hamit's words, and filled with textbook romance. They wanted a black-tie affair on the cliffs of Cornwall, a tent with flowers strung from the ceiling, Queen Elizabeth and 'stodgy' Philip as guests (even though they didn't know them), and the food to be an extravaganza of New England lobsters, oysters, and beef Wellington for those with seafood allergies. They were to leave in a carriage drawn by four white Clydesdales. Their children were to be named Fionnulia and Primrose, if daughters, and if sons, Tiberius, or Ptolemy. Gunther had become unrecognizable. He had been swallowed whole. He went from being a blustering thespian who found comical fault in everything to a spat-out, "gooey-eyed, harlequin ninny" (Hamit's words again). Hamit, who had adamantly declared he wasn't returning to the orphanage, did after spending three days at the club. He brought his new gal with him. She helped him out in the classroom teaching. They never left each other's side. She even helped him with his news briefs in the morning. She claimed to be clairvoyant.

I missed Gunther's friendship, and Golly missed Molly's. Molly and Gunther never apart, Golly became the third wheel, trailing behind them, melancholy, glum, and lost.

Jack and Sarah had to have all sorts of painful shots due to developing a prickly rash on their genitals and strange oozing abscesses on their lips and thighs. They also were abstaining from sex because of other ailments that they kept hushed. Flummoxed and tetchy over the situation, Jack became extra bent and pointy. He had taken up a costive gait and snapped at clothing not folded with neat corners, shoes that weren't perfectly aligned, and children remaining in the shower seconds too long. It wasn't until Catarina started feeding him cigarettes and thimbles of rum with his morning, lunch, and evening rice and beans that his mood became airy and jaunty. The liquor having such a cheery effect caused Jack to come up with a new chapter for his dissertation: 'The Dangers of Boredom.' Through tiny sips of rum, he downgraded his chapter on 'Routine and Consistency' by adding a subtitle, 'Too Much of a Good Thing Smatters of Hell,' and emphasized the dangers of monotony when raising children. He then punctuated his new chapter with an addendum titled, 'Kids Kill Your Sex Life.'

"You mean contaminated mud." He had it all wrong. The kids had hardly 'killed' his sex drive or life. In fact, it hadn't been killed at all, just disabled. But it wasn't worth arguing my point of view. Jack, bleary-eyed but happy over finding a justification for Sarah's and his mud roll, could finally enjoy life again. Even if blaming three-and-four-year-olds was pretty lame. Sarah, on the other hand, had become more obsessed with bugs. She was convinced, as a couple, that they were now incubating a cluster of sarcoptic itch scabies within the skin of their bodies. This caused her to assume the position of a proud mother. I often caught her looking at her limbs lovingly.

And then there was Catarina. Catarina before the party had a lover who she was crazy about. As far as we all knew, her lover was crazy about her too. Then it all fell apart that fateful Rabbit moon night. The night after the party, while Catarina and I stood on the dock having our evening cigarettes, she told me what had taken place with The Scott and two other "Unsavory fellows."

She lamented, "It's hard to know what time, I'd had too many of those punches they were serving, but, well, I think it was late. A man who owned a sesame seed plantation somewhere, and here on a fishing trip, took us back to The Scott's boat in his Bertram, along with another guy who had a patch over his eye—an awfully big boat to be just taking us for such a short ride, but anyway when we were just about at The Scott's boat." She paused here to take a long, pensive drag off her cigarette, then continued. "Hell, I was famished for sex and felt yummy inside, but then The Scott told the man, I think his name was Rubin, to drop me off at the orphanage's dock. The Scott said, 'Not tonight, dear, I have business responsibilities.' He gave me a big, juicy kiss goodbye. I stood on the dock for a while, watching them motor off into the night. They went off toward El Puente. It was so late, I kept thinking. What could they possibly be doing in El Puente?" Biting her lower lip, she stubbed her cigarette out and quickly lit another.

"The plot thickens," I said, wondering what those two fishermen were up to.

"What?"

"Nothing." Then gazing over the river, I added. "His sailboat's gone."

"Yup, gone," she frowned.

Her pain caused the lines around her mouth to be more prominent and her fun-loving spirit to wallow in self-pity. I was at a loss on how to cheer her up. I refrained from telling her he wasn't a great guy, a killer. It wouldn't make her torment any better. Seeing her near to tears, I said, "If it's business he's dealing with, he's probably somewhere up north on the river. I'm sure he'll be back."

"But what was he doing in El Puente in the middle of the night? Who takes off sailing after drinking all night?

"I guess The Scott."

"I have only two more weeks here," she said, which had us laughing because we both felt it was the same as saying months.

"He could be back any day now. If not, why don't you give me a note for him—in case he comes back and you've left." It was nothing but fluff, empty words, but for some reason I wanted her to feel there was hope.

Puffing and blowing smoke all over our arms and legs to fend off the bugs, she said, "I'm looking forward to the Canadian spring air. Oh, well, he was a fun smorgasbord while he lasted. A note? Sure, I'll write a letter, if the salami shows up, yeah, give it to him." Then she laughed while shedding a few tears. "You know, Harry warned me to stay away. I just couldn't resist the surprise. Swimming over to his boat and all."

We both laughed, then stood on the dock for a few minutes in silence before heading to the dormitorio. On the way back, she said, "Let's keep in touch. Write to each other. Hey, if you're still here when I come back next year—won't that be fun?"

Thinking about a year ahead was too much of a leap forward, but I said, "Sure. Sounds like fun." Then out of curiosity, I asked, "What did Harry say about The Scott?"

"It won't last long. He was right."

Before walking into the dormitorio, we both glanced up at the moon. A speck was missing from the left side as it was in a waxing mode. Neither one of us saw a picture of a rabbit or hare, but possibly a human face when we squinted.

"What do you think? That Rabbit moon is gone?" She inquired.

"Looks it."

"Somethings not right though."

"Yeah, I know what you mean," I said. She was right. There was something in the air that was amiss. Again, it wasn't anything tangible. Even Alex, who told everyone and anyone who would listen, including the kids (in German), about Harry's and my shower episode: "*Knallen—so eine schweinerei!*" Wasn't the problem, although more than ever, the obnoxious ass.

I had also found out through Golly, that he had gone off that fateful morning to Doc's place. Since we didn't see him at breakfast, I assumed he had stayed with Doc and eaten with her. Golly felt that Alex had developed a crush on Doc, which made her upset because she had a crush on Alex. "Life can be very miserable," she fretted, making yo-yo sounds.

Golly had become my interpreter. This was a strange occurrence because she was the last person I would think of as a linguist. She liked to tell me what Alex was saying about me. Although we had all doubted her abilities at first, she could understand German. She had spent a summer being a nanny for a German couple in Wachtberg, North Rhine-Westphalia. I was surprised how well she understood the language with only three months of studying under her belt. Her ability to speak was a different issue. Her English was nearly incomprehensible; her Spanish never had any *r* sounds, and the *t*'s were missing. I often wondered if she was making up what Alex was saying, but it sounded like his vernacular. If I had to speak to him, which I tried desperately not to, he would reply, "*Leck mich arsh*"—"Kiss my arse," Golly said—or, "*Gehzum Teufel ficken mopse,*"—"Go to hell, boob!" She sagely translated. Luckily, the little kids didn't understand, and none of the adults cared that I had sex with Harry in the shower. The kitchen ladies laughed at Alex. Aapo, Cadmael, and Eadrich wondered why he was so agitated, shaking their heads and smiling while giving Harry the thumbs-up.

With help from Golly, I learned to say, "*Sich verpissen,* Alex!" (*fuck off*)

As for Harry and me, we lived the way we always had lived, together: staying up late, playing cards, and sipping rum. Only I slept in Harry's bed now, not mine. At night, the fan whirring, the bugs slapping and pinging at the screen, the air thick with humidity, rum, and fruit, we still played Russian Bank. The game never lasted long. Our legs, arms, and torsos would become entwined, the cards scattered and matted to our bodies. It was blissful.

Harry had also stopped bringing up his fiancé's name, Jacquelina, and I stopped mentioning her name too. I also knew Harry's fiancé couldn't have just disappeared. She was there in his head, but what had he done with her? I never brought it up because I didn't want to know. The future wasn't spoken about; we were living in the moment. It was a perfect place to be with him. However, during the day, when walking the kids to school, splashing in the river, tossing the five- and six-year-olds over my shoulder into the deeper waters, when helping Henrik and Raymond carry their plates of food, nudging the kids in and out of the showers, dressing, building forts, I would often gasp at the air for a brief moment over the reality that nothing lasted forever.

Chapter 34

The Sandcastle

It was nearly two weeks since the party, according to Harry's watch, backed up by Molly's daily notches, when a day came around that was hotter than any other day we'd had since my arrival. The rains, having beaten down all night upon the ground, had created muddy messes everywhere. A stream now flowed around the washbasin behind the dormitorio. Once the sun took to baking the earth, the air became thick and heavy. By mid-afternoon, we felt waterlogged from just breathing.

Putting the discomfort of weather aside, Bernarda, Penelope, Charlotte, and I built a sandcastle on the beach. The beach had a light breeze, making it the only place to be during afternoon playtime. The sandcastle was a massive structure. We constructed it by pouring buckets of sand, one after another, on top of each other, creating a mound taller than the girls. This thrilled them to bits, and their tenacity to finish was admirable. We smoothed down the sides and created turrets, a moat, and a courtyard. Collecting rocks, sticks, and pebbles, we made windows and doorways. Charlotte filled the moat up with water; Bernarda helped. Albert, who came over for a while, placed yellow flowers all around the castle walls.

By late afternoon, we were still busy with the details such as straightening out crooked doorways and windows, along with filling the interior with ants and beetles; Penelope found a worm, Bernarda a caterpillar, Charlotte a frog. The birds were singing, and the bright, languid sun had dipped west. It was around this time that I saw something lurking in the bushes near us, on the embankment. The uneasy sense someone was watching us was visceral; then suddenly, with only the warning of a breaking stick, Frankie rushed in. His stout body bundled and pitched, his limbs tight then straightening as he flew through the air, head arched as he landed flat on top of the castle. He then scrambled the sand beneath him into an unrecognizable mess.

It was a surprise attack. We were dumbfounded and immobilized.

I stumbled to get up to grab him. But it was Bernarda—my Chiclet-toothed, dimple-faced Bernarda who got to him first. She grabbed the back of his shirt and flipped him around. She was strong, her anger mighty. She pounded punches into his face and kicked his stomach. I pulled her off, still swinging, hitting the air with her mouth gnarled and teeth bared. Her body hot and tense, I gripped her in a basket hold, trying to calm her down. "Hush. It's okay. We can build another." Shaking, she cried great sobs of frustration. It was then that Penelope picked up a big rock and threw it at Frankie, hitting the back of his head. It was the first and only time I heard a sound out of Charlotte. She screamed.

Grabbing hold of the three girls, afraid they'd torture the boy further, I huddled them together on my lap, holding pieces of clothing and arms. They pushed me away, but I held tight until they finally slumped into me, wailing and mumbling, "Malo Frankie—malo."

Frankie lay on the ground, not moving or speaking. Eyes open, he looked dazed as he searched the trees and the sky. What I found unusual was that he wasn't shedding a tear. His round face seemed calm. Golly and Eadrich, who were nearby, came running over. Golly took the girls; Eadrich picked up Frankie. Golly hugged each girl to her full breasts, and cooed, "Pudd'n pies, me chocolate nuggets. *Don'* cry." Then scrunching her mouth up into her nose, she looked at the castle and Frankie, and said, "Barmy Frankie, dodgy sod."

The back of Frankie's head was red and wet with blood. Crawling from Eadrich's arms to mine, his body sweaty, his weight like lead, he was malleable and clung to my neck with his hands. I hugged him. The girls had punished him enough. Eadrich dabbed his wound with a bandana he had taken off his neck, then wrapped it tightly around Frankie's head. He looked like a Ninja. For the first time, because he was such a troublemaker, I felt sad for him being an orphan with all his energy and no parents to coddle him.

The three of us quickly decided I would take him to see Doc immediately.

The clínica pathway was a long web of overhanging shrubs, branches, swampish puddles, and roots. It was laborious carrying Frankie for the fifteen minutes or so down the path. I almost tripped a few times. The new footwear I'd bought in El Pueblito, a fake pair of Tevas, were helpful. Flip-flops would have been unmerciful.

As we broke out of the jungle, I saw that Doc's clinic was a combination of residence and hospital. A gray, wooden, three-room structure placed on the edge of the shore where the ground jetted out. The peninsula created a fold of swiftly running water that gushed around the spiked curve. The power of the water was felt in the air and underfoot. It gave me the feeling of being overpowered, crushed under its perceived weight. It was an eerie, crazy feeling causing a surreal paranoia to creep up under my shoulder blades and the back of my neck. But Frankie seemed happy. Yet, I'd wished Alex had been around to take him.

Profusely sweating, I put Frankie down once we reached the door. For a kid with a bad bump on his head, he seemed frisky, desiring to run around. Stomping his feet like a bull about to take off, he made tough guy, growly sounds, and showed his teeth. I grabbed his hand. "Frankie, what's up?" I asked in Spanish. He said something about wanting to smash the ant mound over by a nearby tree stump. I picked him up again.

To the side of the front door was a sign painted in big black letters: "CLÍNICA." Attached to the right of the house on stilts was a screened-in porch. Above the door to the porch was a sign that said "ENTRADA." I opened the creaky screen door and walked in with Frankie and placed him down on the floor. He hugged my legs, shyly looking around at the people. Sitting on the benches along the walls were indigenous women, men, and children. The pervasive stench of sour corn made my eyes water. It was too small and hot in the room, even if the windows were open. The people were quiet, solemn, cradling their ailments stoically. Their eyes displayed the reasons for their visit—red-rimmed and sunken, lifeless, and speaking of pain and forsaken hopes, a silent listlessness of deleterious patterns. I found it hard to breathe, yet the birds were singing up a storm. The paradox of abutting worlds.

"*Dah* birds are singing their asses off today," Doc said, walking onto the porch from the interior of the house. Her aura beamed light and sunshine until she looked at me and darkened. "Oh, from the back, I thought you were someone different. A new volunteer. Why are you here?"

"I brought Frankie. He hurt his head." I stood motionless. Her dislike of me was unwarranted. I had never spent much time with her, except that day that I helped, and she pinched me, but I thought she was over it since she had apologized.

Frankie went running over to Doc. She kneeled down and removed the bandana. A woman with her skirt bunched up around her waist, displaying bony knees, grunted. I turned and looked at her. She had a flat face with saggy, dark skin; she smiled. All her upper front teeth were missing. The poverty was raw in the room. I held her gaze for a moment before averting my eyes.

"Come on in," Doc said, waving us to follow her. The three of us went into the examination room. It was basic, with a metal table covered with a green, faux plastic cushion. A large, white cabinet was on the wall, the doors open, exposing medicines and bandages. There was also a wooden school chair in a corner next to a large open window. Looking out the window, I could see the beginnings of a garden. Someone had half-built a large wooden frame and placed a mound of dirt beside it. Rich, dark earth.

"Is that the garden Harry's building?" I asked.

There was a long pause before she answered. "Was building," she corrected. Her voice distant, flat.

Doc seated Frankie on the table, his short, robust legs barely dangling over the edge. She then asked me to fetch the iodine and the butterfly Band-Aids from the cabinet. I did as I was told. When I gave her the stuff, she leaned forward and stepped on my right foot; this was exceptionally painful because Tevas are sandals. I flinched, but she didn't seem to notice or care.

"You stepped on my foot," I said. But she neither looked at me nor said anything back. She hugged Frankie to her breasts, and he nuzzled his little head into the solid, plumpness of her flesh. I stood looking at her, not sure how to interpret her repugnance toward me.

"Have you been well?" I said, thinking her malaria might be back, causing her to be mean.

"Busy," she said.

Frankie, nuzzling, pawed like a lecherous, minuscule old man at her chest. She didn't seem to mind. Her body was the shape of an upside-down violin, her glossy, coal-colored arms glistening as the sun sparkled through the palm fronds into the room. I wondered if Frankie truly knew what he was doing.

"He seems to like you," I said, wishing I had let Golly or Eadrich bring Frankie to the clinic, especially when Doc turned to sneer at my remark. I detected sheer hate embedded in her eyes. What had I done? I asked myself again while watching her use penlight to glance into Frankie's pupil. "He doesn't have a concussion. What happened?"

I explained to her about the castle and the girls, the crazy violence that it had brought on. She sucked in air through her teeth and whistled. "My, my, Frankie, such a little pest you can be. Well, I'll clean the cut, and—why don't you have a seat in the chair." Not wanting to anger her further, I sat down, although I didn't feel like sitting. I was jumpy and wanted to leave.

"What's up with you?" I asked as I sat. She turned and walked over, leaving Frankie on the table swinging his legs. Her height towered over me like an ogre looking at its prey. Had she planned this, me sitting beneath her? Fed up with her nonsense, I sat back, relaxed, and gazed directly into her hooded stare. The blackness of her pupils, tense yet luminous in the indifferent afternoon sunlight, which ebbed and flowed into the room through a lethargic fluttering of the foliage outside. Sweat trickled crookedly down my armpits and along my spine; I forced a smile. "So, what do I do with Frankie? Should he stay here, or should I take him back?" I wanted to leave.

Ignoring my words, she turned back to her patient and put a butterfly bandage on his wound and placed him on the floor, his hands still patting and caressing her breasts.

"If he becomes quiet tonight, bring him back," she finally said.

Frankie touched the bandage on his head and glanced over at me, then to the door. The door shut; I knew he wanted out. He was fine. Being sick didn't have any purpose for him. Doc, seeing what he wanted, opened the door, and he ran out. The kids in the waiting room stopped with whatever they were doing to look up. Doc walked out, and in one of the indigenous languages said something to the sitting children. Then those that could, jumped up and ran outside with Frankie to play. Doc then walked back into the examining room.

"He'll be fine," she said, clearing her throat. "I want to keep an eye on him. Why don't you help me?"

"Really?" Shocked, I said. "Where's Alex, I thought he would be with you?"

"He's shacking up with one of the laundry lady's daughters. Don't see him much."

"Must have just happened."

She laughed and threw me a wild-eyed look, "Lots of things just happen—right?"

I concluded she might be crazy. Hesitant to stay, I, too, looked at the door. It was my escape route.

"*Don* worry, I won't be nasty anymore," she said, smiling. So, she was aware of her behavior. How strange—

Getting up, I looked out the window at Frankie playing. He was running around in circles with kids chasing him. "It's late, and I don't want to walk back in the dark."

"You got a good hour," she said and winked at me.

A middle-aged woman, thin shouldered with an extended belly, was Doc's next patient; her face drooped, pulling her eyes and mouth down toward her chin and neck. Under-five feet tall, she sat on the table swinging her legs, their skin dry and marred.

She wore a tattered bib over her huipil and a thick, woven skirt. Her hair, like that of the rest of the women in the waiting room, was pulled back tightly into a bun. Doc listened to her lungs, examined her eyes, and looked into her mouth and throat, then stood straight and sighed. Turning to me, she said, "This woman is tired. She most likely is anemic and suffers from a poor diet. I will tell her to eat better and get some rest, but it won't do any good. Well, vitamins could help, but they may make her sick to her stomach if she isn't eating."

Then she spoke to the woman in an indigenous language. The woman nodded and got up. When she left, she mumbled to both of us, "*Vaya con dios*."

"I told her not to sell all her fruits and vegetables at the market for money. Keep some for herself. It won't help her family if she dies."

Several more patients came and went. Doc's ability to navigate the different languages was impressive. She spoke Mam, Q'eqchi, Spanish, Garifuna, continually deciphering the issues in English to me.

The last patient was a woman that looked more like a child than an adult. She had large, inconsolable eyes that darted about when she spoke. She also kept scratching her arms and legs, which seemed more out of habit than need.

"She is ill because even though it didn't rain last week, water got in her house, taking her pots and pans away, but what she really means is that there wasn't enough food because her husband used his entire paycheck to get so stinking drunk he passed out, and then when he woke up, he beat her." Doc, wiping her hands on her T-shirt, paused before continuing. "They often speak in rhymes because the truth is too painful. It can also be dangerous. The laws here favor those who have money, and those that don't, well, they're often punished for complaining." Then she asked me to fetch an ice pack from the fridge, saying something about the Club de Bote being a big donor for the clinic.

I went over to a small freezer and opened it. Several blue ice packs were piled on top of each other. "The club." Doc turned and looked at me. "You know the club? The one we all went to. They donate a lot of medical supplies to me; the owners, the workers come here too—for small stuff."

"The owners seem like nice people," I said, thinking I should get going because it was getting late. The sun now directly level with the window.

"Nice enough," she said back. But Doc wasn't through lecturing me about the local population. "They came down out of the mountains a few years back during the counterinsurgency to escape persecution."

"I heard. Lenore told me some of the older kids were orphaned by the war."

"The government took several valleys and much of the terraced mountainous land from them for their friends, industrial farming, and in return, they gave the people the tropics." She stopped talking to shake her head, then continued. "They're mountain people. Now they're river people. The heat, the swamps. They don't have enough land to grow food to sell, just enough to live on, which they sell anyway. They don't know how to find and prepare their medicines. They are forced to pay taxes, something new, and take jobs being paid a dollar a day on the chicken farms, the pineapple plantations. The farms are filthy; they use chemicals. The men drink and beat their wives."

"Aapo left recently to go back to his village," I said.

"They're still plenty of villages in the mountains. The people are angry though. So much has been taken from them. The army still raids them for their boys too, to conscript them into the army. An army that changes them into brutes, so they'll turn on their own people."

She stopped speaking, folded her arms over her chest, and stared at me. I wasn't sure what she wanted, so I waited. The silence was fatiguing; I had missed my nap. She was twitching and flicking the tips of her fingers. I couldn't tell if it was the injustice that was aggravating her, or me—possibly both. Interrupting the silence, I said, "Okay. I'm going. If you need me to help again, I will." I turned to leave.

"Your Harry isn't a good man," she blurted out. "He's selling their land."

Is that what this is about? What's been bothering her? I thought, then said, "He's not mine."

Puzzled by her directness, I leaned back against the wall, letting my eyes roam up and down Doc's statuesque physique. I had heard that the land he was dealing with belonged to Yena, but then possibly he was dealing with other people's land too. Listening to the kids shouting and laughing, I thought hard and long about the situation. Was I ignoring the bad acts of a man because I liked him? I finally said, "I thought everyone was selling because of the oil company coming in?"

She laughed. "What do you want from Harry?"

"I'm confused," I mumbled, finding the question out of place. Then something occurred to me. An epiphany, like when I'm playing Russian Bank, and for several plays, I'd only been concentrating on one half of the game, when I should have been looking at all of it. Once I acknowledged the other half, the next move always became so blatantly obvious.

"Doc," I said.

"Yes?"

"What's your name?"

"You don't know?"

"No, I don't."

"Jacquelina."

"*Que mierda*," I muttered, shaking my head in disbelief.

Chapter 35

Ants

On the walk back Frankie fell asleep in my arms. I took long, aggressive strides over roots and muddy ditches, stumbling. I always caught my fall, but the ground snagged and tore at my feet. Blind to physical pain, as my emotions had spiraled into a banging and clattering in my head like a battery of poorly tuned instruments. But when I mindlessly pushed a palm frond away, and it snapped back and hit me in the face, I stopped. It stung. The slap, a wake-up call. Its' ache burned into my cheek a dismal shout of reality, while the sting bit at my ego. Touching my lower lip, I saw it was bleeding. I sucked on it, cursing under my breath in both Spanish and English. The frond had triggered a descent into self-pity.

The jungle heat steaming around my head, the whine of the beetles, and birds yapping, the darkness made me feel like I was being strangled. I coughed and broke into a sobbing mess but then wiped my tears with the back of my hand. I took a deep breath of the earthy forest air. To waste time brooding wasn't a good idea. My mouth throbbing, I continued walking, the incoming night making the pathway less visible and the jungle shadows deceptive and eerie.

Shifting Frankie onto my other hip, he awoke, but only momentarily to let out a light cry, then rolled his head back onto my shoulder to sleep. A twig cracked behind us. I jerked around thinking Doc, or rather Jacquelina may have followed us.

Before leaving the clinic and a very angry Jacquelina, I had asked her why she wasn't living with Harry? A question I had posed to Harry too. She didn't have an answer while he at least came up with one. Doc heaving with hate, eyes red, her breath bitter like tinny mold when she leaned into me to make sure I understood he was hers-- whatever that meant, I mean, how can anybody belong to another? But to prove her point, she had taken a machete off a shelf and sneered at me before putting it back down. An unsettling action, but I was still curious and riddled her with questions.

"What about Cadmael?" I had asked. She just laughed. Then finding myself confounded, I added, "That day I helped you with your rounds. Why didn't you say you're his fiancé? There was no need to pinch me." She didn't have an answer.

"You knew I existed," she seethed.

"I still don't understand?" Then staring into her fuming eyes, I tried to decipher what all this was really about. "Was it a test? A test for Harry? A test for me? Well, we both failed, so now who wins?" I had said. She had made me angry. The mind game, foolish.

In my disgust with the situation, I flippantly said, "You can have him," and walked out to fetch Frankie. As I stormed down the pathway, Frankie in my arms, her words, 'you knew I existed,' kept running through my head. For months Harry's stories had been filled with her name. He loved her—*todavía la amaba*—he still loved her. The Spanish verb 'to love,' when spoken in the past, is always in the imperfect tense. An action with no definite beginning or end. It made sense, and I felt English should create a verb that did the same because, with my stomach in my throat, my mind churning, I wondered—how does love end?

The sun setting and darkness crawling in like spilled ink, I gazed down the path into the thick foliage. There was no one there, just the jungle and its noises. Above, a bird fluttered leaves upon the ground. Another twig snapped. It caused a chill to flood through my veins even though the heat was monstrous.

I took a step back to see the thicket more keenly. In the shadows about fifteen feet away, under a loping willow, stood a howler monkey. Upright and holding onto a branch he seemed tall. His genitalia, long and pink between his legs, dangled and swayed as he was moving one foot, then the next, in a fixed march. His dark mane framing his large, black eyes gave him the appearance of wearing a mask. I stopped breathing. The boogeyman couldn't have been a more frightening sight. Grinning, his mouth lipless, his teeth yellow, the birds loud, the bugs buzzing, I waited, frightened and not wanting to give him a reason to chase.

He shook the branch he was holding while appearing to be laughing. He then puffed up his chest and opened his mouth wide. The howl that came out, icy and deafening. My stomach tense and knotted, I whispered, "Please go away."

Frankie's eyes popped open, and he began to cry. I hugged him tightly and shut my eyes, and whispered, "Shut your eyes Frankie. Shut your eyes." When the horrific sound stopped, the wind of a swift movement brushed my arms and face. Opening my eyes, I saw the howler was above us in a craggy tree looking down. Then he took off, swinging from one branch to a vine and back to a branch. "He's flying away," I said in a low tone to Frankie, as not to call the creature back. Taking a deep breath, I shifted Frankie onto my other hip, and we resumed our trip back. But I had become exhausted. The monkey had taken the last of my physical strength into the trees. Yet, I continued walking. I then tripped, stumbled, and dropped Frankie into a puddle of roots and mud. He jumped up and threw a rock hitting my knee. "Damn kid!" I hissed, not meaning it, but then again—

He immediately went over to another muddy puddle and stepped in it, splashing muck all over his legs. I groaned at his behavior. To tell Frankie not to do something just made him want to do it more, but I told him anyway to please stop. He ignored me. His mulishness overwhelming, I sat down on a large, round log to rest and think. I put my chin in my hands and my elbows on my thighs. I didn't want to break up with Harry. I loved the silly world we had created. But now it seemed ruined. I imagined the conversation we would have, and it didn't go well, just a battle of who's right and who's wrong. I could just leave, I thought. Leave the orphanage and the whole mess behind. I had been wanting to check out the Bay Islands off of Honduras, and now was as good a time as any to do just that. I smiled at the idea. It was such a simple solution. The thought of doing something new seemed refreshing. I would miss Harry. I then imagined traveling around the Bay Islands and bumping into Harry because he had dumped Jacquelina after quickly realizing he loved me—like some Harlequin, nut job, romance novel. "Shut-up Eleanor," I said out loud to myself.

Frankie uprooted a rock and splashed it into the water. Proud of himself, he came over and leaned on my knees. I patted his back and said in English, "Frankie, I think I need to go away. I'll miss you." He smiled, although I knew he didn't understand what I said. Climbing onto my lap he leaned back against my chest, smearing mud all over my legs. A grackle whistled from afar followed by a guttural, high-pitched honk. The sound spooked me at first, but I knew the bird's call. "Just a cormorant," I whispered to Frankie. Then from some strange place inside me erupted tears that turned into sobs. It felt good to lose control.

I sat for a while on that log enmeshed in my misery rocking Frankie back and forth in my arms. Focused solely on my thoughts and the terrible emotional pain they were causing; I was unaware of what was going on between my thighs and within the folds of my crotch. At first, I noted the sensation as just a tickle. Then something stung, then a hundred more stings. But bathed in tears, I didn't have the will to move. Yet like an elastic band's continuous zap, I finally woke up. The sensation of a small torch sizzling my flesh came to mind. Leaping up, I once again tossed Frankie onto the ground. This time he laughed, reaching up for me to toss him again.

Ignoring him, the biting prevalent and rapid, I looked at my limbs. Massive swarms of pissed-off red fire ants were everywhere. My arms and legs were covered in them. I yelped, swatted, and brushed them off, but there were too many. Rushing over to a stagnant puddle, I splashed the fouled water over my legs and arms. I then took my shorts off and tried to wipe them off, but they were fast and hid behind my knees, and deep into my crotch. The only solution was to sit in the puddle and drown them.

Standing up, dripping wet, my crotch and thighs searing; my fingers had puffed up into pockmarked, blistering sores; my neck was ablaze with pain; I breathed, deep and long. Then clenching my teeth, I picked Frankie up, who was ripping up leaves, and stormed down the last five minutes of the blackened path to the compound. The light over the cafeteria was cluttered with bugs and moths. Everyone was in the dining hall eating. A low hum and laughter crusted the air.

"It's dinnertime, Frankie," I said keeping my voice steady. Putting him down I winced. The walk had increased the swelling of my inner thighs, the feeling, excruciating. Frankie, wiggling away from my hands, ran across the spotty grass and dirt into the cafeteria. Alex, who was standing up by one of the tables, saw him come in and called him over. He picked him up.

Examining his head, he gave him a good tweak of his chin and placed him back down. They walked over to the buffet together. It was a wonderful sight. A solid homecoming for Frankie. As for myself, I wasn't hungry. The only thing I wanted to do, was lie down. Each step across the quad, agonizing. I felt beaten up, physically, and spiritually. I was a mess.

When I limped in through the bedroom door, Harry was on his bed counting money. Piles of money. How apropos, I thought. He was wearing brown linen slacks and his long legs were crossed, jetting out across the floor. His white shirt, unbuttoned and flung open, exposed his chest and smooth stomach, with only a slight ripple where he slouched. He looked sexy, delicious, "yummy" as my dear friend Catarina would say, and despite my throbbing, itching inner thighs and crotch, feverish haze, and the agitation I had towards my situation, I thought of sex.

He glanced up startled at first and went to cover the piles of money with a towel that was on his bed, then changed his mind, tossing the towel to the side. What was the point? He again looked at me, this time with a great, big, welcoming smile that made me feel like I was the only person in the world that meant anything to him. I mistakenly smiled back, but then dropped the grin and frowned. I didn't think I should be friendly. Not because I was angry. I was in too much pain to be angry. I just wished the day hadn't happened. I wished I'd never become his roommate. I wished I liked sleeping in hammocks.

Hobbling over to my bed I said, "What is the verb 'to pretend' in Spanish?" My voice was raspy; my throat felt as though it was closing in on me.

"That's easy. It's *fingir.*"

"Right." I was going someplace with the word but was too befuddled to think of where.

"Give us a kiss."

"I can't," I groaned, flopping down on my bed, the mattress squeaking and bouncing me up and down. "I wish I had some ice to sit on. Do you have any ice?" I asked looking at the ceiling.

"Ice? No?"

Glancing over at him, I watched him. He was still busy with his money. His face had a calmness to it, but then, he was usually calm even though his whole body was full of energy. He looked happy. The air in the room was dusty and hot, my body sweating and itching. My love for Harry frightened me, and the need to throw up, profound.

"You know what the problem with only one temperature is?" I asked, thinking if I had a gun, I would probably shoot myself with it.

"No. What is it?" He was looking at me now. His intense eyes, curious and full of expectation.

"There's no contrast. A person is constantly feeling the same temperature, and it becomes unnerving. Do you think it is something inane in humans that makes us unhappy when everything is the same?" The wooden rafters had several knots of various colors. I began to count how many knots I saw to distract my mind. I was also thinking if I had ice, I might live, but without ice, the desire wasn't there.

"Well, I don't think anything stays the same. With each minute we get older and think differently."

"That Mayan thing, you know, how life is circular." Then changing the subject because I couldn't seem to follow a thread, I asked, "What's with the money?"

"What's wrong with your hands? They're red. And puffy. Did something bite you?"

"No—and maybe." I could no longer move without causing every fiber of my body to twitch. "Are you stealing?"

"What are you talking about?" He put his money into the brown leather bag he had on the bed and put the bag on to the floor. "What's going on?"

Looking over at him, I saw he was buttoning up his shirt. An amoral character, I thought. Adding I never would have fallen for him if I hadn't starved myself of sex. I fell for a dissolute man because I had deprived myself of the joys of carnality for a year. "Never again am I going a year without sex," I said out loud to the ceiling. "Shame on me."

"What?" He fluffed his shirt, something we all did to bring cooler air in; a scent of Old Spice blew my way. The scent of Harry, although he was sometimes minty too. "You haven't seen my locket, have you?" He asked.

"No. Where are you going?"

"I'll be back later."

His remark was more depressing than anything else because what does later mean? I watched in silence as he sat on his bed and put his leather sandals on. I then found myself leaning forward and spitting up part of my lunch into a cup by my bed.

"Good grief," he said, grabbing a bowl he had been eating beans from. He handed me the bowl and took the cup, placing it outside the door.

"Ants' nest. I sat on a red ants' nest," I said, coughing, my throat raw and the need to throw up again making it hard to say anything else.

He laughed. It irked me that he laughed, but then I would have laughed if he had told me the same thing. It was a ridiculous thing to do. So, I laugh, too, although it was painful and caused me to throw up again, this time into the bowl.

"I see you ate rice and beans again today." The joke wasn't funny. Crouching down, he ran his eyes over my body. "This isn't good. Your neck is all swollen." His tone concerned.

Harry gave me his full water bottle. I drank half of it. The tepid liquid was soothing. He then retrieved a jar of Tiger Balm from his dressing table. Unscrewing the top, he kneeled by my side and gently rubbed the balm onto my swollen hands, neck, thighs, legs, and arms. Watching him, I wished he wasn't so caring. I wished he was being mean and evil toward me, but he wasn't. His breath smelled sweet, and I realized he had been eating licorice. Something he never ate when I was around. Catarina had been right, it was the one thing he truly didn't like to share. A wave of tears dripped from my eyes, causing him to pause. He kissed my forehead and used the tail of his shirt to wipe my cheeks. His lips compassionate, the camphor soothing, I allowed myself a deep breath and gained control—that is, momentarily.

When the Tiger Balm jar was empty, he got up and threw it into the trash bin then opened his toilet kit and brought out a bar of licorice. "Here," he said. "Chew on this. It will help settle your stomach."

I touched it to my tongue but couldn't chew. The Tiger Balm was working. It countered the itch, almost nullifying it. My body immediately felt relief, but my convoluted emotions were something to be reckoned with.

"I brought Frankie to see Jacquelina this afternoon," I said, staring at him. He was standing by his table, sifting through items, looking for more salve. "Don't you want to know how Jacquelina is?" I asked.

He turned around and looked at me. "How is she?" He said nonchalantly. Then just stood staring down at me. He looked puzzled, all I could think was, you've been caught. He finally came back over, picking up the throw-up bowl from the side of the bed and placing it by the cup outside the room. "I'll get rid of them both when I leave. The balm should make you feel better. I just wish I had more."

"Why didn't you tell me Doc is your fiancé?" I asked nibbling on the licorice, the anise flavor finally soothing. But then my question to him got the better of me, and I began to shake with what felt like feverish chills. Why wasn't he answering? "Why are you here with me and not at the clínica?"

Standing in the middle of the floor, his shoulders stooped, he cocked his head meeting my gaze and went to say something, but then stopped and looked off at the wall. I had put him on the spot. Not an ultimatum, just answers. Was it fair? Yes, of course, it was. I knew the reality of the situation so why not be honest. Clearing his throat, he looked down at the floor and whispered, "I once did."

Not hearing what he said, too full of blustering and fanciful dilution, I continued, my voice cracking and weak, "I thought your fiancé lived in the city, a distant fairy tale that you dreamed about but rarely saw. But she has been here all along. It makes no sense to me. Please say something that makes sense."

His hands on his hips, his eyes searching the cracks on the floor, made me feel childish. That my tantrum was unwarranted. I wanted to hate him but couldn't. The dense, hot air began to build up around my neck and ears, clogging them and making me shiver even more. I wanted to scream. Instead, I muttered, "I feel so awful. I just feel so awful."

He straightened, twisting sideways to look at me briefly, his eyes displaying thought and torment. Ruffling his hair, he pinched the tip of his nose. We could hear the group coming back from dinner. Jack's voice said something, but it was too hard to hear what. I figured they would have their meeting, but intead, music, loud and boisterous, seeped up through the floorboards. The saucy lyrics memorized: *The golden woman covered in saliva and stars, on the bedroom floor, staring straight into the abyss, naked moon bathed in sweat, climbing his body, never stop—please.*

"Manolo is waiting for me," he said, speaking over the music. His words were cold and void of emotion. He went over to his bag of money, picked it up, and walked to the door. "I'll let the others know about the ants. I'm sorry I have to leave, but it's urgent that I go into town tonight. You'll be okay." His expression was inflicted with worry, or was it? I was having a hard time reading him. Possibly his distressed appearance was nothing more than a furtive mask for his desire to leave. Yet he was twisting once again, stepping out, then back into the room. "When I get back tonight, I'll go over everything with you. I promise. It's not what you think." His voice was smooth but hinted of panic. His bag slung over his shoulder, he paused once more in the open space of the door. "I'm going to get you some more Tiger Balm. They sell it in El Pueblito." And then he was gone. I wanted to shout for him to come back; instead, I lay prone on the raft listening to him walk down the hall, his steps disappearing. The only sound left was the music and its hideous lyrics.

Chapter 36

Recuperating

I spent a good part of the following week in bed with a fever. It had been brought on by the insidious red ant poison. "Insoluble piperidine alkaloids," Sarah had explained. "Can be fatal. Anaphylactic reactions are tricky. You're lucky to be alive."

There had been grumblings amongst my fellow niñeros to get Doc. I begged them not to, as I was convinced the only item in her doctor bag would be the ominous machete. Sarah didn't push the matter. Being the in-house authority on insects, she gave me a handful of some local allergy medication, which made me sleep better and brought the swelling down. However, she felt the only way to assure my recovery was to make amends with the illness's creators. The screwball went down the clínica's path to the red fire ant log and brought back a jar full of the nasty, venomous creatures. She brought them into my room mere days after my injury, when I was in the midst of having fits and turns; when delirious fetishes were causing me to see a red, mean manatee in my room. She put the jar of frantic ants, scaling the glass walls, in front of my face. I screamed, a gut-wrenching, soul-purging sound and swat at the air thinking she was going to put them on me. Instead, she left the jar of ants by the door inside the room, suggesting, "When you're less hostile, tell the ants you're sorry for sitting on their house." She also gave me a lecture: "Ants are the backbone of the earth. Without them, we would starve, trees wouldn't grow, and disease would be rampant. They eat the dead and poop life-giving substances. Always watch where you sit and walk because you've probably already killed millions." Her tone was very accusatory and unforgiving.

Four days later, when I awoke, Golly was standing by my bed with a bowl of black bean soup and a packet of cards, along with a baby she introduced as Ptolemy. I asked her to remove the jar of red ants from my room. They were still over by the door, pounding at the glass, trying to get out. The lid being nothing more than a piece of paper tied with a string, escape was imminent.

She did as I asked, leaving me with the soup and baby Ptolemy. He was round and chewed on his hands. Snot was dripping down his nose, and the diaper he wore was a makeshift, ill-fitting sheet tied on with a strip of ripped, frayed cloth. I ate my soup while watching Ptolemy eat his hands. He was happy and kicked his legs out, excited over something in his head, and fell over. Putting the soup down, I reached out and picked the baby up because he had turtled and didn't seem to be able to right himself on his own. The movement made me dizzy. It was then that I noticed Ptolemy's diaper was wet, and he had stained the floor. Crawling onto my knees, I stood up slowly. It was good to be up. My arms and legs were still swollen and red, and where I had scratched, there were dark scabs. Gingerly, I went over to Harry's side of the room and looked inside his clothing bag. I pulled out one of his T-shirts. It smelled like him, and I kept it up to my face for far too long. Walking back over to the baby, I took his diaper off and wrapped his bottom in Harry's T-shirt.

"He won't mind," I said.

Harry hadn't been back since he left that fateful day with his money. It was disturbing to think he had left me half dead and not returned to see if I was still alive. I figured Harry, the fake Dutchman, had taken his money and run. Where to? Probably his fake country, Holland. Yet no matter how angry or hurt I felt about his disappearance, I missed him.

"How's Ptolemy?" Golly said, coming back into the room. "Molly named him. We've got twelve of these little marshmallows now. We all *gav'm* names because they didn't have any." Molly went over to Harry's bed and pulled the sheet off, placing it on the floor to sit on.

"Where did the babies come from?" I asked.

"Lenore brought them two nights ago. In the middle of the night! A bit *potty* of her. Waffled on about us doing such a *crack'n* job with the kids, then left. They've messed our routine. Spend our time looking after the babies now. The kids have stopped lining their shoes up and walk around all *stroppy*. We have no consistency anymore. It's all goo and random diapering."

"I gather Jack has a new chapter to add to his dissertation now."

"No, he says it's just fine the way it is."

"Really? He must be tired of writing it. Or maybe he thinks it's perfect the way it is."

I had Ptolemy up on the bed with me. When he smiled his round cheeks made his brown, bright eyes disappear. I gave him a piece of mushed-up beans, which he ate, then spat back out, making his mouth black.

"We don't have any bottles or baby food. We've been smashing up the beans and rice and giv'n them milk in cups. More milk gets on their chests than inside their mouths. They poop a lot, so they're getting something inside them. We've started a nappy tally. Drew it on the wall. I've changed over one hundred nappies since they've arrived." Golly tossed me the packet of cards, bent down, and picked up Ptolemy. "I'm going to put a proper nappy on him; when I come back, let's have a go at Old Maid."

"Old Maid?"

"Eat your soup. I'll bring you some water when I return." She wiped the drool from Ptolemy's mouth; he sat with little effort on her full hips, leaning into her breasts. Glancing back down at me, she added, "Glad to see you sitting up. You look better. Not narky anymore."

"Thanks." I was better. Weak, but better. Once she shut the door, the room looked blue and dusty. A disquieting feeling of emptiness set in. I let my eyes roam over the walls and floor while thinking I didn't like the room anymore. Harry's bed still had the mosquito netting flipped up; the creases in the bottom sheets where he had been sitting were still there. His toothbrush, toothpaste, deodorant, hairbrush, and nail clippers, untouched, like ancient statues in a grim landscape. The kids playing echoed up through the craggy boards, along with the sound of babies mewling; one was outright crying.

When Golly came back in, she had Ptolemy and another baby with her, along with balancing a cup of water. She handed me the cup and said, "This is Marley." Marley had a ribbon wrapped around her head tied into a bow. Her shirt was too big, and someone had rolled up the sleeves. It was pink and written with alligator figures was the word 'Benetton' on the front. "I named her," Golly continued. "Marley's me auntie's name. I like me auntie." She placed both babies down on the floor, letting them crawl around. Picking up the deck of cards, she shuffled, then dealt. The babies were quiet and had crawled over to the door, trying to get out. Luckily, it was shut. The room that had grown melancholy while she was away was now full of life. It was good to have her and the babies with me.

Looking at my hand, I asked, "Have you seen Harry?"

"No, but there's been a Harry sighting."

"Yeah, who saw him?"

"Catarina. She drove the workmen into town two days ago. I think she was looking for that Scotty fellow." Golly picked up a card and frowned. "I never win at this game. I need to win. Don't want to be an Old Maid."

"It's just a game," I said, amused that she took it so seriously.

"Catarina said Harry's *stay'n* at the La Vista."

"Without his clothes?"

"I guess? She didn't talk to him. When she came back from town, she wasn't happy. She was all *brassed* off. Gutted, you know. She left yesterday and didn't get to say goodbye to that fellow. I don't know. What did you think of him? A bit *smarmy*, don't you think?" Picking another card, she added, "She left you her address. Wants you to write. Tried to talk to you, but being all dicky, she couldn't."

When the deck was almost spent, I realized Golly had the Old Maid. I tried to figure out which one it was in her hand so I could pick it. But her expression was always the same, no matter what card she was looking at; permanently worried. We played two sets, and she was the Old Maid both times. She left with the babies in a huff, insisting on a rematch.

"Good," I replied, happy to have something to look forward to. My body depleted of nourishment and my emotions brittle; I didn't enjoy being left alone. Too many memories and one giant ghost in the room, Harry. I kept seeing him lying on his bed, fiddling with his toilet kit, sitting on the floor sipping rum. I would also replay various scenes in my head like Doc's behavior and what did Harry mean when he said, "It's not what it seems." As much as I had been trying to hate him, I couldn't. When the afternoon heat arrived and sleep finally took hold, I welcomed it, grateful for its peace.

Golly returned after dinner balancing a bowl of bean soup and Clive and Jubilee in her arms. "Jack named them. We also have a Fido and a Gremlin—Alex's kids. Fionnulia, Tiberius, and Ptolemy, well, you know who named them. Catarina named an absolutely adorable feather-headed girl, Peaches. Sarah named a little boy with a narrow chin Escarabajo—I guess it means beetle."

"More like a nickname."

"We put a baby aside for you to name. But we got bored and named it. Another go at the cards?" We played a couple more hands of Old Maid. Again, she lost. I found it puzzling that she kept losing. But she was determined to win and would be back.

Because I slept sporadically, I began reading my book again. It was difficult reading because of my ability to concentrate was constantly being distracted by my broken heart. But I tried my damnedest to keep focused and to look up words I found confusing. I needed to shut out the noise. I believed its' madness was making me sicker; it ripped at my stomach and tormented my mind.

As the days passed Golly became more and more obsessed with the game of Old Maid. When the kids were in school, she'd come up to my room with various babies. Plop them down on the floor and let them crawl around while playing a game. During snack time, under the pretense of bringing me a green drink, we'd play one quick hand. Late at night, she'd often unexpectedly burst in through the door, insisting on a hand before going to bed. She had put on weight since Molly had started seeing Gunther. To get down onto the floor she'd bend down, then fall onto her bottom. To put one ankle over the other to sit cross-legged, she had to help her legs go where she wanted them to go. She often kicked me by accident because her knees didn't want to bend. She had stopped wearing shorts and now wore a pair of light cotton balloon pants, which were no longer ballooning because they were full. I felt bad for her. She had bright, kind blue eyes. All she wanted was not to be an old maid, but she never won. We were the only two single people in the compound—Cadmael was officially shacking up with Doc, and Aapo still in the mountains.

"Doc and Cadmael?" I questioned.

"Yup, they been on and off for a long time."

"What's a long time?"

"Don't know."

I had this uncanny feeling Golly felt we were bound together in some sort of single sisterhood. I didn't mind. It was nice to have a sister.

Slowly, I began getting up and helping with the morning washing of the children. Without Catarina, with me being sick, and the new babies, the kids weren't being bathed in the same manner. Some even got away without showering. Their clothes weren't being folded correctly, and they were now walking themselves to school. The pooping, peeing, and feeding of the babies had us strapped. I began swimming in the afternoons with the little kids; they liked the attention, but I could tell it wasn't enough. I wore a pair of Harry's boxer shorts and my bathing suit top. The cool afternoon dip doused what was left of my blistering bites with a refreshing coolness. I had also started wearing Harry's T-shirts while sleeping and around the place. I liked how they fluffed easily to let the hot air out and the cooler air in.

One evening, Golly came into my room as usual. It was after dinner. She had Clive and Jubilee and insisted on a game.

"Okay," I said, sitting up, depressed, and feeling moody. I didn't find anything amusing about the orphanage anymore. The whole place seemed sad. I didn't like that the babies had messed up the consistency and routine. The place had fallen apart, and I needed a change.

"New volunteers have arrived," she informed me. "French. Two stinky, scrawny, long-haired boys. They smell like rotten pickles. And the girl? She's jabby. Her name's Noya. Like annoying."

"'*No ya*' means 'not ready' in Spanish. Her name will confuse the kids," I said, dealing the cards.

"They *stay'n* in the attic urine room, fixing it up."

I was happy to hear new arrivals had come. It would make it easier to leave. But like Catarina, I needed to go into town. I needed some answers, closure. I wanted to say goodbye.

Chapter 37

Milla

I walked down the solitary, muddy street of El Puente to where the dirt road and the rutty paved road met. No one had told me, but Catarina had smashed the orphanage's car into Yena's house. A barely functioning vehicle was now a pile of scrap metal. Waiting for the bus wasn't so bad; it was even nostalgic. It was a beautiful morning, the air fresh from a recent downpour. The early hour temperatures, the most comfortable part of the day. Soon the sun would start baking the puddles and the water-saturated trees, creating uncomfortable steam.

The school bus appeared, grinding its gears, and painted with the colorful red and blue face of a dragon on the front. I stepped up and paid the bus driver's young assistant and sat down in a seat near the door. The bus was nearly empty. Ranchero music blasting, the dashboard was cluttered with religious pamphlets, and the windshield was plastered with Christian slogans such as "*Dios es mi guid*" and "*Jesús me ama*." I was in a good mood. The anticipation of seeing Harry made me smile, and I chatted up a storm with the assistant. He was from the area and had eight brothers and two sisters.

The trip to El Pueblito was like a crazy amusement park ride, tossing me into the air and throwing me up against the window. I was all tuckered out when the bus pulled into town. Getting off in the center, I straightened my clothing and hair, and went inside a small tienda and bought a Coca-Cola. Standing on the front steps, I drank it looking around the street. It was still early, and the place hadn't woken up yet. A few dogs were roaming around, and one was sleeping. The La Vista Hotel was just a block away. I stared at the entrance while gulping down large, gasping slurps of the fizzy beverage, thinking it would be fun if I saw Harry walking down the sidewalk. I wondered what the look on his face would be like when he saw me. I think he'd be surprised, and I was hoping in a good way. But no luck. Instead, a man with a lumpy face and pig-like nose stumbled by. He was drunk and was scratching his armpits with a spatula.

Giving the empty soda bottle back to the tienda owner, I made my way to the hotel. A couple of men with glossy, tired, droopy eyes sat under the tattered green awning of the caged liquor store drinking beer. The kook sat on a chair in the cage, looking out, a beer in his hand, and several empties on the table next to him. He hadn't started playing music yet and seemed sullen, almost morose.

On the front wall of the hotel someone had placed a sign that said, "*No soy un baño.*" A woman in a bib wearing a straw hat was sweeping the steps. She looked like she was dancing with her broom. I walked by her into the lobby.

The lobby had harsh yellow walls and a rust-colored tile floor. A gangly spider plant hung from the ceiling, and two giant hibiscus plants had been tucked into the corners by the stairs to the second floor. The place was clean and generic-looking. With no one tending the registrar, I took the liberty of glancing through the guest booklet. Not one name looked familiar. Shutting the book, I leisurely strolled out into the yard. A swath of overgrown vegetation lined the stucco walls. The air was wet and had a rotting odor that I was all too familiar with. A bluestone patio with a glass table and cobalt blue wrought-iron chairs took up most of the grounds, the rest flowers and some grass, and recliners. There was a man with dark wavy hair sitting on a lounge chair near the back fence by a sparse-looking banana tree. The man was facing the sun away from me, but his mop of dark hair and the manner in which he held the paper he was reading made me think of Harry. My stomach fluttered, and I remembered I hadn't eaten anything yet. I wished I had because my head felt light, like it might fall off me. Taking a deep breath, I steadied myself and walked over to the man. Stopping a foot away from him, I stared at the back of his head and cleared my throat.

The man turned and looked at me while folding his paper shut. "Sí."

"I thought you were someone else," I mumbled, immediately feeling depressed. He was an older man with a thin face and delicate features. On his nose, he wore round silver wire-rimmed glasses. His most distinctive features were his eyebrows; they met over his nose and were much too bushy for his face.

"Do you know a man named Harry? Harry Van Cleef?" I asked, my insides gripped with hope.

The man looked at me puzzled, so I said it all again in Spanish.

"No," he replied and then shook his paper in the air as if a pesky fly was bothering him and went back to reading.

Staying put, the front page caught my attention. There was a photo that took up almost the entire page; it was of two young, pretty women, smiling. One was a blonde girl with straight, white teeth, and the other a brunette with sunglasses on. I moved closer and leaned in to see the caption.

"Please. Go away," he said in Spanish. I could tell he was from Spain; he spoke quickly and with a lisp. I didn't leave.

Instead, I kneeled to read. '*Mujer golpeada hasta la muerte en la aldea de la montaña… para vender los partes del cuerpo.*' The words were disturbing; I tried to read the story but couldn't because the lettering was too small.

Standing up, I asked for the paper. "Just for a minute." Frustrated, he got up, bunched the paper into a ball, gave it to me by thrusting it into my hands, and walked away. His hard leather soles made clip-clop noises over the tiles as he left. From the back, although his demeanor was all wrong, he did look like Harry.

I sat down on one of the lounge chairs and stretched out. Unfolding the pages, I began to read. The blonde girl's name was Milla Borja. She was from Finland. The other girl was from Italy. Two days ago, Milla and the Italian had been traveling in the mountains. They went into a village to visit a market famous for rugs and baskets. After leaving the market, they went into the center of the town and were met by a crowd of locals. The locals swarmed around them shouting accusations that the girls were there to kidnap their children to sell them to rich Americans for body parts. The girls were kicked down to the ground and beaten to death with clubs, feet, and fists. The village elder said he had been told from relatives living in the south about atrocities being committed by foreign whites. He gave the police a piece of paper proving the accusations true. There were six words written on the paper: *hacksaw, wood, bags, machete, rope, nails.*

Putting the paper down, I realized I'd been holding my breath while reading and gasped for air. I sat for a few moments digesting the article. The whole thing at first seemed nauseating. A discomfort welled up inside me, coupled with a revolting feeling of disgust. I imagined them, Milla and her friend, trapped within the folds of the angry crowd. The smells of unwashed clothing and madness similar to the stench of hundreds of sickly, underfed chickens, and rabid dogs. The pain of each kick. The raking of skin as each choleric, angry face, and grabbing hand wanted a piece of them. The horror of it was unfathomable, and the list of items and accusations unconscionable.

It was the workmen's village. Aapo had gone back home nearly a month ago to protect his village from the Rabbit moon. He knew Milla, and he knew we weren't harvesting body parts. It was a joke. The letter I gave to Blue-Eyes was Harry's list of items he wanted from the hardware store. Nothing more, nothing less. She could see that all the children were accounted for, all healthy and happy. Did they really believe our inane, made-up blather? Our cynical, bored minds giving way to playful jests; there had been nothing sinister about it at all, just idiocy for our own amusement. I bit my nails, feeling a touch of guilt about the letter mix up. But then who beats someone to death over a list of hardware store items. My mind swirling, I thought about what Doc had said, about the people being angry due to so much having been taken from them. Then I thought of what Gunther had mentioned about our volunteer positions 'they used to be jobs. Paying jobs.'

The paper brushed off their senseless deaths as "fatalism." It had a disquieting nature to it and kept me seated, my mind churning over the horror and the backward simplemindedness of it all. Then, not wanting to think about it anymore because I was already sad enough, I tried to push the incident down deep where I couldn't retrieve it readily, but it kept popping back up. The images. Poor Milla. I found myself silently weeping, but for only a brief moment. Wiping my face with my shirt, I folded the paper up and tucked it into my daypack for the others back at the orphanage to read. There was nothing to do. What was done, was done.

Looking up, I saw that in front of me was a door in the fence to the main road. It wasn't enough to keep out an insane mob, I thought. Did this rundown town think the same way as the people in the mountain village? Then, crinkling my nose, I got up. I'd had enough of the town and felt it was best to leave. Besides, Harry wasn't here, just a Spaniard.

When I walked by the liquor store cage, ranchero music was blasting onto the street. The drunk kook was gyrating his body to the tune. He howled at me when I walked by. When I didn't respond he called me a "*pinche cula.*" Disgust flared up inside me, a foul taste of bile and hate. I hated this place. The rot, the drinking, the poverty, the rich, the lumpy roads. A skinny dog came over to me to see if I had anything for him. I swatted at the air, pushing him away. The sun, already baking the land, made everything putty and moldy. I thought about going back to the States. Was it time?

Grateful to see a bus waiting by the tienda, I ran over to it and got on. The assistant was eating a tortilla while collecting money. I paid and sat down by the door again. I didn't feel like talking on the trip back even though the young helper stood by me the whole way to El Puente. I remained in my head, making future plans, fanciful daydreams of images of better days to come, but none of my thoughts had me returning home. No, I wanted a different country. Not the USA and not here.

Once in El Puente, the sun directly overhead, I decided to try one other avenue to find Harry. Walking over to Yena's house, I knocked on the door. The thin, ragged man who had been at the house that night so long ago, opened the door. When I inquired about Yena, he shrugged and at first told me to go away. When I gave him the history of how I had met her, declaring I wanted to say thank you, he became friendlier. He told me she had sold the house and had gone south with her son and nephew. Looking behind him, I saw the room was completely bare, not that it ever had had much. He must have noticed my curiosity because he added that he was just cleaning up and leaving too. I then asked him if he knew Harry Van Cleef. He laughed and shut the door.

All my means to find Harry used up, my mood dispirited and blue, I went back to the main road. I bought a hot dog from a vendor, took one bite, and threw the rest away. I then secured a water taxi to take me back to the orphanage. It was a smallish canoe with a zippy engine, and we flew over the water. Rounding the bend by the *peligroso* sign, we saw the waters off the orphanage were crowded with small crafts and the *policia de la marina* in their hard-bottomed rubber Zodiacs. I told the driver to check it out. Joining several other onlookers, we idled in the water by the mangroves on the north side of the schoolhouse. There were several *policia,* guns saddled to their hips, faces serious, the caps with gold trim pulled on tight, standing in the water, and searching through the mangroves. Several more emerged from a thicket of mangled roots, branches, and reeds. They were carrying a stretcher with what appeared to be a body zipped up in a black bag. They put the black bag into one of their boats. It was a gruesome sight. The anxiety and nausea I felt over Milla's death was nothing compared to how horrifying and frightening the world seemed now.

Chapter 38

Leaving

I sat cross-legged on the dock with all my possessions, which were not many, a backpack, a daypack, a book, and a water bottle. I had left my bed and all its drapings for the next person. Too cumbersome to carry around.

It hadn't been as difficult as I had thought, to say good-bye to the kids. It was as though they expected it. No sadness, just a small wave of the hand, then aloofness and off to play. Volunteers came and went. In a three-to-four-year-old's brain, how was change comprehended? Was it looked upon as a loss of something known? Or was it of no importance? Since the local staff were the constant and stable adults, we were probably nothing more to them then an aquaintance. Like the coming and going of the air one breathes, sometimes it is sweet and euphoric, most of the time its inconsequential, and every now and then incredibly distasteful. And like most acquaintances, it seemed probable that they gained a new perspective from each one of us, although most likely not much being so young. But then, as I sat staring off into the water, the good and the bad of the place seemed like a moot point because nothing was going to change the past except the future. Woefully gripped with my own inner misery of loss, I earnestly awaited my next journey.

Last night, we had a vigil for Milla and Harry. Molly's wall chart having thirty notches meant the naughty rabbits were gone. This gave us all a sense of relief. Golly finally won at Old Maid. She was also very obnoxious about it. It was as though I had never won a game, and she kept going on and on about me being the old maid and how she was, "*Ge'tin* a *China plate*," which meant she would land herself a wonderful man, and I would only get "*Barnies* and *Porkies*." When she hugged me good-bye, I couldn't get her to let go.

Sitting for the last time on the dock, listening to the lapping of the waves on the shore, I read the last few pages of my book. It had turned out to be a poetic book that didn't help me with Spanish fluency. The words were too literary. Yet, I did chuckle over the psychiatrist in the novel describing the male protagonist 'as a twitchy woman who sleeps around looking for the perfect lover.'

Putting the book in my backpack, I looked up to take in the morning light of the river one last time from the dock. It was mysteriously calm. The middle turbulence had quieted down. Breathing in the splendor of nature, my eyes rested upon the sun rising above the trees, a dark orange color visible and beautiful and so spectacular I figured the day could hold nothing but good tidings.

Across the water, a sailboat was winding its way from the Club de Bote. It was heading toward me, its bow sleek and narrow, a sloop-rigged L. Francis Herreshoff H-28. I knew this because I had been told in detail about every inch of this rig through notes passed to Manolo to Golly to me when I was ill. A twenty-eight-foot boat wasn't large, as seafaring sailboats are sometimes, but this one was long enough, wide, and sported a shallow draft for comfortable shoreline sailing and sleeping, or so I was told. It was the color of night and had a white pinstripe that outlined the lacquered mahogany railing dappled with shiny brass cleats. There were three off-white sails, and the mast flew a yellow flag with a purple imprint of a dolphin. The sails were furled, as the present direction of the boat required the precision of a motor.

"Ahoy, Eleanor!" Dorian yelled, waving an arm while holding the brass helm with the other. He had a ratty-looking straw hat on that shrouded his eyes. I could only see the tip of his nose, mouth, and chin. He stood upright and looked exceedingly robust, his smile kind. Maybe he would grow on me, I thought, sniffing the air; I took a deep breath and stood up.

He threw me a line, and I tied it to the left front piling. Leaning over into the sailboat I handed Dorian my bags, undid the line, and jumped in while pushing us away. Doran kicked the throttle into gear, motoring us back into the outer waters. We planned to motor up the river to the mouth of the ocean, then head to the Bay Islands off of Honduras. They were my plans, and since Dorian did nothing but wander from one shore to the next, they were his plans too.

Passing around the bend, we saw the clínica tucked behind mangroves and willowy vines. A broad opening appeared, and I saw Doc outside, standing in her yard talking to Cadmael. "Harry and Doc were to get married," I uttered more to myself than to Dorian.

"Horrible tragedy," he said.

I remained silent and began to look through my bag for a Spanish dictionary and a notepad. I wanted to look up words and write them into sentences, something, anything to preoccupy my mind as the incident was still deep in my bones.

"They say the body was completely decomposed," Dorian remarked, one hand on the wheel, the other in his front pants pocket. "If it weren't for the locket tucked inside the sneakers bouncing by his bloated, blue head, they never would have been able to identify him. The *policia* seemed to think he had been there for weeks, being eaten up by fish, crocs. Did you know him well?"

When I didn't reply, he continued. "I guess one of the little kids found him. Alfred? His name was Alfred."

"Albert," I whispered, wishing he would just shut up.

"The body was trapped in the mangrove roots that had a bunch of purple and red flowers growing on them. Interesting. That kid *Alfred* likes flowers. I like flowers, too—must have been horrible for him to see something like that. You know, in the papers his name wasn't Van Cleef. It was some long name—lots of names. Possibly French?"

Glancing up, I said, "Chilean. He was Chilean. Well, that's what the police said when they came to get his stuff. He had several different passports. One was Dutch. But I kept asking them what was his name? I mean, what was his real name? They couldn't say, only that they knew for sure he was Chilean. I wonder how they knew that?"

"Really? Yes, that's right, Chilean. Well, he had cement blocks attached to his feet. It never ceases to amaze me how the locals kill people and put cement blocks on the victim when everyone knows they float." He then chuckled, took his hat off, and wiped his brow. His blond hair was matted to his head. He ran his fingers through it making it spiked, then put the hat back on again— but the rim was bent back making him goofy looking. Glancing up at his face, I didn't find him attractive anymore. He had become irritating and plain looking. My whole reasoning for being with him had to do with the idea of a pet. When a pet dies, people like to go out and get another one, so they feel better. But this wasn't working. It was all going terribly wrong. If only he would stop talking—or should I say yapping.

"Do you want some water?" I asked, getting up and going down into the galley.

"Sure, luv." It also bothered me that he called me "luv."

The living area was cluttered with old rags hanging off the cushions, pieces of paper, and other knick-knacks were scattered over the floor and in corners. The air smelled like old shoes and cleaning fluids. I began opening and shutting drawers to see what he had. Flares, a flashlight, a bottle of gin, gum, sleeping pills, more dirty rags. A guidebook on Central America was on the counter by a sink full of filthy dishes that had attracted flies. I picked it up, flipped the pages, and randomly landed on Panama. I read down through the different sections on how to get there, etc., while half-listening to Dorian babbling in the background.

Scuba diving was noted as pleasurable and exotic, and there were surf schools on the Atlantic coast too. Scuba diving seemed more attractive to me. There was a scuba diving language school: language classes in the morning, diving in the afternoon. Now that would be an impressive thing to do, I thought. I also read that I could either take the mailboat or a small plane from the town at the mouth of the river, we were going to, to Panama. Then, for a brief moment, I was taken aback by a visceral sadness. I would go alone. I needed to start anew.

Realizing Dorian was still talking, I began to listen to him again. His voice was like sipping a tepid milk soup. How boring and dull, I thought, pushing my hair away from my face. Standing among the clutter, I huffed wishing I'd gone to El Puente and taken a bus.

"I was talking to the bartender at the club. Max, great guy. You know what he said?" He was shouting now, most likely because I hadn't been saying anything back.

Climbing up the ladder with a couple of waters from the mini-refrigerator, I handed one to Dorian.

"He said Harry had relatives here. I guess an aunt. An Indian woman named Yenara, but he called her Yena. She was from the Muppet tribe in, in—"

"Chile. I think they're called Mapuche." That is what the boy who drove me to the orphanage in his motorized canoe had said. My mind churning, I muttered, "Yena and her family are Mapuche." The connection between what the paper wrote and Yena coming to light. I then thought of another time, an era gone by, and said, "I went to Chile once. Years ago, as a kid. My parents and I went to the Atacama Desert. My father wanted to paint it. Beautiful place." Taking a sip of water, I mumbled. "Before it, all fell apart." I then sat down on the seat next to Dorian, and I asked, "What did you say about Harry having an indigenous aunt?"

But instead of answering me, he was stuck on the word 'muppet'. "He's part Muppet. Didn't look it. I used to see him with the clinic doctor having drinks at the bar months and months ago. They fought like crazy. Don't think they liked each other."

"I think he loved her," I said, not particularly happy to hear about them drinking together at the bar, but glad they fought. Thinking back over the months, I thought about conversations, words that had meant not much then, but that now appeared important. "The aunt from Chile. The bartender said her name was Yena?" I asked with an uptick in my tone.

"I believe it to be Yenara or Yena or both. I wonder whose side of the family she was on. I guess she was wealthy. Moved here with a few family members when Pinochet took over the government. Bought up cheap land, built shit. Smart lady. Oh, he said that she had to leave quickly. Gosh, real cloak-and-dagger stuff going on. Some ministry fellow trying to mess with her deeds. She had sold all her properties and that official fellow, the...the Minister of Interior wanted all her money. Said it was his. There was a gunfight. Must have been when that Harry was killed. Do you know that minister guy and his pack of goons chased her and her family clear across the border in the middle of the night."

I started laughing. How silly of me not to have picked up on all of this until now. Harry had been a teen when Pinochet came into power. No wonder there were rebels and guns in his stories. His stories made sense now; I just had the wrong country. "So, they had to leave in a hurry," I said a surge of enlightenment coursing through my veins.

"What?"

"Did the bartender say anything about a man named The Scott, Dan Scotchwick?"

"Awful fellow. Mean to the help. Disappeared and never paid his bar bill. But get this—They found his sailboat down a swampy estuary. The Club owners claim it's their boat now—It's their payment."

"What did Max say about Harry's death?"

"He laughed. Said he wasn't dead. Wouldn't tell me why though."

I giggled as all the blueness, all the depressing, defeating thoughts that had been plaguing me for days began to melt away. The fantastic feeling of joy was once again enwrapping its life-giving forces around me. "Why that handsome devil," I mumbled.

"What are you saying? And what's so funny?"

"Life. It's so full of surprises," I said, giggling like a schoolgirl.

"A man's dead and you're laughing. This is scary." He took his hat off and wiped his brow, cocked his head at me, bit his lower lip, and asked, "Are you not right in the head? Tell me, do you miss the children?"

"Of course," I said, sobering up. "If I were more together, settled, I'd have taken a few home with me."

"I thought you said most weren't adoptable.'

"Most, isn't all of them. Albert is adoptable. Wonderful, curious, flower-loving Albert. I wonder what will happen to him?"

"Grow up, get a job, get married, have kids. What do you think?

"I don't know."

"Eleanor, you're not going home. Right? We're going sailing," he said with insistence in his voice. I didn't have the energy yet to tell him that I would be leaving. So, I merely replied, "I said if I had it together, but I don't. Anyway, they're in good hands; the French have arrived."

Sitting back, I looked out over the river; a blue macaw sat in a tree as a pelican dove down into the water. In the lazy sunbeams, swaths of flies clouded the air and butterflies flitted in between dark and light. The air smelled of greenish water and sweet linden trees. I relished time and life, the enjoyment of wallowing in a second, making it an eternity. The orphanage had been wonderful at making time stand still, I reminisced, thinking how interesting life could be. Human quandaries and their daily existence, and how at the bat of an eye a leaf that was dangling falls or a hungry bird finds a fish.

Giggling again, I said, "If my friend Gunther were here, he'd say I'm lucky."

"Of course, you're with me," he remarked.

"Well, yes, of course, but also because I have options in life." I paused and bit one of my nails. "But I don't know about my common sense. I did sit on an ants' nest. But if you're lucky, you just end up with a few scars. What do you think?"

"Why, I have a boat and a beautiful girl on it. I'm a very lucky man."

Watching Dorian steer the boat, which took little movement due to the waters being calm and the engine motoring us, I found myself glad to be with him. It was temporary as I had other things to do, like work on my Spanish and scuba dive. But he had become tolerable now, even pleasant to be with; most of all I was grateful not to be alone. My heart felt like it had been peeled thin. It ached. I didn't even know Harry's real name.

"I wonder how many Harries there are in the world," I said.

"Hundreds, thousands. But I don't think you'll find a lot of Dorians."

"Well, guess what? Harry isn't dead."

"Now you sound like Max."

"Harry had lost his sneakers the night of the party. I believe his locket too."

"Then who's the dead fellow, Miss Marble?"

"The mean man—Scotchwick." I laughed again, and then pensively mumbled. "He doesn't know my last name."

"I know your last name. Abernathy."

"I never told Harry. I wonder why?" Lost in thought, I sat back against the gunwale. Even if he knew my last name, I doubted that he would look for me—much too complicated. Then I blurted out, "Serendipitous encounters! Dorian, have you ever lost someone only to find them again?"

"A dog."

"I haven't, but it would be nice. One day. Someplace fun like a mountain top or surfing or scuba diving, or a cafe sipping coffee in a city." And I laughed again.

Then paused.

Running my eyes over Dorian's face and body, I thought of sex and what a nice pet he was turning out to be, yappy, but nice, and said, "Dorian, would you like to stop for a while and rest?"

Acknowledgement

I would like to thank the members of the Westport Rivers Writers Guild: Corey, Paul, Jerome, and Dwayne. They patiently, and at times, not so patiently, listened to the first draft and some of the second draft of this novel. Ugh! No one should have to listen to or read a first draft. However, the Guild was instrumental in keeping me writing. Thank you to my partner, Paul Andonian, for letting me read bits and pieces to him at breakfast, lunch, and dinner. A great big thank you to all the beta readers, proofreaders, and editors.

L. Wendell Vaughan has written for various magazines and newspapers. She has written several short stories which are being put into a book 'The House Fly,' to be published, 2021. Rabbits and Moons is her first full length novel. She wrote a children's book in 2001 called "Andy Ant, What Could possibly Be On The Other Side to See?' The book has been noted for its lesson on diversity and making new friends. Vaughan, a world traveler, has spent a vast amount of time in Mexico, Central and South America. She taught high school history and English for 21 years and lives in the southeast area of Massachusetts with her partner, Paul.